REEVESBANE

GRYPHON INSURRECTION BOOK 4

K. VALE NAGLE

STET PUBLISHING

Cover art by Jeff Brown.

Interior artwork by Brenda Lyons.

Interior graphics by Crystal Gafford of Crafty as a Coyote.

Published by STET Publishing, Denver

WWW.STETPUBLISHING.COM

WWW.KVALENAGLE.COM

10 9 8 7 6 5 4 3

Trade Paperback
ISBN: 1-64392-017-0
ISBN-13: 978-1-64392-017-7

BELAMURIA

ALABASTER
EYRIE

REEVESPORT

WHITEBEAK

CRESTFALL
PALACE

DUCKBILL

ARGENT
HEIGHTS

ABYSSAL NAZE

CRAG
S

NIGHTSKY

NEW
EYRIE

ALWREN

CRA
RA

JADEBEAK
MOUNTAINS

EMERALD
JUNGLE

FLOWER
OUTPOST

SUNKEN
EYRIE

STORMTAIL

RAFTWORK

KING'S
REACH

SUBMERGED
FOREST

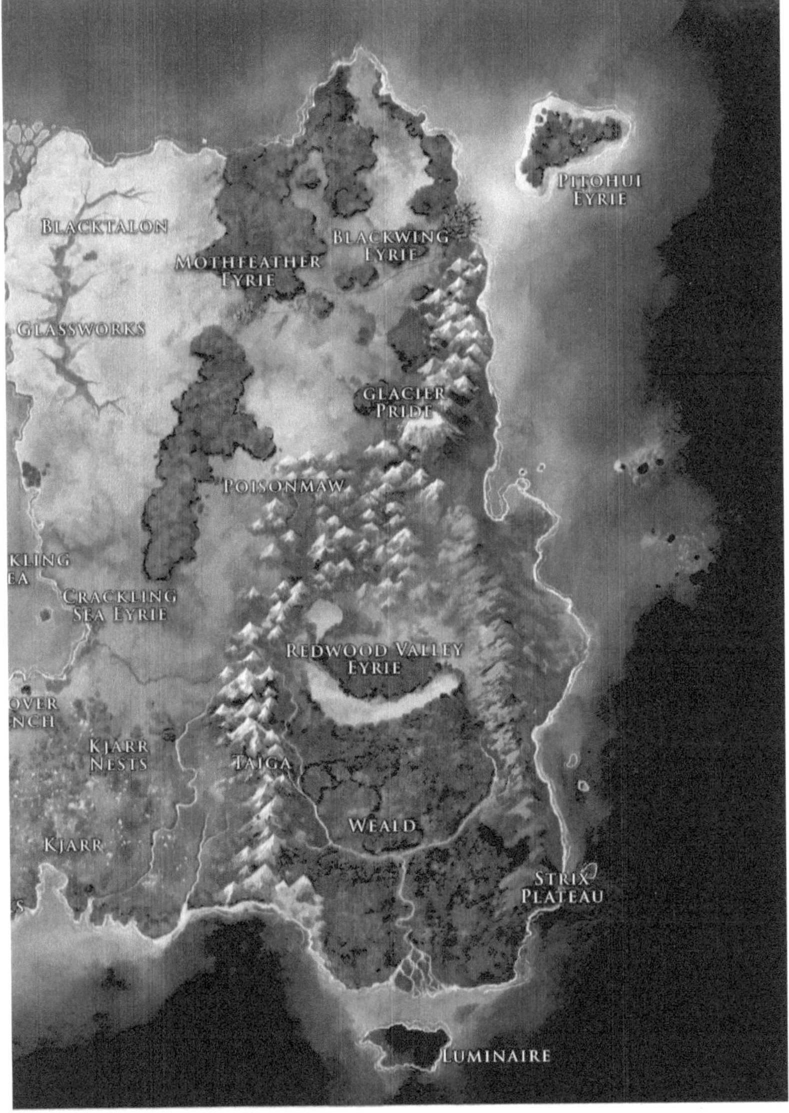

BLACKTALON

MOTHFEATHER
EYRIE

BLACKWING
EYRIE

PITOHUI
EYRIE

GLASSWORKS

GLACIER
PRIDE

POISONMAW

KLING
EA

CRACKLING
SEA EYRIE

REDWOOD VALLEY
EYRIE

OVER
NCH

KJARR
NESTS

TAIGA

WEALD

KJARR

STRIX
PLATEAU

LUMINAIRE

To Larry and Misty, who kindled a love of gryphons in me at a young age. Thank you for all the work you do inspiring each new generation of gryphon authors.

REEVE'S BANE

Headmaster Neider, once leader of the Redwood Valley University, stood in the open council chamber of the Blackwing Eyrie and reconsidered the choices that had brought him here.

In his defense, he thought, there had been a lot of achievements. He'd located the lost eyrie ruins in the bog using nothing more than ancient texts and rumor. He'd provided the information needed to get an assassin into the Crackling Sea's throne room. Under his tutelage, Felicio had unlocked the secrets of saltpeter.

Across the room, he spotted Bario's bright red hues between the glacier gryphon pride leader and a small contingent of trashbirds, the two lowest castes of eyrie society. Felicio's son was careful not to touch the trash-birds' greasy plumage, sticking out from beneath their coverings.

While Neider missed Felicio and had considered him a friend and confidant, he had to admit that Bario had surpassed his father. Where Felicio learned to mine salt-peter, the explosive that had ultimately been the downfall of the Redwood Valley Eyrie, Bario had discovered the alchemical formula to create his own.

Despite what his location in court would suggest, Bario was currently in favor. His nest was situated up in the heights, near the waterfall, and he had only to ask, and anything he wished would be provided. Of course, this also made him too valuable to allow him to be captured alive.

Several blackwing opinici followed Bario wherever he went. Their turquoise scarab brooches meant they weren't bodyguards, they were assassins.

And it's the royal assassins who don't advertise their presence that Bario really needs to worry about.

Bario nodded to the headmaster, and Neider returned the gesture. They'd speak later, at the new flameworks construction site near Mothfeather.

The blackwing reeve, adorned in a harness of polished jewels, sat atop a raised platform. Behind him, a wall of water trickled down a mosaic of gemstones in the shape of an opinicus. The tips of the reeve's feathers had been painted red and orange, and they caught the light coming in from the balcony.

The reeve stood and addressed the guards at the far end of the court. "Bring in the Reeve's Bane."

Neider's eyes got wide. Across the room, Bario shared his look. Their spies in the Redwood Valley had often spoken of Zeph Reevesbane, the gryphon who'd assassinated the Redwood Valley's leader when she attempted to burn down the gryphon's forest and convert it to farms. Last they'd heard, the Bane of the Red Reeve spent his days on an island south of the weald with one of Neider's wayward apprentices, Kia, far from their reach.

Two glacier gryphons, owl-faced, long-eared, short-tailed, and icy-furred, pulled a cart into the throne room, settling it before the throne. They bowed before the reeve, spreading their wings, and then joined their delegation by Bario.

The royal guard, six blackwings with dark leather armor and metal talons, stared with dread. Two of the trashbirds, their oily feathers and fur covered in a cloth for the safety of others, came out and pulled down the walls of the cart, revealing a chained figure.

The prisoner was covered in restraints, each limb secured via leather bracers and chains to a different corner of the wood. His head had a hood over it similar to the ones used on unruly goliath birds with bits of leather tied around his beak to keep him from biting.

Neider stood taller to try and get a better look. He'd only met Zeph Reevesbane once. The gryphon had been escorting Kia through the eyrie fire to safety.

As best Neider remembered him, he was a copper hawk of some sort. Small, unassuming—exactly the sort of creature Reeve Brevin would have hated. If there was an afterlife, she must be chafing against the veil of mortality at having been killed by so meek a gryphon.

Where the blackwings had a single, bright spot of color on the tops of their wings, the creature on the cart appeared to have dark wings with hints of a sickly orange across its entire body. It stayed completely still while the bindings holding its delicate wings were removed. Then, with one motion, it yanked up on the chains holding its forelegs down, and the rusted metal gave with a snap.

The royal guard spread their wings, obscuring the reeve from view, and readied their metal claws.

The creature—no, *opinicus*—lifted its forelegs and, rather than attempting to untie the leather hood, tore two eye holes out with its talons. Then it snapped the straps holding its beak shut and looked around the room.

"Reeve's Bane," the blackwing reeve said. The creature turned to face the eyrie ruler. "You failed to take the Crackling Sea. For that, you've languished in the dungeon for three years."

The creature's eyes found Neider and narrowed in recognition. The headmaster remembered where he'd last seen those eyes. This was the assassin sent to the Crackling Sea. Neider had been his contact; the Reeve's Bane had used his Redwood Valley badge to enter the eyrie and kill the blue reeve.

The headmaster felt sick. He was too old to feel guilt over dead reeves and ranger lords. No one rose to power without becoming a target. What the blackwing opinici hadn't told him was that the reeve's family had also posed a threat.

Neider had opened the eyrie door, and this monster had walked in and killed everyone related to the reeve, taking them apart and leaving them to be found as a warning to others. He'd seen the blue reeve's stone bedroom long after the fact. The marble nest was still stained red.

He hadn't been alone in his nightmares after that. Concerns over seeing her family turn out the same way had weighed upon every action Reeve Brevin took.

"I offer you a chance for redemption," the blackwing reeve said. "A chance to fix the situation you put us in."

The creature, the 'Reeve's Bane,' broke the cheap metal chains on its back legs and stretched its wings, losing a few feathers in the process.

An opinicus chick dashed forwards to try to steal one of the Reeve's Bane's feathers, only to get tackled by a guard. The covered trashbirds came and collected the deadly plumage.

The Reeve's Bane spoke. His voice was eloquent, fitting of an opinicus who had once called himself reeve, and scratchy, as though he hadn't spoken since his incarceration. "What do I get in return?"

"Your freedom," the blackwing opinicus said. When the Reeve's Bane didn't respond, he added, "You will be restored to your reeve status."

The Reeve's Bane hopped down from the cart, spooking the royal guard a second time. He rose on his back paws and looked the Blackwing Eyrie reeve in the eye. "Why should I believe you?"

"Your incarceration was put to a vote," the reeve said. "The other reeves voted five to one to lock you up."

The Reeve's Bane looked to the glacier pride leader, who nodded. Neider had a good idea who the dissenting voice had been. Among the northern eyries who had banded together to fight the Seraph King, there were two gryphon prides, though only the glacier gryphons held the powers of a reeve on the council—the power to cast a dissenting vote.

The Blackwing Eyrie reeve pointed to the trashbird delegation. "Your eyrie has had full privileges while you were locked up. We kept our promise. If you return south and claim the Crackling Sea and Redwood Valley Eyries, you will be restored."

To say the pitohui—*trashbird*—opinici were full members of the alliance was, to Neider's mind, misleading. They existed in the poorest neighborhoods, feeding off of the invasive, poisonous scarabs that had taken over every port city on the continent. Nobody wanted them living in the eyrie, but now that trade had spread the scarabs, nobody could afford not to have a trashbird district, either.

The Reeve's Bane placed a talon under his chin as though thinking. "No, you will restore my reeve status immediately. Then you will provide me with all the supplies I need to lay siege to two eyries."

The other reeves and the glacier pride leader nodded their assent in informal vote.

"You are reeve once again," the blackwing reeve said. "And I will provide you not only with supplies but with an army of our finest soldiers."

"I've seen the bravery of the other eyries," the Reeve's Bane reached out a talon towards one of the royal guard, who leapt back with a squawk, "and I think I'll have to decline your offer. My own opinici and whatever black-wing forces are already there will be more than adequate."

The Reeve's Bane motioned to the trashbird delega-tion. They came forwards and removed his chains and cloth. He stopped them from removing the leather hood. Its broken straps dangled from his head.

The glacier pride leader stepped forwards. "Reeve Rybalt." He used the Reeve's Bane's name for the first time. "You will be traveling down the mountains to reach the Redwood Valley. Allow my gryphons to escort you as scouts until you reach your destination."

"I'm always happy for your company," Rybalt said. He turned and looked straight at Headmaster Neider. "I remember you from the Battle for the Crackling Sea. Is your information on the southerners as good now as it was then? Come with me to my old quarters and fill me in on what's happened these last three years."

Neider stepped through the throngs to join the trash-bird delegation, careful not to touch any of them. While the pitohui opinici around him stayed covered, Rybalt himself was naked. His oily feathers shone in the midday light.

Two steps from the balcony where opinici landed and took off on their way to the throne room, Rybalt turned and looked at the blackwing reeve.

"If you ever attempt to lock me up again, you had best sleep with an armed guard and one eye open," he said. He met the eyes of the other reeves in the room one by one and then leapt off the balcony.

HEADMASTER NEIDER, scholar without a university, stood outside the bedchamber of Reeve Rybalt while a half-dozen attendants groomed him.

When the restored reeve stepped into the main chamber, he wore none of the jewelry or ceremonial armor an opinicus of his station might wear. He didn't even wear a harness. Instead, the opinicus-sized falconry hood was his crown, and the leather straps that once held his beak shut dangled down from it. The leather bindings on his legs remained, though no chains connected to them anymore.

Neider looked for a place to sit but was afraid to touch any of the pillows or pelts. The turquoise shells of several scarabs littered the floor.

The Reeve's Bane seemed amused by Neider's discomfort. "I wasn't given an opportunity to tidy before I was arrested, and my nest has been locked up since I returned from the Crackling Sea so many years ago. You'll have to stand a little longer, I'm afraid. We have one more guest coming. He'll have brought his own cushions."

They waited on the landing, looking out over the

Blackwing Eyrie. Built around a mountain lake, the city had once been no bigger than New Eyrie. Over time, new nests had sprung up along the river as it flowed down the mountains and into the ocean. Looking out now, there was no stretch of land Neider could see that hadn't been developed. The land from lake to ocean had been terraced, cut into districts, converted into orchards, or turned into multi-level nests.

The headmaster swore when a moth bit him and swatted it. Several of the winged pests swarmed around the pitohui reeve. One landed, and its sharp proboscis began to suck the trashbird's blood. After a moment, it started to twitch. Then it fell to the ground, dead.

Seeing the headmaster's look of horror, Rybalt quipped, "Even in the bottom of an oubliette, there were plenty of scarabs to eat. Sometimes I think they keep a few of us locked up just so they don't have to hire an exterminator."

True to Rybalt's earlier promise, the glacier pride leader landed outside. Two of his gryphons landed a moment later with the long cushions opinici liked to rest on while they spoke.

"Iony, it's good to see you." Rybalt put a talon on the gryphon's shoulder.

The headmaster stepped back.

Iony laughed. "You're giving your guest a fright, Rybalt. He thinks he just observed an assassination."

Rybalt withdrew his talon. "Iony's built up an immunity to pitohui venom."

"Aye, my third mate was a pitohui," Iony said. "Seemed wise to build up my resistance if we wanted to have gryphlets."

"Was?" Neider asked. He'd never heard of anyone

developing an immunity. That might be valuable information if he found himself on the wrong side of Rybalt's machinations.

The gryphon nodded. "Someone new caught her eye and she moved west, if you catch my drift."

Neider did not. "And you kept up your immunity so you could touch your friend here?"

"What?" Iony said. "Rybalt's tender hugs aren't worth that trouble. No, my fourth, fifth, and seventh mates were all trashbirds, too."

The headmaster often forgot about the gryphons' strange mating habits. Gryphonology was considered beneath Redwood Valley scholarship, and the very idea was offensive to northern sensibilities.

Rybalt laughed. "I've missed this. You two, grab a cushion. We'll talk on the balcony while my kin clean out the nests."

NEIDER FILLED Iony and Rybalt in on what had happened while Rybalt ate plate after plate of live scarabs. His beak was lined with the turquoise color of their shells.

The headmaster told them what his spies and scouts had relayed, along with his own experiences. While the Blackwing Eyrie's forces, led by Rybalt, had fought against the Crackling Sea, the kjarr gryphon pride had won a victory over the bog pride and attempted to integrate them. Though the Crackling Sea had fought off Rybalt, the fishery and granaries had been burned in the battle. When a kjarr gryphon had been caught stealing pumpkins, the Crackling Sea opinici had killed him and displayed the body as a warning.

Unfortunately for them, the gryphon had been the son of Jun the Kjarr, and war between gryphon and opinici began anew.

"They won by taking the children," Neider said. "Then they cut off the gryphons' wings and forged an army, sure you would return any day."

The Reeve's Bane looked up from his meal. "Had the Seraph King not sent his fleet against my eyrie, I may have returned."

Iony raised an eyecrest. "Had you not been arrested for treason for taking the army with you to defend your home, you mean. That put a halt to it more than your retreat."

Neider looked east at the ocean. Just past his sight was the island nation where the pitohui had come from. Considering how he'd seen the trashbirds treated, he wouldn't have trusted the other eyries to defend their home, either.

"So the Crackling Sea has an army of wingless gryphons," Rybalt said. "That'll make it hard to fight inside the eyrie once they know we're coming. What happened with the Redwood Valley opinici? Did they ever send aid?"

Neider shook his head. "The wingtorn rebelled and overthrew the eyrie. They exist in peace now, of a sort. The leader of the reds attempted to purge the gryphons from the valley with fire, only for them to burn down her eyrie. She was killed near the Snowfeather Dam fighting against a gryphon they call the Reeve's Bane."

Iony perked up. "Another Reeve's Bane? That can't stand. The pride of your name is at stake, friend."

Rybalt scratched his chin again. "Pride has cost me a lot already. So the Redwood Valley reeve is dead? What about the Crackling Sea? Did their new reeve survive the gryphon uprising?"

"Honestly," Neider said, "after you took apart their last reeve's children, no one has been willing to give themselves the title. From Crestfall on south, reeves no longer exist."

"Who rules them?" Iony asked. "The title is a formality. Reeve, Seraph King, emperor, pride leader: they're just a way to describe who's in charge."

"The gryphons are in charge," Neider said.

"About time someone got the right of it," Iony said.

Rybalt laughed. "No. Seriously?"

Neider nodded. "Most of the opinici live in prides now. They all report to Satra the Kjarr, who leads the wingless gryphons. It's not too dissimilar to what the blackwings started up here: several eyries and prides working together for the protection of all."

Rybalt flicked an empty shell off the balcony. "I'm not sure we have the right of it. Had the Seraph King come to us first, things may have gone differently. You can't live off the coast of the Blackwing Eyrie and not take a side. Some days, I think we've only postponed the inevitable."

Neider kept his beak shut. Things said in private had a way of becoming public. He, too, had started to wonder if he'd backed the right side in this conflict. Only the other side's cruelty had convinced him to side with the Blackwing Eyrie. He'd hoped to persuade Reeve Brevin and the rest of his eyrie to do the same, but once Jonas arrived with his plan to burn down the forest and build farms, there was no stopping either of them.

"Is there a forward base already?" Rybalt asked.

Iony nodded. "Yeah, we've been sending excursions in for the past year, trying to get past their owls. There's another valley north of the Redwood Valley that we've been using. I forget the name, but you can't walk ten paces without stepping on the largest monitor lizards you've ever seen."

"Poisonmaw," Neider said, remembering the maps in his office. "It was the ancestral home of the saberbeak pride before the monitors and plague killed all but one of them."

Rybalt rose, letting exoskeletons drop around him. His fur and feathers shone, slick with the poison he stole from the scarabs. "Opinicus pride leaders, gryphon reeves, the last saberbeak, and another Reeve's Bane. We have a lot of targets to kill. We'd best get started."

"There's one more thing." The headmaster tossed a scroll to Rybalt. Inside was a map of the Redwood Valley Eyrie with the treasury circled. The Ashen Weald had not yet recovered Reeve Brevin's fortunes. "Another target our blackwing allies wish us to look into. Two, really. My merchant and scholar spies found something of interest in the ruins."

"Oh good, more scholar books," Iony complained. "I look forward to flying those up the longest mountain range on the continent."

The headmaster didn't correct Iony as to the focus of their search. The glacier pride leader wouldn't be any more excited about flying an eyrie's worth of metal beads up the mountains.

"And the other target?" Rybalt asked.

"It could be nothing," Neider admitted, "but someone we'd assumed long dead has reappeared among the fisherfolk."

REEVE RYBALT

BANE OF THE CRACKLING SEA REEVE

1

THE FREE PRIDES

"The Reeve's Bane has returned!" came the cry from Hatzel's nesting grounds.

Zeph winced a little at the epithet, but he was grateful to be home again. He'd spent all winter with the fisherfolk except for a brief visit to Snowfall for the Blue-eyed Festival. While he'd seen Xavi and Pink Paw there, Hatzel had remained absent. She'd been the one to kill Snowfall's old leader, Vosk, and she had yet to come to terms with that.

Kia floated down after Zeph, landing with a practiced opinicus grace. Several gryphlets and chicks, now starting to look more like fledglings, rushed over to her to show off the new fur and feather paint designs they'd come up with. She spent time with each while Zeph unpacked their harnesses.

He chatted with the various members of his pride while he looked around. With the influx of refugees, both gryphon and opinicus, the nesting grounds had evolved from two simple caves to several buildings and the flyway, a cleared section of the upper canopy to make it easier to fly under the forest.

After a few minutes, Xavi flew down and collected his wayward friend.

"I hope you two don't mind a little more flying," he said. "Hatzel is meeting with Orlea and the old medicine gryphon north of here. She said I should bring you when you arrive."

Kia reattached her harness, but Zeph left his off. It had been common practice for gryphons to wear them among the fisherfolk, but he was looking forward to doing without for a while. They followed Xavi into one of the flyway paths marked with a snake.

"How bad is it?" Kia asked while they flew. It had taken most of the winter for word of Cherine's disappearance to reach the fisherfolk shore and even longer before they'd discovered the Ashen Weald had been the ones to take him. By the time they found out he was missing and packed to head north, things had escalated.

"Six dead," Xavi said. "Four gryphons and two opinici."

Zeph had a hard time believing it. "And you really think it was Ninox?"

"I don't know," Xavi admitted, "but the Ashen Weald sure think it's her."

"What does she say?" Kia asked. "Surely, she's not mad at Hatzel or Orlea's prides."

"We can't ask her," Xavi said. "Her whole pride just disappeared. Parrotface traders came to the camp one day, and it was just gone. Forty owl gryphons, vanished."

Zeph shivered. "And then the dead bodies started appearing?"

"And then the dead bodies started appearing," Xavi confirmed. "Always gryphons or opinici who had gone out after dark."

"They stole Cherine from her, and now she's stolen the night from them." Kia had been unaware of Cherine's relationship with Ninox until word had come of his disappearance through Orlea, who confirmed that Cherine was the father of Ninox's egg. Kia and Cherine's relationship had finally seemed to be over after their last fight, but every now and then Kia got a far-off look that made Zeph wonder if she was regretting leaving for the shore.

They reached the end of the flyway. He'd been so caught up in worrying about Cherine that he hadn't paid any attention to where they'd been going. The path through the canopy dropped them at the Summer Falls, where Reeve Brevin had ambushed him.

A glance confirmed Kia shared his distress. Since the night of the fire, the night he became the Reeve's Bane, neither of them had returned here. He looked around and saw the trees where the reeve had tried to kill him, the ones he'd hidden in, and the one where he'd killed her. His scars ached and burned with the memories of her metal talons.

Perched atop the remains of a massive peacock statue was Hatzel. He'd missed her dark plumage, saber beak, and kindness.

"You two were running late, so we got started without you." She motioned them over. "I'm sorry for the location. This is the one place everyone avoids."

Zeph and Kia settled in. Across from the alabaster-colored peacock's head was the hood of the cobra statue that used to adorn the other side of the Snowfeather Dam. On top of it were Orlea and the lead medicine gryphon.

It was strange for the medicine gryphon to be here. In the absence of Zrim Feathermane, she should be leading the Feathermane Pride. Instead, she'd chosen to remain neutral. Her medicine gryphons treated both the Ashen Weald and free prides alike.

Orlea made more sense. Her opinicus pride, once a small crew of underbough survivors living in crates, had taken over the farms on the grasslands. They'd even managed to get the metalworks up and running again. While they hadn't re-opened the mines, they were melting down scrap and turning it into tools and harness buckles. So far, none of the scrap had been used to make weapons, at least as far as he knew.

The only free prides who were absent were the taiga pride and the Strix Pride. Snowfall was crawling with Ashen Weald preparing to escort the kjarr fledglings from the Strix Plateau to the kjarr nesting grounds through the new mountain pass, and if Xavi was to be believed, Ninox's forty owl gryphons had all vanished.

Orlea turned from Zeph to Kia. "With the addition of the scholar who saved the weald and the gryphon who toppled an eyrie, I declare this secret meeting of the free prides officially in session."

"There's no need to be so dramatic, songbird." The medicine gryphon's voice was honey on bark.

"Is it true that this is all Ninox's doing?" Zeph asked. "Are we sure? Have any of you spoken to her?"

"Nobody has," Orlea said. "I sent some of Ninox's friends up to the Owlfeather Highlands to look for her, but the caves are all empty."

"Owlfeather Highlands?" Zeph asked.

"We, that's Younce and I," Orlea amended, "gave the old Snowfeather nesting grounds to Ninox. That's why she visited me the last time. She was planning on setting up nests there before her egg hatched."

The old medicine gryphon had remained silent on

whether or not she'd talked to Ninox, a fact Zeph hadn't missed. If any of Ninox's pride had come in as patients, he didn't know if the medicine gryphons would admit it. There was a level of privacy to their dealings that the other prides respected. With two dead opinici, however, Grenkin and Orlea may not feel the same way about gryphon decorum.

"Just how attached was Ninox to Cherine?" Kia asked. "Was he a member of her pride?"

"Who knows?" Orlea shrugged. "Does it matter?"

"Well, gryphons don't take permanent mates, right?" Kia prompted. "So he wasn't reeve-consort of the Strix Pride. Was he even a member? I'm trying to figure out if this is Ninox upset over a friend, Ninox upset over a lover, or Ninox upset over having a pride member kidnapped."

"Or not Ninox at all," Zeph added.

"She was always private," Orlea said. "I know Cherine was teaching her how to read. I know they searched the mountains together and found several mass graves."

"What?" Kia asked. "What was that last part?"

"I forget you two spent the winter on the shore," Hatzel said. "The Ashen Weald attack that captured Cherine, as best we can tell from our spies—"

"That's Biski," the old medicine gryphon whispered.

"—As best we can tell from Biski," Hatzel corrected, "the kidnapping took place at a hidden workshop along the mountain pass. Supposedly, it had been owned by Mally the Nighthaunt. When they searched for more information, they found maybe two hundred skeletons, all opinicus mothers or chicks."

Kia had been pacing. She sat down. "I remember her bringing Mally's book to us. That was the last time I saw either of them. I just thought it was part of Neider's library that survived the fire. I didn't think... two hundred? There were *two hundred* dead opinici in the Owlfeather Highlands no one knew about?"

"Maybe...maybe the recent deaths are Mally the Nighthaunt, too?" Xavi suggested. "With the fire and Ashen Weald, a lot has been going on. There are still a lot of gryphons and opinici who went missing the night the Redwood Valley Eyrie burnt down."

"We'd know if he was out there," Orlea said. "You can't just hide a force large enough to do that kind of kidnapping and murder right next door."

Hatzel tilted her head to the side. The jagged, saber-toothed edges of her beak caught the light. "If Ninox is any indication, apparently you can."

Orlea laughed. It was a short, nervous exclamation. "I stand corrected. Okay, let's say this is Ninox. What do we do? How do we stop her from killing more gryphons and opinici?"

"We rescue Cherine," Kia said. "If she's going to keep killing until she gets him back, well, that's our solution."

"Great," the old medicine gryphon said. "How do we do that? Nobody knows where he is."

"If he's at the kjarr nesting grounds, we'll never get him out," Xavi said.

"I don't think he's there," the old medicine gryphon said.

"Your spy?" Hatzel asked.

"Our Biski," the medicine gryphon confirmed. "The island fortress is clear, too. It's crawling with my gryphons. There's no room there, either. Some of the Ashen Weald are nervous about Cherine's disappearance. Since the fantails are living with the kjarr gryphons until the weald regrows, they wouldn't want to risk being seen bringing prisoners back and forth."

"What about the Crackling Sea Eyrie?" Orlea asked. "It's huge. It held hundreds of wingtorn in the lower levels. It has at least one secret passage."

"Makes sense," Hatzel said. "But how do we confirm it? And if it's true, how do we get him out of there?"

"We know some Crackling Sea opinici," Kia said. "Tresh or Quess might be able to get a favor out of them."

"I guess it's back to the shore for us," Zeph said.

The opinicus pride leader seemed to be thinking. She looked up. "Oh, Naya is staying with me. We get regular goliath bird caravans from the shore now that there's a small bridge. You can send word with her."

Hatzel had noticed Orlea's fur-gathering. "What's on your mind? This is a long shot. If you have a better plan, I'd like to hear it."

Orlea chewed a talon. "Okay, it's just...what if we force the Ashen Weald to hand over Cherine?"

"They're not admitting they have him," the old medicine gryphon said. "What are you going to do, kidnap Satra and hold her ransom?"

"No, of course not," Orlea said. "It was a silly idea. We'll see what your fisherfolk friends say."

Something was still wrong with Orlea, however. Zeph could see it in the way she held herself and the swishing of her tailfeathers. Whatever her plan was to convince the Ashen Weald to turn over Cherine, she might go ahead with it on her own.

"When do you want to meet again?" Hatzel asked.

"Ten days?" Orlea suggested. "I don't know how long it'll take to persuade the fisherfolk."

"Just send a messenger," Hatzel said. "The rest of us are all at my nesting grounds."

The old medicine gryphon stood up and stretched her wings. Zeph couldn't remember ever having seen her fly before. She just seemed to appear wherever she was needed.

"I'm heading to the kjarr," she said. "I thought my absence would make some of the Ashen Weald reconsider how they treat the independent prides, and maybe it did. But the young feathermanes aren't looking for some elderly gryphon who can't see to lead them. They're looking for another Zrim Feathermane, and they're starting to wonder if Merin is that gryphon."

Zeph frowned. He thought he'd been doing the right thing by aiding the fisherfolk. Helping them rebuild had let them trade fish that kept everyone fed. But over the winter, a lot had happened in his absence. He was starting to regret his decision to stay away.

He and Kia followed Orlea back to her nesting grounds so they could get word to the fisherfolk. With any luck, one of the Crackling Sea rangers hiding on Luminaire could be persuaded to return home and search for Cherine.

2

NEW EYRIE

"This place is a trash heap," Foultner kicked over a crate of makeshift nesting materials. "You should come live with me in the kjarr."

Henders looked up from his morning grooming. "Are you saying we should move in together? Do you want to share nests?"

"I mean, I guess," Foultner mumbled. That wasn't what she'd meant, but it had been awhile, and it made sense. She'd never expected things to last with Henders, but he'd grown on her the past few months. He was always happy, and it was a nice counterbalance to her poacher pessimism.

She'd been feeling a little lost this winter. Following Satra around and playing bodyguard wasn't the same rush as back when Foultner helped topple waystations and eyries. She was having a hard time feeling like her work here was valued. She thought having a nest of her own and food to eat would make her happy, but instead, she felt adrift and without value.

"I just don't want to fly out to New Eyrie to see you,"

she said. "This whole place should be melted down for scrap. And the smell is terrible, worse than the under-bough used to be."

"Aw, I don't need any more convincing," Henders said. "I'd be happy to move in with you."

"I think someone put your egg in the nest upside-down," she grumbled, but she was inwardly pleased. It might be nice to have someone to come home to.

Henders slicked down his head feathers. "Are you sure it's okay? I know the reds are still less than welcome in the Ashen Weald."

"Hey, the Ashen Weald would be nothing without me. Who's going to tell me no?" She was about to suggest they pack up his things and then throw them out when she heard a commotion from outside.

In her experience, commotions were never a good thing, especially among the poor. Maybe the northern quarter had *commotions* to celebrate a crate of fish arriv-ing. As an underbough opinicus, *commotion* had meant the Reeve's Guard going through her home and breaking things under the pretense of looking for red fern.

She reached for her black harness but stopped herself. Right now, with her generic nest sparrow markings, she was essentially invisible among the New Eyrie refugees. If she walked out there wearing fancy armor and talons, she'd become something else.

She grabbed her old poacher harness instead and told Henders to stay put. She squinted at the bright sunlight. A crowd was gathering inside the walls of New Eyrie. Despite his small salary as a ranch hand, Henders couldn't afford to be within the gates, so his tent and nest were along the shore to the north.

Foultner flew atop the walls and looked down at the

gathering opinici. They were in a half-circle around something metallic and shiny. She flew down and perched atop the burned-out husk of Impir's old workshop so she could get a better look.

The shiny thing was an opinicus.

She blinked a few times. An opinicus in metal armor. That much metal wasn't a show of power. Well, it was a show of power, but more than that, it was a show of wealth. What he was wearing was worth more than all the beads Foultner had accumulated in her entire life.

The rich opinicus was surrounded by ten others. They all had thin metal breastplates, the type you could probably still wear while flying. They were all white with black circles around their eyes. One of them had the tips of his feathers painted gold.

Goldfeather's voice was soft, but he projected well, and it reached her even atop the workshop. It was a nice trick.

Foultner only half-listened to his words, however. She watched the way he spoke and the way the New Eyrie refugees reacted to him. The poor and distraught listened to his kind words of hope, but they looked at his metal-wrapped friend and remembered who they had once been.

While the underbough had joined Orlea's pride, those who remained at New Eyrie had once been merchants, skilled laborers, nobility, or the idle rich. They ate squirrel and snake meat now, but they remembered what it was like to dine on parrot and ocean fish. In the metallic armor, they saw the reflections of what it had been like to live in indulgence.

Henders settled down next to her. He'd never been good at following directions.

"I don't recognize their eyrie badges. Do you?"

Foultner asked. "Did anyone like that ever visit Reeve Brevin?"

Henders shifted nervously. "No, the only eyries that ever came to the Redwood Valley were the Crackling Sea and Crestfall. And even then, Crestfall only sent a trade delegation every other year."

She didn't ask if they were from Crestfall. The color *Crestfall pink* came from the shade of its flamingo-like inhabitants.

She narrowed her eyes to get a look at their eyrie badges. They seemed to have an opinicus head with a spiky crown. She turned to ask Henders a question, but he didn't make eye contact with her.

She grabbed his head and looked right at him. "What are you hiding?"

"We're not supposed to talk about what we saw in the bog," he said. "Merin and Blinky forbid it."

"Yes, you're absolutely correct." Foultner thought this over. "No one except Satra, Merin, Blinky, or me should be told any details that haven't been approved."

She removed one of the boards blocking the way into Impir's workshop. Opinici were a suspicious lot, and it was the only building no one had turned into housing.

She pulled Henders into the hole. "Come on in. We can discuss it privately in here."

"Erlock had a badge like that, before she disappeared into the jungle." He'd been very quick to accept Foultner's ruse. "It said Piprik on it."

"Yes, of course. That's what I expected." Then, after a moment, she added, "Who was Piprik again?"

"He's the fisherfolk who helped cure the starlings," Henders said. "He was white with dark eyes like the opinici outside."

"I see." She climbed out of the musty workshop and onto its roof. She hadn't paid much attention to a medicine opinicus from a backwater fisherfolk town. She knew they'd sent someone, knew he'd returned home after the expedition left, but didn't know anything else about him.

Getting information on the fisherfolk wouldn't be easy. The rangers who'd served under Ellore had all claimed sanctuary the moment they hit Sandpiper's Dune. With news of the parasite having spread after the fiasco at New Eyrie, they were worried about being tried for war crimes.

Rightfully worried, considering how many scholars and opinici of questionable loyalties Merin had rounded up. Foultner reached for the metal talons on her bracers and realized she'd left them back at Henders's tent.

"Hey, at least they're not blackwings, right?" he asked. "Maybe they're friends."

The Reeve's Guard and military often said that the enemy of their enemy was their friend. Foultner, however, was a poacher and knew it was entirely possible to have the entire world against you, no matter their interpersonal problems with each other.

The opinicus with the gold-tipped feathers pulled out a horn and blew it, startling Foultner out of her mental fur-gathering.

A flight of silver opinici appeared from the north carrying boxes, and she reached again for the talons she'd left by Henders's nest. These weren't crates of saltpeter, however. They were of something even more dangerous. They were full of food and clean water. Not just food. This was salted, market-quality food.

The opinicus who was more metal than feathers started handing out fresh harnesses, complete with an opinicus wearing a crown on the badge.

"Fluff," she swore, mindful of Henders's sensitive hearing. "Grab whatever you can't live without from your tent. We're going to the kjarr nesting grounds. When we get there, head straight to my nest."

"Where are you going?" he asked.

First, she was going to get her armor and talons. But after that, "Someone needs to tell Satra another eyrie is encroaching on our territory."

The silver opinicus who'd brought the food was staring at Henders's Reeve's Guard harness. Foultner pulled him back behind the workshop, and they slipped through the crowd and back to his nest.

FOULTNER AND HENDERS FLEW EAST, passing over the Clover Ranch. Habit kept them both over the stretch of sawgrass between the Crackling Sea and the bog. While Urious and Soft Paws had led intensive efforts to keep the northern bog free of starlings, the bog blossoms had only just started blooming, and it would be a while before enough paste had been made to let them clear the entire swamp.

The opinicus couple had just reached the Crackling Sea Eyrie and were about to turn south when Foultner caught sight of several owl gryphons in harnesses coming from the direction of the goliath bird pass. To avoid confusion with Ninox's pride, all of the owl gryphons who had joined the Ashen Weald were required to wear something to show their affiliation.

"Go on without me," she told Henders. "I need to see what's going on."

She hadn't needed to say anything, as he was already

flying to catch up to the owls. He struck up a conversation while Foultner looked at the direction they were heading. A few fantails were posted on top of the trees. She sighed, then headed in that direction, landed, and looked around.

Feathermanes formed a perimeter on the ground around two more dead bodies. Merin was asking questions of Blinky, curled up in a napping pose, who gave one word answers without opening her eyes.

"Nice of you to join us," Merin said. After the Battle for New Eyrie, he'd had gone back into the grasslands and retrieved the bracelets worn by the opinicus commander. It was strange seeing jewelry on a gryphon. Somewhere, he'd picked up an extra bracelet he wore around his tail.

"I was at New Eyrie visiting a friend." Foultner had spent so much time around Satra that she'd built up a camaraderie with Merin by association. "How many are we up to now?"

"Ten." Blinky kept her eyes closed. Her nares opened the tiniest bit. "Tell Henders hello from me."

Foultner stood over the dead bodies. They were both blue heron opinici.

"Grenkin isn't going to like this." She pointed at the feathermanes guarding the crime scene. "Abyssal eels, Merin, you couldn't find one opinicus to come down here? You know how this looks."

"I sent for *you*, but you were off with Henders," Merin chided.

She'd become their go-to opinicus when they didn't want things to look too gryphonic. While the gryphons seemed to think it worked to assuage the fears of the Crackling Sea, she wasn't so sure. Word was starting to spread that she'd been the spy who'd infiltrated several eyries and a waystation to free the wingtorn.

Well, it's too late now. She turned her attention to the victims. One had been cut down pretty quickly. It looked like the other murders. The other, however, didn't have a scratch on her.

"Was this Ninox?" Foultner asked Blinky. "How'd she kill this one?"

"Perhaps the opinicus's heart gave out," Blinky said. "You should have a medicine gryphon look at her."

"Don't fool yourself," Merin said. "The medicine gryphons aren't neutral in this. By refusing to join the Ashen Weald, they're basically working for Ninox."

"We'll find one we can trust," Foultner said. "In the meantime, are we sure this even is Ninox? This is pretty far from her hunting grounds."

Blinky opened her eyes. She yawned and stood up, padding over to sniff the dead bodies. "I do not know."

"Scratch marks, killed at night, left for us to find," Merin listed off the facts. "Sounds like an owl gryphon to me."

"Yes," Blinky said. "But would Ninox want it to look like an owl gryphon? She might hide the kill."

"So if it looks like an owl, it's not an owl, unless that's what an owl would want us to think," Foultner said. "I'm glad you woke up from your nap to tell us that. What about this one?"

Blinky sniffed the other dead body without any scratches. She shrugged. "Who can know such things?"

"We should bring back the rest of your kin and have them inspect the bodies," Merin said. "Maybe they'll find something you missed."

Blinky stood on her back legs to look him in the eye. With the scars across her face, she could look frightening when she wasn't napping. "If there is something in the night that is killing gryphons and opinici, you would do better to let us sleep during the day so we may protect the kjarr nesting grounds."

Foultner reached reflexively for her metal talons, the same weapon that had inflicted the wounds on Blinky when worn by their previous owner. She didn't want to break up a fight between Merin and Blinky. That seemed like a good way to lose a limb. But dragging Blinky to the goliath bird pass during daylight hours wasn't a good way for Merin to make friends. Unlike Satra and Foultner, Blinky had not come to think of him fondly.

"Fine," Merin said. "You're right. Thank you for coming out here. In the future, we'll ask you to take a look at night. I appreciate your protection."

Blinky remained tall for another thirty heartbeats, then lowered herself to all fours and curled back up, putting her paws over her beak.

"There's another possibility," Foultner said. She'd just remembered why she was on her way back to the kjarr and not spending her day off raiding the snacks Henders hid under his nest. "We've got company at New Eyrie. I was on my way to tell Satra. Perhaps you'd both like to join me?"

3

KJARR NESTING GROUNDS

"A new eyrie?" Satra asked. "If only we knew who they were. It would be great to have a scholar to ask. Unfortunately, all of ours have been locked up."

"Mally the Nighthaunt. Impir the Mad. Bario the Phoenix. Headmaster Neider. Cherine the Calculator." Merin didn't back down. "Any of the scholars from the university could be working for their old mentors. As we clear them of wrongdoing, we'll start releasing the innocent ones. Until then, I'm not willing to take any risks with your life. All that's needed to render the Ashen Weald leaderless is one opinicus with enough saltpeter to level this building."

He wasn't entirely wrong, which annoyed Satra. She'd let Bario live, and he killed an island's worth of opinici in his escape. That was on her. And the Ashen Weald had lost a lot of leadership in the struggles of the past year, both the dead like Zrim or missing like Erlock Chartail. One crate of saltpeter in the council chamber and the Ashen Weald might not be able to function.

Satra sighed. She was under a lot of pressure to get the

kjarr fledglings returned home. If politics weren't part of the problem, she'd wait until Ninox was done killing. Satra didn't think the owl gryphon would harm children, but she hadn't expected Ninox to vanish, either.

Satra looked out at her council. Without Zrim and Erlock, she was sorely lacking in allies who would back her without question. The old medicine gryphon had arrived midday to take her place as acting head of the Feathermane Pride. The parrotface elder, after a scrap with Merin's clueless children, had come to make sure her voice was heard. Strix's sons often attended meetings but rarely spoke. She'd come to think of them as fancy clay jars she cycled through on a weekly basis.

She couldn't afford to antagonize Merin. Not if she wanted the council to help her. Not if she wanted it to mean something. Without him, Ranger Lord Grenkin was her closest ally.

"Are we making a problem out of nothing?" The ranger lord cleared his throat. "The New Eyrie refugees have been impossible to help. They refuse to work, refuse to organize, refuse to elect leaders. Why not let another eyrie take them off our talons?"

"If we can get them off their lazy tailfeathers, it would be nice to get a metalworks up and running," Foultner said. "As long as Orlea has scrap to repurpose, she's been luring skilled craftsopinici back to the Redwood Valley."

Satra snorted. "Short of opening trade with Crestfall or taking the ones in the Redwood Valley, I don't see how we're going to get a metalworks or flameworks of our own."

Luckily, Orlea hadn't laid claim to the remains of the eyrie itself. The old Redwood Valley Eyrie's treasury had disappeared beneath the rubble. It would do a lot to re-open trade if the Ashen Weald could quietly remove it from the ruins before any of the independent prides located it.

"What about Crestfall?" the parrotface elder spoke up. "What's happened there?"

"We don't know," Grenkin admitted. "The reeve's pet has migrated to the northern edge of the sea. We can't get close."

"Migrated?" Foultner asked. "I thought it stayed around here. Why would it head north?"

"It, ah, likes to eat opinici," Grenkin explained. "If it's gone north, there are probably dead opinici along the northern shore."

"It's a whale," the parrotface said. "Just go over it."

"It's taken to spitting a jet of water at anything that flies near it," Grenkin said.

"It does what?" Foultner laughed. No one else joined in. "Is someone teaching it tricks?"

Satra's tail twitched back and forth. "I don't want to deal with another eyrie making a move while we're waiting for the blackwings, but it would be nice to have an ally. You're sure you've never seen white opinici with dark eyes, Ranger Lord? They never came to trade?"

Grenkin shook his head. "No, not as such. The one carrying the supplies that Foultner described as a copper hawk except silver, maybe. There was a small eyrie along the argent reaches. Every now and then, they'd send their fastest flyers across the desert to trade with Crestfall and us for medicine. They never had much of value."

Foultner walked to the map on the wall. It had come from the Crackling Sea library. She traced a talon from New Eyrie all the way southeast past the taiga and weald to Swan's Rest. "Henders says the medicine opinicus the fisherfolk sent to help with the starlings was white with dark circles around his eyes."

"Is there a subtle way we could go down there and question him about where he came from?" the parrotface asked. "Or is that some fisherfolk taboo?"

"It is that," Merin said. "But also, the fisherfolk are going to assume anyone you send down there is part of a ruse to arrest Bruen and the rest of Ellore's rangers."

Satra ran a paw through her crest and smoothed down an ear tuft. Ellore was still a wanted criminal, and her rangers had wisely chosen not to return to the Crackling Sea after being rescued by Urious's expedition. So long as they were on the shore, Orlea's pride served as a trade mediator between the Ashen Weald and the fisherfolk.

A quiet voice spoke up. In the low light, her feathers and fur faded into the walls, and her bog blossom blue skull and skeletal patterns stood out. "There is an easy way around that."

"What's that, Soft Paws?" Satra tried to encourage their newest member. While she knew where the parrotface elder and old feathermane medicine gryphon stood, the new bog pride leader was a mystery to everyone.

Urious had returned from the bog with stories of mummies, starlings, and giant turtles. But he'd also returned with a collection of young gryphons painted with skulls and flowers who petitioned to join the Ashen Weald as the bog pride.

Satra had granted their wish, and they'd set up a new nesting grounds along the southeastern mangrove coast with Soft Paws as their leader. All of the young, winged bog witches had joined, but there were still bog wingtorn and crones who held a grudge. After the Heart of the Bog had been flooded—by both water and starlings—they'd disappeared. Satra still hoped to reach a peace with them, someday, but she knew their wounds ran deep.

"Send Ranger Lord Grenkin," the witch recommended. "Have him absolve the rangers of all crimes. Have him honor them for their sacrifice. Have him apologize for not going down there sooner."

Grenkin and Merin shared a look that Satra knew too well. More than anyone else, those two had been the slowest to forgive anyone who had acted without honor during the war.

"Hmm," Grenkin said. "You're right. I hadn't considered forgiveness and contrition as options."

"What do we know about the rangers who refused to come home?" Foultner asked. "Has anyone talked to their friends and family?"

"As best as the inquisitors have found," Merin said, "it's unclear if they knew what the parasite did."

Soft Paws stood. Her paint caught the light. "The bog witches held them for months. They seemed as confused by the parasite as the other prisoners."

Satra studied the young gryphon. She'd spent hours asking questions about the bog pride and their leader. Part of her refused to believe that her sister, Vitra, had led a rebellion. Only Urious bringing back some of her wing feathers had convinced Satra it was true.

Grenkin stood to leave. "Then it looks like I should gather my rangers and fly south."

"No," Soft Paws said. "You will go alone, unarmed. You will come with me to Bogwash, and we will take a raft to Sandpiper's Dune. This is an apology, not a show of force."

Grenkin bowed his long, heron-like neck, and Satra had to smile. While she'd have preferred that Urious or

Thenca take over the bog pride's leadership, she was starting to like Soft Paws.

"While you two do that, let's talk about the new curfews," Satra said. "I don't want anyone flying after dark until Ninox is found."

While Grenkin and Soft Paws left, Satra let Foultner talk about the restrictions. Every time another dead body turned up, the chance that their conflict with Ninox would end peacefully diminished, even if Cherine were found innocent at trial. And, based on the delays, Merin was gathering enough evidence to make certain that Cherine would not be found innocent.

Thinking of the prisoners gave her another idea of someone who might be willing to tell her about their new white eyrie visitors.

AFTER THE MEETING, Satra caught up to Merin outside and they walked through the kjarr nesting grounds. "I'd like to visit the prisoners."

"It's not safe for you to be there." His eyes showed concern. "But if you're sure, I'll take you."

"Thank you," she said. Proper protocol would have the prisoners brought to her, but part of having a hidden prison was limiting travel to and from it. "It's a long shot, but I might be able to find out something about our New Eyrie guests."

Merin's tail swayed back and forth, its metal band catching the light. While he'd gathered four bracelets himself from the New Eyrie commander, she'd been the one to find a fifth matching band. It had been her Blue-eyed Festival gift to him.

"Cherine was a food scholar. I don't think he knows anything," Merin said. "And nobody has gotten a word out of the blackwing."

"Actually, it's the headmaster's pet I'm most interested in," Satra said.

"I hadn't thought of that," he laughed. "You're pretty smart. It's no wonder you're the head of the Ashen Weald."

She thought back to the night of the fire. "Did you think this is how things would end up? Back when you showed up in the northern quarter looking for me."

They crossed the bridge. This was a wingtorn city now, and while there were no restrictions on flight like there were on staying out after dark, most winged gryphons walked within the city out of respect.

"In a way, it is," Merin admitted. "Prides working together, hunting grounds expanded. Cooperation and a better life are what I imagined. In other ways, not so much. I thought Zrim and Erlock would be here to share in it."

"No one could have predicted the starlings." Satra didn't know if that was true. Vitra and Jun may have known. No one had expected Satra to become Kjarr, so she hadn't been taught about their iridescent green neighbors to the west. "Nor the Crackling Sea surrendering."

Merin laughed again. "I remember the expression on your face when it happened. I guess you didn't plan for everything."

She shook her head. "Not the opinici being our allies. I'm glad they are, don't misunderstand me, but I don't think that would have happened if my father had survived."

Merin made his way up the Kjarr River towards the

start of the rapids. "I've come to think of Grenkin and Foultner as friends. When you take an opinicus out of an eyrie, they're not so different from us. When you put a reeve in charge of them, something changes."

She'd had this conversation with Merin several times over the winter. With the war and everything else, neither of them had taken a mate for the season. Not that Satra ever planned to, but it was unusual for Merin. Maybe he'd decided he had enough children. Hopefully he wasn't holding a rushlight for her. Her interest in male gryphons or having children was nonexistent.

The harpy eagle gryphon clicked the metal bracelet on his tail against a rock to get her attention. "Need anything before we go?"

She looked down at the river that split her nesting grounds in two. From up here, the wingtorn looked small, but they also looked free.

"I'm fine," she said. "We'll be back tonight?"

"Depends on how fast you talk," he said. "If it looks like we won't make it back before dark, you can stay in the weald. Askel and Triddle's nests are empty while they help with the path."

4

PRISONERS

Far from the kjarr, Satra wandered through the poorly lit corridors down to where the prisoners were kept. Merin led the way, and two Ashen Weald rangers kept watch over her at all times. She had uncomfortable flashbacks to her time at the Redwood Valley Eyrie.

"How did you find this place?" This was her first visit to the prison. Before, she hadn't understood how anyone could hide anything from Ninox. Now that she'd seen where the prisoners were kept, she didn't think anyone would think to look here, and the running water kept the guards from being overheard by weald owl super-hearing.

"The fires," Merin said. "Specifically, the explosions knocked something loose. One of the scholars we picked up was an architect. He said the opinici had started planning another eyrie out here. Once we knew what to look for, finding this location was easy."

"First Ninox's hideaway, then the prison," Satra added. "Just how many places like this did the opinici build?"

"Your guess is as good as mine." He shrugged. "If you'll

wait here, we'll pull Cherine and the blackwing out for questioning elsewhere so you can be alone with the headmaster's pet."

"No, leave Cherine," she said. When Merin raised an eyecrest, she added, "I'd like to see how they interact. We can separate them if it looks like I made the wrong decision."

"As you wish." Merin motioned for the guards to unlock the last door.

As Satra remained unseen in a side passage, they led the blackwing prisoner back down the corridors to another room. Rumor had it, he hadn't spoken a word to either of his captors—neither Ninox's owls nor the Ashen Weald's rangers had been able to convince him to so much as chirp. While the individual rooms were well-lit, there were no braziers in the corridors.

Once the room was clear, Merin motioned for her to go through. "We'll be waiting outside. Shout if you need us."

"You're not coming in with me?" she asked.

"No, they won't talk with me there," he said. "My children were cruel when they caught Cherine the first time with the saltpeter. He refuses to speak if I'm in the room."

"I see." Some days, Satra was glad for Merin's support. Other days, she wondered about the path she'd set them all down.

She stepped into the cavern. While the other criminals were kept in side passages, the main area was reserved for their three most important guests: Cherine, the blackwing scout, and Headmaster Neider's assistant.

Cherine looked up from his cell. His eyes didn't show any sign of recognition, and for the first time, Satra realized that he probably had no idea what she looked like.

They'd never met, and by his account, he'd spent the conflict helping Orlea's pride after the fires.

"Hello, Cherine." She spoke softly. "I'm Satra the Kjarr."

His curious eyes turned suspicious. He looked from her golden crest of feathers to her kjarr features. It seemed unlikely he'd fail to recognize her in the future.

"I wish to speak to my family and my pride," he said. "Or do I not have that right in your Ashen Weald?"

"You do," she said. "And you'll get to when the trial starts. It won't be long now. If you're found innocent, you'll have my full apologies. I've heard your version of what you were doing with the saltpeter that day. If it bears out, I owe you my thanks. If not, you'll be punished with the rest of the Jonas loyalists."

He remained quiet, and she was left to speculate. He'd told an interesting story. But the fact he'd been found with the saltpeter about to light it on fire was persuasive in and of itself. He'd also escaped Merin's pride and gone into hiding, evading everyone for months. Was that more likely for a scholar or a spy?

Satra turned to the other prisoner. "Hello there. I believe Cherine calls you the cockatiel forger. Do you have something else you'd like me to call you? A name or an alias?"

"How polite." The cockatiel's gape had been stained red by fern use. "I'd expect nothing less from the gryphons' reeve. Call me what you'd like."

Satra questioned the wisdom of giving him access to the red fern again. Ninox and Cherine had attempted to get information out of him by clearing his mind. Merin believed that small doses of the fern would make him more cooperative.

"I'm sure you're tired of questions about your black-wing friends," she said. "I'd like to ask you about other eyries."

Cherine and the forger both perked up.

"I worked with the Crackling Sea scholars a bit on capybara and goliath bird ranching," Cherine said. "And I've read Crestfall's fishing texts, though they didn't do us any good. As best I can tell, only a Crestfall opinicus could live off of their diet. The pink shrimp are toxic to the rest of us."

Except for the question of whether or not Crestfall still stood, she didn't need information on those two eyries. The Crackling Sea's libraries had detailed accounts on Crestfall—the Palace of Fire and Ice in the desert, the glassworks by the sea, the eyrie in the canyon.

"No, these opinici are all white," she said. "They resemble kites, with large black circles around their eyes. Their messengers are different, like silver hawks."

"Where are they?" the cockatiel forger asked. She hesitated, and he prompted, "I can tell you who they are. There's no harm in it for me. But humor me, in case I escape before you execute me. I'd like something to take back to the headmaster."

She didn't see the harm in it. "New Eyrie. They've started providing support for the refugees there."

"Is my family okay?" Cherine asked. This had been the single question he'd asked every time someone tried to question him.

Withholding the information wasn't an act of cruelty. No one in the Ashen Weald knew what had happened to his family. Since the Battle for New Eyrie, the reds living there didn't seem happy to have gryphons about. Even the blues were met with disdain.

"I haven't heard word either way," she said. His posture suggested he thought she was lying.

The cockatiel was staring at her. There was a clarity to his eyes she didn't expect from an addict.

He turned his questions to Cherine. "We were all in the same room together once before. Do you remember, Cherine?"

"At the Redwood Valley, you mean?" The scholar shook his head. "No, I'm sure I would have noticed a gryphon."

"She hid in the back of the room." The forger turned back to Satra. "Her paws were covered. She came in before the lesson started and put a blank journal over her forelegs. Then, she waited until the class left. Everyone saw her harness and assumed she was a Crackling Sea apprentice."

Satra's eyes narrowed. He was correct, but she didn't know anyone had seen her. While she was Jonas's pet, she'd done her best to learn how to be an opinicus. When she asked for access to the lectures, he'd pulled a few strings, and she'd been allowed to visit some of the lower level classrooms.

Of course, Jonas had probably pulled those strings with Neider. It made sense the headmaster's pet would know that.

"Yes, you're correct," she admitted. "I wanted to understand my jailors. Jonas wanted me to learn as much as I could, hoping I'd teach the gryphlets to be members of the eyrie."

"I hear he burned in the fire," the cockatiel said.

"We can hope." Satra had used her resources to look for a body. Foultner had found hundreds, all burned beyond her ability to identify them.

"So you know that a 'reeve' is someone who rules a section of land for the king," he said.

"Except there are no kings anymore," Cherine countered. "The reeves rule the eyries themselves, beholden to no one."

"Well," the cockatiel drew out the word, "there weren't any kings until one of the reeves got greedy."

"Our white eyrie guests?" Satra asked.

"From atop his Alabaster Eyrie, the white reeve declared himself the Seraph King." The forger spoke as though reciting someone else's words. "The true king had died long ago. The white reeve claimed the Alabaster Eyrie had been the first on the continent, said he was descended from the king, and it was time for the other reeves to return to their subservience."

"If that's true, why haven't we heard of him?" Cherine asked.

"Here? In the corner of a valley?" The cockatiel laughed. "If you ask another opinicus to name all the eyries, you're lucky if they include the Crackling Sea, let alone the Redwood Valley. With the starling's pridelord to the west, the Crackling Sea to the north, and the mountains, we were safe because we'd been forgotten.

"And then Bario's father went north and reminded the world that we exist. Then the blackwing reeve nearly took the Crackling Sea. And now the white reeve is on your borders, feeding your starving opinici because you can't."

"*You* would have them surrender to the blackwings like you did," Cherine said. "How is one any better than the other?"

The forger studied Satra's features. "Did Cherine tell you? When we were captured, there were three of us. The other was a gryphon. He was my friend."

Cherine had told them nothing, and this was new information to Satra.

"The Blackwing Eyrie has allied itself with a talonful of other eyries and a few gryphon prides," the forger continued. "But there are no gryphon prides in the Seraph King's lands."

Cherine rolled his eyes. "Scaremongering."

"We all have to make a choice," the forger said. "I just made mine early. You'll need to pick a side. There's no hiding."

She remained quiet. She didn't know how much of this was true. She was speaking to the enemy, to a prisoner. He benefited from every lie she believed.

"You've heard what happened to the Crackling Sea Eyrie's reeve, oh mighty Kjarr? And his family?" he asked her.

"I have." She had no reason to lie.

"You may not call yourself a reeve, but you don't need to. Up north, they call you the gryphon reeve," he said. "If you side with the Seraph King, you will be deposed, but it doesn't matter. So long as you stand against the Blackwing Eyrie, assassins are coming for you. You won't live to see the winter."

Satra stood and left. She'd received enough threats in her lifetime. Whether they were true or not, she wouldn't let them dictate her actions.

5

LITTLE LIGHTNING BOLT

Piprik cried out in his sleep. From within his dreams, he looked at the body of the dead opinicus at his feet. The corpse had been one of the Seraph King's royal guard. His bright white plumage, the dark circles around his eyes, the eyrie crown insignia on his badge. He was bleeding out over the floor.

Piprik looked down at his own bloody, black talons. He'd never killed an opinicus before. He'd believed, incorrectly, that adrenaline and survival instincts would make it easy. Instead, it was like something in his mind had turned off.

In the back of the room, someone was screaming at him. "Mally has betrayed us! The king's forces will be here any moment. Take the elixir!"

His black talons now held a glass vial. A purple substance swirled inside. In his reflection, blood dripped from his beak. He pulled out the stopper and choked it down. It was still hot and scorched his throat. His body began to overheat. He reached down and pulled the badge off the corpse in front of him. It read Piprik.

"Greyfeather Pip?"

He started awake and looked around his small fisher-folk hut. Standing at the door was a peafowl opinicus. Not assassins, then. Levin.

"More bad dreams?" she asked.

His throat still burned from the dream's elixir, so he righted himself and choked down water.

"Yes, just a nightmare," he said.

The small peafowl squeezed his shoulder. "It's okay. I have them, too."

He looked at her. While her time with the fisher-folk had done wonders for her health, she was still small. Between the fire that claimed her mother, the mysterious death of her father, and the blackwing assassins who killed her sisters, it was no surprise that she had nightmares. She had the same hunted look he did.

Still, here at the edge of the world was the safest place for them both. There was something sacred about the fisherfolk's acceptance. Wherever they existed, both prides and eyries gave them space. Or they had, before Reeve Brevin sent the wingtorn here.

He forced himself to eat some salted fish. Food, water, and rest always did wonders for him. Normally, he'd sleep as long as he needed to, but Rorin and Tresh had asked him to take over tutoring Levin now that she was strong enough to fly to Luminaire on her own.

"What's today? Chemistry?" He opened his medicine bag. His eyes were drawn to a purple vial. Was it a trick of his imagination, or did he feel heat coming off of it?

"No, that was yesterday," Levin said. "Today is fighting!"

"Ah, of course. How could I forget?" His body ached at the thought, but he'd been placed in charge of keeping this peafowl alive, and he believed self-defense and knowledge were the only ways she stood a chance.

They left his hut on the edge of Luminaire and went to the beach. It was a cold spring, was always a cold spring, but the sun on his feathers helped.

"Are we learning peacock talons today?" Levin had made her own set of wooden talons similar to the golden ones her mom had worn.

From what Piprik had gathered, she'd learned a bit about striking out like a snake and some very northern-quarter techniques from her previous tutors at the eyrie. "Next time, little lightning bolt. This time, I think we'll learn the secret techniques of the pitohui grapplers."

"Pitohui?" she asked. "Where's that?"

"On an island, just like Luminaire. Except where Luminaire is on the south side of the continent, Pitohui is on the north side, and much deeper in the ocean."

"I live on an island deep in the ocean now, Ashfoot Isle," she said. "How close is Pitohui to the mainland? Farther away than I am?"

"Much!" Piprik laughed. "It's said that if you leave the mainland at daybreak in winter, you must fly longer than the sun to reach Pitohui."

"Hmm," she said. "Is it bigger than Luminaire?"

"Much bigger."

"Bigger than the weald?" she asked.

He nodded. "Bigger than the entire Redwood Valley, weald, and eyrie combined."

"Bigger than the Crackling Sea?"

"Ah, no," he said. "You caught me there. Not that big."

As he always did, he began by explaining what the pitohui opinici believed before he taught her how to fight like they did.

"For them, the body is sacred," he said. "What you eat becomes your muscle and brain, your skin and talons. Every part of you is a weapon, the simplest touch an act of war. You do not invade someone else's physical space unless it is to fight."

"Not big on hugs, then?" she asked.

"Every hug an act of war," he said with a grin.

She laughed, and he joined in. With everything they'd both been through, it was incredible they could find it in them to be happy. He'd never had a daughter, but if he had, he hoped she'd be as resilient as the reeve's last remaining child.

"Greyfeather Pip?"

"Yes, little lightning bolt?"

She returned to her usual serious stature. "When I had fighting lessons with my mom, we never had to learn about what those opinici believed first. Shouldn't this be part of our history day?"

"Well, you only learned the peafowl talon fighting style with your mom, right?" he asked.

She nodded.

"And you're a peacock," he continued. "So you already know what you believe."

"What's a peacock?" she asked.

He blinked.

"What is a peacock opinicus?" he asked, but she shook her head.

"No, what's a peacock?" she asked. "Or peafowl. You and the gryphons use that word. We don't. What makes me a peacock opinicus?"

It was a simple thing not to know. No one would compare an opinicus to a bird in the presence of the reeve or her children.

He grabbed a stick, smoothed out a section of the sand, and began to draw. "These are peafowl. That there is a peahen, the female. And this here is a peacock, the male."

"Oh!" she said. "They're birds that look like opinici!"

He laughed. "You could say that."

She looked at the train of feathers on the male. "But you have it wrong. Those are my feathers. I'm not a male, am I?"

"Birds aren't opinici," he said. "And opinici aren't birds."

She stared at the drawings for a long time. "But why do birds look like opinici?"

"Ah, a question for the scholars," he said. "Now, let's talk about the pitohui grapplers. You asked why we needed to learn about their culture and beliefs before we learn to fight like them. It's simple. Some things are much stronger when you believe in them."

"Like hope," Levin said.

"Yes, I suppose you're correct," he said. "Like hope."

Piprik and Levin trained all morning, taking a break to eat lunch and talk more about the island the pitohui opinici came from, before starting again with the fighting through most of the afternoon. Their combat was only broken up by the arrival of a petrel gryphon.

"Hey Tresh!" Levin called. "Are you here to fight? Pip is getting tired."

Tresh looked from Levin to Piprik. "You and Mi-Lei have been fighting all day? I am surprised you can do that at your age."

Even without anyone nearby, Tresh used Levin's fish-erfolk name. It was the name of a dead girl, but it kept her true identity safe.

"I'm a lot younger than I look," Piprik said. "What brings you out here?"

Out of habit, the medicine opinicus started to inspect her beak. Now that spring had arrived and the weald was starting to regrow, the medicine gryphons had set up a small camp outside Sandpiper's Dune, but he was still in charge of the health of Swan's Rest and the few refugees who had never left Luminaire.

During her expedition into the bog and kjarr to save Quess, Tresh had wrecked her beak. The triangular scar-ring from her youth had grown from the strain, adding to her shark-like appearance. He worried that if she had to bite down like that again, her beak wouldn't survive the experience. His recommendation had been that she invest in some sharp talons.

"Mi-Lei, do you have enough strength to fly back to your family?" Tresh asked. She meant the peafowl fisher-folk islanders who had taken Levin in, the ones who called her Mi-Lei.

"Yeah, I'm a good flyer now," she confirmed. "Do you need me to?"

Tresh nodded. "Please. We have visitors from the Crackling Sea. I do not want them to recognize you."

Levin retrieved her things from Piprik's hut and said her goodbyes.

"Well, sounds like it's time for me to take a nap, then." He yawned and stretched.

"Soft Paws says she needs to speak to you," Tresh said.

"Soft Paws?" he asked. "The bog witch you brought home with you who joined the Ashen Weald?"

"Yes. She is still fisherfolk," Tresh said.

Soft Paws was an odd case. She'd joined Crane's Nest just in time for the village to be dissolved. When Quess and Tresh had returned from the bog with Urious and a bunch of Crackling Sea rangers under their protection, it had been the nail in the coffin for the Crane's Nest refugees remaining.

Few had been willing to listen to Quess's pleas. Those who had joined Swan's Rest with her and Tresh. The others, horrified to find that all major villages had reached a peace with the Ashen Weald, left Luminaire, promising to get their own vengeance on Satra. As far as anyone knew, they'd become islanders, though no one could say what island they now inhabited.

Rather than join Swan's Rest or Sandpiper's Dune, Soft Paws had opened her own village on the other side of the mountains, Bogwash, which acted like both a fisherfolk settlement and a member of the Ashen Weald. Until the infected starlings were cleared out, few wanted to live in the bog, but many of Soft Paws's old pridemates were getting the village ready for that day. In the meantime, a small team of opinici were attempting to get the raftworks up and working again.

"Sure, is she coming here?" Piprik asked.

"She can, but I think you will want to go to Sandpiper's Dune and see her guest," Tresh said. "She brought the Ranger Lord of the Crackling Sea with her."

His eyes widened. "What interesting times we live in."

Piprik let Tresh head back on her own, claiming he needed to eat something and gather medicines before he left. In truth, Tresh always attracted a crowd, and he didn't want the ranger lord getting a good look at him.

He met Bruen and Quess on the flight over. The ranger lord had requested the presence of all the rangers hiding out with the fisherfolk. While it could be a trap, he'd come alone and unarmed with a bog gryphon escort.

A flight of armed sentries passed them by. Rorin, at least, wasn't above preparing for the worst. Whether that was from the ranger lord himself or an assassination attempt on him by the islanders, Piprik couldn't say.

Bruen started up a conversation with Piprik as they flew. The ranger was half-kjarr and had been assigned at the kjarr nesting grounds until the gryphons reclaimed them. Then he'd been part of an earlier, failed expedition into the bog.

While most of the rangers would probably have been forgiven if they'd returned straight home, his situation was unique. He'd served under Ellore and had been promoted to ranger captain. While Ellore, self-styled ranger lord, was still missing, Piprik suspected if Bruen stepped foot into the weald, he'd be brought up on charges in her absence.

Quess chirped at the two of them to stop chatting and land. There was a large crowd at Sandpiper's Dune. Quess and Bruen pushed their way to the front. While she'd come to forgive Urious and the rangers, she probably still had a few choice words for their leaders.

Piprik, as a medicine opinicus, found fisherfolk moving out of his way as he slipped through the crowd. He expected to find Naya's house empty so he could watch the proceedings from there, but when he opened the door, he found Sandpiper's leader unpacking her harness. She was the only fisherfolk leader to regularly travel north for trade. She and Orlea had become fast friends.

"Oh, I'm sorry," he said. "I didn't know you were back. I was looking for a cool place to rest."

"Just got back in time for this mess." Naya gestured to the crowd outside with a wing. "I went looking for Xalt and Jer to see if they'd be willing to do me a favor and found Rorin had gathered everyone outside my house."

While Naya emptied her harness, Piprik helped unpack several of the light crates. While the main bridge over Glacial Run was gone, there was a small, rickety bridge near the plateau that traders were using. If not for the price of fish, it was unlikely anyone would send a parrot across it, let alone a goliath bird.

While rebuilding the original bridge was an option, many fisherfolk felt it was too soon. They enjoyed having a long drop into fast-moving water between them and the wingtorn. The Ashen Weald, in the interest of peace, hadn't suggested rebuilding it. For the moment, there was the one path along with several very light bridges to help wildlife repopulate the south. Those were designed to collapse if anything bigger than a monitor stepped onto them.

The crowd outside became silent.

"Oh, parrot scat. I guess it's time," Naya said. "I'd better go and greet our guest."

Piprik watched the sandy-colored gryphon leave her home and take her place on a stage of packed sand in the open area at the center of town. She stood on one side of Ranger Lord Grenkin, Rorin at the other. Quess, Soft Paws, Tresh, and the expedition sat in front of the stage, looking up.

The ranger lord cleared his long throat. When Tresh

had said he'd come unarmed, Piprik had taken that to mean he hadn't brought any rangers with him. While this was true, he was also missing his iconic prosthetic talons, though he kept his eye patch.

"I know we've spoken through letters and messengers," the ranger lord began, "but something is often lost in translation. I came here for two reasons. The first is for the rangers who were saved from the bog."

Bruen shifted uncomfortably. Quess put a talon on his shoulder. Fisherfolk took the idea of sanctuary seriously. It was unlikely he'd come to harm here, no matter what the ranger lord said. It was why Piprik had chosen this shore.

"Bruen, Mia, Xalt, Jer," the ranger lord continued on to list off the rest of the rangers. "Urious has told me your tale. You acted with heroism during a trying time. You saved as many as you could. You worked together, Redwood Valley, Crackling Sea, kjarr, bog, and fisherfolk. I'm proud of you all."

Piprik didn't see Mia's red feathers in the crowd. Not everyone had hastened to obey the ranger lord's invitation. Was she with her sister, Kia? Or had she gone to New Eyrie to search for the rest of her family?

"I know many of you are afraid to come north, especially those stationed at the kjarr nesting grounds." Grenkin paused. "I want you to know that you won't be tried. Not from your time at the kjarr nests, not from the bog, not for staying here now. What's more, had Ellore survived, I'd also forgive what she did. In the end, she acted to save her rangers. No one will be held accountable for her crimes, either."

Bruen stood. "Thank you, Ranger Lord. Some have injuries, others are weary of fighting. As thanks for our past deeds, will you release any who wish it from their ranger vows?"

To his credit, Grenkin wasn't surprised by the question. "Of course. I brought back pay with me for each of you. Should you return to the Crackling Sea, you can re-enlist as an Ashen Weald ranger if you choose without it counting against you."

Bruen sat back down. As Piprik understood it, most of the rangers did want to head north to be reunited with their loved ones. They only remained out of worry for Bruen. Even Xalt and Jer, both of whom had been Ashen Weald rangers who went with Tresh into the bog, had remained behind despite not having any concerns about being in trouble themselves.

"The other reason I came was to speak to all of you." Ranger Lord Grenkin pointed to the fisherfolk in the crowd. "Not just the protesters who left the Crackling Sea. You left for a good reason. I didn't come to ask you back.

"No, I came to speak with everyone. While I didn't rule the eyrie until Jonas passed, I've spent the last six months wondering what I could have done to prevent what happened to you."

By all accounts, the ranger lord was one of the more honest opinicus leaders. Piprik remained unconvinced, however. Often, it took more than good intentions to stop evil. Certainly, *good intentions* had never been a problem for him when Piprik was younger.

"The answer is...I could have done a lot. I'm as guilty as you probably think me. I'd love to say that my heart was never in any of this, but I was the ranger who took the kjarr gryphlets, ending that conflict and creating the wingtorn.

"I was ranger lord when Jonas made the decision to

send the wingtorn against you, and I said nothing. I saw starving chicks and salted crops and thought the only way we'd survive was with more farmlands. I was thinking of myself."

The crowd was surprised. It was a small blessing that the Crane's Nest refugees had left. They'd be rabid at these words.

"I'm trying to do better now. But I wanted to come in person and tell you how sorry I am. I've devoted my life to making sure that nothing like this ever happens again. I would rather see the Crackling Sea Eyrie scoured from history than have us act without honor one more time."

He looked like he wanted to say more, but he settled back down. Rorin seemed uncertain what to say. Even Naya was at a loss. The opinici from Sandpiper's Dune seemed surprised but still hostile. Jonas and Grenkin were why they'd left the Crackling Sea to become fisherfolk.

It was Quess who broke the silence. "There is little forgiveness left, but we still must move forwards and do the best we can. If what you're saying is true, it will make for a better tomorrow. That's the most I can offer you."

While the rangers made their way to the raft to collect their back pay and decide if they were going home or not, Ranger Lord Grenkin answered questions and apologized to anyone who wanted to hear it personally from him.

Piprik continued his watch from the doorway. Tresh and Rorin were talking, perhaps about whether or not the Crane's Nest refugees would make an attempt on Grenkin's life before he left. Naya collected the two of them and Soft Paws and led them to her home.

"Normally you bring things to trade," Naya said to the bog gryphon, "but this time you brought a guest.

Soft Paws nodded. "I had a question for you on

behalf of the Ashen Weald. While I suppose he didn't need to come, I thought you might appreciate the apology. He figured out that I could ask on my own around Bogwash and still got on the raft, so I take that as a good sign."

"A question?" Rorin asked. "I can't imagine what information we have on the shore that the Ashen Weald needs answered."

Piprik could think of a few, especially if the Reeve's Bane had been seen bringing Levin here the night New Eyrie fell. He was so worried about the little reeve that he failed to anticipate the real question.

"Piprik." Soft Paws looked at him through skull-painted eyes. "A small flight of opinici who look like you have shown up at New Eyrie. They are providing food, shelter, and medicine to the refugees there. They also seem to be recruiting them."

There was no question in there, so he had nothing to answer. For himself, he only wondered one thing: had Mally the Nighthaunt returned home? Everyone did at some point or another. Perhaps Piprik would never be able to, but he'd known Mally would come back here. The Nighthaunt spoke fondly of the Redwood Valley. It was why Piprik had chosen to come here.

The fisherfolk were staring at him. He cleared his throat. "Yes? Is there a question?"

"Forgive me if this breaks fisherfolk laws," Soft Paws said, "but who are you and where did you come from?"

"You do not have to answer that," Tresh told him. She glared at Soft Paws.

"But if you wish to tell them of the opinici who look like you, feel free," Rorin added, earning himself a glare from Tresh.

Piprik weighed his options. There was a lot he could say without talking about who he was.

He chose his words carefully. "In the northwest, there's a beautiful alabaster eyrie. It's made of stone, and its heights reach into the sky. Where the Reeve's Nest that Brevin lived in was a gilded cage, this eyrie has a palace carved into the shape of a massive opinicus."

He took a sip of water. "Or so I hear. I've never been to the eyrie. I grew up in the country, raising goliath birds, before I became a scholar. They say the white reeve found something strange, something he thought would bring him immortality and purity. He began to recruit scholars. He declared himself king."

"Immortality?" Rorin laughed. "A bog tale. Er, no offense meant, Soft Paws."

She shrugged. "Most bog tales are true, if you dig deep enough. They just aren't true in the way you thought you were."

"Matamata," Tresh said, and Soft Paws nodded in agreement. "So is he immortal? Is such a thing possible?"

"No," Piprik said. "I don't believe he is. But he's lived a hundred years and only now is his health starting to fail. He believes he descended from the original king who settled this land. He believes he can return himself and his people back into their pure forms. To that end, he declared himself king and began to take over the other eyries."

"Was he successful?" Tresh asked.

Piprik thought back to the Emerald Jungle expedition. "At first, he was. He began collecting eyries the way you might collect shells. Ultimately, the last free eastern eyries came together under the Blackwing Eyrie and held him back along the desert."

"What does he want with New Eyrie?" Rorin asked.

"A foothold on this side of the desert, I imagine," Piprik said. "There's a narrow corridor between the Emerald Jungle and the desert. The blackwings used to patrol it from Crestfall. After that, he wants to control every eyrie. He believes it's his birthright."

"Crestfall has gone silent," Soft Paws said. "That is what the Ashen opinici say."

"What does purity mean?" Tresh asked. "You said he wanted to make the opinici pure again. How?"

"I'm not sure." Piprik thought of the swirling purple elixir. "They say a ship crashed on the northern shore. Not a raft, a massive ship meant for crossing oceans. On it was a single survivor. A pure opinicus. It died without speaking a word. All rumors, of course. Except...something was found outside the Blackwing Eyrie, frozen in ice. Something with six wings."

"The bog is full of glyphs of six-winged gryphons," Soft Paws said.

"I saw a mummified one, myself," Tresh added.

"What would you advise the Ashen Weald do, Piprik?" Rorin asked.

Piprik thought. "Pick a side or keep your head down and hope the Blackwing Eyrie and Seraph King destroy each other."

It was bad advice, and he knew it, but he didn't have any good advice. He'd never given much thought to the world at large. One way or another, it always went on. He was just concerned about one opinicus.

Mally. Have you come, at last? I've waited for you.

6

THE LONG WALK HOME

Several days of preparation later found Satra back in the weald. Despite warnings from all of her advisors, she refused to wait at the kjarr nesting grounds while the children she'd kept safe for two years in prison were finally returned home. While Foultner's argument—that having her around would increase the chance that their enemies would try something—was persuasive, Satra wanted to believe that the world would let her gryphons have this one, joyous occasion.

She'd taken every precaution. The trip had been split up over three days with well-fortified opinicus waystations built along the path to give them a safe place to sleep at night. The taiga pride had agreed to patrol the skies. As best anyone could guess at the weather, it seemed clear and sunny. It was time. The kjarr fledglings had been given one last chance to fly when they were escorted down from the Strix Plateau and across the weald to the western side, near the taiga, where they now waited.

She met Thenca at Merin's nesting grounds, where the fledglings had been gathered. *Not fledglings*, Satra corrected herself, *at least not anymore.* These were young adults, all hints of baby fat and down gone, but they still had their adolescent feather patterns.

How strange the winds that had brought them all here. Two and a half years ago, Jonas filled cages with gryphlets and transported them across the mountains on goliath birds like cargo. Six months ago, the gryphon insurrection had liberated them from the eyrie, stuffed them into the saddle bags of many of the same goliath birds, and brought them into the weald. Now, for the first time since they'd been kidnapped, they were going home to the kjarr—on their own four feet this time.

The prides gathered to escort the young. Even the so-called free prides had sent gryphons to show their support. Many of them, the taiga pride and Hatzel's pride in particular, had helped rescue Satra and the gryphlets from the eyrie, and their help hadn't been forgotten.

With one hundred young, winged kjarr gryphons to keep track of, they were divided into fives and assigned to a member of the Ashen Weald. She heard a laugh off to her left and saw Askel and Triddle miming a big explosion and then water rushing out for an audience of ten kjarr youngsters. Every time Merin turned around, one of the trouble-makers would try to steal the bracelet off his tail. She smiled in spite of herself.

Several of the parrotfaces went around and talked about mountain safety. While there was a path and several bridges, it was important to make sure everyone stayed with the group. The wind currents in the mountains did strange things, so they weren't to fly unless it was an emergency. If anyone needed a break, they were to let their leader know, and the entire group would step off to the side.

When the parrotfaces finished and the crowd quieted down, Satra stood atop a boulder to address the next generation of kjarr gryphons.

"It's so strange to see everyone with adult feathers," she began. "I still think of you as bundles of fluff and down. Just this summer I was trying to keep you from sitting on ant piles, and now you're all grown up. It's a strange feeling."

The young kjarr gryphons sat at attention. During their incarceration, obeying Satra had kept them safe. In a way, she'd become their den mother in Ari's absence.

"I hope you know that we did everything we could to keep you safe. I know you were without your parents, and having them back in your lives this winter is taking some getting used to. They gave up everything so you'd be taken care of. They love you. Give them a chance."

She thought of her own father, Jun, and everything he'd given up for her.

"When we were taken prisoner, the previous Kjarr, my father, made a promise to me. He said if I could keep you safe, someday we'd see the skies over the kjarr full of gryphons again. You have a long walk ahead of you, but that day is in sight."

It was a pity Jun hadn't lived to see this. Though it was a blessing he hadn't lived to see what had become of Vitra and his mates.

"If you have any questions, ask your leaders. Stay together. Be safe. Take care of each other. The parrotfaces have prepared snacks at the first rest station. I hear it might be fish!"

That was enough to get the young kjarr gryphons moving. Their first stop was a stable at the base of Snowfall Mountain. Satra would meet them there. She hoped that would keep any assassins away from the children.

At Snowfall, Satra found Thenca barking orders to taiga gryphons while Deracho kept watch.

"That's a neat trick," Satra said. "Do they do anything you ask?"

"Within reason," Thenca replied. "If they don't, I just use Younce's voice instead. How'd things go? Are the gryphlets on their way?"

"They're hardly gryphlets anymore," Satra said. "Not even fledglings. But yes, they're coming. Any sign of trouble?"

"Nothing so far," Deracho said. "There was a bit of a snowslide along the path, but it's on the kjarr side. Urious is taking care of it."

Satra nodded. "What about Ninox?"

"Not a whisper," Thenca said. "Her friends don't think she'd stoop this low, but Blinky and Deracho are organizing our owls to keep watch at night."

In the distance, Satra could just make out the start of the procession walking around a lake. She wondered if it was the same path Thenca had taken.

"Where's Younce?" Satra asked.

"He's waiting at the halfway mark," Deracho said.

"I see," Satra replied, and she did. Since the Blue-eyed Festival, he'd pushed for Cherine's release. She told him that she didn't release prisoners as a favor. Cherine would get his day in court to prove his innocence. That was how justice worked.

A flutter of green wings came down from the taiga

nesting grounds, bringing with it a parrotface. Satra couldn't remember ever having seen one fly before now.

The parrotface landed with a *skraark*. "Everything is set up. The food will be ready by the time they arrive."

"Excellent," Satra said. "I think I'll fly down and walk the last bit with them. I used to be quite good at it."

"I'm still good at it," Thenca said.

Satra felt a pang of guilt. She looked at Thenca's bracers, where several wingfeathers from her and her brother were attached.

Thenca considered the Kjarr. "I'm sorry, I didn't mean it like that."

"It's okay." Satra bowed her head. "I'm the one who should apologize. I can't fix the past, but I hope to fix the future."

"You let the bog pride go," Deracho said. "So, in a way, you fixed a little of the past."

"I suppose I did." She didn't know if that were true or not, but it was a nice sentiment. Just a few more days and the kjarr pride would be whole again. She looked west at the frozen taiga. Would the world give her that, at least?

THE GRYPHLETS HAD ARRIVED at Snowfall without incident on the first day and were now approaching the halfway point. The path was holding up. Wingtorn runners patrolled it for any sign of weakness or ambush. So far, things were going in Satra's favor.

Reportedly, even the snowslide had been cleared for tomorrow. If it had been intended to slow down the Ashen Weald, it was a poor attempt to do so.

Satra settled in and snacked on parrots and fish with

the young kjarr gryphons. They enjoyed the meal but complained about the walking. She promised them they'd get to fly once they were away from the strong mountain winds. She didn't tell them about the aerial obstacle course the Ashen Weald had waiting for them on the other side. Better to let it be a surprise.

The gryphlets stayed up far too late, and it was well past dark when Satra finally went upstairs to nap. Her nest was situated between Foultner and Henders. While she'd approved Foultner's request to have her love interest join the Ashen Weald, Satra didn't know how she felt about being protected by a Reeve's Guard.

It wasn't just that he still wore his blue and gold harness, though that was part of it. It was the fact that the Reeve's Guard had failed to prevent the last two Redwood Valley reeves from being assassinated.

He yawned a hello as she settled in. She'd just closed her eyes when she felt the cool air of someone opening the waystation door. Foultner climbed up to Satra and Henders and settled in between them.

"There's a situation outside," the ex-poacher said.

"How's that possible with all of the owls on our side?" Satra asked.

"The owls are watching the path. This happened farther out," Foultner explained. "Two rangers were having a tiff and wandered out to speak privately. Their captain doesn't go in for fighting, so they wanted to settle things where he wouldn't see. Now one of them is dead."

"Killed by his friend?" Satra asked. "Her friend?"

"He says no," Foultner said. "Says someone else did it."

"An owl?" Henders asked.

Foultner shook her head. "No, he says it was a monster."

Satra held back a laugh. "Mally the Nighthaunt? I hope he doesn't think that will get him out of trouble."

Foultner was quiet for a moment. "I don't think it was a monster, but I've seen the surviving ranger. He's shaken up and not in the way they get after they kill someone."

"You think it's like the other murders?" Henders asked. "The ones you and Blinky looked at?"

Foultner paused. "Maybe? Honestly, I don't know if this is something different or not. We're moving the body off the trail so the little ones won't see it. This happened a few hours ago, but I just got it sorted. There's been nothing since then."

"So if this is Ninox, it's just her way of making her displeasure known," Satra said. "Okay. Keep me posted. Don't let anyone go out in groups smaller than four."

Foultner headed back into the cold, and Satra tried to sleep. Many prides and eyries feared the dark. Mally the Nighthaunt, Strix, Ninox. There were several reasons to be afraid.

Of those who didn't haunt the night themselves, there was only one pride who had no need to fear. The taiga pride's eyes hadn't yet lost their blue hue, and the night was as clear as day to them. No monsters haunted their night.

No, the Ashen Weald must have brought this monster with them.

7

HOMECOMING

Once the kjarr's young had left the final outpost, Satra flew on ahead to the nesting grounds to make sure everything was ready for them. The incident the second night seemed to be an anomaly. Whether the ranger had murdered his friend or a strange monster had disappeared into the snow, only time would tell. Deracho had laughed when she'd asked about what it could be, telling her that snow and ice were the only monsters this high up.

As she drew near, she saw Urious standing atop the main building, waiting for her. She tilted left and then right to let him know she'd seen him, and he made his way down to the ground.

She landed and stretched her wings. "So far, so good. There was one incident at night, but it might be nothing."

"I'm glad to hear it," he said. "You have guests."

Her ears perked up. "Guests? Who are they? Are they here for the homecoming?"

Urious pointed to the town hall with his beak.

"They're from New Eyrie. It's the opinici helping with the refugees."

"What do they want?" Now her ears were back. "Did they bring troops with them?"

Urious led the way. "I think they brought gifts."

That was a possibility she hadn't considered. She groomed her fur and feathers, then made her way inside. The three opinici Foultner had seen were all waiting for her—one with gold tipped feathers, one who resembled a grey version of a copper hawk, and an opinicus wearing metal armor that looked impractical to fly in.

They stood when she entered and bowed. The metallic one must have been well-oiled because nothing creaked when he did so.

"Satra the Kjarr," the one with gold-tipped feathers said, "your story has reached even our far shores. We've come to pay our respects. We understand this is a time of homecoming and don't wish to intrude. We will leave the gifts with you and return at a later time, if you wish it."

They didn't make any move to leave.

Ah, politics, she thought. *This is what I learned from Jonas.*

"Please, stay awhile and refresh yourselves," she said. "There's time yet, and I understand you were kind enough to provide food and water for New Eyrie's refugees."

They settled back down.

"You have me at a disadvantage," she continued. "May I inquire as to your names?"

The one with gold tips stood up. "You may call me Goldfeather."

"Is that your real name?" she asked. "It will save gryphons giving you a new one."

His eyes sparkled. "Yes, I had heard that gryphons had

this tendency. Our gryphons remain shy. The starling prides aren't very sociable, though I understand you've seen this for yourself."

"Indeed." She wondered where his information was coming from. The refugees at New Eyrie, perhaps?

The silver hawk stood up. She seemed to be taking her cues from the others. "You may call me Silver."

When Satra tilted her head to the side, the opinicus added, "It's not a gryphonic moniker. It's always been my nickname."

The last opinicus didn't give his identity. "We're here on behalf of the Seraph King. We understand you have a problem with the Blackwing Eyrie. We've been ordered to advise and aid you as best we can."

Goldfeather took over. "We have a small force, but we didn't bring an army out of respect for your sovereignty. We've kept the blackwing invaders from crossing the desert in a war that has lasted years. We know their trickery. We've bested their assassins, relentless though they are."

"That can wait for another day, however," Silver said. "We will be doing what we can to help New Eyrie get back on its feet again. Goldfeather will go back and await further word. I have something I'd ask of you, however."

Satra nodded. "Do tell?"

"I'd like permission to continue on to the ruins of the Redwood Valley. I hear there are opinicus traders there who may have medicine. There's an infection spreading through New Eyrie. I think, with a few local herbs and some we brought with us, I can stop it from spreading farther."

Satra didn't have a reason to deny one opinicus the

trip. She'd heard the reports of New Eyrie from Foultner. They were in need of medicine.

"Of course, go with my blessing," Satra said. "Just don't fly at night. There's been a bit of a misunderstanding. It's safer to travel during the day."

The three envoys bowed, then made their way out of the town hall to leave. Despite the pretense of staying to eat and drink, they had done neither. Once they were gone, Urious came out from his hiding space just outside the room.

"We're done looking through the crates," he said. "There's some dried fruit we've never seen before, spices, salt, and a small fortune in glass."

Her eyes widened. "Glass? It's a strange gift. Do they have their own glassworks, I wonder?"

Urious shook his head. "We had some of the opinici look at it. It has Crestfall's stamp on it."

"A threat, then?" She'd wondered what had happened to Crestfall. Perhaps the Seraph King ruled it now.

"Maybe," Urious agreed. "But this isn't just glass like you'd trade to other eyries. This is glass so fine, it's fit for a reeve. It's the sort of glass not even Reeve Brevin had."

Satra frowned. What were these envoys playing at? And what use did she have for glass? She was a gryphon, not a reeve. She wasn't going to build an eyrie.

WITH HER STRANGE guests gone and their gifts hidden away to distribute among the council later, Satra waited at the edge of the kjarr nesting grounds for the young to arrive.

She'd done her best to remember what all hundred of

them liked to eat, then had the parrotfaces replicate the dishes. Four or five of the children, despite her best attempts to dissuade the behavior, had developed a taste for opinicus food. For them, she'd had Foultner hunt down an opinicus chef and a liberal amount of salt. While their parents may disapprove of the treat, Satra wanted everyone to feel welcome.

Still, she knew what tonight would be like. They may be young adults, but they were about to sleep in a strange place. The parents had spent the last week taking care of their children. It was nice to see. Under normal circumstances, many of these same parents would have let Ari, the den mother, take care of their children. Now, the den mother system was changing, and biological parents were interested in their children again.

It would be interesting to see what happened when the next hatch year broke out of their eggs in a month—kjarr eggs always hatched later than their weald counterparts. With the red fern out of their system, and the kjarr gryphons able to eat the infected wildlife in the bog, the wingtorn had wasted no time creating another generation. In fact, the only children who may not have a relationship with their parents would be the kjarr eggs hatched in the bog.

She looked south, towards Bogwash, and could make out the shape of the ranger lord and Soft Paws flying north. They'd be here soon, probably with enough time to tell Satra how their trip to the fisherfolk shore had gone.

As their small shapes grew larger, Satra checked on her final preparations. Two rangers had been assigned to keep a bonfire going once it got dark. Snacks would be provided all night long to any young kjarr gryphons who couldn't sleep. While Foultner wouldn't let Satra sleep outside, Ari would be out here, and Satra's quarters would be open to anyone who needed to talk.

It would be a rough transition, but she wanted this to feel like home. They'd keep the bonfire and sweets going all week if that's what it took. All month, even.

Having watched the gryphlets on the Strix Plateau ever since their rescue, Ari had opted to come to the nesting grounds early to let the parents have time alone with their children. She'd walked with her own kids until the last waystation, then Merin took over, leading them the rest of the way.

As Soft Paws and Grenkin landed and went to get water, Ari rushed over to give the bog witch a nuzzle. While the stolen eggs may never know who their parents really were, Ari was doing her best to make them feel welcome. And, having caught a glimpse of Soft Paws without her skeletal paint markings briefly during the Blue-eyed Festival when she'd been given new paints, Satra thought there was a fifty-fifty chance Ari might be Soft Paws's mother.

While Ari and Soft Paws chatted, Grenkin grabbed a flask of water and came over to Satra.

"How was it?" Satra asked. She wondered if it was strange for Ari and Grenkin to be together in the nesting grounds after their history. Did his eye and missing talons ache when he saw her?

"Painful," he said, "but a success. Most of the lost Crackling Sea rangers are coming north and will become Ashen Weald rangers. Ellore's second-in-command is staying with the fisherfolk."

"Oh?" she prompted. "He didn't believe you were sincere?"

"I *was* sincere. They're all good rangers." He took a

swig of water. "Actually, I think he fell in love with a fisher-folk. The one Tresh went in to find."

"Lot of love going around, I hear." Satra looked over to where Henders was decorating Foultner's nest with flowers. "Maybe I'll find someone to pair off with and join the fisherfolk."

Grenkin laughed. "I've seen one of my rangers batting her eyes in your direction. She seems too shy to ask out Satra the Kjarr, however."

She laughed. "Okay, enough teasing, I can see the children on the path. What of our new neighbors? Did you find the fisherfolk from their eyrie and talk to him?"

"About that." He lowered his voice. "Sounds like they don't get along with the blackwings anymore than we do. But it also sounds as though their leader styles himself a king and wants all eyries under his control like the old days."

"Great," she said. At least some of the information the cockatiel forger had given her was panning out.

The children were now within view, so Satra did her best to keep her ears perked up and happy so they wouldn't know anything was wrong.

Henders was singing to himself. In the distance, Satra could see Foultner flying overhead to watch the skies around the kids.

"What're you thinking?" Grenkin asked.

Satra pointed to Henders. "I'm thinking we need spies at New Eyrie. I'm thinking maybe we should see if Henders's old nest is still available and if he and Foultner want a job at the Clover Ranch so they can keep an eye on things."

"Hmm." Grenkin scratched the feathers under his chin. "Henders is already working there part time. How much do you pay Foultner? It seems like she's earned her keep a dozen times over."

"I don't," Satra admitted. "If she wants anything, I give it to her. I count five hundred wingtorn who may not be alive if not for her actions. What price could I put on that?"

Ari finished grooming Soft Paws, and the bog witch made her way over to Satra.

"Grenkin told you everything?" she asked.

Satra nodded. "We'll gather more information, see if we can figure out their intentions. I don't want to fight them while the blackwings are nearby, especially if they'll fight each other if we just hang back. What do you plan to do? Are you staying for the celebration?"

While Soft Paws stared out at the procession, Satra inspected her. The war paint had done its job of hiding Soft Paws's identity, but it had also obscured her age. She'd been at the nesting grounds the night the ranger lord had taken them and created the wingtorn. The only reason she hadn't been stolen and tossed into a cage at the bottom of an eyrie was that she hadn't hatched yet.

She and the other stolen kjarr children were a month younger than the gryphons Satra thought of as *children returning home*. Soft Paws had gone through so much, it was impossible to think of her as young, even if sections of adolescent plumage still clung to her feathered half, hidden under paint.

"This is as much your homecoming as theirs," Satra said. "I'm sorry we didn't celebrate it over the winter or think to do so now. Those are your hatchmates."

"Yes," Soft Paws said. "More of my pride are coming from Bogwash with gifts. But it's hard to think of the newcomers as my hatchmates. They hatched here as kjarr.

I hatched in the sunken eyrie nests of the Heart of the Bog. I'm not the same as them."

Satra put one wing over Soft Paws and the other over around Grenkin, and they watched as the first of the young gryphons hit the safe flight glyph and spread her wings, flying home to the kjarr for the first time since she had been stolen.

Satra stepped out of the way as two gryphons ran past her to get back in line for the aerial obstacle course. Several fantails had volunteered to hold targets in the sky while towers offered other objectives.

"Screeeeeee!" shouted a kjarr gryphon as he flew overhead, missing his landing and tumbling into river.

Satra laughed, but Foultner was less amused. Henders had decorated her harness with flowers.

"They're so loud!" Foultner shouted over the sounds of two more gryphons diving into the river.

"They're young," Henders said. "That's what they do. They're loud all the time."

"Yeah, but yesterday it was quiet here," she protested. "Now it's not. Will they keep this up all the time?"

"At least during holidays." Satra admitted that it would take some getting used to, but she was glad happiness had returned to this cursed place. A nesting grounds without the sounds of children was heartbreaking. She'd rather noise than silence. She hated to think what Swan's Rest sounded like.

"I'm going to rebuild my home with twice as much insulation," Foultner grumbled.

"Speaking of housing arrangements," Satra said, "how

would the two of you like to move into Henders's nest at New Eyrie?"

"But I just got here," Henders protested.

"She wants us to be spies, Hends," Foultner sighed. "Okay, fine. What're we looking for?"

"Just keep an eye on the newcomers," Satra said. "Also, you'll be working at the Clover Ranch. That'll let you see if any of them head east."

"Ooh." Henders perked up. "I always wanted to be a goliath bird rancher. Can you make that happen? Right now, they just have me tending the capys."

"Sure!" Satra laughed.

"Great," Foultner said. "Now we'll both get to live your dream."

Foultner and Henders made an unlikely couple. Foultner was too serious by half, having spent every day of her past life scrounging for something to eat so she didn't starve. Henders, by contrast, took everything with grace and humor. That they seemed to balance each other out instead of driving each other crazy surprised everyone.

"When I get back," Foultner said, "I expect my nest to be triple-reinforced and big enough for Henders, too."

"Done," Satra said. "With the lumber mill up and running again, the Crackling Sea is going to try to build some larger nests here for opinici. I'll make sure you get the first one. It'll be across the river, away from the young gryphons."

"Acceptable," Foultner said. "Come on, Henders, let's grab something salty before the eels are all gone."

As one couple departed, two more arrived. Satra chirped a greeting to Urious, Thenca, Ari, and Deracho.

"Looks like you two thought of everything," Urious said. "Food, fires, the obstacle course. You did a great job."

"Mmm," Satra said. "I want to tire them out so they'll sleep well. I picked up a few tricks watching them at the eyrie."

Soft Paws was trying to do the obstacle course. Like the other gryphons from the bog, she was used to flying close to the ground to avoid attracting the attention of the starlings. She clipped her bottom paws on a fantail-held target and was disqualified.

Satra looked at the quiet snowy owl gryphon. "You're welcome to spend the night here if Younce doesn't need you, Deracho. Not that you need my invitation for that."

A few of the gryphons who remained together after mating season had taken advantage of the opinicus influence on the Ashen Weald to make their permanent bond official. She didn't know if Thenca and Deracho had done so yet, but it seemed likely they would.

"We're staying here for a few days to help out," Thenca answered for him, "but then Deracho and I are going to head to Bogwash."

Satra looked at Thenca and Urious. She hadn't considered that they might want to embrace their bog heritage. "Do you two want to rejoin the bog pride?"

"Honestly?" Urious asked. "No. I think I'm happier as part of the kjarr. Seeing how Black Mask and White Stripe looked at me, I don't think I'm a bog gryphon in any way except fur and feathers."

"I felt the same way before I spent time with a few of the bog witches over the winter," Thenca said. "I don't want to rejoin them, but I'd still like to spend a little time down there."

Satra was inwardly pleased. She'd been worried about losing access to both of them. "Why's that?"

"Soft Paws and the others," Thenca said. "They're so

young, and they don't even realize it. We've got Ari and an army of overprotective parents here, but Bogwash is a city where no one is over three years old. There's a lot they don't know about being adults."

Ari nodded her approval. "I think you and Deracho will do a great job down there."

"We'll do our best," the snowy owl gryphon said.

"They also need someone watching out for them," Thenca added. "Vitra is gone, but one of the bog witch crones escaped, and Blinky said she left Black Mask alive. I don't want them to get recruited back into another rebellion against us."

Deracho cooed his agreement.

Satra wondered how he'd feel after they had to shave his fur down for the heat. "I'll miss you two, but I admit I feel better having an established presence at Bogwash. Whatever happened with the Flower?"

"The rangers at the raftworks are still clearing out the rotten food and fixing it up again," Urious said. "Nobody wants to stay overnight there, so teams take short day trips up from the raftworks."

"Starlings?" she asked.

"It's like a beacon to them," he said. "As we collect more bog blossoms, we'll use that to our advantage. Figure out a way to lure them in and finish them off."

"Starlings, blackwings, an opinicus who would be king, and Ninox," Satra mused. "I sometimes worry our fight is never-ending."

"That's not true," Ari said. "Next year at this time, we'll have cleared the infected out of the bog. We have the food problem under control. Ninox will come to her senses once Cherine is found innocent. And, if we can get the flameworks back up and running, maybe it's time to go on the offensive."

"I never took you for a phoenix." Satra looked the den mother over. "Many want the flameworks to remain empty and unused. They don't want the weald to burn again."

Ari's eyes narrowed, reminding Satra and Urious that she wasn't just a loving mother, she was also the gryphon who had bitten off Grenkin's talons. "Opinici always think gryphons are stupid, but if you put Askel and Triddle in the flameworks and ask them to get it going, they'll do so. Then, the next time the blackwings show up at our borders, we can catch them off guard."

"It's a good plan," Satra admitted. She didn't know if anyone would go for it, but she'd love to fill her arsenal with saltpeter. "Now show me how to get Orlea to turn over the flameworks."

Urious laughed. "Don't let Ari solve all your problems for you. You're the Kjarr. Go do Kjarr things!"

Both couples wandered off in different directions, leaving Satra to watch the aerial acrobatics of the hundred gryphons she'd kept safe in the depths of the Redwood Valley. For the first time in two and a half years, the skies above the kjarr nesting grounds were full of gryphons and laughter.

8

SILVER HAWK

Zeph and Kia were busy talking to Orlea when a strange opinicus arrived. She landed outside of the city proper and slowly made her way towards Orlea's nest.

"Who is that? She's headed our way." Kia looked out the curtains. "She looks like you, Zeph. Do you have a sister we don't know about?"

"An opinicus sister?" Orlea said. "Your parents must have been modern. Or fisherfolk."

There was a resemblance. Zeph's ears and paws set him apart, but if he ever needed a double, enough feather paint might turn them into twins.

"Is she Ashen Weald?" Orlea asked. "Fisherfolk? Maybe a combination of Redwood Valley opinicus and copper hawk gryphon?"

Zeph watched the way the stranger moved. He could tell a lot from the musculature of another gryphon or opinicus. While, contrary to Kia's teasing, he never gazed longingly at his own reflection, it was useful to compare the stranger to Pink Paw.

Where Pink Paw's legs were muscular and her

wingspan narrow to allow her to run and pounce under the redwood canopy, the stranger's strength went into her wings, which were longer than a gryphon's. Her tailfeathers, too, were twice the length of Zeph's.

The stranger referred down at her journal several times, then looked up at where they were staring at her. She finally made her way up to them and introduced herself.

"Hello!" she said. "I'm Silver. I was wondering if I could speak to Orlea. I believe that's you, isn't it? Your red beak gives you away."

Orlea bowed slightly. "It is. What brings you here? Where did you come from?"

Now it was Silver's turn to bow. "I'm here as part of a trade delegation from the west. We're trying to help the refugees of New Eyrie, but a sickness has taken hold there. We didn't bring the right medicines, and I heard most things could be bought here."

"For a price," Orlea said. She accepted the piece of paper with a list of medicines.

Zeph read over her shoulder. *Pumpkin, honey, red fern. Whoa, a lot of red fern.*

"We have all of this," Orlea said, "but it's going to be expensive."

Silver reached into a harness pocket and pulled out a string of metal beads. "I saw the metalworks outside of town, so I assume beads are currency here?"

Orlea nodded. Kia's eyes had gotten wide. Zeph's parrotmongering days had never allowed him to reach a point where he could get paid in metal beads, only turquoise. If he had to guess, he'd say that Silver was offering enough beads to buy one of the nicer homes in the northern quarter, back before they'd been reduced to rubble.

"I'll see what I can do." Orlea took the beads. "It shouldn't take long. Zeph and Kia will keep you company while I find Didi and get this packed up for you."

Silver looked at each of them in turn. "What do the two of you do?"

"Scholar," Kia said. "Formerly with the Redwood Valley University."

"Ah!" Silver said. "I saw a building near the metalworks. It looked like there were fields of something being leached. Is that a university experiment?"

Kia nodded. "The flameworks. It's where saltpeter used to be produced."

Silver's eyes narrowed. "I see. I've never seen a—flameworks, you said it was called?—before. They don't have them where I'm from."

"Where are you from?" Zeph asked. He was used to getting replies about how a gryphon wouldn't know where something was located from opinici, but she gave him a straight answer, even if he didn't know what it meant.

"The Argent Heights," she said. "It's a small eyrie, like this one used to be."

"And what do you do there?" Kia pressed. "Are you a scholar?"

"Ah, no. Military," Silver said. "Don't worry; I'm here on a peaceful mission. I'm more of a bodyguard or errand runner at the moment."

"I see." Kia's hackle feathers were on end.

Silver looked at Zeph. "I missed your name before. What did you say it was? What do you do?"

"Zeph Reevesbane," Kia answered for him. "He kills reeves."

"That's a brazen thing to admit in an opinicus camp," Silver's tone remained neutral, though she was watching Kia closely. "Isn't Orlea worried about having you around?"

"We're not big on reeves in the south," Kia said. "That's more of a northern thing at this point."

Silver looked from Zeph to Kia. "We were like that once, too."

"And now? Do you serve a reeve?" Kia asked.

Silver looked outside, where Orlea and a merchant were coming with her order. She turned to leave.

"No," Silver said. "I serve a king."

As she gathered her things and departed, Kia and Zeph were both left wondering what had happened.

"What did you find out?" Orlea asked.

"She serves a king, and she's from the Argent Heights," Zeph said. "That anywhere you've heard of, Kia?"

She shook her head. "It's been too long since I saw the headmaster's map of the eyries. Plus, they weren't exactly labeled."

"Well, that's one more thing our guests can find out for us," Orlea said.

"Guests?" Kia asked.

"Oh, I forgot," Orlea said. "While you two were chatting with the silver hawk, Tresh's friends arrived."

Outside, two rangers were making their way up. One was shorter and walked a few steps behind. The other had a hint of Crestfall pink in his feathers.

"May I introduce Xalt and Jer?" Orlea said. "They're both rangers who owe Biski and Tresh their lives. They're willing to do us a favor and look around the Crackling Sea. Seems the ranger lord has pardoned all of the expedition."

"It's nice to meet you," Zeph said. "Let's find some-where private and talk about where to look for Cherine."

ZEPH STRETCHED out his paws and wings while they settled down to talk. It had taken half a year, but he was starting to feel like himself again.

Well, physically he felt like his old self—fit, nimble, and ready to pounce on a parrot. Mentally, he'd changed. He wanted more than to be left alone to hunt. A sense of empathy had awoken within him after helping save the kjarr gryphlets. It had grown when he helped with Sand-piper's Dune and Levin. Ultimately, what he'd spent the winter doing was learning from the fisherfolk. Somehow, in their secluded villages, he'd come to see himself as part of a larger world. His winter hibernation was now spring action, and the first thing he wanted to do was save Cherine.

"How do you know he's in the eyrie?" Xalt asked. Inside Orlea's hut, his feathers lost their pink sheen. Jer sat next to him and nodded along.

While Tresh's influence made them willing to show up for this meeting, they weren't on board with doing anything that might get them locked up. This would take a little convincing. Thankfully, Kia was up for the task.

If their winter on the shore had taught Zeph to channel his empathy, it had turned Kia into a leader. Not like Satra the Kjarr or Reeve Brevin. Not even like Rorin or Hatzel. She was a leader in a broader sense. She commanded fisherfolk and taiga gryphons from Sand-piper's Dune, Swan's Rest, Luminaire, Hoarfrost, and Williwaw on how to manage their food stores better. It was a different kind of power. It wasn't political, but it reached further.

"We don't know he's there," she said. "He could be anywhere. They could be hiding him in the middle of the bog for all we know."

"Not bleeding well going back there," Jer mumbled.

"But while you're crossing the Crackling Sea off the list of possibilities," Zeph continued, "we'll be searching other locations: the taiga, the weald, the kjarr, and the Owlfeather Highlands."

"You think they'd hide him in the northern mountains?" Jer asked.

"No, but I think Ninox is up there," Zeph said. "If I can get her attention, there are places she can help us rule out."

He actually had a few ideas about where Ninox, or at least her pride, were hiding. He'd rule out the closer locations for signs of habitation first. If those didn't pan out, he'd see if Hatzel could lead him up to Poisonmaw, the abandoned home of the saberbeaks. It was overrun by monitors, but it would make a good hideout. As the birthplace of the monitor plague, it had a reputation for being cursed, making it a great place to avoid company.

"Where are you going to look?" Xalt asked Kia. "Except for New Eyrie, you'll stick out wherever you go."

"My sister is checking New Eyrie for me," Kia said. "I'm going to search in a different sort of way."

"Oh?" Xalt asked. Despite his confrontational attitude, he seemed to be genuinely curious.

"When we looked for Cherine the first time, before the fire, most of our discoveries came by looking through his journals," she explained. "Prisoners and jailors both need to eat. When the rimu mast is in full swing, food will be so plentiful that no one will keep track of where it goes. But it's been a tight winter, and the parrotfaces are working hard to make sure no one goes hungry. If I can find out where the food goes, it might help us narrow down the general area of the prison."

"You're a smart opinicus." Jer didn't seem to mean it as a compliment. "Be careful, or they'll lock you up with your friend."

Kia's voice no longer held the uncertainty it had as an apprentice. "The wingtorn would be dead along the coast and their children eyrie vassals if not for me. If that doesn't hold weight with Satra, there's no hope for the Ashen Weald."

Orlea poked her head through the door. "Silver's long gone and the Ashen Weald traders have gone back to the parrotface nesting grounds to sleep."

"I don't feel good about that one," Kia said about Silver.

"Xalt, Jer," Orlea said, "you two can stay here with me. Zeph, now's your chance to get back to Hatzel. And, Kia...I gathered everyone you wanted to talk to."

"Oh, good!" Kia said. "It'll be nice to start this tonight."

Orlea shook her head. "Ninox seemed pretty sure there was a spy here. I hope she's wrong, but just in case, try not to go anywhere alone, all right? Bring someone you trust along."

Zeph slipped out of Orlea's hut and made his way to the edge of the reeve's hunting grounds. It would be good to sleep back in his home nest again.

"W<small>AIT</small>, what do you mean you gave it away?" Zeph asked. "It's not a great nest, but it's the only one I have."

"Is it?" Hatzel said. "Then you've been sleeping on sand all winter?" She didn't wait for a reply. "We have limited space here. I opened up the winter nests, but even then, we needed as many caves as possible to keep the gryphlets and chicks safe. So the little ones get the big cave and the medicine gryphons get the smaller cave."

Zeph's ears and tail drooped. He didn't want to sleep outside. There were bugs outside, and sometimes it rained. Well, here at the start of spring, it rained almost all the time. The entire weald, burned and pristine, were both covered in a cool mist.

Hatzel rolled her eyes at his droopy ears. "However, our opinicus members might have something you'd be interested in."

She led him along a new path between the winter caves and her pride's usual nesting grounds. About halfway between them, he nearly walked straight into a wooden pillar.

He looked up. An opinicus building made of redwood stretched from the ground to just below the tree tops. The bottom floor was just pillars, but after that, it was divided into covered and open areas.

"Looks fancy," he said. "Where'd you get all of the wood?"

"A good number of redwoods were destroyed by the saltpeter but extinguished before they caught flame," she explained. "Orlea got the eyrie lumber mill repaired, and here we are: housing for everyone in the pride."

Several paths stretched out from the building, weaving between covered nests that provided some level of privacy. He could smell salted meat stored in crates on the second level where monitors couldn't get to them. Past that, he heard laughter and talking.

"We were organized for thirty magpie and copper hawk gryphons," she went on. "Now, we have room for about a hundred gryphons and opinici of all types."

"How do you keep everyone fed?" He flew up to the second story to look inside. He found a crate that wasn't secured shut and opened it up.

He was reaching for something salty when Hatzel said, "Monitor meat." He put it down.

"Once it's salted and cooked, the opinici don't mind eating it. Gryphons are still squeamish, me included. I know I'm immune, but unless things get dire, I'm abstaining."

It made sense. The monitors along this stretch of the weald had grown massive. Now, instead of a menace, they were a meal. It also made sure the large monitors were culled before they reached a truly monstrous size.

He looked at the covered nests up high. "Where are Xavi and Pink Paw staying?"

"They have my old cave," Hatzel said, "since they're watching the kids. Their eldest hasn't regained his sight yet, so he feels safer on the ground, at least for the time being. He's in the medicine cave next to theirs."

It was starting to get dark, but he still had a little blue left in his eyes from the winter and could see more construction farther down. It was hard to tell, but he didn't make out any nests.

He pointed with a wing. "What's that?"

"Right now, we're storing the food here," she explained. "I'd like to make this one all nests, then add on more buildings for storage, curing meat, cooking, and teaching."

"Teaching?" he asked.

Hatzel nodded. "We have a few scholars. Not university scholars, mind you, but the sort that teach opinicus chicks. Now, they'll teach gryphlets, too. After what happened, I want all of my pride to know three things: history, hunting, and writing."

Zeph looked up at the nests in the heights. "Which one is mine?"

"Depends," Hatzel said. "Are you staying this time? Or is this just one more stop before you go off and live in the taiga or shore for the other half of the year?"

While her tone and question were both practical, that was how she often showed she was hurt. He didn't blame her.

"I didn't mean to stay for so long," he admitted. "I just felt like I needed to be there, like I was needed there."

He pointed his beak towards all the pride members. "You've learned a lot from the new members, especially the opinici. I learned a lot from the fisherfolk. I love the weald, but I feel like I might be needed somewhere else."

Hatzel was quiet.

"I'd like to promise I'm staying," Zeph began, "but I think once we free Cherine, we're going to need him to help hunt down Impir, Bario, and the headmaster. The world is like the sea during a storm. Everything is choppy. I just need calm water before I can go back to hunting parrots."

"Oh, good. You even sound like a fisherfolk now," she said. "Well, I guess you had to get your adult plumage in at some point. Come on up. You're nesting with me on the top floor."

9

CLOVER RANCH

Foultner's first few days at the Clover Ranch were uneventful and, if she were being honest with herself, kind of enjoyable. She liked working with the giant domesticated birds.

Tilly, the head goliath of the herd here, seemed to remember her from when she'd come through with the wingtorn after taking the Crackling Sea. Everywhere Foultner went, Tilly followed behind and *mronked* at her if she did something wrong.

Once the goliath birds were happy, Foultner would check on the capybaras. How the previous ranch owners had kept the large rodents in check, she didn't know. They were always gnawing through their pens and sneaking into the bog. Thankfully, they were easy to trap and bring back. And it gave Foultner an excuse to roam around and look for signs that the Seraph King's opinici were straying from New Eyrie.

She was leading several wrangled capybaras back to the ranch one afternoon when she saw Silver and a half-dozen opinici fly overhead. Foultner raised a wing to wave from the ground.

Several days later, it happened again. This time, Silver waved back. The next time, Silver landed.

"Hello there," Foultner said before Silver could speak. "I don't suppose you have any water? I forgot how long it takes to walk back and didn't bring any with me."

"Oh, sure." Silver pulled out a flask.

Foultner took a long swig. It was better than the ranch's well water and she said so.

"There's a carrot farm west of New Eyrie with an impressive watering system," Silver explained.

"Well, I'm much obliged to you." Foultner considered telling them about the carrot farm's sinister history, but she decided it might be more exciting to let them figure it out on their own. *Carrot* had become her codename for Impir when she was talking to Merin or Blinky.

Silver inspected one of the large rodents. It made a chuffing sound at her. "Do you walk them to the bog every day to graze?"

"Oh, no," Foultner said. "They keep escaping from their pen. I don't know how the blues kept them in check. I usually go out and try to recapture a few when I finish taking care of the goliaths."

"Have you been deep in the bog?" Silver scratched the rodent behind its ears.

Foultner scratched at the back of her head idly out of habit. "Can't say that I have. I did date a blue who said he went into the bog once. Said it's full of turtles. Not the smartest bird in the flock, but pretty feathers. You know the type."

Silver nodded. "You've probably seen us at New Eyrie.

We're trying to help out by looking for some reds who went in searching for food and never came out again. Do you know who owns the bog? Is it gryphons or opinici?"

That didn't seem like a useful distinction to Foultner in the current age. "I suppose with the bog and kjarr prides in the Ashen Weald, it's their land, now. If they can pry it out of the starlings' claws, that is."

Black Mask and the last crone were still unaccounted for, so this section of the bog remained free of Ashen Weald outposts until Urious and Soft Paws finished their search, but Foultner didn't feel any need to tell Silver that.

After a few more pleasantries, Foultner made her way back to the Clover Ranch. Once the capybaras were secured, she headed north to meet up with Henders.

While he was sketchy on the details of the expedition, he'd opted not to go into the bog again, even to track down missing capybaras. Instead, when he was done with his main ranch chores, he went to the edge of the Crackling Sea to fish. The dock was designed with safety in mind, standing six feet above the water to keep sailfins from crawling on top of it.

Of course, that would do little good if the reeve's pet came calling. Foultner would rather take her chances with the starlings. Splitting up, though, let them keep watch in both directions.

"Howdy there, Foult," Henders said. "How goes the wrangling?"

"That's not how ranch workers talk," she snapped. "We need to work on your accent."

He frowned. "I don't do a lot of spy work. That's not really how the Reeve's Guard works. We mostly stand around and guard things."

She didn't have the heart to tell him he probably wouldn't find work guarding another reeve. Or, if she were being honest, did she think him particularly good at that line of work. She wasn't even sure she wanted him to guard Satra. Incompetence aside, when an assassination attempt happened, he'd be more likely to get himself killed.

Before the night of the fire, he'd worked as a flower guard. Foultner misunderstood this to mean he'd gone with the Headmaster's expedition into the bog and guarded the trading outpost there, but he later clarified that he'd guarded the botanical gardens—literal, not architectural, flowers.

"How goes the fishing?" she asked, hoping maybe he had a knack for it. "Catch anything?"

He pointed to a large jar of water. She looked inside. None of the fish were big enough to eat.

"I'm just keeping up appearances," he said. "I'll toss them back when no one is looking. Did you see the king's opinici again?"

"Yep." She settled down next to him. "I spoke with Silver a little. She says they're looking for missing reds in the bog."

"Huh. We didn't hear anything about anyone missing at New Eyrie." He pulled on the line. By the displaced water, he'd finally managed to catch something big. He'd just brought it close to shore when a sailfin surfaced and ate it. "That's the tenth time today. I'd have better luck fishing somewhere else."

"Better luck at fishing, but not better luck at spying." She skipped a rock down at the sailfin. "A lot of reds have gone missing, but not in the bog. I've been watching. I'd say a third of the refugees outside the walls have packed up and gone north wearing white harnesses."

"Can you blame them?" Henders asked. "If you're not part of the Ashen Weald or a member of the free prides, there isn't really a place for you out here. Maybe they're better off at Crestfall or the white eyrie."

"There's no way Crestfall is still standing," Foultner said. "A bunch of flamingos and glass? I'll bet they wouldn't last against a single gryphon pride."

Most things in life were too good to be true. She didn't know what the white eyrie had promised, but she'd put the odds of them having a better life up north at just above nil.

Henders caught another fish and put it in the jar. It was just big enough to eat. "None of the white opinici have flown across the Crackling Sea since Silver came back from Orlea's pride. On our side, I'm not even seeing blues head to New Eyrie, either. It's like they've forgotten it."

"The whites are probably biding their time until the rest of their army gets here." Foultner pulled the fish out of the jar and swallowed it in one bite. "That, or they're really here to help. Or maybe they're after something in the bog. Was there anything of value?"

He swatted her talons when she reached for another fish. "The bog gryphons had a huge stockpile of things stolen from the Crackling Sea. It's not common knowledge because we don't want opinici sending expeditions in to try to steal it from Soft Paws's pride."

"What kinda stuff? Like pretty jars or like... stormcloth?" Foultner asked. The strange, thick cloth was a relic of when the Crackling Sea had first been made. It was thick, strong, translucent, and surprisingly light. As best anyone could tell, it was made from the fibers of a plant that didn't exist anymore.

She managed to pull another fish out of the jar when he wasn't looking. This one was too small to eat, so she tossed it back into the water. As far as she knew, the Crackling Sea treasury was still under lock and key, unlike the Redwood Valley Eyrie's.

"A little of each?" he guessed. "Jars, some with the parasite still in them. They were going to send an expedition to try to find those. And at least some stormcloth."

"Hmm." Foultner couldn't imagine anyone risking the starlings just for a little stormcloth. And, as best she knew, only the Ashen Weald, fisherfolk, and free prides knew about the parasites—outside of the blackwing spies.

"We should pack it in," Henders said. "Finish up at the ranch, then go home to New Eyrie. Maybe you'll run into your new Silver friend."

Foultner pushed over the jar of fish, sending them back into the water. She'd let Henders finish up their Clover Ranch chores. She'd promised to check in with Blinky after work.

A FANTAIL MET Foultner just outside the ranch and guided her straight east, passing her usual turnoff towards the kjarr nesting grounds. There'd been another killing. This one was in the aneda woods outside of the Crackling Sea Eyrie.

Blinky was awake and overseeing the scene. A group of parrotfaces wandered around looking for clues, careful not to step on the bodies of two dead opinici.

"Do you want me to lend you Henders?" Foultner

asked. "I'm sure the Reeve's Guard had some process for figuring out crimes."

Blinky looked up. "That is not necessary. How are things at the ranch? Do not eat any of the birds. They do not like it when you do that."

Foultner didn't have to ask how Blinky knew that. There was a wanted poster on the side of the barn with a scarred owl face drawn on it. "It's fine. Maybe I'll be a ranch owner one day. What happened here?"

"Two dead opinici," the owl gryphon said. "Crackling Sea. One is a ranger, the other is a butcher. They were selling meat from the stores for a high price."

Foultner wondered if they were the same couple she'd stumbled upon when she'd freed the wingtorn. "They knew better than to be out after dark. Not that they deserved to die for it. Any witnesses this time?"

She'd come pretty close to being killed a few times for her poaching exploits back in the old days, so she had a particular dislike for opinici who tried to profit off the starving. On the other talon, she knew she hadn't deserved the death penalty for poaching, and she did have sympathy for these two.

"One witness." Blinky pointed her tiny beak towards a shaking feathermane. "He was here to buy food, though that is not how he tells it. Says he came upon the bodies and saw an owl flying away."

"An owl?" Foultner asked. "Not a monster?"

"Monster?" Blinky's brow creased, moving the scars on her face. She turned towards the sea, where the reeve's pet often hid. "It is too far for something that large, is it not?"

Foultner looked up at the trees. "The witness in the mountains said he saw a monster."

Blinky relaxed. "The one who was fighting with his friend. I do not believe him."

"Or maybe he finds owls monstrous," Foultner countered. "Seen any weird owls about? Other than you?"

Blinky started to turn away but stopped. "Actually, yes. Biski's grey owl assistant travels to and from the Ashen Weald and free prides to trade goods. He was seen near several murder sites. I do not suspect him, though. He seems to be everywhere."

"We should track down every lead. Is Biski still at the Crackling Sea Eyrie?" Foultner looked at the sun and sighed. She might not get home before dark.

Blinky made a soft cooing noise. Another owl poked his head out of an aneda tree and cooed back.

"Yes," Blinky said. When Foultner got up to leave, she asked, "These deaths were avoidable. How do we keep the opinici from leaving the eyrie at night?"

Foultner thought it over. "Be scary. Make noises when they try to leave so they think there are monsters. They'll tell others, and everyone will stay indoors."

Blinky considered this. "The tales of Mally the Nighthaunt. They were made to keep children in the nest at night?"

Foultner thought back to the underbough. She'd seen strange things there as a chick. And as an adult, if she were being honest. Though nothing as monstrous as the reeves. "Sure, exactly."

She made her way back west to the eyrie on the cliffs. Just this afternoon, she'd complained about having to walk the capybaras back from the bog. Now that she was getting to stretch her wings, she didn't feel any better.

FOULTNER HATED the smell of fish. She liked to eat fish—cooked, salty fish—but she hated how it smelled raw. The sea air, the humidity, and the mist coming off the Crackling Sea always made her feel like she was soaking in a broth.

She flew around the amphitheater in the center of the city, the hollowed-out egg shape, but didn't see any sign of the bright orange and blue medicine gryphon. She considered perching on a balcony and shouting. There weren't even any familiar faces around. Most of her friends now were gryphons, and the wingtorn wouldn't have anything to do with the eyrie.

She ended up going to the throne room. She figured it'd be empty, but there might be whatever the ranger equivalent of a Reeve's Guard was standing about who would know where the medicine gryphons were.

There were no guards, but she saw the ranger lord sitting on the steps leading up to the throne.

He looked up. "May I help you?"

"Ranger Lord Grenkin," Foultner said.

Realization sparked in his eye. "I didn't recognize you without your harness. Is there something to report? I heard there were two more deaths."

She nodded. "A butcher and a ranger selling contraband in the aneda forest at night."

"It seems insane to risk one's life for a couple of beads." He stood and walked away from the throne. From what Foultner heard, even Jonas had been afraid to use it, lest he tempt the blackwing assassins.

"Biski's grey owl assistant was seen near a few deaths," she said. He raised an eyecrest. "I don't think he's involved. He just flies around everywhere fetching things for Biski. But he might have seen something out of the ordinary."

"She's next door." Grenkin led Foultner out of the throne room and towards the library.

"The butcher and the ranger, they were lovers." She felt compelled to speak. "Their relationship was a secret, but I stumbled upon their tryst when I freed the wingtorn during my first trip here."

He studied her. "What else did you see?"

"You," she admitted. "You and a ranger up late at night."

He blushed, his nares turning red.

"Oh, no," she stuttered. "I mean, she'd come to report to you. She wanted to poison the wingtorn. She said that was Jonas's standing order if he didn't report in. You told her no."

Grenkin considered her. "I was never strong enough to stand up to Jonas. We missed our reeve, and he was the next best thing. But when he left for the Redwood Valley, I began to find my bravery. And when he didn't return from the eyrie fire, I knew what I had to do."

He opened the door to the library, where Biski was chatting with several rangers. "I'll leave you to it."

Foultner watched the ranger lord leave. Many of the top blues were dead, hiding, or locked up under suspicion of being a Jonas loyalist. If something happened to Grenkin, she didn't know who would step up to lead.

"Oh, hey, Foultner." Biski sniffed the air. "Why do you smell like a goliath bird?"

"I've been working at the ranch to earn some extra beads," she said. "I'm thinking of maybe starting up my own, if I can find the birds. What's going on here?"

Two rangers, one with hints of Crestfall pink in his blue heron plumage, were looking over a map of the eyrie.

Biski introduced them. "Xalt, Jer, meet Foultner."

"Oh, Henders's girlfriend," the pinkish one said. "He wouldn't shut up about you."

"That's...I don't know what that is," she admitted. She didn't talk about Henders with anyone, not even Blinky.

"Sweet," the other ranger said. "I think it's sweet."

Biski rolled up the map and gave it to them. "Thanks for showing me around. I never got to look around the place in the past. I'm glad you two came back from the fisherfolk. If you need anything, don't hesitate to ask!"

Foultner watched both rangers exit the library and fly off the ledge before she turned to Biski. "Okay, what's going on? That was weird. Nobody has a map party in the reeve's library."

Biski considered Foultner for a full minute. When she spoke, there was an accusatory hint in her voice. "I was hoping they might know where Cherine is being held. Where the Ashen Weald is holding him."

"Hey, you're as Ashen Weald as I am," Foultner said. "I don't know where they're holding the Jonas loyalists. You'd have to ask Merin about that."

Or Ranger Lord Grenkin, she realized. His Ashen Weald rangers were transporting the prisoners.

Biski was trying to stare her down. "Cherine's not a Jonas loyalist. He's not even Ashen Weald! You locked up an opinicus from a free pride."

"*I* didn't do it," Foultner protested. "*Merin* did. What do you expect me to do about it?"

"Merin's your friend. Find out where he put Cherine so I can rescue him." Biski puffed up her mane.

Foultner laughed, she cut her laughter short when she saw the look Biski was giving her. "Okay, okay. You're little, but you've done a lot. I heard about your experiences from

Henders. Nobody is going to tell me where your scholar is at. And if you rescue him, you're going to start an incident. Let the trial go on as planned. If he's innocent, he'll be set free. Speak in his defense if you need to. Medicine gryphons all get some sort of law training, right?"

Biski was still glaring at her.

"Look, I didn't come here about your rescue operation," Foultner explained. "I'm looking for your apprentice. Have you seen him?"

Biski shook her head, her mane swaying back and forth. "No, but I sent him to try to find some starberries for me about two weeks ago. I think he's still trying to find them."

Two weeks ago? Foultner wondered. That was a long time for him not to have reported in. "It's still early in the season for starberries, isn't it?"

Starberries were blue and plump with a small star design on the bottom of each berry. They were tasty, but most types matured in the summer.

Biski shrugged. "He said he'd seen some in the northern mountains that ripened in spring."

Well, this was a waste of time, Foultner mused. "All right, well, if you think of something, let me know. Send word through the kjarr nesting grounds."

Biski's posture was still confrontational. "Only if *you* let me know when you find out where they're holding Cherine."

Foultner considered throwing Grenkin under the feathermane's frightful gaze but thought better of it. She was more likely to need a favor from him than from a medicine gryphon. Instead, she left the library and did her best to get to New Eyrie before it got too dark out.

She debated cutting across the water, but every now and then it'd light up like lightning, so she reconsidered. There were rumors that the reeve's pet used the crackling jelly swarms to hide, and she didn't want to become a snack.

10

HEADMASTER NEIDER

Neider wandered around the camp as far as the blackwings would let him. This close to the Redwood Valley, they seemed concerned he'd try to go home. It was a quaint sentiment—his home had been the university, and it had burned in the fire.

He stayed away from the northern section where the prisoners were kept. He worried that if he went there, he might see someone he knew, someone he would feel compelled to help. Better to stay far away from that unpleasantness. So he wandered the southern edge where the trashbirds congregated, bypassing a corral full of an ever-growing number of captured weald monitors who hissed at him as he moved past.

"Hey-la, Headmaster," one of the pitohui said. He was unbothered by the hissing reptiles nearby.

Neider hadn't bothered to learn any of the opinici's names, never bothered to learn anyone's name, really. It was too much trouble. He was always mixing up names.

Which wasn't to say he didn't know who this opinicus was. He knew that the trashbird had a family staying in the slums of the Blackwing Eyrie. He took these missions, the dangerous ones, because it allowed him to send money to his sister on the pitohui island. She invested that money into fruit groves of several sorts that were starting to turn a profit. In another year or two, the opinicus here could take his family back home and work the groves.

Neider knew who this opinicus *was;* he just didn't know his name. He knew the blackwings, too. Most had worked as prison guards before being suddenly reassigned as scouts.

The headmaster wandered among the trashbirds, careful not to step on any of the teal scarabs that had infested the camp. To maintain their poison plumes, the pitohui had brought some with them, but they preferred to eat them live, and the bugs had a knack for escaping from harness pockets. He'd been given a vial of antivenom for emergency purposes and told he wouldn't be given a second one.

"Is the Reeve's Bane here?" he asked.

The trashbirds looked up from their game. "He's checking out the coastlines for your mystery opinicus, the white opinicus who miraculously reappeared. Iony just got back, if you want to talk to him. He's cleaning up by the falls."

"Ah, I see," Neider said. Considering what had happened in the Redwood Valley, it was strange to find the pride leader of the glacier gryphons working with the blackwing opinici. It made Reeve Brevin's plan seem positively speciesist.

He meandered to the waterfall and found Iony standing under the water, letting it wash off several layers of grime. A weald medicine gryphon harness lay nearby, taken off one of the locals they had locked up near the monitor cages.

"Dear me, more cave exploration?" the headmaster asked. "Did you find where it comes out?"

Iony shook off the water, drenching the headmaster. He was losing more of his winter coat every day but still managed to soak up an impressive amount. He lifted a paw to try to get the water out of his long, pointed ears.

"I did," the gryphon said. "The path leads from here all the way down through the mountains to the Summer Falls. Only problem is that it's underwater since your apprentice blew up the dam. Found a few opinicus bones in there, too, and a section that smells like gryphons."

Iony had been tasked with finding a path from Poisonmaw to the Redwood Valley that didn't run afoul of Strix's daughter. The red-and-black owls were as likely to kill blackwings as to let them live. It was only after they'd run into the trashbirds unique adaptations that the owls backed off.

From what the headmaster's contacts had told him, Ninox was also looking for the Ashen Weald prison. It seemed she thought the blackwings would lead her to it eventually. When the Reeve's Bane had asked Neider if he thought they could work together, he'd been clear: the weald owls weren't like Iony's glacier owl pride. They were serial killers, more beast than sapient creature, and they killed without a second thought.

The Reeve's Bane seemed skeptical, but the bodies of his scouts persuaded him.

"Have they grown suspicious?" Neider asked Iony.

"No," the gryphon said. "It's been a stroke of good luck, but no one has even stopped to question me. Unfortunately, I haven't found anyone who knows about the prison."

The headmaster worked hard to keep his voice calm. "Any word of Cherine or Kia?"

Iony's ear went sideways. "Your friend by the Redwood ruins says Cherine is locked up with our scouts."

"Hmm," the headmaster said.

Iony climbed out of the water and got closer to the headmaster than he was comfortable with. "The black-wings will kill him when they rescue our scouts. They'll kill your little forger friend, too, if they think he talked."

The headmaster was used to having his loyalties tested and didn't rise to the bait. Iony was staring into his eyes.

"I'm sure my assistant will do just fine. He's remark-ably close-beaked, on and off the fern," Neider said. "And I think you'll find Cherine is a treasure trove of informa-tion. If you can keep him alive, of course. Kia, too."

"Ah, the brightlycolored one," Iony said. "She's been poking through your old office. A team of reclaimers located it. The entire ruins are crawling with gryphons and opinici looking for metal. Nothing in your old library that our blackwing friends wouldn't want found, eh?"

"Of course not," the headmaster said. "Though perhaps there should be."

Iony's ears both went forwards. "I'm listening."

"We have a tome of information on the Seraph King," Neider continued. "With a few alterations, we could slip it into the wreckage to be found. A few lines about gryphon purges and the Ashen Weald might take the fight to the king on their own."

Iony finished preening the water out of his feathers. "I'm headed back first thing tomorrow to meet with your underbough spy. Leave it outside my nest, and I'll plant it in the ruins."

"Of course." The headmaster would have to stay up late to get it done in time, but it was worth it if it kept him in the good graces of his blackwing allies.

THE HEADMASTER FINISHED his additions to the Tome of the Seraph King and left it outside Iony's nest. With that out of the way, he retired back to the closed hut. While the Reeve's Bane was out scouting, Neider had it to himself. He'd just taken a drink of water when the warm, cinnamon taste hit him. Most opinici added a little to their water for flavor. The headmaster never did because it made it too easy to miss the taste of poisons or, if his palette was correctly attuned, hallucinogens.

He sat down on the edge of his nest. Everything started swimming, and the light went out.

—*Headmaster.*

Had a voice spoken? Or was it just in his head? His talons gripped the floor, trying to stop the spinning.

—*My dear Neider, that's no way to greet an old friend.*

Through the windows, the headmaster saw a shape moving outside the hut.

—*Do you remember our first day at the university? I told you we would do great things together.*

"Have we?" Neider managed. "Have we done great things?"

The shape spread from one window to the other. Soon, it filled all the windows in the hut.

—*Great, terrible, wondrous things. We killed so many opinici together.*

"Saved," he slurred. "We saved so many opinicus chicks together."

—*Do you ever do the math? Add up the chicks you saved from death, then subtract the number I buried in the mountains? I wonder if we were a net positive.*

"You killed them. I didn't do that. You did that on your own."

—*I was surprised that you ran to the reeve to tell on me. You were kind enough to leave me a note first. What was it you said? 'Flee, and die a free opinicus'? I didn't die. I still live.*

Neider tried to focus on the shapes outside his window, but every time he looked up, he was overcome with vertigo. "Are you cured?"

The shapes coalesced in the doorway, becoming a single opinicus. Neider couldn't tell what was real and what he was hallucinating. He saw black eyes, too many wings. He saw red talons and a dark red beak.

—*No.*

"Then you're still dying. At what cost do you do this? How many have you killed since we drove you from the mountains?"

—*Legions. Whole prides of gryphons are now extinct. An eyrie on the border of the Emerald Jungle no longer exists because of me.*

"Was it worth it?" he asked. The shape entered the hut. He could feel its hot breath against the feathers on his face.

—*I will see this continent devoid of opinicus life before I allow myself to die. Show me one other organism that would not do the same. I act within my nature, said the monitor to the parrot. I say the same to you here and now.*

The shape retreated. Neider's head cleared a little. The

black eyes remained. "You kept the Seraph King alive. Why not do the same to yourself?"

The shape held up its claws, stained red with iron its body couldn't process.

—*It cannot fix my flaws, only reset them. I have reached the end of my soul. The next time I drink, it will be the last. If it does not work, I will die.*

"And your masters?" Neider asked.

—*The Seraph King is the same. He has used up his lives. The next elixir will give him his godhood or kill him.*

"Why tell me this?" His eyes were beginning to focus again. The dark shape was now outside the hut, at a window, at several windows at once.

—*Because there are a talonful of opinici who may crack the elixir before I do, and they all came from the university. You were able to use my research to stop the disease in eggs and chicks. If you can draw the red from my talons, I will give you the white eyrie. Failing that, tell me where you're hiding the Seraph King's prize so I may buy myself more time to experiment.*

"The dig site," Neider began. His beak had stopped chattering. "The dig site northeast of where the Jadebeak River enters the bog. Your prize is there, chained to a pedestal."

—*Goodbye, old friend.*

The headmaster stood and went for the door, but then caught the smell of incense. Its sickly-sweet scent took him back to his days raising bees, and consciousness left him.

HEADMASTER NEIDER AWOKE to the sound of dripping on the roof. His body jerked awake when he remembered the previous evening. The door to the hut was still open, and the Reeve's Bane was leaning on the frame and watching him.

"Looks like you had one hell of a night," the trashbird said. "Careful of the stuff Iony ferments. You have to water it down first. Only the glacier pride can drink it raw."

Neider's mouth tasted of stale cinnamon. The hint of incense was still in his nares. "Mally the Nighthaunt was here."

The Reeve's Bane stiffened. "That's quite the statement. Is he locked up with the prisoners, or did you just have a bad dream."

Neider's headache worsened with each droplet that hit the thatched roof. "He was here. Ask the guards outside."

"They went to get breakfast," the trashbird said.

But they never leave to get breakfast. They're too afraid I'll sneak away.

Neider pulled himself up onto all fours and crawled out into the day. He had a good idea what hallucinogenic Mally had put in his drink based on how sensitive his eyes were to the light. He'd be more careful about what he drank. There were few precautions you could take against the Nighthaunt. It was best to give him what he asked for and pray he didn't kill you before one of your assassins got him.

Neider and Rybalt followed the sound of dripping to the back of the hut. There was a puddle of red spreading next to the crates of dried fruit.

Above, impaled upon tree branches, were the guards.

The Reeve's Bane shouted for Iony. His owl gryphon

second-in-command arrived with several blackwings in tow. They all looked up at the bodies.

"How did this happen?" Rybalt asked. "Who was supposed to relieve them?"

"It was me." One of the blackwings looked sheepish. "I just kept sleeping because they never came to get me. I figured they'd found someone else."

"Our blackwing friends need a reminder of how guard duty works. Perhaps watching the monitors every night for a week will help with that." Iony turned to Neider. "Why weren't you killed?"

The headmaster didn't feel a need to lie. "I told him what he wanted to know."

"Which was?" the Reeve's Bane asked. "Not the location of our camp, obviously. We're going to need to pack up and move into the caves at the other end of the valley."

"I gave him the location of the seraph in the swamp," Neider said. "That is part of our mission, isn't it? To make sure the Seraph King finds it?"

Iony and the Reeve's Bane shared a look that suggested they may have had a different goal than the Blackwing Eyrie, a goal they weren't willing to state in mixed company.

"There's another seraph?" the guard who slept through the massacre asked. "And we *want* the Seraph King to get his talons on it?"

Believing there was power in knowledge, the headmaster spoke up. "This isn't like the one frozen in the ice. It's degraded too far to be of much use. And... there's a gift inside it. A weapon."

The Reeve's Bane looked him in the eye. "Do you understand the consequences if the Nighthaunt takes it back to the white eyrie? There are almost ten thousand opinici who live there."

"I would bring about the end of the war," Neider said.

"You would bring about the apocalypse," Iony snarled. "The flowers and pumpkins that limit its spread only grow here in the south. The Ashen Weald doesn't have enough antidote to keep themselves safe, and you want to unleash that upon a city of thousands. I see why you and the Nighthaunt were colleagues."

Neider felt the words in his soul but stood resolute. "Two eyries fight until one is wiped out. Only half of the winning eyrie remains alive. Now, we have a dozen eyries on both sides fighting. How many are wiped out?"

"I don't question your math, opinicus," Iony said. "I question your ethics."

"It's a long shot," Neider countered, "but if it works, I could wipe one eyrie off the map and win the war. Without the Seraph King, the eyries he's conquered would reclaim their independence. This *is* the ethical thing to do."

"The Seraph King sent an army to try to wipe out my eyrie three years ago." The Reeve's Bane's voice was a whisper. "If you make a move like that and you miss, it's an opportunity at peace you've killed. Your opponent will send everything he's got at you. You'll just galvanize the western eyries against us."

The blackwing guard looked shaken. He was unaware of their trap in the swamp, it seemed. "But isn't it worth it even if it doesn't kill the king? Surely, without Mally the Nighthaunt, he'd die of old age?"

Neider thought back to his old friend's words. Was it true that the Seraph King was on his last elixir? There were only so many times you could force opinicus biology to accept it before the body became strained and tattered. Still, if anyone had found a way around that, it would be Mally. All his words could be lies. His only true loyalty was to himself.

The headmaster cleared his throat. "If you want the Seraph King to die of old age, you need to figure out where he's getting his elixir from."

"I'm working on it, old bird," the Reeve's Bane said. "Some idiot locked me up before I could find out last time."

The blackwing looked like he wanted to protest the honor of his reeve, but a drop of blood landed in the puddle and splashed onto his leg and he leapt back.

"What about our other objectives?" Neider asked. Now that he knew Mally haunted these woods, he had better things to fear than blackwings and trashbirds. "Any word of the Ashen Weald's reeves or their...nest."

"The gryphon reeve is well protected," the Reeve's Bane said. "And there are smarter gryphons than us looking for the location of the prison and Reeve's Nest. If we wait, one of them will find it."

"That sounds like where we were when we arrived," Neider said.

"Not exactly." Rybalt pulled one of the guards down. "Now that we know Mally the Nighthaunt is here, we might be able to lure him out."

"With what bait?" Iony asked.

"His top lieutenant, the opinicus who recruited him into the Seraph King's army," Rybalt said. "The headmaster's intelligence checked out. Piprik isn't dead. He's been hiding out with the fisherfolk all this time. He's on the far side of the largest island."

"You're certain?" Iony asked.

"I know, it hardly seems possible. Three armies wiped the small eyrie bordering the Emerald Jungle off the map. Still, there was a lot of confusion. At least a dozen scholars managed to disappear." The Reeve's Bane turned from his friend to the blackwings. "Clear up the camp. Move us to the south end, by the cave and the monitors. Maybe the lizards can keep better watch. I'll take a few pitohui and some gryphons and see if we can get to the shore. Let's hope the owls in the woods are feeling generous."

Neider looked at the two dead guards. How much of the previous night had been real? Mally the Nighthaunt stretched long in his memories, with black eyes. Only the red talons and beak remained the same.

What happened to the opinicus I used to love like a brother? he wondered.

Unlike Mally's crusade to save his own life, the head-master had always considered the greater good. Better the Blackwing Eyrie stop the Seraph King than all the eyries fall under his rule. It was too bad Reeve Brevin had never been smart enough to see that.

ZEPH PARROTBANE
BANE OF THE REDWOOD VALLEY REEVE

11

ZEPH AND KIA INVESTIGATE

Zeph's investigation took him to the medicine gryphon cave at Hatzel's nesting grounds. Despite explaining that he was working with their leader, the young medicine gryphons wouldn't tell him anything.

"Watch my mane shake nooooo," the feathermane said as she shook her head back and forth. "I'm not answering any of your questions."

Zeph ended up catching breakfast with Xavi and Pink Paw. Breakfast, in this case, was a small goliath bird and catching it meant chasing it through the aneda forests that bordered Hatzel's hunting grounds.

Pink Paw delivered the killing blow. "You think the medicine gryphons are hiding Ninox?"

Zeph shrugged while he ate. It felt good to hunt something that wasn't a fish. "If one of her pride were hurt, what other option do they have?"

"If they were hurt, they wouldn't just stick around the cave, right?" Xavi asked. He was still grooming dust and small rocks out of his blue and white magpie feathers.

"Sure," Zeph said, "but the type of injury could give us a hint as to where they're hiding."

"The plague caves are still open," Pink Paw said, "even though there are medicine gryphons in every nesting ground since the night of the fire. It's where I'd check first."

"Sounds good." Zeph finished his meal, chatted a bit with two of his favorite gryphons, and then headed to the caves.

It had been a while since he'd last been here to trade fern seeds for bees. His skin itched just thinking of all the stings he'd endured to get the hive south. It was a small consolation that the bees seemed to be doing well by the pumpkin patch. Following in his footsteps, more hives had been transplanted as the southern weald started to grow again.

He called out from the entrance to the cavern. No one answered. He came inside and found a brazier lit. Unlike his previous visits, there was no young firetender watching it.

He wandered into the back room and disturbed the old medicine gryphon and several apprentices. They were making compresses out of aneda and charcoal, a common treatment for lace monitor venom.

She dismissed them, and they walked past him. "Zeph Beeflight, I send you out to investigate, and you opt to investigate me first."

"The woods are full of danger," he countered. A gryphon's epithet could vary from pride to pride, based on what they believed a gryphon's most impressive accomplishment was. "If one of the Strix Pride were harmed, they'd come here for treatment."

"Sounds plausible," her sticky voice said. "I wouldn't tell you if it had happened."

There was a curtain propped up by several crates, blocking off the back of the cavern.

He moved a little closer to it. "Knowing what injuries they had might tell us where they're staying."

"Oh for parrot's sake," she swore. "You're as subtle as a gryphlet."

She pulled back the thick woven curtain revealing a nest and several boxes of aneda resin. "This is where we kept Pink Paw's son. It's for gryphons whose injuries make them sensitive to light."

Zeph blushed. "I'm sorry. I had to check, though."

"I don't blame your gumption," she said. "I just question your speed. Why are you still here instead of checking the next place off your list?"

"Sorry." He felt like a scolded gryphlet as he left the cave with his tail between his legs.

Well, one place down, ten more to go.

Zeph landed atop Snowfall. He hadn't realized until the Blue-eyed Festival how much he missed his mountain-top birthplace, especially its hot springs. The taiga gryphons greeted him with cheerful chirps and told him that Younce was still asleep.

So he walked right into Younce's cave and hopped on the fluffy gryphon.

"Oomph," Younce said without opening his eyes. "Let me sleep another hour. You know where to find breakfast on your own, Tresh."

"*Skraark!*" Zeph shouted, and Younce leapt out of bed.

"Monitorspawn," he swore, "you're starting to turn into a parrot yourself."

"Sorry to wake you," Zeph lied, "but I had a few questions about the old nests at Snowfeather."

Younce yawned. "I see where this is going. I gave them to Ninox, but I don't think she ever got to use them. I don't know where she is. Not in the taiga, as far as I can tell. There's only been one murder here."

Zeph made a mental note to ask about the death. What he actually needed now was Younce's love of history. "You once said that all taiga nesting grounds had an emergency escape path, right?"

"Sure," the taiga gryphon said. "You found Hoarfrost's when you fled from the starlings. Deracho used the one here at Snowfall to sneak Satra back to the kjarr when she and Mignet were caught at the hot springs. What's it to you?"

Zeph tried to groom his hatchmate's fluffy tail but quickly gave up. There was a reason weald inhabitants joked that taiga gryphons were all preen and no hunt. It took forever to get so much fur in order. "So if all taiga nesting grounds have them, where's the one at Snowfeather?" Zeph asked.

"Nobody knows." Younce admitted. "The Connixation was generations ago. It froze everything, even the emergency escape paths. Snowfeather's could still be frozen solid even today."

"Is there a pattern or something to look for?" Zeph asked. "Did Deracho find one at Williwaw?"

"We've only uncovered about a tenth of Williwaw," Younce said, "but the islanders who fled from there told me about theirs. You should be able to check for a pride glyph. Snowfeather's was two crossed white feathers with black bars. Good luck finding that under the snow."

Zeph sighed. "This might be a fool's errand."

Younce scratched at his fluffy ears. "Whichever way the main caves face, look for an escape path leading the opposite way. If nothing else, it'll give you a place to start."

Zeph bowed and mantled his wings. "Thank you, oh mighty taiga pridelord, for taking time to meet with your subjects on this spring day."

Younce wrapped his large paws around a shiny rock and threw it at Zeph before curling up to go back to sleep.

ZEPH PICKED up Kia before he headed into the Snowfeather—or was that Owlfeather?—Highlands. It seemed fitting that they should return here, considering they'd blown up the dam along the Snowfeather River.

"Crater Lake is looking pretty sad," Kia said. "How does everyone know it was us who blew it up?"

"Triddle," Zeph explained. "He told Askel about the explosion, and Askel told everyone else. Now, when they tell the legend of the Reeve's Bane, they say I killed Brevin atop the dam and, upon her last breath, she exploded."

Kia laughed. He started to talk again, but she held up a talon to tell him to pause and kept laughing.

"Okay, I'm done," she said. "You know, I didn't get to be a Reeve's Bane. I was there, too."

"Would you like an epithet?" he asked. "I could give you one."

"Ha, no, I'll come up with one myself," she said. "*Like the fish who leapt from the water, I will praise myself if no one else will.*"

"Your Rorin impression is pretty good!" He laughed. "Honestly, though, it was the floodwaters and a stray owl that killed Brevin as much as it was me. And if you hadn't caught me out of the sky, I'd have landed on the ground and died. You're welcome to the title if you want it."

"Mmm," Kia said. They were over the Owlfeather nesting grounds now. "Looks abandoned to me. Shall we investigate?"

Zeph looked in a cave. There were a few opinicus supplies strewn about, probably from squatters after the eyrie fire. Several frost chickens had taken over the others.

"Nothing up here," she called down. "Just a lot of very territorial chickens."

"Nothing down here, either," he shouted. "None of these caves go into the earth, though. A taiga pride would want some place to keep warm."

They didn't have the tools to dig and look for a deeper cave, so they flew around the mountain, looking for a crossed feather glyph. It would be faster to split up, but he worried there were stranger things than owls in these woods if Younce's claim that a monster had killed a ranger in the taiga were to be believed.

Off to the east, he saw Biski's apprentice. When he shouted a hello, the apprentice disappeared into the aneda woods.

"Strange gryphon," Zeph said. "I guess he's not social."

"Do you remember him from your taiga days?" Kia asked.

"The whole year and a half?" He shook his head. "No, he was born after me. There's usually a gryphon or two with the grey markings, bobbed tail, and long ears— northern taiga markings. He's the only one at the moment, though."

They wandered through the woods, eventually coming across several broken branches on the other side of the mountain. They landed to look around.

Kia tilted her head to the side. "The broken branches sort of look like crossed feathers, if you look at them right."

"I think you've been flying too long without taking a break to eat," Zeph said, but when he tilted his head, he could see it.

He flew up and searched behind the tree branches, finding the barest hint of a white glyph. "There's something here."

She joined him. "It's pretty faint. It could be just about anything."

Still, they searched around and found a small cave. While it looked like an opinicus had taken refuge there, the cave didn't go far back before the walls had collapsed, and they gave up.

"Well, we can cross the medicine caves and the Owlfeather Highlands off our list." Zeph stretched his paws. "I guess the spirits of Snowfeather wanted us to find the exit, even if there weren't any owls here."

They did one last pass, but the angry frost chickens had enough of the duo and chased them into the sky.

"Any luck with your book searching?" Zeph asked as they flew back into the weald.

"Not nearly as much as I'd hoped," Kia admitted. "I did convince the parrotface elder to speak with me. I'm headed there tomorrow."

His eyes widened. "A leader of the Ashen Weald is willing to talk to you about Cherine's disappearance?"

"Well, she said I could come talk to her," Kia said. "I don't know if she'll tell me anything. It's worth a try, though. Orlea said the parrotfaces were trading with the Strix Pride before they vanished. I'm still hoping if we follow where the supplies are being sent, we'll find the prison."

"Huh," Zeph said. He'd assumed Ninox had no allies. Instead, he'd found out that Younce and Orlea had given her the Owlfeather Highlands and the parrotfaces had been trading with her. It would be much more difficult to find her if she had gryphons helping keep her hidden.

12

RANGER LORD OF THE CRACKLING SEA

Z eph arrived back at Hatzel's nesting grounds to find a letter waiting for him on his nest. It was sealed with wax, a Crackling Jelly insignia.

He'd been discussing his adventures when Hatzel said, "You have mail," and pushed it over to him.

"Mail?" He tried to gnaw the seal off of the letter. "When did we start getting *mail?*"

She took the seal back and cut the top off with her claws before giving it back to him. "Right now, I suppose. I think Younce sending Blue-eyed Festival invitations on paper started giving gryphons and opinici ideas."

Zeph held the letter under the moonlight to read it better. His blue eyes were nearly gone now and his night vision with it. "Ranger Lord Grenkin says he wants to meet with me about our mutual friend. Says he might know of a place to look."

Hatzel's brow furrowed. "I don't like it. He's loyal to Satra. He wouldn't betray her."

"Unless the information is really coming from Satra?"

Zeph ventured. "She could be using Grenkin to send us a message without Merin or the Ashen Weald knowing."

Hatzel took the letter from him and read it while shaking her head. "He wants to meet in the middle of the night? With all of the murders going on?"

"Well, that'd be the best way to keep prying eyes away," Zeph said. "And it's right by the Crackling Sea Eyrie, out of the forest."

"Whatever you do, don't go alone." Hatzel went back inside and settled down on her nest. "It's probably a trap."

He curled up in the nest next to her. "Don't worry; I have a plan."

"Aren't you supposed to be back at the kjarr nesting grounds doing Ashen Weald things or saving your pride or something?" Zeph asked the old medicine gryphon. Instead of coming in announced, he'd managed to sneak past the outer caves and had nearly made it to the curtained off area before he was caught.

"I came back to discuss things with my medicine gryphons." She was physically blocking him from going near the back of the room this time. Her voice held more annoyance than usual.

"Mmm." He tried to look past her, but saw only the earlier compresses for treating monitor bites. "Well, I just wanted to tell you that Ranger Lord Grenkin sent me a letter asking me to meet him outside the Crackling Sea Eyrie later tonight. He says he'll let me know where Cherine is being held."

"Why are you talking so loudly?" she scolded. "Fine, go talk to Grenkin. Either it's some sort of trap and this is all going to hell when he tries to arrest the Reeve's Bane, or he's just trying to get information out of you."

"Well, I'm going to go by myself," Zeph said. "I just wanted to keep you informed."

He started to leave the cave but ducked into a corridor. The medicine gryphon, whom he'd left alone in the room, seemed to be having a conversation with someone. Zeph could only hear her side of the conversation.

"Yes, he's a bit of an idiot. It's probably a trap. Best to stay away."

Ha, I knew it! he thought. With any luck, his backup should show up on their own.

ZEPH FLEW WEST, careful to stay south of the goliath bird pass, firmly in taiga territory. He came across two sets of taiga gryphons on his way. Where a patrol used to mean a pair, the murders had increased that number to five.

He stopped to chat with both sets. Anyone born at Snowfall was welcome in the taiga. Even during times like these, no one was distrustful towards him. It felt good to be liked, though that was no longer his biggest concern.

He cut north before he hit the kjarr, flying low against the aneda forests. While he felt safer around the taiga patrols, he didn't want to attract the attention of the Ashen Weald. They might ask what he was doing here, and he didn't have a good excuse to be this close to the Crackling Sea.

He found an aneda tree with a section burned off and made a nice little lookout for himself. His brown feathers matched the color of the bark. He could just make out the rocks where the meeting was to take place in a few hours, four outcroppings called Sailfin Point.

The sun disappeared over the Crackling Sea. The temperatures dropped. Even in spring, things could get fairly cold. Some of the medicine gryphons said the world would keep getting colder every year until all life was frozen. That was past his lifetime, but it was a chilling thought. He put a paw over his beak to keep from laughing at his own pun. He hoped he'd been right about the old medicine gryphon. If not, he was in trouble.

With the last hint of night vision blue in his eyes, he could make out the ranger lord landing at Sailfin Point. Six rangers stood back, though still visible.

Zeph frowned. His letter had said to come alone. Well, he supposed a ranger lord couldn't risk it. Zeph was the Reeve's Bane, after all.

He came down from the tree. The rangers were looking to the skies, so Zeph crawled the rest of the way to the meeting point. He stood tall before he left the safety of the trees. He didn't want to startle them into doing anything unwise.

"Ranger Lord Grenkin," he called. He'd forgotten the blues didn't have good night vision.

Grenkin's escort jumped, but the ranger lord ordered them to stand down. "Zeph Reevesbane. I don't know that we've ever had the pleasure to meet. You'd departed the Battle for New Eyrie by the time I arrived."

It was a strange opening for someone who had invited Zeph here. It sounded confrontational. Was that just in his head?

He approached, careful to keep several monitor lengths between him and Grenkin. "I had an opportunity to save lives if I acted swiftly, so I took it."

"Did you save them?" the ranger lord asked.

"I did," Zeph acknowledged. When he'd last seen Levin, she'd grown into a young adult and was learning about the world from Piprik. "But I don't imagine you called me out here over a gap in the attendance records. Your letter said you were willing to give me the location of Cherine?"

The ranger lord's talons went to his net, and Zeph crouched low.

This is a trap.

"I didn't send a letter," Grenkin said. "I received one from you."

A trap, but not from the ranger lord.

From the sea side, hidden by the smell of salt and the sound of the crashing waves, came a third voice.

"There's no need to be alarmed," it said. "I sent the letters. Ranger Lord Grenkin, I don't know if you'll remember me. We met years ago."

The figure, an opinicus, stepped into the moonlight. He had black and orange feathers. What Zeph first took as dark plumage around his head turned out to be an over-sized goliath bird hood modified for use on an opinicus. The straps hung loose, dangling when the opinicus walked. Around the eyes, the leather had been clawed away to allow sight. There were shackles on his legs, the chains between them also shattered.

"I hope you'll forgive the intrusion, Zeph," he continued. "Strictly speaking, I didn't need to forge a letter from you in particular. I've always wanted to meet a Reeve's Bane, and I thought this might be my only opportunity."

"You were at the fish market before the blackwings attacked." Grenkin's talons didn't leave his net. "Were you a trader? You came with a message from the reeve."

"That one was forged, too," the stranger admitted. "The reeve was already dead."

The rangers with Grenkin had secured their metal talons but held back.

The stranger turned back to Zeph. "I'm afraid I misspoke a moment ago. I meant to say that I'd never met *another* Reeve's Bane."

With that, Grenkin realized who the stranger was and charged, letting loose a haunting heron war cry. The stranger charged the ranger lord, closing the gap.

From the sea came twenty more dark-plumed assassins. Half were a mixture of black and sickly orange, the others were blackwings.

Zeph tried to rush forwards to the ranger lord's aid, but a blackwing knocked him back.

Zeph hissed.

"Gryphons, always so dramatic!" the blackwing laughed. His talons and polished black leather armor shone in the moonlight.

Around him, the rangers were falling. Even Ranger Lord Grenkin began to stumble.

Something was wrong.

The blackwing slashed at Zeph, but Zeph crouched. The opinicus reared up and Zeph pounced, catching the opi's forelegs with his paws. He pushed to keep the metal away from his important bits.

The gryphon and opinicus bit back and forth at each other, beak-to-beak. Just when the opinicus was starting to pull his talons free, Zeph used the momentum to lift up, then came straight down, digging his dewclaws into the legs of his opponent.

When the opinicus cried out, Zeph caught his neck and killed him.

He turned to go to the ranger lord's aid, but Grenkin was on the ground twitching. The stranger stood over him.

"Don't worry, my dear Grenkin," the Bane of the Crackling Sea Reeve said. "We'll take you some place nice and comfortable and have a chat about where you're holding my scouts."

The other rangers were also on the ground twitching. Zeph was torn between a desire to attack and confusion at what had happened. How had so many been subdued so quickly? He thought of the jelly toxin, but his opponents weren't wearing metal talons.

He could fight or flee. If anyone had heard the ranger lord's cry, help was coming.

He crouched down.

The other Reeve's Bane inclined his head slightly towards Zeph and untied his metal talons. He lowered himself down low, like a gryphon, and they circled each other.

"What did it feel like to crush the life out of the red reeve?" the stranger asked. "Did you taste her blood? Did she become part of you?"

"It was terrible," Zeph said. "I'd have let her live if I'd had the choice. More than anything, I felt shame."

"You ended a tyrant!" the stranger said. "What could be more glorious than that?"

"What did it feel like to kill the blue reeve?" Zeph had never heard anyone speak the name of the Crackling Sea Eyrie's leader.

"Necessary," the stranger said. "It was something that needed to be done."

Zeph hadn't expected a utilitarian answer. "Why did you let Jonas live?"

The stranger flexed his talons. "I'd been ordered to kill the reeve, his flesh and blood, and the parents of his children. As his male consort, Jonas wasn't any of those things. I didn't see any reason to kill him."

Zeph was taken aback. "You didn't kill him because of an oversight in your orders?"

"I'm a professional," the stranger said. He was just opening his beak to explain more, but Zeph took the opportunity to pounce.

The opinicus didn't dodge. Zeph's claws went into the stranger's shoulder. The opinicus pulled Zeph close, inhaled deeply, then pushed him away.

Zeph felt slick with the stranger's sweat. Sweat, or oil like Tresh had in her plumage to keep her waterproof?

He licked his feathers and the effect was immediate. He fell to the ground. He began to twitch slightly.

The stranger pulled a bandage from his harness pocket and placed it over the claw marks on his shoulder. "It's always nice to meet someone who doesn't know about the pitohui. Among all of the eyries who allied themselves with the blackwings, ours is the most feared. The blue reeve wasn't the first I'd killed. He won't be the last, either. You, however, are my first Reeve's Bane."

He pushed Zeph onto his back and walked over to the ranger lord. "I've heard of the trouble Jonas caused. Maybe it would have been better if we'd killed him. For the strife he caused you, I offer my apologies."

The stranger motioned to the blackwings, who seemed hesitant to pick up Grenkin while he had the pitohui oil on him.

"Tie each of his legs with leather straps and carry him that way, if you're so squeamish," the stranger said. He looked down at Grenkin. "You had a blackwing, a cockatiel, and a gryphon in your care. I brought with me someone who cared about each of them. If they're all alive, you may yet survive this night."

Where the foreign Reeve's Bane's entrance had been boastful and loud, Ninox's was neither of those things. One moment, four blackwings were trying to lift off with the ranger lord. The next, a portion of the night sky detached itself, and the opinici collapsed, misting the air with blood.

The other blackwings fell a moment later, and Sailfin Point filled with owls.

The pitohui hesitated.

"You must be the one picking off my scouts." The assassin looked from Ninox to the ranger lord. "My fur and feathers are poison. One touch, and the neurotoxin takes effect. You have no choice but to retreat or face death even in victory."

Ninox didn't speak to him. She hooted once, and her pride fell upon the pitohui.

The other Reeve's Bane fled into the aneda forests. Instead of following him, Ninox turned and walked back to Ranger Lord Grenkin.

"You took my mate." She placed her face up against his, beaks touching. "You will tell me where he is located, or I will let the poison kill you."

Several of Ninox's owls collapsed and began to twitch. The others rifled through the blackwings' harnesses and pulled out vials of a liquid that looked red in the moonlight. They fed it to their wounded and the spasms stopped.

"There is still time," Ninox said. "Soon, the damage will be permanent. Give me any reason to let you live. Is he at the Crackling Sea?"

The ranger lord shook his head. Or, at least, that's how Zeph saw it. It was possible it was a trick of the spasms. He felt his own body twitching harder. One of Ninox's owls with dark brown plumage brought him some of the antidote.

Ninox began listing locations. "Kjarr? Bog? New Eyrie? Redwood Valley? Bogwash? Fisherfolk villages? Taiga?"

The ranger lord shook his head no at each of them.

"Weald?"

The ranger lord hesitated. The other owls were staring at Ninox.

"That is enough to be useful." She nodded to the same owl who had cured Zeph, and Grenkin was given the antidote.

The owls were turning to leave when Ninox paused. "Probably, they will lock up the copper hawk if we leave him. Bring him along."

While the spasms slowed, Zeph felt suddenly sick. He vomited and blacked out.

13

DARKFEATHER HIGHLANDS

Zeph gasped awake. He reached for Hatzel, but she wasn't in the nest next to him. He looked around. The old medicine gryphon was standing over him.

"Dumber than a bag of rocks," she said. "How could you not know it was a trap?"

He caught his breath. The world still felt like it was moving too quickly. His heart raced. His paws were sweaty.

"I knew it was a trap," he said, "but I figured Ninox would show up if you told her about it."

"Did you, now?" the medicine gryphon asked. "And how'd that work out for you?"

He thought back to Ninox letting the other Reeve's Bane go and interrogating one of the leaders of the Ashen Weald. "Her plan and my plan were a little different."

"You wanted me to kill the pitohui," Ninox said.

Pitohui? Zeph couldn't remember if he'd heard that term. His head was still spinning. He looked around and realized he wasn't in the medicine gryphon's caves. In fact, he had no idea where he was. There were cave paintings with white feathers. Someone had added crossed red and black feathers. *This must be the Snowfeather nesting grounds.*

"Well, I didn't know he was coming. But yes, that would have been nice." Zeph stared at the cave paintings. "We searched Snowfeather and didn't find you."

"The chickens guard the only way in," she said.

He laughed. The only cave they hadn't explored had been full of guard chickens. Askel and Triddle would be proud.

"The pitohui is smart," she continued. "It is better to watch him and see if he finds Cherine before I do."

Zeph didn't agree with her reasoning and let her know it. "An opinicus crafty enough to kill the Crackling Sea reeve is too smart to leave alive. All the Ashen Weald leaders could be in danger."

"If they wanted to be safe from the blackwings, they should have left my pride alone to guard the north." Ninox shrugged. "If they are killed, it is their poor choices that brought them here."

"I like Cherine as much as the next gryphon," Zeph said, "but you're letting a lot of innocent gryphons and opinici die just to get him back. How many of the dead bodies came at the claws of your pridemates?"

Ninox stood over him. She looked bigger than he remembered. She still had her winter coat. "None."

"It was all the blackwings?" he asked.

She gave him one last look, then began to leave the chamber. "No, something else haunts the woods. Something that does not need blue eyes to see in the dark."

He watched her go, but she stopped and motioned for him to follow.

"Now that you are better, it is time for you to leave," she said.

He stood up, and his head began to spin. He took a few steps, but his legs were wobbly.

"He's allergic to the antidote," the medicine gryphon explained. "You should feed him first."

Ninox looked from the medicine gryphon to Zeph. "Fine. Come with me. I hope you tolerate salt well."

He allowed himself to be led into a large cave decorated with Snowfeather glyphs. A brazier illuminated the caves. He hadn't smelled smoke when he searched, so the ventilation must come out somewhere strange, maybe by the Summer Falls.

Fluffy gryphlets squealed and chirped as they ran around in circles, beating their wings to practice flying without feathers.

The old medicine gryphon pointed at three of them. "Cherine's children."

Zeph wasn't sure what to say. He hadn't really believed that Cherine and Ninox had anything in common. Now, he was staring at their offspring, one of whom was an opinicus herself. "What're their names?"

Ninox turned back, her hearing as keen as ever. "I did not name them. I did not know if opinici did something special for that. I will discuss it with Cherine once he is free."

The old medicine gryphon opened a crate of food marked with an Ashen Weald insignia. Inside was salted jerky and marshmallows.

Zeph ate as much as his stomach would allow while he watched the gryphlets play. Owls came from different directions into the main cavern, bringing reports to Ninox.

"I'm guessing you built a few ways in and out away from the main caves," he said.

"They were already here when we arrived," she said.

"Snowfeather was built to withstand a siege, not a Connixation."

He wondered aloud who they expected to be attacked by.

"You were born in the taiga," Ninox said. "You tell me."

He didn't know and admitted as much. "Now that we've found each other, what happens next?"

"Nothing," Ninox said. "You go back. If you find Cherine, send word. Otherwise, that is that."

"We'll work better together," he countered. "Do you believe Grenkin, that Cherine is in the weald? If so, where have you searched? We can look in the other locations."

She regarded him. "Everywhere. I have searched everywhere. If Cherine is in the weald, I cannot think of where. I sifted through the ashes of the Feathermane Pride's nesting grounds. I dug out the entrance to the fantails'. I flew the length of Glacial Run several times."

"What about the cave where he was kept the first time?" Zeph asked.

Ninox's ears perked up slightly. "Where was this?"

He walked over to a section of the cave wall that included charcoal and ash maps. He traced a claw down the Snowfeather River to where it disappeared underground in Hatzel's hunting territory.

"Just south of here," he said. "Hatzel and Triddle pulled him upstream to get him out. Did you check there?"

"That's Merin's territory," the old medicine gryphon said. "You're not going to be able to get close. He has owl night guards watching it."

Ninox didn't speak.

"You can't be considering this," the old medicine

gryphon said. "Let me find an excuse to send an apprentice, maybe Biski to take a look."

"No, you ask too much of Biski already," Ninox said. "I will keep watch from afar and see if the guards are lazy."

The brown-feathered owl came in to report to Ninox. "One of Grenkin's rangers recovered enough to get help. The Ashen Weald will be there any moment."

"Thank you, Grax." Ninox said. "Take Zeph out the fourth tunnel, then seal it closed once he is gone."

"How will I find my way back?" he asked.

Ninox looked him in the eye. "You will not. If the blackwings capture you, I do not want you to be able to lead them here."

He started to protest but gave up and followed his owl escort down a long tunnel. At least he had two new pieces of information: Cherine was somewhere in the weald, and the blackwings were looking for the same thing he was.

14

THE HIDDEN WORKSHOP

I t took Kia a while to locate the hidden workshop the owls had been using to conceal their blackwing prisoners, but she finally found signs of a skirmish in a grove near the waystation and figured out the door mechanism.

After spending the day going through parrotface trade routes under the pretense of helping out, she'd decided that the flight-averse parrot gryphons weren't sending an unusual amount of food anywhere. That left her with a few other options. The Crackling Sea's farms were producing brackish vegetables. They could be holding the prisoners there or sending food somewhere else, possibly into the bog, that the parrotfaces were unaware of.

That could wait until tomorrow, however. For now, she wanted to get a look at where Cherine was taken to see if any of his notes remained. Thankfully, Cherine had included instructions on how to find it in the letters he'd sent to her back when he was seeking help with the translations. She felt a pang of guilt for not responding as she pulled one of them out and searched out the grove near the abandoned waystation.

The air inside the workshop smelled faintly of bee-calming incense. Cherine's journal and quills were still on the desk. Based on the dust level, several other pieces of parchment or vellum had been taken by the Ashen Weald rangers.

She searched the workshop from top to bottom several times hoping to find a clue of some sort. Instead, she just found more dust. She was about to leave when she heard a scratching sound coming from one of the stable pens. It sounded like stone scraping against stone. She pulled herself in the side room, careful not to step on any glass, and held her breath.

—*Home sweet home.*

It wasn't right to call what Kia heard a voice. It was like hearing a beast talk. There was a click and buzz and resonance to it. Yet there was also a clear Redwood Valley trill, though at a much lower register than Kia was used to hearing.

"You were this close to the valley and Brevin never caught you? Why didn't you build your workshop deeper in the mountains?" The second voice had a bit of Crackling Sea twang to it. Speaking sent him into a coughing fit. Kia recognized the sound from the survivors of the eyrie fire.

—*I was still collecting specimens from the underbough. I couldn't be too far away for that, now could I?*

The Crackling Sea voice was silent.

Something must have passed between them because the red voice spoke up again.

—*Not having second thoughts, are you? When we found you in the ruins, buried sixteen feet under rubble, you said you only cared about one thing.*

"Nothing has changed," the scratchy voice said.

"Whatever it takes to bring down the Blackwing Eyrie, I'll pay the cost."

Kia smelled the ointment used on victims of the fire. Her own oil burns itched in response.

—*Always a merchant.*

The red voice had moved. Kia heard the sound of scraping and something falling away.

—*Ah, here we are. Maps of the mountains and the bog. The very ones the Blackwing Eyrie provided to Felicio, in fact, before his death.*

She kept her breathing even. Felicio had died before she attended the university, but she'd heard the rumors that his son, Bario, had killed him.

"Bleeding Redwood scholars." More coughing. "Were all of you traitors?"

The red voice laughed, a sound that seemed both bestial and opinical at the same time.

—*I'm sure there were some who were not. They probably burned in the fire. Not a very noble end, now was it?*

"I nearly burned in that fire," the blue said.

—*You kept a gryphon as a pet and treated her like a daughter. You deserved to burn, but we saved you.*

The sounds of talons walking around the workshop caused Kia to try to hold her breath again. Four pair of clicks, not two.

"All your friends went blackwing," the blue voice continued. "Why did you join the Seraph King?"

The Redwood Valley accent turned away from Kia's hiding place.

—*At first, I didn't choose a side. I did my experiments, progressed alchemy as far as I could take it. I perfected the elixir that kept the Seraph King alive but stayed away from his agents.*

"And then?" the blue prompted.

—*And then I was approached by one of the Seraph King's only true friends, an opinicus named Piprik. The blackwings had been a little squeamish about the murder thing when it was eggs and newly-hatched chicks. Piprik told me that if I could turn the king into a god, purify him, I would never lack for test subjects.*

"Did you?" the blue asked. "Purify him, I mean? Or make him a god?"

—*No more than I did to myself.*

The red laughed, and the blue joined in, leaving Kia to wonder what they were laughing at.

—*Soon. Soon, he'll have his ascendancy. If we find what the headmaster hid in the bog, before summer. If not...well, that's a military matter. I never dip my talons into talks of strategy and tactics. I'm a scholar, not a fighter.*

The sound of scraping stone echoed throughout the workshop, then it went silent. Kia waited for another hour, afraid that when she looked out from her hiding spot, she'd see the two strangers.

When she finally exited, she found the dust around one of the pens disturbed. In the other side room, the desk had been opened up to reveal a hidden compartment. There was no indication of what had been inside.

Kia slipped out the front door. She walked through the aneda trees to the goliath bird pass, careful to stay along the side of the road. She walked for an hour before she felt safe enough to fly.

15

FOULTNER, RANCHER
EXTRAORDINAIRE

The Seraph King's mystery expedition had flown over Foultner and her capybaras without stopping for several days, leaving the Redwood Valley opinicus wondering if she'd said or done something wrong. This morning, however, that changed.

Henders had woken up an hour early to get to the ranch while it was still cool because he was needy and wanted to be liked. Foultner knew Urious had pulled some strings to get her assigned to the ranch and assumed she couldn't be fired, so she'd slept in an extra hour and was only just getting her harness on and stepping out the door to head to work.

She nearly trampled Silver, who was waiting right outside the tent.

"Oh, I'm sorry," Foultner said. "What brings you to the refugee tents?"

"Oh, no, I wasn't watching where I was going," Silver apologized. "I was too busy trying to figure out the numbering scheme. Your tent has a 372 glyph on it, but your neighbors say 161 and 163."

So she was looking for me, Foultner thought. "Whoever lived in 162 was eaten by starlings, so we moved our tent up. A lot of the numbering changed that night."

"So I hear." Silver looked past Foultner into Henders's tent. Foultner let her because there was nothing suspicious in there. "Your neighbors said you and your mate met as captains in the Reeve's Guard?"

Foultner didn't particularly want anyone poking into her past, but she was grateful she hadn't bothered to tell anyone here she was a spy.

"That's right," she said. "We don't tend to talk about that since, well, we didn't really do a great job at guarding the reeve. Honestly, when people ask what I did before the war, I tell them I was hunter."

"Before the war," Silver mused. "It means something different here than it does up north. Have you eaten? May I offer you breakfast?"

"Sure!" Foultner had already eaten, but she found if the meal was good enough, she could always find room. "I have about an hour before the capybaras will miss me."

She let herself be led away from New Eyrie and into the foothills west of the town. It was hard to call them mountains having grown up in the valley, but it was nice to get some altitude.

They landed atop a small farm with an empty stable. There were a few guards about, but otherwise, it was fairly empty. What caught her eye was the supplies left out. While Silver had chosen to bring her here while no one was around, Foultner would estimate around fifty opinici were stationed at the farm.

The top of the small building had food already set out. They settled in across from each other on a table built into the roof, and Foultner began tasting each dish, starting with smashed red berries. They were sour enough to invert her beak, and she quickly moved on to salted fish.

"I'll admit, I have an ulterior motive for inviting you up here," Silver said.

Here it comes; recruitment. Foultner braced herself. She wasn't sure if it would be better to join or decline the offer and just watch.

"I was hoping you might be interested in loaning us some goliath birds," the grey opinicus said.

Foultner blinked. "What?"

"We'd pay for them, of course," Silver assured her. "I just wanted to do a little more trading with the Crackling Sea Eyrie and Orlea's pride before we leave. There are some things it's hard to fly with."

Foultner pretended to think it over. "We can figure something out. How many birds do you need?"

"Ten for a week, if you can spare them." Silver slid a small bowl of the craneberry mash into her beak without flinching.

Foultner's eyes watered in sympathy. "We can probably swing that many for a week. That's a lot of trading, though. Does the opinicus pride have that many things of value?"

Silver pointed down to a wagon and several large crates on the ground. "I plan to use seven to start sending our supplies back north. It's about time to leave."

Foultner remained calm, but she'd been around long enough to know that when someone changed their story mid-conversation, something else was going on.

Are you borrowing them for work here, or are you going home with them? Or are you up to something more nefarious?

Whatever they really wanted the goliath birds for, it

wasn't something they wanted her to know. Definitely not for trading, that much was certain.

Silver counted out a large number of metal beads. "Will this cover the birds and you delivering them?"

Reminding herself that New Eyrie opinici were desperate and wouldn't haggle, Foultner said, "That'll do it. I can bring them this evening before sundown. Will that work?"

"Mmm," Silver said. "There's a path into the hills I can show you. I'll have someone meet you there."

"Great," Foultner said. "I should probably get to work. Thanks for the breakfast. I always appreciate a good meal."

She started to depart, then turned back. "Do you really have to leave so soon? It's been pleasant chatting. You should let Henders and I show you around."

"A tempting offer," Silver said, "but I'm afraid we put you all in danger by being here. We've come across a few blackwing scouts. If we stay much longer, they'll rally a force from Blacktalon to send at us."

Foultner wondered if her own forces had caught any blackwing scouts or if this was just a ruse.

Silver stood. "I can't help but think that all your misfortune in the south started because of the Blackwing Eyrie. I wouldn't be able to forgive myself if we brought their wrath down upon you a second time."

Foultner placed an equal amount of blame on several parties, mostly Jonas and Brevin, but didn't say that out loud. "Well, maybe we'll meet again. I'll swing by this evening with the birds."

To the north, a flight of several opinici appeared, led by the one with gold feathers.

"Looks like your Goldfeather friend is back," she said.

Silver nodded, but her posture stiffened a little. She led Foultner to the edge of the farm. "He'll be pleased to know I solved the goliath bird problem."

"Whatever happened to your metal friend?" Foultner said, deliberately taking her time to see how nervous it made her new acquaintance.

"Making sure the path home stays safe," Silver said.

Just as it seemed like she'd push Foultner into the sky to get rid of her, Foultner lifted off on her own with a "Take care!" and flew east towards the Clover Ranch.

As much as she wanted to believe the Seraph King's forces would be withdrawing in a week's time, she couldn't help but think that if they did leave, they'd return with an army. She'd let Henders know to get the birds ready, but then it was time to check in with Satra.

FOULTNER KNEW she'd be sore from all of this flying by the evening, but for the moment, she was happier in the sky than trying to find and prepare ten goliath birds.

The head of the Clover Ranch had, in fact, fired Foultner. Thankfully, Urious had been there to smooth things over. He and Soft Paws were planning another expedition to search for signs of starlings in the north and the ranch was a good place to organize, so the Ashen Weald had taken over the bottom floor.

Now well past the ranch and sawgrass flats, Foultner landed outside the kjarr nesting grounds and walked the rest of the way in. She didn't want to risk being seen by one of the foreign opinici. She'd left her swirled metal claws and black armor in storage and kept her head down.

It would be just as bad if one of her friends noticed her and was questioned later by Silver.

Foultner was surprised to hear laughter. Several young kjarr gryphons ran past her. One of their friends had been lagging behind and flew to catch up.

It's become a different place. Satra finally got her wish.

Foultner slipped in the back of the council building. She caught Satra's attention, and the Kjarr cleared out the room claiming it was time for a break.

Once the room was empty except for the council members, Foultner stepped forwards and explained about the goliath birds. "They say they're leaving in a week's time because they don't want to draw down the wrath of the blackwings upon us."

"It's a bit late for that," the old feathermane medicine gryphon said.

Foultner's brow furrowed. She looked around the council chamber and realized no one was representing the Crackling Sea. "Did something happen to Ranger Lord Grenkin?"

"Blackwing assassins," the medicine gryphon explained. "The same ones who killed the blue reeve, he says. They tried to take out both him and the Reeve's Bane."

Foultner was nonplussed. She'd assumed Silver's claims of blackwing scouts was part of the ruse. It took her mind a moment to kick back in, but when it did, she had a lot of questions.

"What happened? What were Grenkin and the Reeve's Bane doing in the same place?" She paused as she realized they needed a distinction. "Zeph, I mean. And how did they survive? The tale of the blue reeve being killed is legendary."

"Ninox," said one of the Ashen Weald owls. Foultner only knew this one because his colors were backwards. He was a dark red with a black undercoat. "She showed up to save the day and threaten Grenkin if he didn't tell her where her mate was."

Almost as surprising as his news was his use of a contraction. Ninox's brothers had immersed themselves into the common language and were starting to lose their accents.

"The assassins don't look like the blackwings, though we did find dead blackwings there," Merin said. "Grenkin said the blackwings call them *trashbirds.*"

"Charming." As an underbough denizen, she'd been called trash by all manner of northern quarter opinici and Reeve's Guards.

"They're coated in poison," the medicine gryphon added. "We found two vials of an antidote. We're working on figuring out what's in it. Two vials aren't enough if they attack again."

Foultner had a solution for that. "You should ask the emissaries. If the Seraph King and Blackwing Eyrie reeve have been fighting for decades, they'll have come across these assassins before."

Satra nodded. "It would give us one more opportunity to get as much information out of them as we can. We'll have a feast and invite all three."

The parrotface elder sighed. Things were starting to grow again, but the stockpiles wouldn't handle another emergency.

"We'll write up the invitation and send a courier to deliver it," Satra said. "We'll have to find an opinicus to write it for us."

Foultner tried not to be offended by that. "Don't send a

courier. Send Merin. He's the most imposing leader who isn't missing or dead. It'll look better coming from him."

Satra looked him over. "I don't know, Soft Paws is probably more imposing."

"Thanks," Merin said.

"But she's also pretty young," Satra continued. "Do you want us to send an armed escort with you in case the blackwings make another move?"

To Foultner's surprise, Merin looked like he wanted to say yes. In the end, when his hooked beak opened, he said he'd be fine.

By the time Foultner made it outside, she didn't have a moment to spare to find Blinky and check in with her. Foultner would have to hear her friend's thoughts on the assassination attempt later. For now, she had goliath birds to deliver.

16

BEACHHEAD

Piprik lounged in the shade while Levin practiced diving at various targets set up along the beach. He'd asked her to let out a screech or a war cry as she hit. While a silent attack was more deadly, this let him close his eyes and still keep count. On the twentieth dive, he called her over to drink something and cool off.

"Whatever happened with the pitohui grapplers?" she asked while she groomed sand out of her feathers. "And why do they grapple? Isn't it easier to slash or dive?"

"Because they're venomous." He opened an eye and saw Levin staring at him, incredulous. "Poisonous, rather. They secrete a neurotoxin. So if they brush up against their target even once, their opponent begins to lose control over their muscles."

"A poisonous opinicus," his young apprentice said. "I've never heard of such a thing. What happens if they fall in love with someone who isn't a pitohui?"

"Poetry," he said. "A lot of poetry. And a song or two."

Levin wouldn't let up. "But how do they, you know, have chicks together."

"That's a question for your foster mother to answer, Mi-Lei," Piprik said. When she didn't take the hint, he sighed. "It takes over a year, but you can slowly build up an immunity. That allows for, well, cuddling. The catch is that, if you stop taking a dose of the toxin, you become hypersensitive to it."

"No wonder they're not very popular," she said. "Everyone is afraid to touch them."

"That's why they live in the worst parts of the eyrie," he said. "And they cover themselves when they go out. Not just a harness, everything. If you see one without a covering, they're going to murder someone."

"Or just fixing their feathers," Levin countered. "Or just in the privacy of their own nest. No one wants to go around with a sheet over their head. I don't even want to wear my harness half the time."

"You could go live wild with the gryphons," Piprik said. "Then you'd never have to wear a harness."

"The taiga gryphons wear harnesses," she countered.

"Well then, don't be a taiga gryphon." He pointed to the targets. "Go clean those up, then we'll talk history. It's about time you learn about the wider world, starting with Crestfall and Reevesport."

Levin cheered and ran off to the beach. While they used sand opinici as targets, they dressed them up, and those items needed to be brought in so they weren't washed out to sea.

Piprik went to his hut to fetch food. His young pupil was smart. She was capable. She could defend herself. Soon, she'd need to decide if she wanted to stay a fisherfolk or return to opinicus civilization. While he hoped she'd stay here, she often talked about how she didn't think all of her sisters had died. If she went north and told opinici who she was, at least some of them would look to her as a leader.

In his experience, leaders came in two types: those who ruled and those who served. His investment in the southern eyries was minimal. In the grand scheme of the world, he figured they'd fall to one side or the other. But he was invested in seeing leaders who set an example. Even if he wasn't invested in New Eyrie or the opinicus pride, he was determined to help Levin. He had a lot to teach her before she went north to find out if she was the last of her family line.

He opened a clay jar and looked inside. He was getting tired of salted fish bars. Maybe it was time he learned to cook for himself. If nothing else, it would give him something to do while he bided his time.

He was on his way back when he saw Levin looking down at something on the beach. His first thought was a crab, but when he saw its vibrant teal color, his heart stopped.

"Get away from it!" he shouted.

Levin jumped back. The advantage of never having yelled at her before was that she didn't question it.

He tossed the fish out of the clay jar and smashed the scarab with it, over and over again, until it stopped moving.

"Did you touch it?" He was shouting again. He went through his harness pockets, searching for his red vial. "*Did you touch it!?*"

"No, no, I didn't!" She was shouting back at him now. "What is it? What's *wrong* with you?"

He stopped to catch his breath. He used the lid of the jar to move the scarab inside. Then he began to scoop the sand where the scarab had been into the jar.

"I'm sorry I shouted at you," he finally managed.

She was still staring at him, wild-eyed. She must think him mad.

"The pitohui live on an island paradise." He used his scholar voice to calm her. "The crops they grow there feed a dozen eyries. Ships travel to and from the pitohui carrying food, fish, exotic birds."

The look she gave him showed she still thought he'd lost his mind.

"But the ships also bring insects. Wherever the traders from the pitohui's island go, they bring scarabs." He pointed to the clay jar. "Scarabs that can kill you.

"Other opinici call them trashbirds and force them into slums, but they can't cast them out. Because once scarabs start to infest a port, there's only one type of opinicus that can stop them. The so-called trashbirds."

Levin's eyes widened in understanding.

He put the lid on the jar of sand and teal insect parts. "The pitohui eat the scarabs and become poisonous themselves. But it stops the scarabs from taking over and spreading."

"You said wherever there are scarabs, the pitohui are, too," she said. "Does that mean there are pitohui here now?"

He looked around. The scarab couldn't have swum out to Luminaire. He started to call her Levin but corrected himself in case anyone was listening. "Mi-Lei, listen to me carefully. Go straight home to your foster family. Stay there. Lessons this week are cancelled. I'll send word when it's safe again. Do not tell *anyone* about this, understand me?"

Levin nodded. He hated to bring fear into her life, but

fear was a part of everyone's life. She needed to learn to survive on her own.

He waited until she had flown so far over the water that he had trouble making out her form, then he hurried back to his hut to prepare.

PIPRIK'S HUT was too exposed and too easy to keep an eye on. He grabbed his supplies and went deep into the redwood thicket that made up the heart of Luminaire. He got as far from the other fisherfolk as he could get. He didn't want any of them harmed. He even shooed away a large salamander. While he couldn't tell them apart, Tresh had a favorite, and he didn't want to cause her distress.

He finished his preparations as best he could and settled down on a rocky outcropping.

He didn't have to wait long.

Shapes appeared along the edge of the glen, alternating pitohui and glacier grey. He didn't see any of the bright shoulder markings of the blackwing opinici.

Ahead of him, two of the shadows entered the sunlight. With his hood and broken bindings, it took Piprik a moment to recognize the Reeve's Bane. By how close the glacier gryphon was standing to him, his companion must be Iony.

Piprik had met them both, long ago. There was no recognition in their eyes now. It was a pity. On the whole, they wanted the same thing: to find the Nighthaunt.

"Reeve's Bane, Pride Leader Iony," Piprik said.

They froze.

"You're well informed for a fisherfolk," the Reeve's Bane said. "But I suppose the Seraph King has eyes everywhere. In fact, I heard you were once called the Eyes of the Reeve, back before he styled himself a king."

Piprik didn't rise to the bait. "I mean you no harm. I don't intend to get in your way."

"I doubt that," the Reeve's Bane said. "Even if it were true, you delivered the Nighthaunt into the king's care. The blood on his talons has stained yours, too."

"I hold no love for Mally," Piprik said. "Together, we could find him and bring him to justice."

"So that's it?" Iony said. "You had a change of heart and that's why you joined this strange commune?"

"The fisherfolk aren't so strange," Piprik said. "Sometimes, I think they're the only opinici or gryphons who have things figured out."

The Reeve's Bane took a step forwards. "What happened in the Emerald Jungle, Piprik? By the time we arrived, all of our scholars were dead or missing. Did you execute them? Or does Mally have them locked up somewhere?"

Piprik suppressed memories of bloody talons and chittering starlings. "Mally betrayed all of us."

"That's not true," the Reeve's Bane said. "There were a lot of dead starlings that day. There were even more blackwings. But we only found a single white-feathered corpse. In fact, we thought that corpse was you. Whose body did I burn in the jungle, Piprik?"

There was no point in telling them what had happened there. Not even the Redwood Valley scholars would believe what they found. It was better they thought the Seraph King mad. It was better they thought Mally insane. It was better than knowing they were right.

"You're just an administrator, a bureaucrat," Iony pressed. "I lost gryphons that day, too. If you come back with us and answer our questions, we'll lock you away in my nesting grounds. You'll never fly free again, but the blackwings won't execute you."

"Or I can take you to my island," the Reeve's Bane said. "We're offering you a chance at life in exchange for information. We know you were always a go-between. You aren't the mastermind. You weren't one of the scholars. If you make us fight for it, I can't promise how things will go."

Piprik leaned on his back paws and lifted up his talons. "By all means. If it helps you catch Mally the Nighthaunt, that's all I ask."

The Reeve's Bane moved slowly, just close enough to rub his own arm against Piprik's. The neurotoxin began its work. Soon, he was on the ground.

"I guess your potency is back," Iony said to the Reeve's Bane.

"I guess so," his friend responded. "Or Piprik is so old it hit him hard. We're going to have a hard time getting him back in the daylight. What're the chances no one is looking for us after the failed attempt on the ranger lord?"

Iony laughed with his whole head, his ears wobbling with the motion. "If we're careful and fly low, we can probably get him to the bamboo grove and take the long way around after nightfall."

Piprik looked up at both with his one eye that was still open. A little drool came out of his beak. The Reeve's Bane was supposed to be the craftiest in the blackwing reeve's arsenal—an opinicus so dangerous he was locked up when not sent on a mission.

"Do you think he's really after Mally?" Iony asked.

"The strangest part of war is that opinici do, in fact, have a change of heart from time to time." The Reeve's

Bane stared down into Piprik's open eye. "If that's true, he's going to make the perfect bait. I can't imagine how a bureaucrat stayed hidden for this many years. Or how he faked his own death."

The Reeve's Bane looked from Piprik's open eye to his beak. He'd recognized something was wrong, but he didn't seem able to put his talons on it.

Piprik's own talons clutched the flint. Just when the Reeve's Bane recognized the red tint of the puddle of drool as matching the color of the antivenom he'd kept in his medicine pouch, Piprik struck the flint together, igniting a dozen fuses that spread out in every direction. While he'd sent two vials of the saltpeter Bario had left behind with Biski when she went into the swamp, Piprik brought back an entire crate with him from the Crackling Sea's island fortress. This was some of Felicio's original, mined saltpeter. Not Bario's pale imitation.

Iony's gryphon cry began and was cut short by the explosions. The gryphons and opinici around the outer rim were vaporized. Only the Reeve's Bane and Iony were smart enough to duck down.

Piprik got up and made a dash for cover. Iony grabbed his leg. The gryphon's mistake was in treating the fisherfolk like an old money-counter. He wasn't prepared for the strength of the slash Piprik gave his opponent's forepaw.

"He's a bleeding phoenix," the Reeve's Bane shouted over the echoing in their ears. "How did we miss *that*!?"

Piprik's wings were shaking from the blast and wouldn't let him fly. Pieces of redwood and rock were lodged in his feathers. He made it to the edge of the glen. His blackwing pursuers took a few steps forwards, then stopped.

Quess, Bruen, and Levin appeared at the edge of the glade, all holding spears.

"We found them!" Levin turned and shouted behind her. "They're here, kill them quickly!"

The Reeve's Bane and Iony managed to get airborne and flew towards shore, shedding tree branches and blood as they went.

Piprik looked behind Quess, expecting an army. He saw only trees, some scorched.

"Everyone else was on the mainland," Levin explained. "I just thought it would sound scarier if I had an army behind me."

Piprik laughed. It was a loud, rough sound that echoed in his ears.

"Can you fly?" Bruen asked. "There might be more of them on the island."

Piprik looked back at the glade. Six pitohui, six glacier gryphons. It was unlikely anyone uninjured had stayed behind after the Reeve's Bane had fled.

He was starting to try to say that when shadows blocked out the sun. Tresh, Rorin, and twenty sentries arrived at the glade from Swan's Rest.

"What happened here?" Rorin boomed.

Tresh rushed over to check on Quess and Levin. When she'd determined that they were safe, she turned to Piprik. "You have some explaining to do, but first, let us get you to someplace safe."

He allowed himself to be carried across the water to Sandpiper's Dune, the closest settlement with a medicine gryphon who wasn't him.

As SPLINTERS and rocks were pulled out of him, Piprik debated how much to tell Rorin and Tresh. He considered them both friends, but he didn't think anyone would understand what he'd seen and done.

"They thought I was Piprik," he said before he realized how crazy that sounded. The medicine gryphon began looking for a head injury, but Piprik waved her off.

He settled on a lie that would have the same effect as the truth. "I'm not. Piprik, that is. They found his body. I... I killed him. He was a bad opinicus who did terrible things, and I killed him with my own talons when I realized he'd sold us out."

Levin's pain and confusion hurt the most. He hated to think that his actions and story would undo the values he'd taught her.

"I should back up a bit. I was a scholar on a Blackwing Eyrie expedition into the starlings' jungle," he began.

The jungle was hot and humid. We were sent in to find out what happened to the previous expedition. They'd disappeared without a trace. You already know what green wing altruism is, but we didn't know about it at the time.

17

THE EMERALD JUNGLE EXPEDITION

"I don't know what green wing altruism is," Levin said.

Quess and Tresh shared a look.

"I'll explain when we get to it, little lightning bolt," Piprik said. "At first, we didn't even know about the starlings."

Broad, thick leaves blotted out the sun on the edge of the Emerald Jungle. Flowers and ferns seemed to grow out of trees, and the jungle floor was thick with vegetation. Every so often, a millipede the size of three gryphons standing in a line would scuttle by, sending leaves and startled birds into the air.

Piprik wandered through the ruins of the previous expedition's camp. Based on the large exoskeletons, it appeared they'd found a way to eat the giant bugs. Several wooden structures remained upright, but all of the tents had been destroyed. He found a multitude of cages. Inside were several gryphons who had starved to death. This wasn't why he'd become a scholar. This wasn't why he'd agreed to come out here.

Mally held an emerald feather in his talons. His nickname was known even among the blackwings, but they'd been forbidden from calling him the Nighthaunt. The Redwood Valley opinici were a superstitious lot, and the blackwings didn't put much stock in the rumors.

"*We were wrong not to,*" Piprik said. "*Whatever you've heard about him, it's true. He is every tale told to frighten chicks.*"

Levin shivered. She was the only one who had grown up at the Redwood Valley.

The expedition had several days of quiet where they cleared out the cages, fixed up the basic structures. What wasn't apparent at first was that they were in an eyrie, or at least the outskirts of one. The camp's buildings hadn't been constructed out of stone by the previous team; they'd been reclaimed from the jungle. As Piprik explored farther, he found other structures. He continued on until he discovered strange glyphs, then he brought the news back to Mally.

"Excellent," he said. "Let's set traps and capture some of the native gryphons so we can study them. We seem to be between four sets of territory markers. We should be safe."

Piprik didn't say what he was thinking—that the previous expedition probably believed the same thing. He'd been ordered by the blackwing reeve to give Mally anything he wanted.

"*I do not understand,*" Tresh said. "*You were a blackwing opinicus?*"

Piprik nodded. "*Stay with me a little longer. It'll make sense. We were all blackwings except Mally.*"

South of the Seraph King's eyrie were two stretches of land he hadn't been able to conquer. That was what they were there to study. What had held back his forces, and could the Blackwing Eyrie harness that power?

To the north was the Abyssal Naze. At a glance, it appeared to be a forest like any other. Upon closer inspection, rock holding it up had been eaten away by acid rain in several places, and the ground could give out at any moment. Streams and rivers cascaded down into massive holes, disappearing into nothingness. The naze was safe enough to fly over during the day, but none of the Seraph King's patrols ever stayed the night.

"Owls?" Levin asked.

"I don't know," Piprik admitted. "We turned our attention south, to the Emerald Jungle."

It took a month for the new expedition to finally catch a starling. When they did so, against everyone's protests, Mally dissected it. He called gryphons an invasive species. It was the first sign of his madness, but it wasn't the last.

Two more months passed. The blackwing scholars continued to study plant and animal life while Mally studied the starlings themselves. He checked their beaks and talons for something.

"At the Blackwing Eyrie, Mally had hidden his illness well," Piprik said. "After several months in the jungle, it became apparent he wasn't okay. His red beak and talons weren't stained with blood like the tales say. They were caused by his body's inability to process iron. He was dying, and he believed the cure lay in the jungle."

"This is a mad tale," Tresh said.

"Wait until you hear what happens next."

Five months in, Piprik noticed their stores were running low. They were still sending their research out, but supplies weren't coming in. When he asked about it, the courier became confrontational.

Piprik shrugged it off at first. Shipments were late sometimes. Perhaps the eyrie was getting ready to recall them. While new insects and plants were exciting to him, they hadn't unlocked the secret to keeping the Seraph King at bay. They picked off starlings who came near the border, but without knowing how many were out there, they were afraid to push deeper into the jungle.

And then the supplies started up again, and everyone was happy, Piprik was relieved to eat fresh fruits and vegetables. They'd discovered some edible roots, but they lacked any discernible flavor. With the shipments came new spices, and the roots became enjoyable again.

A week passed before he realized that the crates didn't have the Blackwing Eyrie mark on them. The spices, too, tasted different. He didn't know how to confront Mally about it. Perhaps one of their allied eyries was now providing supplies. There were several possibilities.

While Piprik continued cataloging plant types, Mally had the workers create sound-proof cells so the starlings could be kept apart without calling for help. He stopped dissecting them and seemed to be waiting for something.

"Wait, you said you'd explain green wing altruism," Levin interrupted.

"It is a kind of bond or hive mind the starlings share," Tresh explained. *"It is why when they are exposed to the parasite, the infected starlings do not turn on each other."*

"It's a little more than that," Piprik added. *"Have you ever awoken to find a large weald crawler in your bed?"*

Levin nodded and made a face that showed her disgust.

"That's how starlings feel about all gryphons and opinici who aren't starlings," he went on. *"There's a visceral, disgust-and-kill reaction even when they're not infected."*

What arrived next had the insignia of Crestfall on it. Strange, treated clay containers held purple essential salts. Mally began to boil the salts into an elixir and use it to give his iron disorder to starlings and then try to cure them of it.

"*I don't understand,*" Rorin said. "*How is that possible? What was the elixir?*"

"*I don't have a name for it,*" Piprik admitted. "*Its effects are how the Seraph King has lived for as long as he has. It causes a reaction in gryphons and opinici on a very basic level. By itself, the chemical does nothing. But if you add stress to the opinicus...or a change agent...things happen.*"

"*Like giving a healthy gryphon an iron disorder,*" Rorin said.

"*Yes,*" Piprik confirmed. "*Exactly like that.*"

Levin opened her beak to talk but closed it again. Piprik wondered if she'd heard the rumors of Impir and her mom. He suspected he'd find out by the end of his tale.

Mally had taken Piprik under his wing. Piprik took notes and offered suggestions. Whatever his ethics had been a year ago, nine months under the Nighthaunt's tutelage had changed him. When they caught a lost taiga gryphon, he didn't think twice about killing it. Somehow, he'd become a monster himself.

Yet it was exciting. Mally became sicker, but every day brought a new experiment that could teach them how to remove the iron disorder. Anything felt possible.

Then the courier turned up dead. That was when things began to fall apart. For the first time, the scientists asked where the supplies were coming from. Without a courier to send the order out, they were still arriving. On the edge of the path, crates would be left with no sign of who had brought them there. The one scholar who tried to hide along the path to discover their source disappeared.

It took two weeks to bring the blackwing scholars near

mutiny. That was when the last shipment arrived, and with it, the Seraph King's forces, led by Piprik.

"W<small>AIT</small>, I thought you were already there," Rorin said.

"He said Piprik isn't his real name," Levin said.

"What is your name?" Tresh asked.

"Khalim." It felt strange to say it out loud after all this time. "Khalim of the Blackwing Eyrie. I was born at a ranch outside Blacktalon, one of five chicks. My father was from an eyrie that borders the desert, but he wanted us raised somewhere safe. When the Seraph King's forces took his home, he died trying to retake it. I became a scholar to get away from the fighting."

Khalim realized at once what had happened. Mally had sold them out to the Seraph King. Piprik, the real Piprik, put the other scholars under guard. Only Khalim was allowed to roam free as Mally's assistant.

They repeated the experiments for the so-called Eyes of the Seraph King. Piprik demanded they test the experiment on Mally. If he could really change the essence of an opinicus, he should prove it by curing himself.

But the elixir wasn't ready yet. While it reversed the effects and bought Mally time, it didn't cure him completely. Still, it was enough for Piprik. He ordered everything packed up that night. The next day, everyone would fly over the Abyssal Naze and into the Seraph King's territory.

"I couldn't allow that." Piprik-who-was-Khalim said. "I finally found my strength. We'd come to understand the problem the starlings presented, their green wing altruism. I decided I would rather risk all of our lives than have us turned over to our worst enemies. So I released a single starling."

The starling wasn't missed. It fled into the wilderness. Khalim returned to Mally's quarters and waited.

Hours before dawn, the starlings arrived, and Khalim was able to see why the Seraph King feared the Emerald Jungle. Piprik led a small force into Mally's quarters to fetch him and Khalim.

"Mally was already out the door when I acted," Khalim said. "I killed Piprik with my own talons. Mally locked me into the chambers and there I waited until the other scholars found me."

With the starlings outside and the Blackwing Eyrie's forces coming at any time, Khalim and the other scholars were forced to make a choice. They'd helped Mally for months not realizing he'd switched sides. When the blackwings arrived, they'd all be executed as traitors.

Ultimately, the scholars decided they would wait for the starlings and blackwing forces to fight, then they'd flee into the Emerald Jungle. Only Khalim had a different plan. He tore the eyrie badge off of Piprik's uniform. He would disguise himself as one of the Seraph King's agents and hunt down Mally the Nighthaunt. He bleached his feathers, leaving the black around his eyes, and adopted the mannerisms and appearance of Piprik, taking even his name.

Khalim thought back to the taste of blood and the vats of purple elixir. The dead starling in the corner. The other scholars pleading with him to join them. He wouldn't tell Tresh, Rorin, or Levin about that. Not yet.

"How did they get through the Emerald Jungle safely?" Tresh asked. "Is that who Erlock went to find, your friends?"

"I don't know, I didn't go with them," he said. "And yes, one said he'd hide along the Jadebeak River."

"How did you bleach your feathers?" Levin asked. "Why don't they regrow black? How much like Piprik do you look?"

"Identical," Khalim said. "And you would be surprised what one can accomplish with alchemy."

His friends, the fisherfolk who had harbored him for years now, mulled this. He let them think it over. There would be more questions soon.

18

KHALIM

"So the blackwing assassins don't know you're Khalim?" Rorin asked. "They believe you're Piprik, and that's why they tried to kill you?"

"Yes," Khalim said. "No one knows who I am—or that I'm still alive—who isn't in this room right now."

"You said Mally could change the starlings' essence," Levin said. "And Impir is Mally's apprentice, right? Is that why my sisters were all green except Ivess?"

"Yes," Khalim said. "The easiest time to change a gryphon or opinicus is when they're in the egg."

He pulled out a piece of paper and began to sketch the gryphon prides across the world. "The purple elixir speeds up the process, but it's been happening naturally all along. Look up to the taiga. What birds live there?"

Levin settled in like this was another lesson. "Gyrfalcons, snowy owls, goliath birds."

"Yes and yes," Khalim said. "And the gryphons look the same way, right?"

She nodded.

He sketched the gryphons. "They didn't when they

came here. Over hundreds of years, they began to resemble the birds. Their eggs took on those traits."

Tresh frowned but didn't form a question.

"You'd never seen a peacock before, right, Mi-Lei?" he asked. The medicine gryphon had left before he told his story, but he couldn't be sure when she might return.

"Right," Levin said. "Well, just their feathers on the wall."

Khalim sketched a peahen and a peacock. "I'm going to guess the feathers from six emerald peafowl and one blue?"

Now Levin's eyes got wide. "Yes, one over each of our nests."

"Normally, half of the reeve's children would be peafowl, the other half would have their father's traits," he said. "On average, that is. It's a bit of a simplification. But with the right chemicals and peacock blood, you can force the change while the chick is in the egg."

"So Ivess being blue wasn't a mistake," Rorin said. "That was Impir proving he was choosing how they look."

"I didn't know Impir," Khalim said, "but I assume that's how he did it. The peacock feathers came from importing the birds from Reevesport on the other side of the continent. Gryphons take on the attribute of the birds that live in an area. It's how they adapt to an ecosystem."

"I...do not believe any of this." Tresh's tone wasn't confrontational. It was reserved.

"Cranes, diving petrels, sandy terns." Rorin listed off the most plentiful birds along the shore. They were also the most common fisherfolk appearances.

"Once Mally could change chicks in the egg, his research became the *Nachlass Mal*," Khalim said. "It explains how to stop the blood iron disorder before the chick is born and how to detect it in eggs of a level of development. The child mortality rate east of the desert halved the year after his research became common knowledge. Suddenly, every eyrie knew the Redwood Valley existed."

"But he wasn't a chick," Levin said. "He was an adult. He was trying to cure himself that way?"

Khalim considered the metaphorical path they were walking down. He took another step. "Yes. Eggs and pregnant mothers are easy. Feed her the blood of the bird you want. Place the egg in heated blood and salt. Most of the time, that's all it takes. But he was an adult."

Rorin put a wing over Tresh, who seemed lost in thought, before turning to Khalim. "You said he had success with the starlings. What was different about them?"

"I don't know," Khalim admitted. He tried not to think of Mally using his own blood and concoctions to give the starlings his iron disorder. "The discovery of the elixir and purple salts? Perhaps if he'd allowed the iron disorder to settle in for years, nothing would remove it. I can't say."

"But it had some effect," Tresh said. "Not like with Levin, not completely, but it works on adults."

He nodded. "A little."

"It just takes bird blood." She was staring into the dark circles around his eyes. "Or opinicus blood. Piprik's blood."

"Ah," he said.

"The other scholars hid in the Emerald Jungle by *becoming* starlings," she continued. "You hid by *becoming* Piprik."

Levin put a talon on his. "You're like me, then."

He managed a smile. "What gave it away?"

"The birds," Tresh said. "You said you dyed your feathers, but look closely. You are not a red-winged blackbird bleached white. Your shape is not right. You are something predatory."

"A white-tailed kite," Khalim said. "They're all over the northwest, where the Seraph King rules."

"Wait, what does that mean, they *became* starlings?" Rorin asked. "They were opinici, and they became gryphons?"

"We left in a hurry," Khalim said. "I haven't seen how they turned out. Once the green wing altruism took hold, I was afraid they would see me as an enemy."

"Do you miss your face?" Levin asked. "Your real face?"

"I do," Khalim said. "I miss my name, too. But Mally must be stopped, and this is the only way I can get close to him while he's under the white eyrie's protection."

"Can you change back?" she asked.

"Honestly, I don't know," he admitted. "I'm not sure how it would be possible. I'd need large quantities of my own blood from before the change."

"Before, you said the Seraph King searches for purity," Tresh said. "Is that why he wanted Mally's help? To change himself?"

"They say as a young fledgling, he pulled a six-winged opinicus out of the ocean," Khalim recited. "The opinicus told him of the homeland of all opinici. But to get there required six wings to make the flight. The king called this opinicus a seraph. He wishes to be remade in its image."

"But that's just a story," Levin said. "There aren't really seraphs."

Tresh stood and went to the door and made sure no one was outside. "I have seen one."

"What?" Rorin said. "Where?"

"The bog," she replied. "It is the source of the parasite that took the starlings."

"There's another frozen in ice," Khalim said. "The glacier pride guards it for the Blackwing Eyrie. That's what the Seraph King is really after. That's why he pushes east."

"The Ashen Weald needs this information," Rorin said. "Satra needs to know why the white eyrie is really here."

"How do you tell them so they believe you?" Tresh asked. "How do you do it without betraying Piprik—sorry, Khalim?"

Levin looked down at her talons and green plumage. "I don't know how I feel about any of this."

Piprik ruffled her crest. "Every Redwood Valley opinicus is engineered now, just a little, to keep them healthy. It means nothing, lightning bolt. What matters is what you do after you're born. Everything before that means nothing."

Their questions were interrupted when Quess and Bruen opened the door.

"We've cleaned up the glade," Quess said. "We put the pitohui bodies aside for you to give them a proper burning like you requested. We were very careful of the oil on their feathers. The gryphons we gave a taiga burial."

"Are they fisherfolk, then?" Bruen asked. "Gryphons and opinici working together?"

"The Blackwing Eyrie will take any allies it can get," Khalim said. He didn't actually know the pitohui burial rites, but he had other plans for their dead bodies. "They'll work with anyone willing to stand against the Seraph King, gryphon or opinicus."

"I've always thought of them as right—" Bruen noticed Levin and changed his term to something less offensive, "frost chickens."

"If the Seraph King held Crestfall or the Crackling Sea, he could launch an attack on the Blackwing Eyrie itself," Khalim said. "I don't say that to excuse what the blackwings did to your reeve, Bruen, but that's why they did it."

"Yeah, we'll put that in the history books," Bruen said. "As for me, I'd be just as happy to see every blackwing opinicus dead."

Tresh and Rorin both looked at Khalim, but neither revealed his secret.

"So," Khalim pretending to be Piprik said, "who wants to give Satra the news?"

THE FAKE PIPRIK finished packing a satchel. He was done with the bodies of the pitohui and now had new vials of antivenom. It was time for him to depart.

The best thing he could do for the fisherfolk was to leave his old hut vacant on the shore and find a new place to continue searching for Mally. With him gone, the Blackwing Eyrie shouldn't have any reason to harass the fishing villages.

He affixed the storm barrier. Overhead, Swan's Rest sentries kept watch over Luminaire. He'd given them the remains of the scarab and descriptions of the Blackwing Eyrie's allies.

Green peacock feathers wove between the white and red crane shapes of the sentries overhead, and Levin landed next to him. "I'm going with you."

"I'm not sure where I'm going, yet." He finished securing his harness pockets.

"You're looking for Mally, right?" she asked. "Well, Soft Paws said the white opinici are all up at New Eyrie, where my subjects are. We can start looking together. I'm worried about what'll happen to the Redwood Valley opinici. I think they need me."

"They don't need another reeve," Piprik cautioned. "Half of the opinici your mother used to rule are now in Orlea's pride. Another quarter have joined the Crackling Sea or gryphons. All that's left at New Eyrie are the ones who refused to let go of the past."

Levin wore her mother's snake necklace and golden talons. "I've been thinking about that. Can't I declare myself Redwood Valley reeve and disband the eyrie? There's got to be something I can do to let them move on. I won't know how to help them without talking to them."

He thought it over. His first stop was Snowfall to see the taiga gryphons. He could join the fisherfolk traders on their flight north. By himself, he shouldn't attract too much attention. A green peafowl opinicus would be harder to hide, especially wearing the trappings of the former reeve.

He wished Zeph and Kia hadn't given Levin her mother's things. "You're not going dressed like that, are you?"

Levin shook her head. "No, I just wanted to try them on one last time."

Piprik sighed. "Okay, let's go find Naya and see what she can do about a disguise."

PIPRIK AND LEVIN walked into Naya's home at Sandpiper's Dune and found her deep in conversation with Rorin and Tresh.

"If we could have a moment of your time?" Piprik waited for them to quiet. "Mi-Lei would like to come along and speak to the opinici at New Eyrie."

Tresh and Rorin looked at each other.

Naya just looked confused. "Why are we sending islander fledglings to speak to eyries?"

"Ah." Piprik cleared his throat. He'd incorrectly assumed Rorin and Tresh would have told Naya about harboring Reeve Brevin's youngest child.

"My name is Levin," she said. "I fled New Eyrie when my sisters were killed by Impir and Bario. Mi-Lei drowned. Her family have been taking care of me ever since."

Naya looked around the room. "And I'm the only one who didn't know this?"

Piprik didn't mention his own identity issues. The nice thing about fisherfolk was that they never questioned anyone's past. He suspected many of the opinici who pulled in nets of fish and built reed nests along the shoreline had their own sordid pasts, now long forgotten.

"It was not our story to tell." Tresh turned to Levin. "Are you sure you want to reveal yourself? You still have a lot to learn."

"And growing to do." Rorin had to duck to keep his crane-like head from hitting the sandstone ceiling of Naya's home.

"I'd like to find out what's happened with New Eyrie first," Levin said. "Maybe there's nothing I can do to help, maybe they're better off with the northerners, but I need to know."

"So I need you three to disguise her," Piprik said. Everyone was looking at her train of bright green peacock feathers. "Make her look like a fisherfolk so they don't see her mother in her."

"It's not easy to hide a peacock," Naya said. "I have some blue dye, but not enough to take care of those tail feathers."

"The blue peacock opinici from the Redwood Valley Eyrie have green in their tails, too," Levin countered. "So do a lot of the islanders. It's just my chest we need to change."

Tresh pointed to Rorin's plumage. "Give her a splash of red dye on her chest like one of Rorin's sentries."

"And have her trade in her metalwork for some of Tresh's sea monster trophies and flippers," Rorin added. "Those're two things you never see the weald or eyrie wear."

"The reeve had seven daughters, right?" Naya asked. After she received confirmation, she said, "Well, just be male, then."

Levin blinked. "What?"

"Nobody's going to lift up your tailfeathers to check," Naya said. "Be a male fisherfolk while you travel."

"I don't understand. I mean," Levin blushed. "How do I do that? What's the difference?"

"In my experience," Piprik began, "if you have a masculine name and opinici call you *he*, nobody will question your gender no matter how you act."

"Levin is a feminine name at the eyrie," Levin said. "It was my great-grandmother's name. Mi-Lei is a feminine name on the shore, isn't it?"

Tresh nodded. "Didn't Zeph call you Lei? That is a masculine name here."

"It's a masculine name among the eyries, too," Piprik said.

"Lei," Levin tried it on. "Yes. I like it."

"Wait, *Zeph* knew, too?" Naya let out another audible sigh to show her displeasure. "I guess I spent too much time up north looking for answers and missed that my islander neighbors were harboring a reeve."

Levin ruffled her feathers. "I don't want to be a reeve. It's just that a lot of opinici at the eyrie were kind to me. I want to make sure they're okay. I keep wondering if I could have done something if I'd stayed."

"All right, I'll help," Naya said. "We'll dye you today. I'll convince the traders to wait `til tomorrow, and I'll make sure there are a few peafowl fisherfolk in the caravan."

Tresh picked through a crate of goods from Orlea's pride. "Do you have white or black, Naya? We should fix Piprik, too."

"Nothing permanent," Piprik said. "I may need to speak with some of the white eyrie opinici."

"We should do this in one of the abandoned houses the dunes have reclaimed," Tresh said. "There could be spies in the bamboo forest still."

19

THE INVITATION

Foultner and Henders led ten goliath birds through the tall grass to the carrot farm. Ever since the starlings attacked New Eyrie, she didn't like walking through here. While the Ashen Weald had done their best to clear out the bodies, it was still common to stumble across skeletons.

Henders chirped to himself as they walked. She didn't ask him to stop because it had a calming effect on the goliaths. He paused now and then to peck at bugs crawling up the tall stalks.

"One of these times, you're going to get a stink bug," she warned.

He laughed but also took more care with which insects he ate.

Foultner fluttered above the grass to confirm that they were on the right track. "Not much longer now."

Overhead, the sun glinted off of five metal rings. Merin let his impressive shadow pass overtake the two opinici. Foultner and Henders were supposed to arrive just as Merin was leaving. The timing looked good.

"I want a tail ring," Henders said. "Do you think I'd look good with a tail ring?"

"You're not a gryphon. How're you going to get rings to stay on your tailfeathers?" Foultner rolled her eyes. They continued walking in silence. It was just like Henders to worry about fashion when they were on a mission.

She paused at the edge of the grasslands. Merin looked like he'd delivered his message. Silver and Gold-feather were bowing. Silver slipped away to fly north, probably to report back to the opinicus in the metal armor, if Foultner had to guess.

Foultner led the birds towards the ranch. Merin leapt into the air, then pretended to notice Foultner and Henders for the first time. He landed down next to them.

"Pride leader," Foultner said loud enough for the white opinici to hear. She and Henders bowed.

"I recognize you." Merin played along. "You two were part of the Reeve's Guard, weren't you?"

"Captains Foultner and Henders." Henders pulled his old badge out of a harness pocket and held it out to the gryphon.

Merin sniffed at it once, then looked away. "When you're finished here, bring three goliaths to the kjarr nesting grounds. Monitor lizards killed our last caravan, and we're in need of replacements."

He took to the air and headed back east. This encounter had been Foultner's idea. She needed a reason to visit the kjarr without raising suspicions. This gave her that and allowed her to speak to Merin.

Henders and Foultner led the birds up to the ranch, where Goldfeather was waiting.

"Ten goliath birds, just like Silver requested," Foultner said. "The payment has been taken care of, but we're happy to wait while you inspect them. We can bring any replacements by in the morning if necessary."

Goldfeather made a show of looking the birds over. Foultner had only been a rancher for a week, and she already knew enough to spot someone who was clueless. Henders made a show of dusting off the birds. Nobody had asked him to do that, but Goldfeather seemed to appreciate the effort, so she let it go on.

"The gryphons don't care much for ex-Reeve's Guard, it sounds like," Goldfeather said.

"They don't care much for the reeves, either." Foultner attached a pack of her supplies to one of the birds while he looked the other way. It contained several items that looked personal and a nontrivial number of beaded currency. With any luck, Silver would stop by to return it tomorrow.

The foreign opinicus laughed. The metal decorations on his harness jingled. "Well, I'm certain you did the best you could. We've seen the blackwing's assassins. They employ the best."

"Nice of you to say." She'd been expecting this part. "Doesn't make it any easier to get work from the Ashen Weald, however. They're not keen on us New Eyrie opinici, especially not those who served in the guard. Thankfully, the goliath birds aren't so picky about their company."

"Mmm." Goldfeather watched Henders shine the beak of the last bird. "Well, there are plenty more reeves in the world to guard, should you want to return to your old line of work."

"Honestly, I prefer the ranching life," she lied. "When the goliath birds try to kill me, they don't use metal talons, explosives, or poison."

Goldfeather laughed. It was a practiced sound. "Well, there are ranches in the north, too. If you change your mind, we'll be here a while longer."

Foultner bowed and mantled. "I'll think it over after dinner. Speaking of which, are you done with the birds, Henders? We need to return."

Henders nodded and thanked Goldfeather for his business. Foultner took one look back to make sure her pack was still attached to the goliath bird, then they made their retreat.

FOULTNER DIDN'T HAVE to wait until the next morning to meet up with Silver. After she and Henders finished cleaning up at the ranch and reporting their findings to Urious and Soft Paws, they began their flight back to New Eyrie to go to bed.

They were over the walls of the city when Foultner saw the white harness and shiny plumage of Silver waiting outside their tent.

"Go inside and sleep when we land," Foultner told Henders. "I want a few minutes alone with our hawk friend."

He didn't need much prompting. He'd already dozed off once on the way home. When they landed, he mumbled something polite, then went inside to sleep. A couple of moments later and his whistling snores serenaded the night.

"Sorry about Henders," Foultner said. "He's my, um, nest-sharing opinicus friend."

"We call that a 'mate' where I come from," Silver said. "And I should be the one apologizing. I didn't mean to intrude so late, but you left your pack on one of the goliath birds, and I wanted to return it."

She passed over the satchel. Foultner resisted the urge to open it up and make sure everything was there in favor of politeness, but then realized that's exactly what a New Eyrie opinicus would do.

"Thank you so much for returning it!" Foultner counted the beads. "It's all there, my cut of the goliath bird deal. Thank you so much. Can I get you something to eat?"

"Oh, no, thank you. I'm headed home to sleep," Silver said, but she was wearing the same gear she wore when Foultner saw her leading expeditions into the bog.

Are they sneaking in after dark now? That's a dangerous place during the daylight. I wonder if Blinky has anyone watching New Eyrie at night to see who's going in and out of it.

"Well, I really appreciate you coming all the way out here," Foultner said in her rancher accent. "Say, your Goldfeather friend offered me a job up north. Said there were reeves that needed guarding and birds that needed ranching. What's it like working for him?"

Despite the drawl, she'd phrased her question carefully. The Ashen Weald hadn't been able to figure out the hierarchy of the king's opinici. She hoped that risking an insult might help clarify.

"I wouldn't say I work *for* Goldfeather." Silver remained coy about her rank. "He's more of the king's messenger. My armored friend and I are from different eyries assigned to help out here, so it's nice to have someone who can adjudicate when there are disagreements."

"Oh, I'm so sorry, I didn't mean any slight," Foultner

said. "I just see him sitting at the ranch while you do the heavy lifting, so I assumed—well, I assumed wrong."

"No insult taken. He definitely likes sitting pretty." Silver paused. "I don't know your situation. Most opinici here would be much better off under one of the king's eyries, that much is true. But things along the eastern range aren't safe. Blackwings test our borders monthly, and most of the goliath herds need workers because the old ranchers moved closer to the capital."

Foultner gestured to the torn, dirty tents around her. "We're on first name terms with danger around here. We're not on speaking terms with a good meal."

Silver seemed to be sizing up Foultner. She finally withdrew a piece of parchment and dipped one talon into ink, writing by the weak rushlight.

She wiped her makeshift pen off on a cloth before giving the parchment to Foultner. "If you decide you want to come north, give this to the recruiter. It'll tell him you're assigned to the Argent Heights, where I live. It can be rough up there, but nobody ever goes to nest on an empty stomach."

This was what Foultner had expected. "Why, thank you so much!"

"You don't seem averse to hard work. We'd be happy to have the company," Silver said. "Plus, we have some of the cheapest syrup tarts in the north. Our chefs will turn one of you salty reds into a sweet beak in no time. Now, if you'll excuse me, I'm needed in the south."

Foultner watched as Silver flew off. Saying she was needed south was probably a slip of the tongue considering Silver's cover story was heading back to bed, but it confirmed Foultner's suspicions.

Now she just needed to decide if she wanted to go be a

spy. It wasn't the sort of work she could bring Henders along for. She had a good thing here. She'd love to sit back and let someone else handle whatever problems the Ashen Weald ran into next.

She was curious what a syrup tart tasted like, however.

FOULTNER HAD JUST CLOSED her eyes when she felt the airflow through the holes in her tent change.

"Hello, Blinky," she said.

The owl gryphon settled between the two nests. "I thought you two would share a nest."

"A big nest would look suspicious out here. No one can afford one," Foultner said. "And Henders says I kick in my sleep."

"Yes, you do seem like an opinicus who would do that." Blinky blinked. "I was listening when Silver spoke to you. Will you go to these Argent Heights?"

"Not unless I have to." Foultner looked at Henders, who was still snoring. "I don't have a good feeling about what they're up to out here. This doesn't feel like an invasion, at least not yet. They steal some of our refugees, fine. But Silver headed south. I'd need to be after something pretty important to risk infected starlings at night. What do you think?"

"I think the blackwings are what we should be worrying about," Blinky said. "I think Ninox knows where they are, but she will not tell us."

"You're friends with Biski, right?" Foultner asked. "Tell her where they're hiding Cherine in exchange for the location of the blackwings. She's looking for Cherine, so she's probably got a direct line to Ninox. Chirp, tweet, flap, and problem solved."

Blinky shook her head at Foultner's colloquialism. "You think Cherine is innocent? Merin wants to execute him. He is very certain."

Foultner yawned. "Orlea's pretty sure he's innocent, and that's good enough for me. Look, I'm going to sleep. Can you find out what Silver is up to in the bog?"

Blinky hooted and a half dozen shapes landed around the tent. "Yes, we will find out. Do not come by the kjarr grounds tomorrow. I do not want Silver to see you there."

"I just spent all day coming up with an excuse to be able to go there," Foultner whined.

Blinky did not blink.

"Fine, have it your way." Foultner rolled over and put her back to the owl gryphon.

As Blinky and her escort slipped south, Foultner wondered if there were enough owls left to guard the eyrie and kjarr.

20

BOG WISPS

In the early hours of the morning, Kia slipped into the upper halls of the Crackling Sea Eyrie to meet with Biski and Mia. Orlea had loaned her a tattered Crackling Sea harness. They'd stayed up late talking about the mysterious voices in the workshop, but in the end, they hadn't been able to figure out who it could be—just another red and blue disenfranchised with the war.

Kia yawned. She'd had to risk flying before sunup to reach the Crackling Sea in time to slip in unnoticed. Xalt and Jer met her along the mountain pass and flew her in. A red with two blues was less suspicious than a lone Redwood Valley opinicus.

Biski and Mia were waiting for her in the library.

"It feels like it's been years since Sandpiper's Dune." Mia groomed her younger sister's feathers. "I searched New Eyrie for the rest of our family, but they're gone. They went with some refugees north, from what I hear. They didn't leave word, but I found a tent with some of Olan's things in it."

Kia pushed down a lump in her throat. It was enough

that Mia was alive, but she missed her parents and brother.

Biski pointed to a bookcase that was off-kilter, revealing a door behind it. "We've searched most of the secret passages, but we haven't found any sign of Cherine. This place is like a maze."

"We did find something," Jer said. "A lot of weird sounds."

"Bog wisps," Xalt muttered. "They're coming from the old reeve's rooms."

"Is it Grenkin?" Kia asked. Were there bog wisps inside buildings? She didn't know. "Has he taken up residence there?"

Biski shook her head. "I've been keeping an eye on the ranger lord when these two go in. He'll spend time in the throne room, sometimes, but he doesn't go into the old passages or the reeve's quarters. All the Crackling Sea opinici stay away from them."

"That's `cause they're *haunted*," Xalt said. "That's why. I heard one of the spirits whisper the old reeve's name."

"We're out of passages to explore," Jer said. "If they have him hidden here, he's not in any of the tunnels the ranger corps or books knew about. You can search them yourself, if you'd like."

Kia shook her head. "I'm not here to search the tunnels, though it sounds like we should check on the old reeve's quarters."

Xalt and Jer both moaned.

Kia decided she'd bring Biski and Mia along for that one. "What I'm really hoping to explore are the records. The parrotface elder was nice enough to let me look at theirs since I'm a food scholar and they trade with the fisherfolk. What I want to see is if the Crackling Sea documents match. You can't have prisoners without feeding them. The extra food's coming from somewhere, and if we can find out where it's going, we'll find Cherine."

"The ranger lord holds onto those records himself," Biski said. "You'll have a hard time sorting through them."

"We can get him away from the ledger for an hour." Mia stood next to Xalt and Jer. "I'd like to talk to him about the bog and see what his feelings are on Bruen and Ellore."

"I think I know what I'm looking for," Kia said. "An hour should be enough time."

"I can keep watch," Biski said. "He's not going to be up for a few hours yet, though."

Kia grinned, something she'd been learning from the gryphons. "Perfect. That gives us time to search for bog wisps in the tunnels."

Xalt and Jer complained anew.

Mia laughed. "Come on, you two. We saw the real bog wisps already. They were just wingtorn with paint. You can't really think there are spirits, can you?"

"You didn't hear the stories about what happened to the reeve's family," Jer said.

"Yeah," Xalt added, "if any place is haunted, it's this one."

"Well, I'm not afraid of bog wisps," Biski said. "Let's go exploring!"

MOST OF THE secret passages had been built during the initial construction of the Crackling Sea Eyrie, back in time immemorial. Only a talonful had been added later.

These were easily identifiable by the crude construction and bricked walls.

Kia and her entourage followed a passage from the library to a small garden above the cliffs.

"Did we take a wrong turn?" Kia asked.

"Nope, this is one of the more unusual paths," Xalt explained. "None of the passages go directly into the reeve's quarters, probably to prevent assassins."

"Well, that didn't work out too well for him," Mia muttered.

"But there is one passage from the reeve's quarters to this garden," Jer continued. "Actually, most secret passages are escape routes like the one Impir used, and several of them lead here."

"We started looking around and found a mark behind the pond," Xalt said. "We traced it back to a petrified tree. Underneath its roots, we found the passage to the reeve's quarters."

"You two did a good job," Kia said. "When we get back, I'll let Biski know."

Their medicine gryphon had stayed behind to keep the door in the library safe from prying eyes.

Kia hid her surprise as Xalt and Jer pulled down the petrified tree, revealing the passage below.

"We'll stay here and keep watch," Jer said.

"And not because we're afraid of the ghost," Xalt added.

Mia laughed, and the two sisters pulled themselves into the passage. There were several braziers, and after a little discussion, they decided they were probably safe to light them.

Mia put her ranger training to use. "The dust on the ground has been disturbed. It could just be our Crackling

Sea friends outside, or someone else could have been coming in this way."

"We should let Grenkin know once we're done here," Kia said. "He'll want to close up the entrance or put guards in the garden."

"Good luck explaining how we stumbled across this," Mia said.

Fifty feet of winding passage emptied into the reeve's quarters. They confirmed that the door between the rest of the eyrie and the room had been sealed off before lighting more braziers. They gave off no scent of fish.

"They're fairly modern," Mia commented. "Bario invented the scentless version, didn't he?"

Kia didn't respond. With the braziers lit, the room sparkled. Mother of pearl lined the walls. A stone altar with nesting materials had been built up in the center.

"That's a shrine *and* a nest," Mia snorted. "What, did they worship him while he slept? And they call us reds ostentatious."

Kia had to flap her wings to reach the top of the nest. She nearly lost her breakfast when she saw what lay on top.

While the body had been removed, the blood of the reeve and his family still stained the nesting materials and stone.

"Don't come up," she coughed to Mia. "I think this is where they found him after, well, you know."

They explored the shelves, full of history books. They examined a wall of strange carvings and toys. They came across a painting from the top artist in the Redwood Valley depicting the reeve in all his glory surrounded by another opinicus and the reeve's dozen children.

"That must have been hard," Mia said. "They say he

took a male consort and didn't enjoy the company of female opinici at all, but he still felt like he had to continue his bloodline. I can't imagine how his mate felt about that."

Male consort. The face was much older when she saw it, but she realized where she'd seen the opinicus next to the reeve in the painting.

"Jonas." Saying the word aloud felt strange.

"That's right," Mia said. "From rancher to consort to... well, he was basically acting as a reeve by the end, wasn't he?"

"I always thought of him as a merchant." Kia's mind went back to the meeting where Jonas had talked about his plan to kill the gryphons in the weald. "And a murderer."

"He was that." Mia shifted uncomfortably.

Kia squeezed her sister's shoulder. "There are definitely some unredeemable opinici out there, but you're not one of them."

The lights flickered.

"Bog wisps?" Kia asked.

"No, it's a breeze," Mia said. She licked her talon and held it up. "Maybe the door into the eyrie proper isn't sealed up tight?"

"No, the flames are pointing in the wrong direction." Kia watched the braziers before heading to the very back of the room. "Did Xalt and Jer miss a secret passage?"

They spread out and began taking books off the shelves. They covered the length of the room before giving up.

"Is it on the ceiling?" Mia asked. "Where's the switch hiding?"

Kia looked around. She saw bloodstains dripping

down the side of the nest. "If it's another escape route, it would make sense that the switch is on the bed."

They got to work disassembling the nest on top. The blood was long dry, but Kia couldn't shake the feeling that her talons were covered in something sticky. Ultimately, they found their answer in the four ornaments on the corners of the bed. The jelly and fish ornaments were stuck in place, but the seahorse and flower ornaments could be twisted.

"The flower opens the way to the garden from this side," Kia said. "That makes sense. But what does the seahorse represent? Where does that go?"

"I think it goes to the reeve-consort's quarters," Mia mumbled.

"What?" Kia asked. "Why do you think that?"

"Well, you know, seahorses. For the Crackling Sea rangers, they represent, um, mating." Mia's nares turned red.

Kia blinked. "I don't get it. Why do seahorses represent that?"

"I'll explain when you're older," Mia said. She turned the seahorse and heard a click. The breeze intensified.

"No, really, why *seahorses,* don't you know how they mate?" Kia began, but Mia shut her sister's beak, and they made their way down the new passage.

KIA LIT the braziers in the consort quarters. Mia had been correct about what the seahorse represented.

"At least there's no blood in here," Mia said.

Kia checked the ornaments on the consort's bed, but they were all solid except for the seahorse. The main door connecting the room to the rest of the eyrie was still sealed off. "Only the reeve and his children were killed. The consort was left untouched."

"Do you think he was in on it?" Mia asked. "It's pretty suspicious that he survived."

Kia thought back to the haunted look in the consort's eyes when he wandered the Redwood Valley. "I don't think so, but who can know? I don't think anyone ever suspected him, at least."

"If I were the reeve's consort, I'd want a much nicer room than this," Mia said.

The chamber was a quarter the size of the reeve's. The walls had tapestries and paintings on them but no mother of pearl. The reeve's chamber had smelled of a common incense used to hide the smell of death, probably courtesy of the poor souls who had to clean up the room afterwards. The consort's room, similarly sealed off, smelled like...

Kia sniffed again. It smelled like burn ointment. She climbed on top of the bed and looked down at the floor. Her and Mia's parrot-like footprints were joined by a third pair of heron-like, Crackling Sea foretalons.

"Someone's been here," Kia said.

"You're right." Mia pointed to the far corner of the room where the dust was disturbed in the shape of where an opinicus had once been sleeping.

"We found Xalt and Jer's ghost," Kia whispered.

"Great," Mia said. "Now let's get out of here."

They quietly extinguished the lights and closed the passages behind them.

21

ACCOUNTING

Kia, Mia, Xalt, and Jer slipped back into the library where Biski was napping.

Mia nudged her. "I thought you were supposed to be keeping watch."

Biski awoke. "I do that by napping. Nobody is willing to come in and wake a sleeping gryphon, so the library stays empty."

Xalt and Jer shrugged.

"There's no ghost," Kia said. "But someone has been staying in the old reeve's quarters."

"No, that's not quite right." Mia preened some of the dust out of her sister's feathers. "Someone has been staying in the *consort's* quarters. They just had to go through the reeve's quarters to get there."

"Who?" Biski asked. "And why? There are much easier places to sleep at night."

"I don't know," Kia admitted. "Someone who knew about that passage even though the rangers and books didn't."

"There are *easier* places to sleep," Xalt said, "but not *safer* ones. It could be a scholar or fugitive of some sort."

"It's a bad time to be a scholar," Jer confirmed.

"Could it be Ellore?" Kia asked.

The four opinici who had been on the bog expedition all shook their heads.

"Her eyes were already going silver when she left to blow up the dam," Xalt said. "I don't think she had much life left in her."

"I mean, she's probably *out there,*" Jer said. "Just the same way the infected starlings are *out there,* trying to bite anyone who comes near them, no soul left."

Mia frowned. From what Kia had heard, her sister had grown close to the traitor ranger lord.

The dulcet sound of the current ranger lord issuing orders echoed from the throne room to the library.

"That mystery is going to have to wait for another day," Biski said. "If we want to catch Ranger Lord Grenkin off guard, now's our chance."

Mia straightened her harness and looked at her sister. "You and Biski stay back. Once we get him to put down the ledger, we'll walk with him out to the balcony. That's your opportunity. We'll park Biski at the entrance to the throne room. Read as fast as you can, and when Biski chirps, put it down and run into the library."

Kia nodded. She moved a notepad to her front harness pocket and dipped one talon into an inkwell on a library shelf so she'd be ready to scribble down any notes.

Mia, Xalt, and Jer finished preening, then stepped through the passage from the library to the throne room.

"It's good to see you up and about so soon after your attack, Ranger Lord," Mia said.

Grenkin had set up at the bottom of the stairs, well away from the throne itself. "Redwood Ranger Mia, Crackling Sea Rangers Xalt and Jer. To what do I owe this visit?"

Mia cleared her throat. "They'd like to thank you personally for pardoning them. I'd like to take a moment to see if you were sincere about pardoning Bruen and Ellore. I spent a lot of time with Ellore, and while I don't deny her crimes, I think I understand why she did them."

"Oh?" the ranger lord said. "Well, do tell. I could use some insight into the former captain's actions."

He allowed himself to be pulled out towards the balcony by Mia, limping as he walked, and Biski pushed Kia into the throne room.

"Be quick," the medicine gryphon chirped. "Mia's a talker, but Grenkin might get weak and need to come back at any time."

Kia opened the ledger and skipped to the most recent writing. Zeph had said that Grenkin told Ninox that the prison was in the weald. If that were true, it hadn't existed as a prison before the founding of the Ashen Weald. She looked through the different scribblings. All the prides were getting supplies equal to their membership except for Merin's.

From the Parrotfaces, his pride was getting the same supplies as everyone else. But from the Crackling Sea shipments, he was getting around twice as much per gryphon as any other pride.

Maybe he just likes fish? Maybe Satra's rewarding him for rescuing her? Kia tapped her beak with a talon, a sign she was thinking about Cherine. *Or maybe he has prisoners to feed.*

The good news was that Merin's pride lands were small. He'd benefited the most from the creation of the

Ashen Weald as his pride could now hunt almost anywhere in the weald or kjarr. The bad news was that they didn't have many places to hide prisoners.

Unless... could they be hiding him where they captured him the first time?

Biski chirped a warning, and Kia closed the ledger and scurried back to the library.

"Thank you for your insights, ranger," Grenkin said. "I stand by my decision to forgive all past crimes by Ellore. I believe she's dead, but we'll cross that mountain range when we come to it. In the meantime, I'll see what I can do to make sure the opinici with kjarr or gryphon heritage don't feel isolated. It was a lapse of judgement on my part that made Rakesh and Ellore susceptible to Blackwing Eyrie recruitment. I'll endeavor to do better."

Mia, Xalt, and Jer bowed and mantled towards the ranger lord.

"That's all I can ask," she said.

Grenkin stretched his good talons. "What about you? The Redwood Valley rangers are essentially gone, as are the Reeve's Guard. Any chance you'll join the Ashen Weald rangers?"

"If the offer comes with a promotion," Mia said with a smile. "First, I need to find out what happened to my family. They were at New Eyrie but left with the last group to head north. I think they'd like to know I'm alive."

Grenkin nodded. "I hope they're okay when you find them. You had a sister, didn't you? One of the Redwood scholars?"

"Kia, sir." Mia's posture stiffened.

"Yes, that's right." The ranger lord settled down and put his talon prosthetics over the ledger. "I heard she's handling all of the trade between the fisherfolk and the weald prides. I'd love to meet her, sometime, and see about opening up negotiations between the sea and ocean."

Mia shifted. "I believe she's afraid of being arrested if she comes north."

"Ah yes. *It's a bad time to be a scholar,*" Grenkin quoted. "I hear that everywhere I go. It's understandable. Things should be back to normal pretty soon now, once they execute the opinicus who tried to blow up Merin's nesting grounds. Tell your sister to come visit me after the trial. In, say, a week."

Kia gulped from her hiding spot. She'd assumed she had a lot more time to find Cherine. The Ashen Weald's prison had stayed hidden for months. Now she had days to locate it before Cherine was executed.

"I'll let her know," Mia said. "If you'll excuse me, Xalt and Jer promised if we ever escaped the bog, they'd take me fishing."

"Of course, of course." Grenkin waved a talon to dismiss the three of them. "You're welcome here any time, especially if you're looking for work."

The three rangers exited out of the balcony and into the amphitheater to keep from drawing attention to the library.

KIA SCRIBBLED down everything she could remember from the ledger.

"What's the plan?" Biski asked.

Mia rifled through the books in the library to keep checking for hidden passages. She poked a carving of a seahorse several times, eliciting a giggle from Xalt. "Find Cherine in the next week or kiss him goodbye."

"I think he's in Merin's territory." Kia looked up from her notes. "Nothing else makes sense."

"Great," Biski chirped. "How do we search his territory without being noticed?"

"We need our own owl gryphon," Xalt said. "We need Blinky."

"Blinky is on the Ashen Weald's side." Jer worked on patching his harness while they planned. "What about one of the taiga gryphons? They've got owls, too, right?"

"Well, they do love me up at Snowfall," Biski said. "It's pretty hard to sneak a bright white gryphon into the weald. I'd ask my long-eared, grey assistant to look around, but he's still missing."

Kia thought of Deracho. "The taiga owl gryphons aren't really the same as weald owls."

"There's the volatile option," Mia said. Everyone looked at her. "We could tell Ninox he's there and let her find out for us."

Kia tapped her inky talon on the stone floor. "That would be great if she'd just go and scout it out for us. But it seems just as likely that she'd try to take Merin's territory by force. What happens next if she kills even one of Merin's children or, stars forbid, hurts Merin himself?"

"Nothing good," Xalt said.

Jer nodded.

"Besides," Kia continued, "I think we can find out where he hid Cherine last time and check there first. It should be easy, right? Hatzel will know how to do it."

SABERBEAK

Zeph listened while Kia explained what she wanted Hatzel to do. Her words echoed off walls of the medicine caverns. Orlea and the old medicine gryphon listened in. While he'd been busy getting kicked out of Ninox's hidden pridegrounds, Kia had gone through her own set of adventures.

"So that's it," the scholar said. "I just need you to go back to where you found Cherine the first time and see if he's there. I'm sure Merin is hiding him somewhere in his territory."

Hatzel stared at her. "Last time, Triddle tossed the longest rope I'd ever seen into the river and let it get carried into an underground, underwater cave where Cherine tied it around his waist, and I pulled him out."

"Oh," Kia said. "So how do we get back down there?"

"You'd have to ask Triddle," Hatzel said. "He knew where the cave was. I only ever saw where the Snowfeather River went underground."

Zeph's ears drooped. "As much as I love Askel and

Triddle, they're both loyal to their pride. They'd never betray their pridemates."

"Why not?" Orlea asked. "Triddle was happy to turn on Merin the first time, when he saved Cherine. Why not a second?"

"If you ask him, and he says no, he's going to go tell Merin what you're planning," Hatzel said.

"What's our other option?" Orlea asked.

Zeph looked at the old medicine gryphon. "We could tell Ninox we think we know where Cherine is being held."

"Do you think that's wise?" The medicine gryphon's voice was scratchy.

"No," Kia admitted. "Mia and I discussed that before I came. I think both plans have problems with them."

Zeph's ears showed concern. "We need a new plan."

"There's a third option." Kia pulled out Orlea's journal and tossed it back to her. Xalt and Jer's stories were the latest additions, which they'd been discussing on the way over. "Tresh swam through an underground river in the bog to rescue the Ashen Weald expedition. Can you get us a petrel fisherfolk?"

Orlea frowned. "Do you really want to risk igniting conflict between the fisherfolk and the Ashen Weald?"

"You're right," Kia said. "We should just let Cherine die. Is that what you mean?"

"You know it's not." Orlea's hackle feathers were raised. "I *like* Cherine. He's nice. He helps out others. He's a good opinicus. But why *not* tell Ninox? She can hide from the Ashen Weald if things go south. The fisherfolk can't."

Zeph's tail twitched back and forth. "If it was the blackwing assassins killing the Ashen Weald at night, there's still a chance for Ninox and Satra to reach some sort of peaceful agreement. If Ninox kills all of Merin's pride guarding his territory, that chance goes away."

After a long silence, Kia spoke up again. "I'm sorry for yelling at you, Orlea. You're not wrong. At what cost would Cherine want to be rescued? What would he want us to risk? And what happens to him after our rescue?

"We can't take him to the fisherfolk. So far, the weald and eyries are respecting the fisherfolk's right to peace. But everyone is being told that Cherine is the one who set the bombs in the weald. They're not going to let the so-called mastermind of the conflagration live out his days peacefully eating fish. All hell will break loose."

"Do you trust the Ashen Weald's judges to find him innocent?" Hatzel asked. "'Cause I don't. Even if he has to live out his life in exile, I think that's better than being killed for a crime he tried to stop."

"If only there were a way to rescue him *and* prove he's innocent," Zeph said. "I don't know how you do that, though."

Orlea chewed on a talon. "You do it by revealing what really happened."

Zeph shook his head. "Who knows what really happened?"

She stayed quiet, but she was staring at her journal, leaving him to wonder what was on her mind.

Hatzel stood. "I'm going to Snowfall. Triddle is near there. Maybe we can find out where the cave entrance is. If not, there might still be fisherfolk traders. And failing all of that, we go to the owls."

The medicine gryphon shook her head but didn't offer any better solutions.

"I'll go with you," Zeph said. "The fisherfolk are more likely to talk to Kia or me."

"Great, you all know what to do," the medicine gryphon said. "Now stop conspiring in my caverns and go accomplish something other than setting the fisherfolk, free prides, and Ashen Weald at each other's throats."

"Orlea?" Zeph prompted.

She started. "Sorry, I just had an idea. I'm not going to Snowfall. I'm going to the kjarr nesting grounds to see Foultner. I'll catch up to you later. If you need rope and harnesses to re-enact Triddle's old plan, talk to the merchants in the eyrie ruins. Didi should have both."

Didi, the blue splotchy merchant, had a soft spot for Zeph, or at least his wares. A few parrots and she'd quickly find whatever they needed. He watched everyone else exit, leaving him alone with the medicine gryphon. "What're the chances Ninox would be willing to send an owl to scout out Merin's territory for us?"

"Do I look like the Strix Pride den mother?" the old medicine gryphon scolded. "Get out of my caves. If Ninox wants to speak to you, she'll find you."

23

SNOWFALL

Piprik resisted the urge to wipe the white feather paint away from his eyes. His bones ached in the cold air. He'd forgotten Snowfall was so tall. The last time he'd come through taiga territory, he was fleeing for his life, trying to locate the fisherfolk villages. This time around, he was able to take in the sights. The sights, in this case, being spring snow.

"How're you holding up, 'Lei'?" he asked Levin. They were waiting to see if they'd be allowed use of a nest here to begin their search.

"So far, so good." Her chest feathers were a mix of red and blue, all hints of green gone except for her tail. She wore a pair of petrel gryphon flippers that had no traction on the ice. She kept scratching at where one of Tresh's necklaces irritated her neck. Naya had added what she called *decorative netting* to Levin's harness to make her look more fisherfolk.

"You look ferocious," Piprik said. "Like some sort of deep sea padfoot."

"All I need is a raft," Lei laughed. Her voice was a

little scratchy. Despite Naya's assurances that male and female opinici both had a wide vocal range, Lei had spent the flight trying to adjust her voice to sound more like the only male peafowl she'd spent any time around, Impir.

Quess and Naya were busy discussing trade deals with Younce across the amphitheater. The leader of Snowfall kept looking over and squinting at Piprik as though trying to work something out.

Quess finally left the negotiations and padded over to Piprik and Levin.

"How's it going?" Piprik asked.

"Well, he finally figured out who you were," Quess said. "Though he has no clue about Lei."

Levin puffed up her chest with pride.

"Actually, recognizing you is what changed his mind," Quess continued. "He hasn't forgotten you stitching him back together after the Battle for Sandpiper's Dune. Since he doesn't have any offspring, you can use the cave next to his, Mignet's old quarters."

"What do the other taiga gryphons think we're doing here?" Lei asked.

"Trade," Quess said.

The peafowl opinicus nodded. "Oh, that's a good ruse."

"It's not a ruse." Quess opened a satchel full of salt. "I expect you to sell as much of that as you can."

Piprik ran a talon through the salt. Ocean salt was much higher quality than what the blue opinici's salt-works produced. "This gives us a reason to be at the Crackling Sea or New Eyrie. Good thinking."

From the east, several weald gryphons arrived to speak to Younce. Piprik saw the familiar outlines of Kia's vibrant colors next to Zeph's copper hawk browns. They caught Quess's eye and changed direction.

Zeph started to speak, then recognition flickered in his eyes when he looked at Lei.

"Hello, Reeve's Bane," Quess said. "I don't know if you've met Lei and Pip? They're islanders from Ashfoot Isle, and they're here on a trade mission. For Lei here, it's *his* first time coming north of Luminaire."

Zeph looked confused, but Kia caught on.

"Lei, Pip," she said with a bow. "Welcome to the taiga. You should definitely try the sugar frogs while you're here."

Zeph pulled Piprik away from the prying ears. "Is this wise, bringing her this close to her home?"

"Him," Pip corrected. Lei had been clear that, even in private, he wanted to use the new name and gender. He seemed happier than Pip and seen him before, and it did prevent any owls from overhearing his old identity. "That's not for us to decide. He wants to get a look at New Eyrie and see if he can do anything to help. We can hope he sees that they don't need another reeve and returns to the fisherfolk, but that's his choice."

Zeph shook his head. "I know you're right, but black-wing assassins nearly got me and the ranger lord a week ago. *He's* much safer at the shore."

This was news to Piprik. "Rybalt and Iony paid me a visit two days ago. I had to blow up part of Luminaire to get away."

Zeph's head tilted to the side, and Piprik realized his mistake. He'd grown comfortable with Lei and often spoke of the world beyond the shore without a care for giving away his identity.

"Rybalt is the name of the assassin who killed the

Crackling Sea reeve," Piprik explained. "Stories say he's always accompanied by a grey glacier gryphon, Iony."

"Rybalt," Zeph said. "He's the one I met. Is he after Satra? Or just the prisoners?"

"I don't know," Piprik admitted. "He has a reputation for killing reeves. That's how he became a reeve himself, killing the leader of the pitohui eyrie when she refused to join the Blackwing Alliance. He hasn't been heard from in years, not since the Crackling Sea incident."

"You haven't heard anything from the shore, you mean?" Zeph prompted. When Piprik didn't respond, he added, "Nice feather paint."

Piprik considered what to tell Zeph. His copper hawk friend had a certain knack for getting things done despite his small size and lack of military training.

Piprik shrugged. "Rybalt and Iony were searching for Mally the Nighthaunt. I came north to try to find him."

Zeph's hackles rose. "On the shore, you said the two of you took apart a taiga gryphon. Is he your friend?"

"No." Piprik was adamant. "If I find Mally, I plan to let one of his enemies know. He has enough of those. He left me to die on the edge of the Emerald Jungle."

"Just make sure Levin has gone home by then," Zeph said. "She's not safe around someone like Mally."

"*He*'s not a child anymore," Piprik corrected. "*Lei* needs to decide where he belongs."

Kia waved them back over. "Quess is willing to go cave diving for us before she heads home, Zeph."

"I can't promise to help you with whatever crazy scheme you've come up with this time," the petrel opinicus said, "but I can at least tell you if the cave is empty or not."

"Biski has taken over the library at the Crackling Sea,"

Kia said to Pip and Lei. "I'm not sure what you two are after, but she seems to know a lot of what's going on along the sea coast. You should check in with her. She can probably get you nests at the ranch, too, when you're done here. They rent out the upper levels."

"Ah yes, my wayward apprentice," Piprik mused. Then he remembered his cover and added, "Rather, the apprentice of Swan's Rest's medicine opinicus. We'll consider it after we check a few things with Orlea's pride."

"Well, Biski's a full medicine gryphon now," Zeph said. "I don't think anyone promoted her, but she started calling herself one and nobody corrected her and it stuck."

"Oh, here comes Younce to show you to your caves," Quess said.

"We need to check in with Askel and Triddle," Zeph told Quess, "then we'll head back to the weald."

Younce landed next to the suspicious grouping of non-taiga gryphons. "Those two are already halfway back to the kjarr. We found a new hot springs, and they're bright-eyed and fluffy-tailed trying to figure out what to do with it. They'll be back here tomorrow to stock up. Why don't you return in the morning?"

Zeph and Kia exchanged a look. Piprik wasn't sure what they wanted with Askel and Triddle, but it seemed their call wasn't a social one.

"Pip and Lei, however, can come with me," Younce said. "I'll show you to your quarters. It's been a nice spring, but it still gets below freezing here. What I'm saying is, don't use the hot springs and then go outside. You'll become an icicle."

Piprik allowed himself and Lei to be pulled away. He'd have to find out from Quess later what Kia and Zeph were up to. He'd been around enough scheming gryphons to know when something was going on.

Gressle and Carru were leading a caravan up from Swan's Rest to the ruins to trade. Pip, Lei, and Quess were going to meet them there, then Pip and Lei would take the Caravan west towards New Eyrie.

24

ORLEA'S GRAND SCHEME

Orlea flew north to bypass Snowfall on her way west to the kjarr. She didn't want Kia or Zeph tagging along for this one. They didn't necessarily share her quest for the truth at any cost, instead trusting that things would work themselves out. Hadn't the gryphons and opinici in the south ultimately come together, after all?

Orlea and Naya felt differently and had found kindred spirits in each other. Hidden within the crates of supplies coming to and from the shore were notes, interviews, snippets of information gathered from both ends of the Redwood Valley.

For Naya, her motivation was simple. Sandpiper's Dune was a city whose opinici had cast out all of their gryphons under the first sign of duress. Her brother, an opinicus, had been in charge—and yet Naya and found herself wandering the frozen taiga with a pride's worth of sick gryphons. She wanted to know why that had happened and what she could do to prevent it in the future.

The next time a Rakesh shows up at our gates, she'd written in her last letter, *I want Sandpiper's Dune to refuse to his demands and stand united. We are not gryphons. We are not opinici. We are fisherfolk.*

Orlea's thoughts were more convoluted. Some days, she thought they were better off now than ever before. Despite food shortages, everyone was fed. She hadn't been able to shake the feeling that she'd missed something the night of the fire. She'd led the gryphons in to rescue Satra, but it should have been simple: grab the gryphlets and fly. Instead, she'd watched as the level above her melted and a waterfall of oil and fire engulfed the underbough.

It was an image that had never left her.

There'd been talk about how Reeve Brevin had planned it all, but that didn't add up for Orlea. There'd even been talk that it was an accident, a stray spark from the flameworks. She didn't believe that, either. The fire, the oil, had come from above, and despite it possibly being against her best interests, she couldn't rest until she knew the truth.

And after all of the interviews, particularly those with the guards assigned to the jail cells in the northern quarters, she now had a pretty good idea of what had happened the night of the fire.

She still had questions, of course. There were gryphons who refused to be interviewed, like Merin, and those who had died the night of the fire, like Strix. But there was one gryphon she thought might talk to her—if she could find a way to get him alone. To do that, she first had to make a stop to see an old friend.

Orlea flapped her wings conspicuously and landed just outside the kjarr nesting grounds. She made a show of carrying a small package in her beak as she walked towards Foultner's nest.

A guard with a feathery mane spotted her and slipped off towards the main building where the Ashen Weald met. She'd just reached the empty nesting area where Foultner used to live when a large gryphon landed beside her. Orlea transferred the package to her harness to let her speak.

"I didn't realize you'd been invited here tonight," Merin said. There was no malice, but his voice wasn't friendly, either. "Foultner isn't coming. She's on assignment elsewhere."

Orlea looked at the metal bands. One of those bracelets would have bought a lot of squirrel meat in the underbough. "Looks like she took everything she owns with her."

"What?" Merin looked at the empty nest. "Oh, they must have moved her already. She requested a larger nest that would hold both her and Henders. I'll walk you there."

The gryphon pride leader had a saunter when he walked, the tuft on his tail swishing back and forth. Orlea had to double her speed to keep up with him.

"You know, I've been trying to sit down and hear your version about the night of the fire," she prompted.

"What for?" His tone was neutral. A stranger wouldn't know about the months of requests she'd sent to speak to him. "We were together for most of it saving the kjarr gryphlets."

Yes, it's those moments when you and your kin left my side that I'm most concerned about, Orlea thought. "Don't sell yourself short. You managed to rescue Satra all on your own. That's what I'd like to hear about. Did your pride help you?"

With Merin in the lead, other gryphons and opinici made way. Off to the west, near the larger bridge over the river, several white opinici arrived in shiny armor. She recognized Silver, who waved a talon in greeting.

Merin guided Orlea away from the guests. "We spread out to look for Satra. I just happened to find her first."

"Askel and two of your children?" she prompted.

Merin nodded. "I believe that's right. I haven't really given it much thought. I found Satra alone in the northern quarter. She'd already rescued herself; I just let her know what the plan was and guided her out of the city to the gryphlets."

Orlea had the advantage of having talked to Hatzel right after the conflagration, so she knew that Satra had blood on her that night. Orlea also knew that Satra lived in the under-bough and not the northern quarter, having helped babysit the first kjarr gryphlets to fledge on one or two occasions.

In fact, Orlea had even tracked down a map of the northern quarter and figured out what building Satra had come out of and who had previously lived in it. Had Satra killed Jonas? Was she hiding it to avoid causing problems with the Crackling Sea? Whose blood was on her paws that night?

Orlea didn't think Merin would give her those answers, but it was curious that he lied.

"Here it is." The large gryphon pointed up to a second story dwelling not too dissimilar from what a nicer Redwood Valley home had looked like. There was no ground entrance, a curious choice as Foultner was living in the city of the wingtorn now.

"She said to take my usual payment for the ferns in the beads hanging by her nest," Orlea lied. She detached the small package and swayed it in the air, letting the scent of red fern hit Merin.

He drew his beak back. "Just how much fern do those two go through? Do opinici not have a mating season? Never mind, don't tell me. I'm sure I don't want to know."

Orlea laughed and flew up to the landing. "Oh, everything is still packed up. It may take me a few minutes to find. She said she had some ink for me this time made from a type of Crackling Sea squid. Thank you for answering my questions, by the way."

Merin looked back towards the guests and the celebration at the council building. "Take your time, but please head out once you find it. Things are a little tense right now with the diplomats."

"Sure, no problem," Orlea shouted down. "Say, I have a new tinder fungus for Askel and Triddle to try. Do you know where they're at?"

Henders and Foultner's things had already been unpacked, but Merin hadn't come up to check.

"They're at the first waystation on the kjarr side of the path through the taiga," Merin said as he took to the air to rejoin the celebration.

Good, Zeph and Kia won't head out there tonight.

Once Merin was back across the river, Orlea grabbed Foultner's shiny black armor and swirled grey-metal claws and slipped out of the kjarr nesting grounds.

Now for part two of my plan.

It took Orlea a while to find Askel and Triddle as they weren't actually at the waystation. Instead, they had a small covered nest set along a path leading into the mountains towards a waterfall.

She watched as they went to and from a cave. Triddle's words about the type of springs they'd found echoed between the rock faces. Askel was just as excited about how hot the water was. Once they'd settled down to sleep, Orlea got to work.

First, she slipped on Foultner's hardened leather armor. According to Foultner, she'd killed a Blackwing Eyrie captain on her own and took his armor and metal talons as trophies. Having known Foultner for some time, Orlea suspected that one of the owl gryphons had done the actual killing.

While Foultner and Orlea had been the same size when they were starving poachers, Orlea found that the armor was a little snug on her now. While the conflagration, starling attacks, and wars at New Eyrie and the Crackling Sea Eyrie had caused a food shortage in general, Orlea was eating better now than she had as a poacher.

The merchants in her pride attempted to curry her favor with food, and proper nutrition had returned her to a normal opinicus weight. Unfortunately, a normal opinicus weight for her was larger than a normal opinicus weight for Foultner.

Ultimately, she did her best and left parts of the armor undone. She blackened her bright red beak with a dark paste and slipped the swirled talons on, then moved towards the tent.

I'm lucky they go to sleep before the sun goes down. It's going to be a chilly flight home from here.

She reached the tent, of Crackling Sea opinicus design, and looked for the opening when she found a small nest.

Are Askel and Triddle raising an egg together?

She peeked inside but didn't find an egg. Instead, an angry-looking ground parrot stared up at her. She realized the small parrot nest was actually built into the ground.

You've got to be kidding me.

Ground parrots usually made the *skraark* sound imitated by their gryphonic lookalikes, but during the mating season, the males would dig holes and emit a loud booming sound to attract mates. Here, with rock all around, the sound would reach down to the waystation.

Orlea went through her harness pouches until she found one full of mixed berries. She sorted them out in the evening light until she located a dried rimu olive and held it out for the bird.

It ignored her.

She poked it.

It puffed up, and when it opened its beak, she stuffed the olive inside.

The parrot started chewing and settled down into the warm nesting material, allowing Orlea to open the flap of the tent and slip inside.

Triddle had burrowed under the nesting, while Askel snored loudly on top, splayed out in all directions.

Orlea poked Askel's back paw. In her best Foultner voice, she said, "Hey, Askel."

Askel's foot twitched, but he didn't wake up.

She tried again. "Hey, Askel, wake up."

He blinked. "Foultner?"

She didn't contradict him. "Can I talk to you outside quickly? No need to wake Triddle."

Askel shook his head, sending a few stray feathers across the nest, and crawled outside.

He cast a disapproving look at the parrot in the nest, who was now fast asleep. "You're not much of a guard parrot, Boomer."

"I'm surprised nobody has eaten him yet," Orlea said.

Askel stiffened. "You're not Foultner."

She wiped the black off of her beak, revealing its bright red color.

"Orlea?" He asked. "What are you doing here? Why are you dressed as Foultner? Is she okay?"

"She's good from what I hear," Orlea said. "I borrowed her armor because I wanted to give you a familiar opinicus to see when you woke up so you wouldn't sound an alarm or wake Triddle."

Once she was following the path, she also wanted to hide her own identity from any onlookers. She didn't mention that part.

Askel's chestnut-colored plumage looked as dark as Merin's in the fading light. His ears were back. "Why didn't you want Triddle here?"

Orlea settled down, partially to keep her legs warm, but mostly to help Askel relax. She realized the metal talons were strapped over her own, so she tied them back on the leather bracers.

He relaxed the smallest bit.

"I think Triddle would try to talk you out of what I'm about to propose," she said. "I'm going to tell you a story, and I want you to tell me if I'm right or not."

His ears moved forwards, and he settled down with his paws under him.

She cleared her throat. "I believe, back in the summer, you slipped away after I led you into the Redwood Valley

Eyrie. I think two of your pridemates, Merin's offspring, went with you. I think you went to the market square."

He sat still. Not frozen, but only adjusting to stay warm.

"I believe that the night before, while Zeph, Hatzel, Cherine, and I planned to rescue Satra's gryphlets, you were with Merin. I think when your pride leader heard that the opinici were planning to burn down the weald, he decided to give them a taste of their own medicine."

Still no confirmation from Askel.

"I think there's only one gryphon who understood fire and oil well enough to pull it off. And you had some of the saltpeter they found Cherine with. I think you're the one who started the fire that burned down the eyrie."

"Did Foultner tell you that?" he asked at last.

Orlea shook her head. "If Foultner knows your secrets, she didn't tell me."

Askel stayed quiet. The wind blew through the taiga.

"What do you want me to do?" he asked at last.

"You know Cherine? The one Triddle saved?" She wasn't sure if this was going to work or not, but he hadn't raised the alarm so far.

He nodded.

"They're going to execute him before the week is out for starting the weald fire," she said.

"Triddle says it wasn't him," Askel said. "That he just found the saltpeter."

"That's not what Merin thinks," she said, "but I think Triddle's right. And I think there's a way we can save Cherine, but I need your help with it."

His ears were fully forwards now. "What do you need me to do?"

She took a deep breath. "I want you to confess to the eyrie fire and let me put you on trial."

Askel looked at the tent and nest where Triddle was sleeping. He looked down at the waystation. He even took time to consider Boomer the Ground Parrot.

Finally, he looked back at Orlea. "Okay."

25

ASKEL THE PHOENIX, APPREHENDED

Orlea and Askel flew through the evening and into the night, bypassing Snowfall and Hatzel's hunting grounds to reach the bright brazier lights of her home. Several merchants and guards were outside her home, wondering where she had gone off to.

Askel landed next to her, kicking up some dust. She didn't know if he was a bad flyer or having second thoughts.

"Arrest this gryphon," she commanded the nearest guard, an old Reeve's Guard who'd joined her pride from New Eyrie. "He's the gryphon who burned down the Redwood Valley Eyrie. His trial begins at dawn."

Orlea went into her quarters and tossed off the black armor. She hung the talons on a peg next to the entrance. She'd prepared Askel on the way over. He knew what to say and what would happen next. It wouldn't be pleasant, but he could have turned back at any moment during their flight here.

The leader of the traders, Didi, followed Orlea in without ringing the chimes. "What do you think you're doing? The Ashen Weald are going to burn this place down to get him back!"

"They already did," Orlea said. "Askel isn't denying it. He told me everything on the flight over. He was under orders from Merin. What are they going to do, burn down the eyrie a second time?"

"That...that can't be right!" The merchant was in a tizzy, which was understandable. The Ashen Weald owned the land all around them.

"It is right," Orlea said. "And it's about time the truth came out."

The merchant tried to preen herself calm. "We can't just disappear into the night like the Strix Pride."

Orlea hung up her harness next to the keys the old prison guard had given her. "The Ashen Weald seems to have forgotten it's made up of several prides and eyries. It's accountable to every pride leader. I've had enough of their secret prisons, enough of Merin's children and Ashen Weald rangers skulking around my borders."

"This is about Cherine?" Didi said. "He's one opinicus! We lost nearly a thousand the night of the fire. Let them have him if it keeps the peace."

"Cherine isn't the only Redwood scholar they're holding," Orlea countered. *Does everyone know about him?* she wondered. To her knowledge, the Ashen Weald hadn't released his name and had just described him as the scholar who started the saltpeter explosions. "If Merin thinks he can execute members of my pride with impudence, it's time we show him this goes both ways. We'll see if his Ashen Weald allies stand with him then."

"We're *executing* Askel!?" Didi was hyperventilating.

"It won't come to that." Orlea hoped it didn't come to that. She'd gotten Askel into this. "Order all our guards to watch Askel. Construct a cage out in the open so any gryphons flying over can see him, but make sure he's comfortable, well fed, and has a section where he can sleep away from prying eyes."

"We don't have guards!" Didi protested. "We didn't think we needed them with Ninox watching the north."

"Didi, calm yourself," Orlea commanded. "Reassign the opinici guarding the red fern at the hospital. You know everyone under our protection. Find all the old Reeve's Guard, Redwood rangers, and any of the military who survived New Eyrie. We just need enough to dissuade a rescue mission before we can start the trial."

Didi wandered out, missing the door the first time. After the clink of Foultner's metal talons falling to the ground and the jingle of the prison key on the peg, the merchant made it outside.

Orlea curled up in her oversized nest. Tomorrow, the Ashen Weald would realize what she'd done. Tonight, she needed to get as much sleep as she could manage.

ORLEA AWOKE to the hooting of an owl. She knew better than to think it one of the birds.

"Ninox or Blinky?" she asked.

"You cannot tell us apart by our voices?" came the reply.

Not when you're speaking owlish, I can't. Now that she'd heard the gryphon's reply in common, she knew the answer. She opened her eyes to confirm it. "Nice of you to finally pay me a visit, Nox."

The owl gryphon was looking through a stack of books. "Why did you kidnap Askel?"

"How'd you find out?" Orlea asked.

"The Strix Pride watches the pass near Mally's old workshop," Ninox said. "They saw you fly by, then I saw Askel in the cage outside."

"I needed a bargaining chip to get Cherine back." Orlea wiped the sleep out of her eyes but didn't leave her nest.

Ninox tilted her head. As an owl, that put it upside down. "But why Askel? Why not Satra or Merin?"

Orlea laughed at the suggestion, then wondered if Ninox had seriously considered going for Satra. "I took Askel because he started the eyrie fire. If he admits to it tomorrow, the Ashen Weald has to decide if it's time to put the night of the conflagration behind us. If they do that, they're more likely to turn Cherine over unharmed even if they find him guilty."

Ninox considered this. "What is a conflagration?"

"A connixation made of fire," Orlea said. Her owl friend's vocabulary had become much better, but she was still missing a few of the less common words.

Ninox pulled out a book on geography scavenged from the university. "What else have you found?"

"We've narrowed down Cherine's location." When Ninox's ears perked up, Orlea added, "But I'll only tell you if you promise that you won't rush in after him until we've checked it out first."

Ninox considered her words. "Unless things are dire, I will not rush in myself tomorrow. Is that enough time for a promise?"

"I'd rather make it three days, but it sounds like Cherine may not have much longer," Orlea said. "Kia found out that the Ashen Weald is sending extra food to Merin's territory from the Crackling Sea. We're going to check Cherine's old prison from the first time Merin caught him."

"We looked at all of the unburned weald and found nothing." Ninox preened a feather that already looked perfect. "I do not know where Cherine was kept the first time. I would not ask now, except that it could be important. What happened to his beak?"

Orlea's eyes widened a touch. She hadn't considered that Cherine wouldn't tell Ninox about his past. The scholar and pride leader had grown close enough to have children together, so Orlea had assumed he'd told Ninox everything. Then again, it was hard to know how gryphon relationships worked.

Orlea shrugged. What would it hurt? "He was keeping the capybaras in the grasslands. Do you know about the herds?"

"Yes. We killed and ate them while he was gone," Ninox said.

"Of course you did." This was new information for Orlea. She'd never stopped to consider what had happened to the large rodents that had started Zeph and Kia on their path which had allowed the weald gryphons to evacuate in time. "He followed rangers into the forest and found some saltpeter crates, fuses, and oil. He was testing the saltpeter to see what it was when Merin caught him. They thought he'd brought the explosives in and held him in a cave with an underground river. Hatzel and Triddle used a rope to pull him upstream, but Merin's pride had already broken off the tip of his beak."

Ninox licked a paw. "This is why he is afraid of Merin."

Orlea grabbed a quill and ink from beside her nest and opened a journal. "When I asked you about the night of the fire, you told me you helped secure the way out for the gryphlets, but you never told me how you did that. Do you know what your father was up to that night?"

"He tried to kill the reeve," Ninox didn't say any more than that. Her tail swayed back and forth.

"I know he fought Reeve Brevin, or at least her commander, Wolden," Orlea said. "But are you telling me he went into the eyrie that night to find and kill her?"

Ninox bowed her head.

"None of the Reeve's Guard helped fight the fire that night, at least not in any organized fashion," Orlea continued. "When you say you secured the path out of the eyrie, what do you mean?"

"I killed twenty-six of them." Ninox's voice had no shame. "I held the Reeve's Guard headquarters while my brothers took the outposts. My father went to kill the reeve. He failed."

Orlea became aware of how quiet the area around her home had become.

"You said you wanted to know about the night of the fire," Ninox pressed. "The eyrie was like a pride with a bad leader. It was harming the prides around it. My father nearly put an end to that. Zeph did. Now you have become leader. A better leader than your reeve. Your pride has become safe."

Orlea wasn't so sure of that, not if the Ashen Weald chose to attack rather than act in a rational manner. She just had one more question. "Did Strix know that Merin was going to set the eyrie on fire?"

"I do not know," Ninox said. "They spoke after the meeting, but he did not tell us."

Orlea put the pen away. It was better not to write this down yet.

"A question for you," Ninox said. "Would you have led

the gryphons into the eyrie if you knew about my father's plan? About Merin's?"

"No," Orlea said. "I only helped because I believed no one would be harmed. I have no love for Reeve Brevin, but Askel's burning oil turned the underbough into an inferno. I wouldn't have helped if I'd known that was going to happen."

"I see." Ninox picked up the small tome on geography. "I would like to bring this with me. I will return it later."

"You may," Orlea said. When Ninox stood to leave, she added, "Three days, Nox."

The owl gryphon looked at her. "I promised one."

"Neither you nor your pridemates go into Merin's territory," Orlea stressed. "Give us time to check the cave and see what the Ashen Weald does about Askel."

"Not me nor the Strix Pride will do anything," Ninox confirmed. "It is like a puzzle. Cherine liked puzzles. With the hatching of his eggs, the mating pact has ended. He was not able to see the eggs hatch. That is wrong. Satra should not have kept him from the eggs. She should not have attacked my pride holdings. She has made many mistakes."

Orlea didn't know what to say to that. She didn't disagree.

Ninox put the book in her beak and slipped up through some loose boards on the ceiling. Orlea would have to make a note to fix the roof of the old storage shed she'd converted into a home.

The night was quiet. She kept hearing Ninox's comments about a promise being a puzzle that needed to be solved. Orlea regretted telling her about Kia's information. She couldn't help but feel that she'd set something else in motion that wasn't part of her plan with Askel.

26

DIPLOMACY

S atra led the guests into the council chamber. The leaders of the Ashen Weald were sitting in a semi-circle, including the parrotface elder and head medicine gryphon. Despite their feelings on Merin's efforts to track down all of the scholars spying for the Blackwing Eyrie, they'd heeded Satra's call.

Ranger Lord Grenkin formed the center of the Ashen Weald side of the circle, flanked by the eldest pride leaders. He looked worse for wear but had insisted on coming to this meeting. Satra had chosen to sit along the edge, next to Silver, and put Merin by Goldfeather. It had been Blinky's idea to see how their guests reacted to seeing the lone Ashen Weald opinicus leader in a seat of importance.

For now, that reaction was confusion, as they weren't sure if they should thank Satra or Grenkin for the invitation.

Silver solved the problem in a different way. "Thank you, Pride Leader Merin, for extending the invitation. It's good to dine in the halls of the Ashen Weald one last time before we go."

"Please, just Merin is fine." His tail twitched in agitation as he spoke. Satra knew he'd have preferred his full honorific, but she'd convinced him that the purpose of tonight was to gather information.

"I do appreciate a lack of formality now and then," Goldfeather crooned. "It's nice to get away from the capitol."

"Does the informality hold for Reeve Satra and Reeve Grenkin, too?" Silver asked.

There was a confidence to the small hawk that she'd lacked on her last visit to the kjarr nesting grounds. If Satra had to guess, the white eyrie's expedition had found what they were looking for and were no longer required to play nice.

Several opinici and gryphons brought in a selection of food. Most of the crops from the Crackling Sea still tasted brackish, but several parrotface scavengers had located wild berries and eggfruit. The servers were careful to serve the less salty food to the guests.

Several bog witches brought in bowls of water. Where weald and kjarr gryphons would drink from any running water, the bog pride held a reverence for clear, clean water. They gathered it from special springs, stored it in stolen opinicus barrels, and tossed in goldmint or pumpkin leaf to flavor it.

Satra sipped at her bowl. Goldmint. She'd have to be careful she didn't drink too much of it.

"Kjarr Satra takes her title from the land around her," Merin said, "as did Jun the Kjarr."

"Did the Kjarr title come after they conquered the bog pride?" Goldfeather asked. "Was there a time when the kjarr used the term pride leader?"

Silver shot him a glance. "We mean no disrespect to the bog pride."

"Many of the kjarr pride are now bog pride. Many of the bog pride are now kjarr pride." Soft Paws's voice was quiet. She and Urious had been searching the bog the past few nights under the pretense of clearing out starlings, and she looked half asleep.

Satra would have to think of something nice to do for the youngest pride leader. "The bog pride are here because they want to be. They're no longer a conquered pride. I didn't agree with my father and grandfather's choice."

"Southern politics are a fascinating departure from the northern eyries." Goldfeather picked up a craneberry and tossed it into his beak. "These are good and tart. I saw the flooded fields on the flight over. You did a great job, Reeve Grenkin. I never would have guessed these came from lands salted three years ago."

Satra rolled her eyes. Their guests were amateurs if they thought the Ashen Weald leaders were susceptible to such small prods and innuendos.

"Ranger Lord, please," Grenkin corrected. "And I suppose your friend set the initial expectation of not needing titles when she failed to include her own. I apologize for not recognizing your badge earlier, Reeve 'Silver.'"

Silver dipped her head. "Reeve is more of a ceremonial title where I'm from. I'm afraid the Argent Heights aren't as large and exciting as the Crackling Sea and Redwood Valley eyries. We don't stand on formality or titles. Despite my best efforts, I've not been able to get the goliaths and thunder birds to salute me."

At Satra's suggestion, Grenkin had gone through the trade logs to find out as much about their guests as possible before tonight. While the Seraph King was still a mystery, he'd uncovered several old trade deals with the Argent Heights.

"Still," the ranger lord continued, "it's good to see the badge behind all of the trade requests. How are the Heights? Did our medicines work?"

"Aye," Silver said. "Many chicks were saved."

"On that note of cooperation," Merin said, "I'll admit that I did invite you here with ulterior motives and not just to feed you."

Goldfeather picked up a starberry with a single gold talon and popped it in his beak. "We suspected as much, though we do appreciate the food."

Silver took a sip from her bowl. "And the water. I've never tasted anything quite like this before."

Satra wondered if Goldfeather's talons were naturally gold or if it was a thin layer of paint. Either way, it seemed a bad idea to eat with a metal talon.

She cleared her throat. "You mentioned fending off the Blackwing Eyrie's assassins in the past. There've been several attempts this week on the Ashen Weald and fisherfolk villages. The assassins were coated in poison and their blackwing allies carried an antidote. We were wondering what you knew about them."

"And how to make the antidote," Soft Paws said. Even here at dinner, she wore a pouch of herbs and medicines around her neck.

"I'm afraid we don't know how to make the antivenom from scratch," Goldfeather said. "It requires a sample of the poison itself to craft, usually from the scarabs."

Silver didn't make eye contact.

Goldfeather went on. "As for Rybalt, perhaps my

compatriot would be so kind as to tell our hosts how she became a reeve?"

"The Reeve's Bane led one of the attempts on my home eyrie." Silver looked up from her bowl. "I was the commander of the Reeve's Guard at the time. Like you, we were allied with neither the blackwings nor the Seraph King. Like you, we were naïve."

She paused to drink. "We're a small eyrie with little of value. If you placed the Argent Heights anywhere else, no opinicus would pay us any mind. But we're the first eyrie on the other side of the desert, the first eyrie north of the Emerald Jungle."

Lord Grenkin's research had also located several maps. They were a little flowery, marked with monsters and myths, but they helped show the wider world. Crestfall's endless deserts spread north of the Crackling Sea, dividing the Blackwing Eyrie's mountains from the Seraph King's coastal plains.

It made sense that both sides would search for a foothold across the desert and sea. In Silver's words was a warning—having a foothold along the southern coast of the sea would be almost as useful for either side.

"We rebuffed the Alabaster Eyrie's diplomats," Silver continued, "including my gold-feathered friend here. The Blackwing Eyrie didn't bother to send diplomats. They sent assassins."

"The Reeve's Bane?" Merin asked.

"Reeve Rybalt of the Pitohui Eyrie," she confirmed. "I was guarding our reeve when he was killed. I only survived because I tore the red vial from a dead blackwing and drank it before my body gave out. We pushed Rybalt out of the eyrie, but his blackwing allies were nearly across the desert by then."

"Thankfully, in his wisdom, the Seraph King had sent an army to help," Goldfeather said. "One of our scouts caught sight of the army flying over the desert and brought word."

"If not for the Seraph King, I wouldn't be here today," Silver said. "They'd have finished off the rest of us and taken the eyrie. That's the foe you face now—an assassin who poisons you so the Blackwing Eyrie can slip in and finish you off."

Merin looked at Satra before speaking. They'd hoped for more practical advice. "Do you have any suggestions for fending them off? How does the Seraph King do it?"

"The forces of the king are unmatched," Goldfeather said. "The Golden Sky army is a sunrise that illuminates the heavens from Reevesport to Whitebeak."

"It sounds like bravado, but it isn't," Silver added. "We outnumber the blackwings four to one. If the desert wasn't so wide, it would be easy. There's no way to take an army across the desert and have it in fighting condition on the other side. You can't even reach Crestfall in one day's flight."

Something was bothering Satra. "The desert can't go all the way north, can it? Surely it reaches the ocean eventually. Is the coast any better?"

Goldfeather's gold-tipped plumes drooped. "A few opinici, perhaps. Not an army. The coral forest and blood rains look safe, but the red water carries something in it that kills bats, gryphons, squirrels, and capybaras outright. Not even opinici are fully immune."

Satra nodded. Perhaps there was some truth in the myths and horrors on Grenkin's map. She changed the topic to less troublesome matters, food and weather, and the conversation stayed pleasant all the way through the sugar frog desserts.

SATRA'S HEAD felt fuzzy by the time their guests got up to leave. Next time, she'd stick to regular water. Goldmint wasn't as strong as gryph mint, but she'd consumed a lot of it over the course of the evening.

She let Merin walk her across the bridge to her nest. As Goldfeather and his guards flew north, a white shape detached itself from the formation and landed on the other side of the bridge.

"Reeve Silver," Merin said.

"Pride Leader, Kjarr, thank you for the nice evening." Silver didn't move from the bridge.

"How may we help you?" Satra asked.

The moonlight shone off of Silver's armor. "You should join us against the Blackwing Eyrie."

"Did Goldfeather order you to tell us that?" Merin asked.

She shook her head no. "He's seen enough to know that we can take the Crackling Sea by force if we need to. He's no longer concerned with diplomacy, should it come down to it."

"That's not much of a pitch," Satra said.

"When the Seraph King's armies fill your skies, you want them to be there to liberate you, even if the liberation is a lie," Silver continued. "You don't want them to show up as conquerors."

"What happened to Crestfall?" Satra countered. "Were they liberated? Or did they fall to the Blackwing Eyrie?"

"If you want more information from me, you'll need to

provide some of your own." To Silver's credit, her feathers remained smooth and her voice calm. "Make no mistake. We *are* winning this war. We control most of the continent. There's little the Blackwing Eyrie can do to stop us now. If we bide our time, it's only because we're deciding on how we wish to win."

"I'll take your advice under consideration," Satra said. "Swift winds."

"May the assassins not catch up to you before you arrive at your nest," Merin added. "Our owls watch the nesting grounds, but you've a lot of grasslands to cover. You'd best leave now."

Silver took to the air, leaving behind Satra and Merin. They passed by a single bonfire left burning all night in the center of the nesting grounds.

"Between the blackwings and the wingtorn, the Redwood Valley and Crackling Sea have been gutted of opinici," Satra said. "Our silver friend isn't wrong. We don't know how large their forces are."

The smoke from the fire reminded her of the first time she and Merin had met, escaping from the burning eyrie. Things had seemed dire then, too, but she'd put her faith in what turned out to be fifty gryphons and come out of it okay.

"If they try to fight us here, they're in for a surprise." He nodded to several feathermane guards. Under his tutelage, the feathermanes were starting to find their roar again since Zrim's death. "If we can get the flameworks and metalworks running again, we'll have an advantage."

Satra considered this. "Orlea controls both. Jonas considered building a second flameworks, but it takes a lot of time and effort to get one running. I doubt Bario's blackwing masters have theirs up yet."

"There's also the parasite." Merin's words were tentative, as though he feared rebuke. And she should have rebuked him, but she didn't know what tomorrow held.

The parasite had been intended as a weapon against the southern eyries, but they'd figured out a cure. If they could grow enough pumpkin and bog blossom, there was no reason they couldn't use the blackwing's weapon against the Seraph King.

Except common decency. Satra's head still buzzed from the mint.

"We'll try diplomacy first," she said. "When it comes to opinici, I trust Foultner, and I almost trust Grenkin. But when an army of diplomats arrives and they're all opinici, I question what happened to their gryphons."

"Are you trying diplomacy on the king or Orlea?" Merin asked, referring back to his comments on the metalworks and flameworks.

"Both," Satra said. "Orlea likes us, though. Now that trade has built up, I suspect we'll be able to reach some sort of arrangement without too much trouble. If nothing else, I'd like to re-arm the wingtorn who were declawed. That seems like a basic level of decency even Orlea could get behind."

"You should see if she feels the same way about us tomorrow," Merin said. "The scholar we caught with the owls goes on trial, and there's talk Orlea might claim him as one of her own pride."

Satra had been content to let Merin handle rooting out spies and Jonas loyalists, but she had a bad feeling about this one. "It's strange that the arsonist you caught has friends and lovers amongst the underbough and Strix Pride. How sure are you?"

Merin chirped a code as they approached Satra's den

and four invisible owls hooted back. "Certain enough to put him on trial. Uncertain enough that I didn't kill him when we caught him either time."

Satra stopped outside the den. As a rule, she didn't let other gryphons or opinici inside when she was heading to sleep. "Make sure the trial is fair, Merin, even if it means he goes free."

"The evidence will speak for itself, Kjarr." Merin flew off.

Perhaps Satra had insulted him by suggesting otherwise. She could worry about that tomorrow. Tonight, at least, nothing eventful should happen.

27

THE WISDOM OF OWLS

"I s this wise?" Headmaster Neider asked. "We're very close to the eyrie. We might get recognized."

He was squeezed into a fishing hut outside the remains of the Snowfeather Dam. Iony and several glacier pride were in here with him. Farther upstream, Rybalt waited with the remaining blackwing opinici who hadn't been eaten by monitors or blown up by Piprik.

"We haven't seen anyone come up this way," Iony said. "Well, no one except your spy."

Neider rested his talons on a stolen key but didn't comment. If all had gone well, his cockatiel forger would still have the matching key. He'd cultivated a lot of relationships during his time as headmaster, but he'd never asked anyone to do anything that might cause them harm. He hated leaning on his contacts now, but time was growing short.

"I'd rather be back north," he said.

"We needed someone who speaks owl," Iony replied.

The headmaster titled his head halfway around and poked at Iony's long, pointed ears. "You don't speak owl?"

"Not weald owl." Iony paused. "Not even glacier owl, I suppose. I'm surprised these 'Strix' gryphons held onto their language for so long."

"I saw *the* Strix pride leader once. This was years ago, you understand, in the bog." The headmaster rubbed his talons together for warmth. "He ate one of my apprentices."

Iony rolled his eyes. "Gryphons don't eat opinici. That's just a medicine gryphon's tale."

"Most gryphons don't," the headmaster confirmed, "but you don't know the Strix owls. They're...something different. Feral."

"Don't let them hear you talking like that," Iony said. "It's about an hour to sun up and no sign of little Strixette. Is this a trap?"

"There's only one way to find out." The headmaster stepped several steps before Iony tried to call him back. "Don't be absurd. I'm far too important to kill."

He was partway across the drained remains of Crater Lake when several owl gryphons materialized around him. He hooted a greeting in owlish.

"Tell your friends to come out, too," a dark brown owl commanded.

Once Iony and the glacier gryphons were visible, the brown Strix gryphon hooted and Ninox landed.

"Pride Leader Ninox," Neider said. "Please, allow me to introduce Iony of the glacier pride. You might consider them the northern cousins of the taiga pride. We received your message. Normally, we would not be summoned like this, but we do appreciate you not killing our scouts."

Ninox looked from the headmaster to Iony and back. "Your cockatiel friend and the blackwing with him are being held in Merin's territory."

"Why tell us?" Iony asked. "What makes you think we aren't going to assume this is a trap?"

Ninox considered him. "It is a trap. You will find the prison and open the way. I will come in after, murder you, and save Cherine."

"There's no need for that," the headmaster grumbled. "Cherine was like a son to me. I wouldn't allow harm to come to him."

Ninox was unimpressed. "He did not mention you."

"And what is a gryphon to him?" Neider hated to admit when his ego was hurt, but he had put a lot of time into grooming Cherine and Kia into becoming the next generation of scholars.

"He was taken before he saw his eggs hatch," the gryphon said. "If all of my mates are kidnapped before the eggs hatch, it will make it hard to find new, better mates the next season. This is basic math. Did you not say you were a scholar?"

Iony grinned. "How can we contact you if we have more questions?"

"You cannot." Ninox hooted to her gryphons, who disappeared into the last of the night. "We will be watching to see if you can locate the prison. If so, you should not come back out, or we will kill you. Make sure no harm comes to Cherine."

Headmaster Neider watched the gryphons disappear into the night before turning to Iony. "What do you think she meant about his eggs hatching?"

Iony laughed. "I think your boy settled down with a nice gryphon."

Neider blinked. "What could he have seen in that creature of the night that he didn't see in Kia?"

"Scholar, spy, headmaster, and matchmaker?" Iony

chided as they left. "You can't tell opinici who to fall in love with. And a mating season doesn't necessarily mean love. Just ask my last six mates."

"Well, we need to tell Rybalt not to harm Cherine," Neider said.

"You can make a case if you want," the glacier gryphon said, "but orders are orders. We're here for a few very specific things. Any scholars who can't be converted need to be killed. We don't want another Mally the Nighthaunt."

THE HEADMASTER SCRIBBLED in his journals. His conversation with Rybalt had not gone the way he wanted. The pitohui seemed intent only on locating the two prisoners and what they carried.

That wouldn't do. He needed new apprentices to train. There was so much he had yet to teach Cherine and Kia.

He thought back to the night of the fire. "I should have brought you with me then, Kia. How will you become a scholar without my tutelage? I have been irresponsible with my apprentices."

—*Headmaster.*

He started. The sun was out, though the camp was mostly asleep after waiting for hours for Ninox to show herself. They'd moved from the northern end of the valley to the southern, clearing out the monitors from a large cavern and putting them into cages for later.

A dim candle lit the headmaster's new den. "You're quite brave today, coming out into the light."

—*Surely, you did not think daylight could vanquish me?*

The voice echoed through the cave.

"In truth, I wonder sometimes if you can be killed at all. Step into the light, old friend. Let me see what you've become."

—A strange thing to say. I have been dying as long as we've known each other, mortally wounded by fate, doomed at birth. I just die slower than most.

Neider thought back to his early days at university. His friend had been a peregrine falcon named Mal back then with a black beak and talons. As the disease progressed, his talons had turned grey, then white, then the red of iron filled them like vials.

"Was I the first opinicus to call you Mally?"

—Getting sentimental? I didn't come here to reminisce.

"What did you come here for?" The headmaster asked the darkness around him. The flickering of the lone candle suggested that there was some movement just beyond its illumination. "Didn't you find what you were looking for in the swamp?"

—I did, thank you. Your brightly colored apprentice is sticking her beak into my old workshops. I could smell her when I returned there. I thought, as one old master to another, I should warn you of her fate. Since you were kind enough to warn me of my apprentice's arrest.

It was a courtesy from the pre-university days when the old masters would send their apprentices out to spy on other scholars. He'd left a note for Mally warning him of Impir's pending arrest. Mally hadn't come to his apprentice's rescue. Neider hadn't even been sure the message had been received, and they were on the same side back then.

Mally leaving Impir to be captured was one of the few reasons the mad peafowl was still trusted by the Black-wing Eyrie. Where Neider handled the spies and Bario was in charge of saltpeter, Impir now oversaw programs to hatch healthier chicks. It was a level of trust Neider had warned against, but if his northern allies were more concerned about fighting a war than their own children, that was their mistake to make.

"There's little I can do about her now." He wished he had a way to warn Kia, but she seemed unlikely to heed his warnings.

—*We located the seraph in the swamp. You should leave, come join the Seraph King. Your blackwing allies are only biding their time before they kill you. Why else send you to the front lines with an assassin?*

Mally's voice seemed to come from the walls themselves. Had Iony not gone over the caverns in excruciating detail ahead of time, there was no way Neider would have known about the small fissure along the ceiling.

The headmaster rested his talons under the journal. "None of that talk, old friend. Leave me be, that I may grow old teaching young opinici again."

—*I could take you from here. You would disappear into the darkness. I have need of scholars like yourself. There are few more dedicated to knowledge than politics. Perhaps we are the last two.*

"And live like cave gryphons? I think not." The whiskers on Neider's face vibrated the smallest amount as the pressure in the room changed.

The headmaster closed his eyes and lit the fuse on a new type of saltpeter light. It burned with the intensity of sunlight, illuminating the shape descending from the ceiling.

When the light filled the cracks under the weather barrier, Iony and Rybalt took their cue and led a small army into the headmaster's room.

"By the depths, what *is* that?" Rybalt shouted.

The headmaster opened an eye. There was nothing left of the peregrine falcon who had once been his friend Mal. The shape above him was twice as long. Its back legs were misshapen talons. Its tail was long and gryphon-like with a feathered spade at the end. Its eyes were pure black orbs recoiling from the light.

But its body was long and lithe like the mummified seraph in the swamp.

"You...you really consumed one," Neider said. "What have you become? You're more Nighthaunt than opinicus."

Each limb sprouted feathers, becoming four protowings in addition to his long, thin wings that no longer resembled a falcon.

"What are you waiting for?" the headmaster shouted at Rybalt. "Kill him before he escapes!"

He knew his words had come too late. The Nighthaunt slithered through the crack in the ceiling and disappeared into cave system, becoming like the very cave gryphons they'd told stories about as young apprentices.

"You didn't tell us he was a monster," Iony said. "What is that thing?"

"Mally has always been a monster," Neider said. "The bright lights just confirmed what we always knew."

"Very poetic," Rybalt replied, "but how did he *become* like that? He was one of you reds once, wasn't he? I can't imagine that *thing* teaching classes at the university."

"I believe that's what happens when you try to become a seraph and fail." The headmaster picked up his journal and ink and left the room. Mally the Nighthaunt wasn't the sort of opinicus you could vanquish with a trick of the talon. Neider would be sleeping with the glacier pride tonight.

Iony and Rybalt went to check on the rest of the camp. Neider followed along, not quite ready to be away from more tempting assassination targets than himself.

"I'd assumed alchemy was just about protecting chicks from disease," the Reeve's Bane said. "But he did that to himself? Is that what the seraphs look like?"

Iony's ears were back. "That's not what the one in the glacier looks like."

"We have to kill it." Rybalt rifled through his packs looking for something. "What're the chances we can lure it back one more time?"

"I don't think we'll be seeing the Nighthaunt again," Neider said.

"We have a mission," Iony said. "If we lose the rest of our forces chasing monsters, we won't have enough for the jailbreak. There's no coming back empty-taloned this time, Ryb. The blackwings will annex your eyrie if you do."

Rybalt swore. "We have enough monitors. Our spies have located Reeve's Nest in the rubble. All we need is the bleeding cockatiel."

"Everyone will know we're here if we make a move on an Ashen Weald prison," Iony said.

"Half of the fisherfolk's island blew up. I think they know we're here," Rybalt countered. "It's just a matter of time before they check this valley. What of your spy, Headmaster? Can your opinicus search a gryphon pride for us?"

"I suppose we'll find out," Neider said. "When do you plan to try all of this unpleasantness? Tomorrow night?"

"No, I believe the Strix gryphon when she says she's

going to come in after us." Rybalt located several small vials of a failed saltpeter mixture that caused loud noises but little fire. "We'll do the jailbreak during the daylight when Ninox can't hide."

Iony looked out of the cave entrance towards the remaining glacier gryphons, blackwings, and trashbirds. Neider had never seen him look so worried.

The headmaster left the two behind to find a safe place to nap. When he passed by the entrance to the cavern, he thought he heard the whisper of a single word from between the caged monitors.

—*Pity.*

28

UNDERWATER CAVE ADVENTURE

Quess tested the water of the Snowfeather River and shook her feathers out before grooming a few back into place. Freshwater was easier than saltwater, but she hadn't been grooming oil into her fur and feathers on the flight north. There wasn't a lot of liquid water around Snowfall.

"I should be fine," she said. "Tresh held her breath for twenty minutes in the bog. I'm sure I can manage three."

Kia tested the harness and ropes while Hatzel went over how the plan had worked last time. Zeph chased a leaf-nosed snake through the underbrush nearby.

"Where does the river come out?" Quess asked. "There isn't a nice lake or something on the other side, is there? It'd be easier than swimming against the current."

"Glacier Run, if Triddle is to be believed." Hatzel had given Quess several chances to back out. "You're sure you want to do this?"

"What's the worst that can happen?" Quess asked. Both Kia and Hatzel rolled their eyes at the obvious answer: *A lot.* "Look, I know what it's like to wonder if your friend is okay. I'm just going to poke my head up, see if this Cherine is anywhere around, then swim back. Easy."

Zeph padded back over with a snake in his beak. "Sorry. Did you tell her about the harness?"

"I was just getting to that," Kia said. "If you do find Cherine and he's alone, toss this around him and tug three times. Hatzel will be ready to pull him out just like last time. Easy, right?"

"It was a close thing last time," Hatzel said.

Quess looked at both of them like they were a little crazy. "You sure that's what he'd want?"

"I'm open to other plans," Kia said, "but we know this one works. I've also been practicing the fisherfolk techniques for getting water out of lungs in case it doesn't work quite as well as we're hoping."

"It'll be fine," Zeph added. "Either Cherine's not there and now we know, or Merin's kin probably left him alone. They're very dumb."

Quess shook her head. Zeph, Kia, and Hatzel's plans seemed to work a surprising amount of the time when Zeph was the one telling the tale. She didn't know how she felt about being made part of the team, but she remembered being lost and imprisoned in the bog. She wanted to help.

"Okay, let's do this." She grabbed the harness, tested the rope to make sure it worked, and slipped into the water.

The current moved at a fast pace. That was good for helping her find the cave but wouldn't be great when she needed to make her retreat. Her flippers allowed for her talons to fit through them, and she held onto top of the tunnel carved by the river when it went underground.

I didn't realize it would be so dark. Did Tresh really do this for twenty minutes? I feel like the sides of the river are squeezing shut.

She continued on cautiously. Pulling Cherine out had taken Hatzel a minute, but Quess could afford to take her time. She went carefully, checking to find the hole in the top of the submerged cave. She was surprised when she saw a faint light ahead.

That's not a good sign. Someone is living down here.

She held onto an outcropping and let the water push past her. Through the light, she could just make out one large shape. When it turned its head, she caught sight of a curved tip at the end of its beak that resembled Carru's.

Cherine was supposed to be a golden eagle in the face with a metal beak. This was more of a harpy eagle. She considered heading back, but one gryphon didn't mean Cherine wasn't there. That could be his guard.

Just one little peek, then I'll slip away.

She watched through the water. The gryphon turned his back on the river, and she poked her head through.

The cave was one small passage. There was barely enough room for one gryphon here. It wouldn't make much of a prison.

She was about to duck back down when the large shape turned and pounced without looking.

It held her up in two massive paws and looked at her. The tips of its claws cut into her sides.

"A little swimming opinicus? Down here?" He laughed. "Now we know how Cherine got out the first time. We have some questions for you."

Quess wiggled one arm free and grabbed the rope. She threw the harness loop around the gryphon's neck and tugged on the rope three times.

"Eh?" was all the gryphon managed before Hatzel

pulled with all of her might, and the gryphon was jerked into the water, kicking and thrashing.

With his paws more concerned about trying to keep him out of the water, he let go of Quess. She took two steps up the passage, but heard the sounds of a dozen gryphons coming down.

She looked at the river. Upstream was a splashing, angry gryphon twice her size.

Downstream it is!

She slipped into the water and let the current take her into the depths.

ZEPH PUSHED Hatzel from behind while Kia grabbed the top of the saberbeak's harness and tried to use her wing muscles to help.

"Why is Cherine so heavy?" Zeph asked between pushes. "I carried him back at the medicine cave."

"You carried him a few feet," Hatzel said between gritted tomia. "I carried him up the mountain. He's surprisingly big."

"His beak is coming up!" Kia said. "Push harder!"

Zeph was so busy pushing that he didn't notice the shape of the beak until the opinicus was on the shore. "We have a problem."

Kia unhooked the rope from Hatzel's harness. "Wait, that's not Cherine."

"Is he dead?" Hatzel asked. "Just what happened in there?"

Kia rushed over and began to push just below his rib cage. "Flip him over. Hatzel, you're stronger, push here. Zeph, watch his head. Do what I do, okay?"

It took a little effort, but the Merin-kin coughed up half the river and started breathing again.

Zeph pushed the rope into the water, letting the river start to slowly pull the rest in.

The Merin-kin pushed himself up on his paws, stopping to catch his breath. Kia and Hatzel looked at each other, unsure what to do or say.

Zeph retrieved the snake he'd caught earlier and swallowed it in one bite while Hatzel gave him a questioning look. He walked over to the half-drowned gryphon.

"What, what happened?" the hook-beaked gryphon asked.

Zeph got right up in his face, trusting his snake breath to give truth to the lie. "Hello, fellow gryphon! We saw you wrapped up in a seven-foot-long cave snake. If not for me and my companions, it would have swallowed you whole. You owe us your life."

He practically spat the syllables in *swallowed you whole*.

The gryphon recoiled from the smell. "Cave snake?"

"Y-yes, that's right," Kia said. "The university pulled one out of the Snowfeather River a few years ago. You're lucky it was so small. The big ones are as big as three Hatzels."

The rescued gryphon was still coughing. He seemed skeptical but disoriented.

The rope Zeph had tossed into the water pulled the rest in, and with a loud *plop* the harness went in after it.

"The snake is back!" he cried out. "Quick, take this poor gryphon to safety!"

Hatzel pushed the gryphon away from shore while Kia let out an improvised gasp and followed suit. Only when they were away from the water did they get to work preening the poor gryphon dry.

"Cave snakes don't normally come that close to the surface," Kia said. "Were you spelunking and got lost? I heard about a gryphon swallowed whole just last year around this time."

The gryphon shook his head. Whether he remembered what he had been up to or not, he appreciated being groomed dry.

"Come on, our nesting grounds aren't far from here," Hatzel said. "We'll get you warmed and fed before you return home. By the beak, I'd say you're part of Merin's pride?"

"He's my father," the gryphon coughed.

"Well, I can't help you with that," Hatzel said. "But we'll make sure you're flight-worthy before we send you home."

"Was anyone with you?" Kia asked. When he shook his head, she continued, "We should probably be certain. I'll fly back and check the shoreline. I think I left my journal there."

As Kia took off, Zeph and Hatzel shared a look behind their guest's back. Just what had happened to Quess?

ONLY WHEN TEN minutes had passed did Quess realize that she should have caught her breath before leaping into the water. The current picked up as several other underground tributaries fed into the Snowfeather River.

She forced herself to stay calm. The river had to end somewhere. Ideally, that was somewhere with air.

As new currents fed in, she was pushed against the

sides of the cave. The scrapes and lost feathers were adding up. She kept her wings close to her body, using tiny half-strokes to keep away from the sides.

Five more minutes and her lungs were at their limit. She belatedly wondered what would happen to Bruen if she died here. Would he head back north or stay with the fisherfolk? She often felt that the only thing tethering him to the ocean was her, and if she passed, he'd go out in search of the deposed ranger lord, Ellore.

He's probably the only opinicus who still believes in Ellore. Whatever we think of her on the shore and in the weald, he thinks of her as someone who always looked out for him.

Quess's lungs burned. She resisted the urge to breathe but let out a small gasp when the river dropped and sent her speeding down. She was coughing water when it finally spit her out the side of a chasm and down towards the Glacier Run.

She coughed up water, back beat her wings to try to slow down, and crashed into the other side of the cliff face. She managed a few breaths before she plummeted into the rapids below.

She tested her wings. They were seaworthy, and that was worth something. She'd find out in a few moments if they were flightworthy. Several feathers were broken or pointing in the wrong direction. She felt like a dugong tossed between two serpentine whales.

She'd swum the rapids of Glacier Run once before. Back then, she flew above them, dipping in to try to catch Tresh, who had run away as a fledging. That had been in late summer, when the water level was at its lowest.

With the spring runoff, Glacier Run was a new type of beast. Quess slipped between rocks and tried to center herself. Coming up was where the runoff from the taiga met the runoff from the Strix Plateau in the center of the weald. If she was still in the water when that happened, chances were good she'd get pulled under and drown.

So when she saw a large, relatively flat rock coming up, she began trying to swim against the current. She made just enough headway that when she was pushed into the rock, she was able to hold onto it. She let the surge move past her, then climbed on top.

While the water often crashed up the rocky sides, she saw the charred remains of a bridge up ahead. It would be a good place to dry off before heading back to find Kia and Zeph, if her wings would take her that high.

She looked behind her to see if there was a calm in the river coming up just in time for her rock to get submerged in a wave. She pushed off, pushed through the water's surface, and beat her wings as hard as she could.

She got a little lift, but nowhere near enough to reach the bridge above her. She settled for a clump of vines, letting them bear her weight while she tried to get her feathers dry and straight again.

While she preened, she looked up at the skeletal bridge. A gliding squirrel landed atop the end of a strut and chewed at a bit of green sticking out of the blackened wood.

This must be the same bridge the wingtorn used to march down to destroy Crane's Nest and Swan's Rest, she thought. It was wide enough for several goliath birds to walk shoulder-to-shoulder. *They probably blew it up to keep the fire from spreading from the southern weald.*

By the time Quess had returned to the shore from her bog misadventure, the fisherfolk had already asked Zeph and Kia all manner of questions about the night of the weald fire. Quess had taken pity on them and not asked her own set. Instead, she tried to glean what had happened from the conversations around her with limited success.

In the end, the only way she'd been able to forgive the wingtorn and rangers was by *not* immersing herself in the details. That obsession was what had caused the rest of Crane's Nest to leave the shore and become islanders. In their grief, they couldn't let go.

Quess wouldn't say she'd let go, but she had found a sort of stasis between grief and hatred. She still couldn't think of her lost children and mate without breaking down.

Bruen has witnessed that often enough.

The Crackling Sea ranger had become a temporary rock for her. Her greatest surprise had been that Tresh had given her that solace without judgement. Quess didn't know where things would go with Bruen, but she'd given herself permission to grieve however she needed to. For now, that meant not going through it alone.

She looked up at the charred bridge and tried to see it as just a bridge, not the method by which an army had arrived on her shores. When it was fixed, it would allow a faster trade route up to the eyrie ruins. She should talk to Rorin about that. Maybe this was the next step in peace between the fisherfolk and Ashen Weald.

While she was watching the bridge from her tangle of vines, she saw a heron neck peek out of the northern, unburned weald side of the river. Looking for all the world like a bird building a nest, an Ashen Weald ranger flitted out from hiding and under the bridge, landing on the underside of its southern edge.

Before Quess could think to say or do anything, two more rangers and a splotchy blue merchant flew to the same area. She heard the sound of metal on metal, then a rusted door opening, and three of the four disappeared.

The last stood watch. He stared up and down Glacier Run from his hiding place under the bridge. He looked at the tangle of vines several times didn't notice anything out of the ordinary.

Quess stopped her grooming. She froze in place, letting the scout's eyes go over her without seeing her. She waited the better part of an hour before he went back inside.

Do I try to go back to Kia? Or down the river to Swan's Rest?

The thick vegetation on the northern side of Glacier Run could be hiding more scouts. Instead, she decided to fly along the cliffs to the east. Eventually, she'd arrive at the small, temporary bridge near the Strix Plateau that the fisherfolk sent goliath birds up. She wouldn't look out of place there, assuming no one caught her before then.

She beat her wings a few times. They didn't feel great, but she wanted to put some distance between her and the bridge before the next scout came out to look around.

She flew for the rest of the morning and into the afternoon, stopping every so often to cling to the rocky cliff face and rest. She was nearly there when she heard the sounds of opinici talking up top.

"I'm telling you, I saw an opinicus down in the water," the first voice said. Male. Resonant. She caught the hint of a hooked beak against the sky.

"Nobody's going to swim in Glacier Run in the spring," the second, female voice said. This one had a bit of song to it, though it also had a salty edge. "Look how fast the current is moving. It would be suicide."

"Look, I'm telling you what I saw," the other said.

"Look for yourself."

Two faces looked over the side of the temporary bridge. One had the hooked beak of Merin's pride. The other was the blue heron of an Ashen Weald ranger.

Both of them stared right at her.

She swore, got ready to flee, then started laughing.

"Quess?" Gressle called down. The Sandpiper's Dune opinicus was in charge of the fisherfolk trade caravans. She turned to her companion. "Well, don't just stand there, Carru. Go help her up!"

"I'm okay!" Quess shouted back up. "Give me a moment, and I'll fly up to you."

It took some doing, but she finally crested the top of the cliffs overlooking Glacial Run and collapsed among the confused fisherfolk.

"I thought you were going to Snowfall?" Gressle asked. "How'd you end up on the east side of the valley?"

Carru tried to preen her feathers back into place, but his beak was a little too big for the job. "Is everything okay? What happened to your companions?"

Quess caught her breath. "I'll catch you up once we arrive at Orlea's pride. For now, do you mind if I hop on top of one of the goliath birds and take a nap?"

Gressle shrugged in confusion but shifted aside some of the goods in a cart to make room. Quess half-heartedly preened a few more feathers, then fell asleep. Between the underground river and the rapids, she'd burned through a week's worth of energy.

She meant to tell Carru to wake her when they reached the grasslands, but all that came out of her beak was, "Grass," before she fell asleep.

"Hmm? Did you call for me?" Gressle asked. "Poor dear. She's already asleep."

29

PRISONER ESCORT

Word from the waystation didn't reach Satra before she left for the weald. She wanted an opportunity to speak with Cherine ahead of the trial and see if she could get more information from him or the blackwing spies.

She left before sunup to cross the taiga. She missed having Foultner as a bodyguard, but Blinky and Merin kept her company. She wasn't comfortable with the Ashen Weald rangers watching her, so several of Merin's pridemates served as her guards.

Blinky wanted to hide Satra's bright crest to make her harder to spot, but Satra had dismissed the idea. She didn't have time to spend hours grooming feather paint out before the scholar's trial began. Besides, most of the attacks had come at night. It was unlikely the Bane of the Crackling Sea Reeve or Ninox would make a move during the day.

They landed outside of Merin's pridegrounds on the side closest to the grasslands, at a small gathering area. With the caves and rocks, she recognized the layout.

"Was this a nesting grounds once?" she asked.

Merin nodded. "This is where my father died stopping a stampede of goliath birds from trampling a nest of eggs."

"The report to Reeve Brevin didn't mention gryphons at all." Satra had learned to read on old eyrie reports. "It said they'd gotten loose and only half had been recovered."

"A dozen gryphons were trampled because no warning was given." Merin's response was cold. "The eggs survived, though my father didn't. He stared down the goliath birds until the end, and when they hit him, they changed course."

It explained why Merin felt the way he did about opinici. Satra was surprised he'd softened as much as he had with Foultner and Grenkin. The fact that the food experiments had ultimately killed his father explained why he held ill will towards Cherine.

They walked south to the cliffs overlooking Glacier Run and waited by the remains of the bridge. They watched, but no other gryphons came by. Glacier Run's rapids were too much effort to fish from for another few weeks. Merin had until then to find a new place to hold prisoners.

The door under the bridge opened and several rangers flew out, escorting the same blue merchant Satra had purchased goods from at the Redwood Valley Eyrie.

"Is that Didi?" Satra asked Merin. "Are we letting merchants into our prisons now?"

Merin shook his head. "You'll have to ask the rangers. My guess is she was able to provide something from the black market that the Crackling Sea couldn't get us."

The splotchy merchant looked like she hadn't had a good night's sleep in several days. Blinky stepped in front of Satra to hide her from view as the opinicus flew past.

"Selling black market goods doesn't seem to agree with her," Satra said.

"Quiet," Blinky commanded. "You are not good at sneaking."

Satra figured that was most likely true and kept her beak shut until they were inside the old opinicus prison.

The first set of doors used the same key all opinicus prisons used, adding to the theory that this one had been built around the same time as the Redwood Valley Eyrie and then forgotten until the destruction of the bridge revealed it.

Most of the cells holding Jonas loyalists used identical keys. The Ashen Weald had managed to gather a few from New Eyrie refugees, who were happy to part with them for twice their weight in metal beads. Foultner had lifted several more from New Eyrie's barracks after the starling attack.

The final cells, however, were something different altogether. Tall and ornamental, they were prisons fit for reeves—though they currently held Cherine and the unnamed blackwing spies. The key for these had proven much more difficult to come by.

Merin had a small pouch on his bracer. He dug into it with his beak and pulled out an ornamented key in the shape of a peacock. The head formed the tip of the key, and several of the feathered prongs on the other side had broken off. He gave it to the opinicus jailors, and they opened Cherine's cell.

While the guards prepared the chain and bindings for Cherine to fly him to the Strix Plateau for the trial, Satra examined the peacock key.

This one had come from Reeve Brevin's corpse. The Ashen Weald had paid a small ransom in food to get ahold of it not because they'd found the prison yet but because Satra knew of one other door the key opened: the Redwood Valley treasury located under the Reeve's Nest building.

Orlea and several other interested parties led teams of scavengers into the eyrie ruins. The Ashen Weald wasn't one of those interested parties. Instead, Satra had waited... and watched the metalworks. The first bits of scrap metal to be melted down were low quality. They'd come from harness buckles or metal supports.

A week ago, however, the metalworkers had begun to work with a fine silver. The same silver used to decorate the interior of Reeve's Nest. Now that the capitol had been found, it was only a matter of time before the treasury beneath it was unearthed.

If the vaults had cracked as the Reeve's Nest collapsed, so be it. There were worse opinici than Orlea to have access to that much currency. But if they were still locked, Satra wanted to be ready with her key.

There was one more complication, however. Both the headmaster of the university and the commander of the military had their own copies of the peacock key. Headmaster Neider had fled the night of the fire. If he'd left his key behind, Satra's spies hadn't found it in his quarters, though the latest search revealed the intriguing *Tome of the Seraph King*.

The commander at New Eyrie hadn't held a peacock key, either, suggesting that his predecessor, Commander Wolden, the opinicus who died fighting Strix, had taken his key with him to the grave.

Satra didn't like loose ends. Especially not when an eyrie's worth of treasure was at stake. Even during a war, there were opinici on both sides willing to sell goods. *Especially* during a war. Crestfall was well-situated along the trade routes and would make a useful ally if the Ashen Weald could liberate them.

The jailors finished preparing Cherine and presented him to her. She realized that, as the Kjarr, she should probably say something.

"You've been accused of espionage, arson, and crimes against the Ashen Weald," she told him. "You'll have a fair trial and a chance to defend yourself. If you're found guilty, the sentence is death. If you're found innocent, I'll send messengers to every pride in the Ashen Weald proclaiming your innocence."

"Will my home pride be allowed to participate in the trial?" he asked.

Merin looked like he wanted to speak, but Satra had asked him to refrain from doing anything that would jeopardize the fairness of the trial. Instead, he twitched his tail. The metal bracelet on it clinked against the stone floor.

"I don't believe you have a home pride, Cherine." Satra motioned to the guards to start guiding him towards the exit. "As best I can tell, you used to be a Redwood Valley scholar. But you didn't flee to New Eyrie or Orlea's pride after the eyrie fell. You stayed with Hatzel's pride for a few weeks, perhaps, but I've never heard anyone claim you're one of hers. And then you were assisting the owls."

"Padfoot," Merin said in spite of himself. "Or perhaps a spy. Should we invite the Blackwing Eyrie?"

"Mind your manners," Satra scolded Merin. "Hatzel's

pride, Orlea's pride, and the taiga pride are all welcome to watch the proceedings. I've sent invitations."

"I'm a part of the Strix Pride," Cherine said.

Whether this was true or he was just attempting to vex her, Satra didn't know. "Ninox has disappeared, so we were unable to notify her. She's currently a suspect in several murder investigations herself. I wouldn't expect your owl paramour to show up."

"Surely the accused's mate has a right to be there?" he asked.

She'd heard the rumors about him and Ninox from the inquisitors, though it was interesting to get confirmation of it. "Yes, of course. Though gryphons don't mate for life. Legally, you were only Ninox's mate from the mating flight until the egg hatched. Unless you two became fisherfolk?"

A significant amount of Satra's time had been spent trying to combine the laws and customs of seven gryphon prides and two eyries into something everyone could agree on. The fact the bog pride considered Bogwash to be a joint fisherfolk holding had just complicated matters further.

She was pretty happy with what they had figured out. The current laws felt fair and as uncomplicated as possible. The only area where things were still fuzzy was when it came to gryphons and opinici who weren't members of the Ashen Weald, such as Cherine.

"If Ninox shows up," Satra said, "I'll make sure you get to speak with her. And if you're innocent, you can go search for her yourself."

"I *am* innocent," Cherine said. "I just don't know if you'll recognize that."

Merin huffed but didn't speak up this time.

"Only time will tell." Satra led Cherine into the bright daylight and they began their flight. They'd just landed at the plateau when the messenger arrived about Askel.

30

FOULTNER'S BAD DAY

"We have a problem," Foultner said. She'd come by the kjarr nesting grounds to drop off a report and found the council chamber empty except for Triddle. He'd just discovered Askel was missing. Both he and Foultner had come east together looking for Satra, which was when they'd found out about Orlea.

Satra blinked. Apparently, she hadn't considered this possibility. Honestly, Foultner wouldn't have guessed Orlea had this in her.

"Is it true?" Satra asked.

"What?" Foultner said. "Yes, he's been kidnapped. Of course it's true."

"No, his claim about the fire." Satra looked a hundred yards away at Merin, who was guarding the prisoner. "Did Askel set it, and did Merin order him to?"

"Askel says he did it, at least according to my sources," Foultner said. Once she had food to spare, it had been easy to re-invigorate friendships with some of the merchants and poachers at Orlea's pridegrounds. Foultner ran into several along the grasslands on her way here.

"Okay," Satra said, "but *is it true?* Gryphons confess to things that aren't true all the time. I saw enough of that in the eyrie. Did he really set the fire? Or is this some sort of ploy to get us to release Cherine?"

Foultner weighed two answers in her mind, her head swaying back and forth with the choices before she settled on the left one. "Yes, it's true he set the eyrie fire. Well, both eyrie fires, if we count New Eyrie. I don't know if it's true Merin ordered him to do so."

"This was information I could have used half a year ago," Satra said. "Why didn't you know it then?"

"Spying is hard." Foultner shrugged. "I didn't find out on my own. If Askel hadn't told me in confidence, I wouldn't have known before today. And it's a lot harder to report on something someone just tells you. There's a certain etiquette and trust to it all."

"Orlea figured it out on her own," Satra said.

"Orlea has a pride at her disposal," Foultner countered. "She also got to interview all of the Reeve's Guard who survived New Eyrie and joined her pride. She's persistent. You won't find anyone with the same knack for getting information."

"You're right. I don't mean to blame you." Satra's eyes were on Merin. "She's demanding we trade Cherine for Askel, I'm guessing?"

"There were no demands." Foultner frowned. "Maybe she's waiting for us to make an offer?"

Satra was still, her crest slicked back. The lack of an offer bothered Foultner as much as the rest of it. It had to be a ploy to get Cherine back, but there'd been no demands. By all appearances, Orlea was actually going to try Askel and find him guilty.

Satra spoke slowly and quietly. "What prides would

stand with us if we execute Cherine and let them execute Askel?"

"What?" The question caught Foultner off guard. "Uh, Grenkin is with you. He's got that whole martyr thing. You don't have a closer ally in the Ashen Weald than your former enemy. If the bog pride was controlled by Thenca or Urious, I'd say them. There's no way to tell what the bog witch is thinking. I'd put beads on them leaving entirely."

"And the weald prides?" Satra prompted.

"The feathermanes will split. The medicine gryphons will stay independent; the rest would join Merin." Foultner stopped herself from overpreening. She'd prepared for a lot of things—blackwing assassins and Seraph Kings—but not this. "The fantails seem loyal. You're lucky Erlock Chartail put you in charge of them before she disappeared. The owls and parrotfaces are anyone's guess. I think they'd prefer to stand with you, but their nests are about as far from the kjarr as a pride can get."

"What happens if we return Cherine and get Askel back?" Satra asked. "Assuming that is what Orlea has planned."

"Merin and half the feathermanes will revolt." Foultner considered her words carefully. "But the rest of the Ashen Weald should hold together. They value kindness and forgiveness in the shadow of all the conflict that formed them."

Satra's stillness gave way to pacing. "There's always a chance that both Cherine and Askel are found innocent."

Here Foultner disagreed. "Askel has admitted to the crimes and named Merin. There's no innocence there. All that's left is a sentencing."

Satra somehow kept her voice even. "Then we hope Askel's sentence is forgiveness. Orlea seems like the type."

"And Cherine?" Foultner asked.

"Merin has had all winter to prepare to explain to the council why the scholar is guilty." Satra looked up at the sun. "You have about two hours to find the best witnesses you can to prove he's innocent."

Foultner swore in the way she couldn't when Henders was around. "I'll figure something out."

"Find Kia and find one of the Strix Pride," Satra said. "And send messengers to the fisherfolk and taiga. I want every so-called 'free pride' leader possible watching. I want the council to feel the weight of their decision."

Foultner turned to find Blinky, then thought of something. "What about Merin? What about the accusations against him?"

Satra's ears and tail were unreadable. "I'll handle that."

FOULTNER DELEGATED the task of finding a Strix Pride owl to Blinky and flew straight to the patch of debris Orlea called a home, landing by the giant cage out front.

Triddle was pushed against the bars, preening Askel. When Foultner landed, he padded over.

"There's no talking him out of it," Triddle said. "He thinks he's doing the right thing. And who knows? Maybe he's right. I'm proud of him."

Foultner didn't have time for this. Stress had her feathers standing on end like she was charged with static. "You know they execute traitors, right? That a thousand opinici lost their lives in the fire?"

Triddle didn't respond, but his crest and ears both drooped.

"Try harder," Foultner said before she stomped her way past some merchants to Orlea's shed of a home.

Hanging on the wall next to an empty key peg was Foultner's black armor and talons.

"That's how you got to Askel?" She hated the thought that her friendship with the fiery gryphon had led to his capture.

"Hello, Foultner," Orlea said. She was napping, probably because she'd been up all night kidnapping gryphons. "You're welcome to take them back now."

"You can't just *steal* gryphons and put them on trial," Foultner fumed. "It's not right."

"I didn't steal anyone," Orlea countered. "I politely asked him to confess and let me put him in a cage."

"You kidnapped my armor and claws," Foultner challenged.

"Those aren't gryphons or opinici, they're just things. And I borrowed them." Orlea wiped a stray bit of black fur paint off her cardinal beak. "The Ashen Weald actually broke into Ninox's home and stole her mate. I don't know why you think you have the moral heights here."

Orlea wasn't wrong, but that made Foultner madder. "What's your plan for Askel? To trade him for Cherine?"

"Askel already said he did it," Orlea said. "He wants to offer a longer confession to the inhabitants of the underbough tonight, then we'll sentence him. There's no trading here. If you want to release Cherine, and you should, you need to do that on your own."

"You and Satra are *both* crazy," Foultner said. "Askel is a good gryphon. The Redwood Valley Eyrie was in the middle of purging the weald and fisherfolk when he lit that fire, and don't you forget it."

"He'll have an opportunity to explain that," Orlea said. "You know who's a good opinicus? Cherine. I was in the medicine gryphon caves with him. He saved a quarter of the weald, and thanks to him, they evacuated most of the south before the wildfires took the nesting grounds there. Ask Triddle how he knew where to find the crates of saltpeter in the north."

"Askel is my friend," Foultner said. "Don't you dare let any harm come to him."

She stormed out of the shed and went to fetch Triddle. She had no idea how he knew about the crates of saltpeter, but she needed witnesses, and he seemed like a good starting point.

"I'm not leaving Askel's side," Triddle began, but she shut that down.

"You want to give Askel a good chance of getting out of this alive?" She didn't wait for a response. "Great, because this is how we do it. Soon as you're done, you can come back."

She looked at the sun and swore. "Go and report *directly* to Satra. Don't stop at Merin. You hear me?"

Triddle nodded. She waited for him to get into the air going in the right direction before she turned and headed to Hatzel's nesting grounds. She hated dealing with gryphons who thought they were too good to join the Ashen Weald, but if anyone could help her locate Kia in time, it was the saberbeak.

Foultner was halfway there when Orlea's words came back to her. *I was in the medicine gryphon caves with Cherine.* If Foultner was going to help Cherine, she needed to figure out where he'd gone after he escaped from Merin. Her first stop should have been talking to him instead of running around like a ground parrot with a monitor on its tail.

"MERIN'S LOOKING FOR YOU," Foultner told a very confused hook-beaked gryphon who was lounging about in the middle of Hatzel's nesting ground eating parrots and chatting like it was the Blue-eyed Festival.

She hated the thought of what might happen after Askel's testimony about Merin got out, but she'd stress about that later in the day. The thing about stress and anxiety was that it was better to pace herself.

Only after Merin's oversized brat was gone did she talk to the trio in front of her. "Tell me everything you know about Cherine."

Zeph and Hatzel looked at each other and didn't talk.

Kia spoke words, but they were useless. "He's really into calligraphy and feather pens. There used to be a flying squirrel that lived outside his nest at the university. He tried feeding it, but it would sneak in while he was at class and eat all of his food."

"No, stop, what?" Foultner said. "He's on trial *right now*. I don't have time for this."

She looked at Kia. "I need *you* to testify on his behalf, and I need to know where he was after he escaped from Merin right before the fire. And he was in a medicine gryphon cave, right? I need to know about that, too."

"I can do that. I was the opinicus in charge of finding him." Kia looked around like she'd been waiting for someone but didn't elaborate.

"And *you*," Foultner turned to Hatzel, "*you* need to go watch the trial. That's an order."

"You don't get to order me around," Hatzel said. "But I'll escort Kia there."

"You're very pushy," Zeph said.

"What I need the Reeve's Bane to do is to shut up," Foultner said. "If I had time to be polite, I would be! But I still need to track down the head medicine gryphon."

"Oh, I saw her fly overhead with Biski," said a gryphon who looked just like Zeph except taller and with a single pink paw. "She's probably already there."

"Great!" Foultner said without enthusiasm. "Let's get going, then!"

To her surprise, all three of them started flying in the right direction. She didn't really need Zeph there, but he was popular, so maybe he'd say something about fish and it'd make a difference. At this point, Foultner's panic level was high, but she'd gathered as many witnesses as she could.

It would be a miracle if Blinky could locate a Strix Pride owl in time, but Blinky was incredibly competent. She had a certain level of finesse and stealth Foultner envied. If anyone had the subtlety and grace to locate one of the missing Strix Pride, it was Blinky.

31

THE OWL GRYPHON WHO BLINKED

Blinky peed on the rocks outside of the abandoned Snowfeather nesting grounds and kicked up dust. She walked a few steps away and waited.

There was a softening to the air currents that suggested several owls were now hiding nearby. She waited for twenty minutes before one finally materialized out of the forest.

A dark brown and red gryphon walked up to Blinky. "Go pee somewhere else. You are not welcome here."

Grax. None of Blinky's scouts had caught sight of this owl gryphon since the pride disappeared. There had been a few sightings of the other owls, glimpses before they disappeared into the highlands, but none had reported seeing dark brown plumage.

That was good. That meant that Grax was probably Ninox's second in command or possibly the den mother.

"I need one of you to come with me," Blinky said. "It would be better if it was Ninox, but you will do."

"Ninox is sleeping." Grax's tail swished back and forth. She was off guard and unsure what to do.

That worked in Blinky's favor. "Then it is up to you to help Cherine. I am in charge of making sure he is found innocent. My assistant, Foultner, is gathering Hatzel, Kia, and Triddle. I need one of your pride to help."

"I'm not sure," Grax said. Blinky hid her surprise at the contraction. Even among the Ashen Weald owls, the common language's nuances gave them trouble.

"It is okay, Grax." Ninox's voice came from the forest. "I am certain Blinky would not hurt one of my pride just to get at me."

Ninox had used Blinky's name in owlish.

"It would be better if you came yourself," Blinky said. "It would mean more to the other pride leaders."

"I do not think so." Ninox appeared along the edge of the aneda trees. She'd always been well-groomed, but every feather was impeccable. She hadn't been sleeping. She was ready for action. That didn't bode well for Satra's plans today.

"I will return Grax as soon I can," Blinky said.

Once Ninox disappeared into the woods, Blinky led Grax towards the Strix Plateau. According to Ninox's brothers, none of the Strix Pride were welcome there. Blinky hoped an exception would be made for the trial. Until ten minutes ago, none of the owl gryphons on different sides of the divide had spoken since the split.

FOULTNER ARRIVED BACK on the Strix Plateau in time to find an owl problem. At least, this was what she assumed an owl problem looked like.

A dark brown owl was making harsh cooing noises at Ninox's brothers while Blinky tried to fend them off.

Foultner couldn't tell one owl from another without the help of extensive facial scarring, so she just assumed Blinky had done her job and found one of Ninox's pride.

"Do any of you speak owl?" Foultner asked her guests.

"Nobody speaks owl except the owl gryphons," Hatzel said. "Do you want me to intervene?"

Foultner was developing an appreciation for any gryphon large enough to boss Merin around, but she had to trust things would work out on their own. "No, you go take your place at the council seating. You may be called upon to testify. If you can keep the other 'free' pride leaders from leaving, that would be great."

Hatzel peeled out of formation and glided down towards the southern edge where the trial was being held. The staging area where the Ashen Weald had been born now stood as an impromptu court.

"I can help with the owls," Zeph said. "They like me."

"The owls don't like you," Foultner scoffed. "They think you cheat at hunting."

Zeph laughed, which only annoyed Foultner more. She guided them down next to Blinky.

"This is Grax," Blinky said. "She is second to Ninox, who would not come. Grax says she has spent many days with Cherine and can prove he is part of the Strix Pride and not a padfoot."

"Padfoot?" Kia asked.

"Opinici do not have this word?" Blinky asked.

"A prideless gryphon, usually a criminal of some sort," Foultner explained. She turned to Grax, who was still cooing obscenities at Ninox's brothers. "Speak in common, please. How can you prove that?"

"He taught me how to speak common," Grax said. "He said he could help me through the *lexical complications* and perhaps owlish would help fill in the lacuna inherit in the language."

Zeph and Foultner blinked.

"That does sound like something Cherine would say," Kia admitted.

"It is just words," Ninox's eldest brother said. His siblings stood on either side. "It proves nothing."

Grax cooed something that made Blinky's eye go wide, then said, "I'm better at common than you'll ever be."

The owls gasped at the use of two contractions in the same sentence.

"I guess that'll have to do." Foultner made note of Grax's owlish profanity in case she needed to use it later, then looked at the collection of owls before her. "Which one of you is in charge of the pride this month?"

The red owl with black underfeathers stepped forwards. Foultner couldn't remember his name. She only ever dealt with Blinky. "Great, that's what I thought. Take your seat on the Ashen Weald council. The trial is already going."

Foultner led Kia and Grax away from the others. Zeph followed along like a lost gryphlet.

"Do you know anything about Cherine?" Foultner finally asked him.

"I was there when Hatzel brought him to the medicine gryphon caves," Zeph answered. "I remember Younce had offered him a place to stay in the taiga, too, after he healed."

"Excellent," Foultner said, "we can implicate the leaders of two more free prides even as Askel throws accusations at Merin."

"Wait, what about Askel?" Kia asked.

"Nothing. He's just helping Orlea with a small project

unrelated to what we're doing here." Foultner pushed them towards the witness waiting area. It was probably better if they didn't know just yet. If Triddle went first, maybe they wouldn't find out until later. She really needed everyone here to testify if Cherine was going to have even a parrot's chance in a monitor den.

As they neared the circle, she saw the last of the pride leaders landing. Only the ranger lord was too weak to fly across the mountains.

Merin's voice echoed across the plateau. "Gryphons, opinici, we gather here today to put to rest the events that destroyed the Redwood Valley Eyrie..."

32

MERIN THE ACCUSER

"Gryphons, opinici, we gather here today to put to rest the events that destroyed the Redwood Valley Eyrie." Merin paused to let his words sink in. So many had been seeking closure, and he could finally bring it to them.

"There's been a lot of blame to go around. The deeds of the Blackwing Eyrie are well known—who hasn't checked their eyes for silver after developing a cold ever since the starling attacks?—but I'd like to talk about someone else's schemes."

He reached into a crate behind him and lifted out a peacock feather stained in blood. One of the fisherfolk in the audience, a small peacock, gasped. His white-eyed friend put a wing over him.

Whether it was seeing the peacock feather or the reminder of what Reeve Brevin had done to the fisherfolk, Merin didn't know. He continued, "Where the Blackwing Eyrie sought to use parasites to scourge the south of all life, Reeve Brevin sought to kill all of the gryphons."

He paced, letting the sun catch on his bracelets. "No,

that's not quite right. She may have wanted to burn out the gryphons from the weald, but there was another group she let die off through neglect."

"Neglect, in its most extreme form, is indistinguishable from malevolence." He kicked back with his leg and the old crate collapsed. Bones spilled out.

This time, it was more than one peafowl fisherfolk who raised a commotion. The Ashen Weald's council members were especially agitated.

Good. They should be.

"Who were these lost chicks and mothers?" He dug through the bones and pulled out several posters of lost and missing opinici. Some were just pieces, the rest having burnt away the night of the fire. Orlea and Ninox weren't the only ones who had teams searching through the ruins of the red eyrie.

"They were members of the Redwood Valley Eyrie. *Opinici*, not gryphons," he stressed. "Reeve Brevin gave them to her scholars to experiment on. The same scholars who created the saltpeter explosives that purged the gryphons from the weald."

He lifted a wing to gesture to the southern weald. While the kjarr nesting grounds or Crackling Sea Eyrie may have been better equipped to handle a trial, he'd chosen the Strix Plateau because it overlooked both the burned and pristine weald. It had been nearly a year since the fire, but he wanted everyone to remember it like it was yesterday.

When he'd kicked over the crate of bones, that had been his cue for several Ashen Weald rangers to light a bonfire upwind. His nares picked up the slightest hint of smoke.

Perfect.

"Do you know what opinici stayed at New Eyrie? The merchants. The scholars. The rich. The northern quarter nobles, Reeve Brevin's pets. They never came home because they were all complicit. In Reeve Brevin's utopia, they lived well. In Reeve Brevin's utopia, there were no gryphons. In Reeve Brevin's utopia, there was no underbough."

"But Reeve Brevin isn't on trial here. She's already faced her sentence." He kicked dust over the bloodied peacock feather. "Today, we're interested in the opinici who made her weapons. The opinici who made the world a more terrifying place. The opinici, without whom, her plan would have been impossible."

He returned to pacing a measured prowl around the ring. "Felicio the Phoenix discovered saltpeter and weaponized it. His son, Bario the Phoenix, discovered how to make it without having to mine. His workshop was stuffed full of the crates used to burn down the weald.

"Headmaster Neider. The opinicus who organized the scholars disappeared into the night when Brevin died. Mally the Nighthaunt was only the first. Which brings us to the last remaining scholar responsible for the night of the fire, Cherine."

He stopped in front of the accused. Cherine's metal-tipped beak shone in the light. The opinicus looked tired but defiant. His eyes kept going to one of the witnesses, a brightly colored parrot.

"Who is Cherine?" Merin asked the crowd. "To answer that, we need to look back at the reasons why Reeve Brevin wanted the weald for herself."

He dug into the pile of bones once more and pulled out a charred book. He dragged it to the center of the ring.

"When the world went up in a blaze, I wanted to try to

understand it. I think that's something we all felt, right? When I found out Reeve Brevin was dead and most of her scholars had fled, I thought I would never know what had happened."

He flipped open the book. Inside were facts and figures. "I was wrong. All I really needed to know was how to read. Their plans, their schemes, the reasons for the murders—their books contain it all!"

"I'll save you hours of sifting through this tome," he continued. "When the fire years ago allowed Brevin to create the grasslands, she began to grow crops and raise goliath birds and capybaras. You want to know to know why the reeve burnt down the weald? That's why. She'd rather give a bunch of ground squirrels a place to wallow in mud than let gryphons live."

Here was the tricky part. He took a deep breath and let it out.

Calm.

"Brevin goes into great detail. Hatzel's land should support two more capybara herds. My land would have raised starberries. The parrotface nesting grounds were to be flooded to grow craneberries."

He turned to the parrotface elder. "The next time you eat craneberries, remember there was an opinicus who believed them more valuable than the lives of your young."

He'd been watching Cherine's face. While Merin had talked, Cherine had been looking at the page the book was open to. Understanding crossed his face.

"What sort of opinicus looks at gryphon lands and calculates what's best to grow there? What sort of opinicus weighs the lives of parrotface gryphlets against a crop of berries or a herd of capybaras?"

Merin pointed at the accused. "Cherine. He calculates how much food can be grown over a set area. All of the facts and figures you see in this book? The ones Brevin used to figure out whom to murder? Cherine calculated them. This is all *his* work."

Cherine was speaking with his advocate, a medicine gryphon. Judging by the tone of their whispers, whatever they had been expecting, this wasn't it. Merin had the advantage.

"Bario the Phoenix. Impir the Mad. Mally the Nighthaunt," he listed them again. "Scary tales to frighten chicks, no doubt. But perhaps the scariest of all was the opinicus who could look at a nest of children, scribble in his notebook, and tell the reeves what value their life was worth."

He returned to the center of the ring and looked up, not at the council of leaders, but at the common members of the Ashen Weald. "Let the trial of Cherine the Calculator begin!"

KIA
BANE OF THE REDWOOD VALLEY REEVE

33

BISKI FOR THE ACCUSED

Whe Biski had been approached by Foultner regarding Cherine, she'd expected to be told the location of his secret prison. In fact, Foultner's words had been, *I need your help saving Cherine*, so it was easy to see where Biski had gotten confused.

Biski had not expected to play advocate for the accused. In fact, she wasn't sure what had happened to Cherine's assigned counsel. Something about an incident with netting and a very stern talking to by an owl with facial scars. All Foultner had said was that the previous counsel didn't have Cherine's best interests in mind.

Cherine looked a little panicked. That was good, Biski thought. She'd never actually been anyone's advocate before, but she'd had to learn the basics as part of her training. Due to their impartiality, medicine gryphons were sometimes called upon to settle disputes between prides. She hadn't studied particularly hard, but she'd been considered good enough to carry on with her studies.

"Let the trial of Cherine the Calculator begin!" Merin

concluded, indicating to Biski that it was time for her to begin.

She let out a loud, exaggerated yawn. "My goodness! I love a night time story as much as the next gryphon, but that one nearly knocked me out."

The look on Merin's face was priceless.

"Did he really say that Reeve Brevin wasn't on trial here?" She licked a paw and pretended to groom sleep out of her eyes. "That's strange. It sure sounded like she's on trial, what with her *murder journal* and all. He even went to all the trouble to dig up her grave and grab one of her feathers."

She lifted it up in her beak and waved it, emphasizing how tiny it was before dropping it. "Our dear, departed Brevin was much smaller than I remember." She licked the blood stains.

"Also a fan of craneberries judging by the taste." She turned to Merin. "Please, tell me you didn't murder some poor bird just for your parrot and squirrel show, Merry."

The blood on the feather was actual blood, but he'd have to let others inspect it to prove that. She was banking on him not wanting people to get a good look at the size of the feather.

She padded around the outer rim of the ring just as he had. Instead of stalking, she almost pranced, showing off how ridiculous it was.

"Merry here makes a lot of good points about our past. It's great that we've all been brought together. I'm extra glad that Brevin and Jonas were both stopped."

She paused in the center of ring, doing one last stretch. "There were a lot of heroes of the last year. Some fought, some healed, some stood up for what was right. All are things that have to happen for society to work.

You've probably noticed that most medicine gryphons were run ragged patching up survivors. You should ask any of the wounded if they would have survived without our care."

She turned to Cherine. "In fact, that's where I met old metalbeak here. He'd been beaten within an inch of his life. Seems strange the same gryphon who broke his beak should be prosecuting him, but I'm not the one who makes the laws."

Satra was unreadable. Biski wasn't sure if that was a good sign or a bad sign. Foultner had a reputation for being mercenary from her old days, but as far as Biski had seen, the poacher was dedicated to Satra's interests now. If the Kjarr was behind Biski's sudden assignment to help Cherine, she'd like to know.

"I think there are a lot of heroes whose names aren't nearly as well-known as they should be," Biski continued. "I saw Younce fight a floating city surrounded by sea monsters, but I also saw him break taiga neutrality to give the sick gryphons from Sandpiper's Dune a home while they recovered.

"Do you have salt? Have you eaten in the last two days? Were you able to eat preserved meat all winter long? You should thank Kia. She's a food scholar like Cherine here, and she made that happen. With *calculations*.

"You've heard tales of the incident in the bog. You may not know that the party of Ashen Weald explorers, myself included, were trapped in a pit beneath a flooded, buried eyrie. You know who saved us? A fisherfolk and an owl. I know I'm grateful to Blinky and Turresh!"

While Naya and Rorin were in the stands, Tresh was still on the shore. *Well, shoot.* Biski had forgotten that Tresh was no longer a leader. The so-called free prides and fisherfolk were allowed to ask questions or speak at the proceedings, though they didn't have a vote on the guilt or innocence.

"I'd like to talk about an opinicus who's been over-looked for far too long. The opinicus that saved the northern weald: Cherine." She pointed her wing towards the unburned weald in a mirror of Merin pointing towards the burnt weald.

"As advocate for the accused, I would like to call Kia to the ring to answer some questions." Biski sat back down next to Cherine. He looked a little calmer.

34

THE BLUE, GREEN, AND RED WITNESS

K ia listened while Biski addressed the council. "She's surprisingly good at that."

Zeph nodded. "I'm not sure what I was expecting, but both Merin and Biski surprised me."

"I hope Quess is okay," Kia said.

Zeph nuzzled her. "Xavi's watching for Quess back home while Pink Paw searches the river."

Kia held one of Cherine's feather pens for comfort. "What happens if they find Cherine guilty? And does he go back to the cell tonight? How long does a gryphon trial last?"

"Who can know? This isn't like any gryphon trial I've heard of," Zeph admitted. "In the old days, it was just hunting in someone else's territory and the punishment was food-related. This is something different, something Ashen Weald. For all I know, they could execute him without giving us a chance to save him."

Kia considered this. "Well, this trial is kind of another chance for us to rescue him. But just in case, you should check Orlea's pride for Quess; she may have checked in with the fisherfolk traders there if she saw Merin's son at Hatzel's nesting grounds. If she found where they're holding Cherine, we can rescue him tonight."

"Won't that make it look like we think he's guilty?" Zeph asked. "If he's found innocent, everything goes back to how it was."

Kia thought about the fires, the Crackling Sea, New Eyrie, and the Ashen Weald. She thought about Xavi's eldest son, about Merin's words.

"I don't think so," she said at last. "I don't know that Cherine is ever going to be safe here. If anyone believes Merin's words, he'll be in danger."

Biski was finishing up her speech and getting ready to call Kia up front.

"Slip out while I'm up there and find Quess. And what's happening with Askel," she added. "Even if Cherine is absolved before going back to his cell, we need to make sure those two are okay."

Zeph nodded and disappeared as Kia stepped into the ring to answer questions.

KIA WASN'T sure if she should face the council along the northern edge of the ring or if it was better to address Biski and Merin along the southern edge. She decided it was more polite to face the direction of whoever was asking her questions.

Biski was first up. "How long have you known Cherine?"

"More than a few years now," Kia said. "We met in a class on weald fauna. I was trying to locate some bats for a school project, and he saved me a lot of time."

"How's that?" Biski asked. "How did he save you time?"

"He pointed out that while everyone *talks* about bats, you never see any, do you?" She paused. "Basically, I was never going to finish my project on bats. He said it was a bit of a trap and suggested squirrels instead."

Biski nodded. Her mane, too young to rest against the ground, bounced a little at the movement. "You were the scholar assigned to locate Cherine, weren't you? What did you end up finding?"

"He was supposed to be watching a herd of capybaras along the grasslands," Kia explained. "With the help of some local gryphons, I found his blood-stained journal along the edge of the weald. I brought it back to the university and gave it to the headmaster, who had me present it to Reeve Brevin."

Biski made a *tsk* sound. "So Cherine's research, which Merry says was used by the reeve, was actually from an abandoned journal? He didn't give it to her directly?"

Kia nodded.

"What else was in it?" Biski asked. "Specifically, what brought you to the medicine gryphon caves."

"Cherine studies, well, *everything*." For the first time, Kia looked over at him. He looked miserable, but he perked up when he met her gaze. She felt a small pang of regret at not returning his letters or visiting him. "They sent him out there to figure out how to grow enough food to support everyone. Thing is, they underestimated how smart he was. He figured out that they were *already* growing enough food to support the Redwood Valley Eyrie. What he didn't know was that they were also trying to support New Eyrie and the Crackling Sea Eyrie."

She stood and walked a little to keep feeling in her paws and talons. "He couldn't figure out where the food was going. But in his notes, he began to see crates of something mysterious making their way into the weald. He started tracking the rangers, making notes of where they were going. He tested one of the crates and found it was full of explosives."

"This feels made up," Merin said. "Yet another scholar story."

"Are you denying that you found Cherine testing a crate?" Biski directed her question at him and not Kia.

"I'm not here to answer your questions," Merin said. "Kia's your witness."

Hatzel stood up from the guest leader section. "I think you opened yourself up for the question when you commented. You were there when Cherine was captured. Is Kia lying?"

"Yes, I saw Cherine lighting the saltpeter crate on fire," Merin said. "I don't see how it makes Kia's fabrication any truer."

"That's because you're not as smart as I am," Biski chirped. "But not many gryphons are. It doesn't make any sense for Cherine to light the saltpeter on fire if he's the one sneaking it into the forest. No other opinicus tested the saltpeter."

"One of the saltpeter crates went off by Hatzel's nesting grounds," Merin said. "That happened before the night of the fire."

"With all due respect, pride leader," Kia spoke with a grace she didn't necessarily feel, "I believe that was one wounded ranger. Hatzel's nesting grounds were attacked when the rangers found out I was speaking before the gryphon pride leaders at your nesting grounds. One of the dying lit the box on fire before he passed. It was a last ditch attempt after they'd lost."

Merin stood and preempted Biski's next question. "Scholar Kia—or is that apprentice?—I feel you've misled us a little. Are you and Cherine lovers?"

"Are we...?" Kia asked. "Certainly not. You've had him locked up for half the year and nobody has been able to see him. Unless you two have a secret romance, I don't imagine he's had any lovers since you stole him from Ninox's pride."

"Before that," Merin clarified.

"Yes. The relationship ended two years ago, though." Kia realized now she should have said something earlier. She didn't like being called a liar, especially not when she had left out something important.

"That must have been rough. I hear opinici mate for life. You have my condolences," Merin said.

"We weren't mated," Kia protested. "We were just dating. I don't know if there's a gryphon equivalent. Courtship?"

"Still, I can imagine you were fairly upset with him. It's natural for opinici to break up on bad terms, isn't it?" Merin's voice had a genuine quality to it Kia didn't trust.

"It was hard for a while," Kia said, "but we were friends. I believe our past friendship is why the headmaster asked me to find Cherine."

"Headmaster Neider, Blackwing Eyrie spy?" Merin commented. "Well, that's very big of you to follow Neider's orders to find Cherine. Still loving your close friend after you break up is admirable. Still loving and caring for him while you lie for him."

Kia's feathers ruffled. "That's not what I said."

"I'm afraid Cherine used your past love to blind you to the truth," Merin said. "He knew you'd say nice things about him."

Kia started to open her beak again, but Biski held up a paw, her sign that Kia should stop talking.

The mismatched feathermane looked up into outer ring. "Pride Leader Hatzel, since you were nice enough to speak earlier and you've witnessed Kia and Cherine together, how would you describe their relationship?"

"They never shut up," Hatzel said. Several of her pride in the audience laughed in agreement. "They argue all the time. They think that because their curtain blocked out the light, it also blocked out sound, but anyone who has come within a hundred pawprints of them has heard their bickering."

Biski nodded knowingly, much to Kia's chagrin. "So not, as the opinici might say, love birds?"

"Is that a question?" Merin asked.

"No, I suppose not," Biski replied. "I just don't put much stock in your theory that Kia is here testifying two years after an opi relationship ended because she's trying to win Cherine back from Ninox. I've broken a lot of hearts in my days. That's just not how it works."

"Are we done with this witness?" the parrotface elder said. "Not that hearing about the accused's love life isn't interesting, but I don't have all day."

"I apologize, pride leader," Merin said.

"I'd apologize, but that's actually my next line of questioning," Biski said. "Kia, go sit down. Grax, you're up next!"

35

THE OWL WITNESS

M erin objected before the owl gryphon could reach the center of the ring. "Ninox's pride are wanted in relation to the night time murders. We should be locking her away, not asking her questions."

"Strix Pride," Grax corrected him. "We're called the Strix Pride."

Strix's red-and-black son ruffled his feathers and said something to Grax in owlish.

Grax cooed back something fierce.

"Language," Satra cautioned.

Merin knew Satra didn't speak a word of owlish, but both owl gryphons straightened up.

"I won't be arresting any witnesses today," the Kjarr continued. "Grax, you're free to return home after you've testified. We'd appreciate your help in solving several murders, but that's a case for another time."

Grax nodded.

"Biski, your witness," Satra finished.

Merin turned back to his current favorite child and

whispered, "One of Ninox's pride doesn't just show up on their own. Something is going on. Find out what."

His blue-feathered offspring bowed his head and disappeared. Merin had a problem on his paws. This should have been a simple trial. There shouldn't be a counsel for the accused, let alone witnesses. He was no longer certain of his victory.

He looked to his fourth favorite child with brown plumage. He considered handing over the peacock key but decided it may be better to hold off on that. "Stand guard by our emergency witness, just in case. Bring him over if I send word and the key."

Grax had finished her introduction and was now answering questions about Cherine. "I spoke a little common before the fire. Strix required the new gryphlets learn it. But I spoke it badly, like him."

She pointed her paw at Ninox's brother. He squinted back but didn't coo anything obscene.

"How did you improve?" Biski said. "Your common is excellent. I know how hard it is to learn."

"I sat with Cherine, guarding the prisoners. He talks a lot." Grax looked towards Kia, who nodded her agreement. "So when he'd say a word, I'd say it back to him. Contractions are hard. Words should not combine like that. But I figured it out. You think of it as a new word, not two words."

Merin rolled his eyes. "The prosecution is willing to stipulate that Cherine can make words with his beak. I imagine with his tiny taloned claws he can knit warm little harnesses for parrots, too. Is this relevant?"

"It goes to character," Biski challenged. "Do you know any other owls who had a gryphon or opinicus sit down and work with them on the oddities of common? I don't.

But if opposing counsel is getting bored, I can help wake him up. Hey Grax, Merry here thinks Cherine and Kia still have something going. Tell me about Cherine's love life."

Cherine, who had been ordered not to speak without permission, held his face in his talons.

Merin could relate. "I object."

"To mating?" Biski said. "You have twelve offspring."

Merin looked helplessly towards Satra for help.

"Biski, we're not here for the scandal," Satra said. "Ask what you need Grax to testify to and leave it at that."

The crowd in the outer ring looked disappointed, especially the fantails.

"Ninox mated Cherine this last season," Grax said. "They have two gryphlets."

"I don't see how Cherine having two eggs with Ninox is relevant," Merin said.

"Three," Grax corrected.

"What?" he asked.

"Three eggs," she said. "Two gryphlets. One opinicus chick."

"I think it's as relevant as any of the things you asked Kia." Biski shrugged. "Here's the real reason I called Grax here today, though. Is Cherine a member of the Strix Pride?"

Grax nodded. "Yes."

"So Cherine wasn't a padfoot," Biski continued. "He was kidnapped from another sovereign pride that wasn't at war with the Ashen Weald?"

"Correct," the owl gryphon said. "He's one of us."

"I'd argue they *were* at war with the Ashen Weald," Merin grumbled.

"How's that?" Biski asked. "Ninox helped secure the

pass to the Crackling Sea for the wingtorn. Six of her scouts were with us all the way to New Eyrie."

"I'd argue they weren't her scouts, they were her brother's scouts," he countered, "but if she was really our ally, then why was she hiding Cherine and the blackwing scouts from us?"

Several audience members raised their voices as they learned this for the first time. He could see Satra's disapproval.

Well, they'd figure it out when the cockatiel comes to testify tomorrow.

"We were not... not allies," Grax protested. "The black-wings were caught by the Strix Pride in the Owlfeather Highlands."

Biski interrupted her. "Ninox isn't on trial here."

"She's right," Satra said. "I realize the nature of Cherine's capture raises questions on both sides, but let's keep this to whether or not he's guilty of treason."

Merin couldn't quite figure Satra out. Half the time, she sided with Cherine. By limiting the trial to exclude both Cherine's capture and Ninox, however, she prevented Biski from claiming that Merin had been wrong to arrest him at all.

That made Grax a much less worrisome witness.

Merin cleared his throat. "No more questions from me. Biski?"

The mismatched medicine gryphon seemed to be thinking. At least, that's what it looked like to him. She had a kind of blank-yet-determined look on her blue jay face. The wind ruffled her mane.

He'd always been suspicious of Biski. She was too close to the free prides and fisherfolk for him to trust her loyalties. She hid behind the medicine gryphon's sanctuary oaths, using them as a shield.

"I believe Grax had something she wished to ask." Despite the subject of Biski's words, she was looking at Satra.

As was Grax. "You should have released Cherine to be there when his eggs hatched. You should let him go tonight to see them."

The temporary representative from the fantails finally spoke up. "I don't believe there's a safe way to take Cherine there and get him back in his cell, Kjarr."

"Let's compromise," Satra said. "If he's found innocent, he'll be home soon enough and can see them for himself. If not, Ninox can bring them here herself to see him after he's sentenced."

"Mating season is over," Merin protested. "There's no reason to honor that request."

"You failed to honor it during the season," Biski protested. "You didn't let him out then. This is the right thing to do. He didn't even get to see his mate during that time. You've held him for months. He didn't see Ninox once since his arrest."

"Merin's right," Satra conceded, "but the laws are new. I'd err on the side of compassion, if the Ashen Weald is with me?"

The other leaders nodded their heads, then turned to look at Merin. For a moment, he'd been so busy acting as an advocate of justice that he'd forgotten his part as a pride leader in the Ashen Weald.

He wanted to deny Cherine any access to the chicks and Ninox. He had a hard time believing there was any love between those two. Merin tended to forget his mates entirely until after the gryphlets hatched, as he assumed they did about him. But he knew opinici were different, and the Ashen Weald was a place for both species.

"In general, I agree," he said at last, "and I'm sure we'll spend hours discussing it after the trial. For now, if Ninox is willing to turn herself over, I have no problem if she sees Cherine tonight since she couldn't see him before now."

Grax and Biski both tried to protest that it wasn't safe for Ninox, but Satra held fast. If the so-called Strix Pride's leader was willing to turn herself in, she'd be permitted to see Cherine.

Merin was feeling pretty good about how the surprise witness turned out until Biski announced the next one.

"Next up," the feathermane chirped, "I'd like to hear from Triddle."

36

THE WATER PHOENIX WITNESS

B iski chirped encouragement to Triddle, who looked overpreened. Based on Foultner's information, he was going to need his paw held through this.

Merin was unreadable. That was good, Biski thought. The only reason to look unreadable was if what your opponent could read into your stance was something in their favor.

"Thank you for taking time to come up here to the plateau," she said. "I understand you helped with the pathway through the mountains and are doing exciting things with hot springs. The Ashen Weald thanks you for all of your hard work."

Triddle nodded slightly. Biski hadn't had time to tell him what the questions would be about.

"Loyalty to the Ashen Weald is important," she contin-ued. "We've all heard about your exploits at New Eyrie. You're...a water phoenix of sorts. Not many gryphons can say they brought down the walls of an eyrie!"

Still no response.

That was fine. She just needed to establish him as a hero before Merin got going. "So help me out. We all know Cherine was captured by Merin's pride. How did he escape? Where did he go?"

"How would Triddle know that?" Merin asked.

Hatzel shifted in the stands.

"Do you know the answer?" Satra asked. At Triddle's nod, she added, "I guess we'll find out, then."

"Take your time," Biski said. "In your own words, what happened?"

Triddle didn't look at Merin. "Cherine was in bad shape. We were hiding him in a cave, and part of his beak had broken off. I thought he'd get beak rot and die if I didn't do anything. He was kind and smart. So I... I rescued him."

"How did you do that?" Biski asked.

Triddle looked up into the stands at Hatzel, who nodded. Merin's stony stance broke a little with a twitch of the tail.

"I had a theory that the underground river in the cave was the Snowfeather River after it disappeared underground." Triddle's crest perked up every time he said *theory* or *river*. "So I borrowed some harnesses from the eyrie trash heap, along with some rope, and pulled him upstream."

"You're a nice gryphon, Triddle. No one could fault your empathy." Merin's eyes flicked to Hatzel and back. "In fact, I'd go so far as to say that someone preyed upon it."

"Tsk," Biski scolded as Merin walked in front of them.

"Of course, you're a small gryphon." Merin bumped Cherine, forcing him to stand. "Our accused opinicus is fairly large. Probably a gryphon ancestor or two there, eh? You pulled him all the way out of the water on your own?"

"Cherine's not big, he's just lanky," Biski protested.

"Let Triddle answer, Biski," Satra chastised.

Triddle didn't respond at first. A nod from Hatzel finally opened his beak. "I asked Hatzel to help me. She did the heavy lifting."

"You broke into my territory and stole my prisoner?" Merin accused Hatzel.

"The Snowfeather River is in my territory," she challenged. "Your father's paw print marks the territory there. It was his gift to me when I took over the copper hawk and magpie prides. Triddle was visiting us, and, unlike you, we don't capture every guest who flies overhead and break their beaks off. Are you really going to lecture me on pride boundaries after you stole Cherine from Ninox's?"

"I call Hatzel as a witness," Merin said. "It seems she knows more than she told us the night of the fire."

Hatzel stood to glide down into the ring, dislodging several opinici with her impressive wingspan before Biski stopped her.

"One moment!" Biski said. "I have more questions for Triddle. I want to know what happened later."

One of Triddle's ears went sideways with confusion. "I only saw Cherine again the night before we went to the eyrie, when I went by the medicine gryphon caves. He was still unconscious."

Merin was busy giving the old medicine gryphon a dirty look. He only looked back when Biski's questions got more pointed.

"So," she said, "how did you know how to stop the fire?"

"Oh!" Triddle perked up again. "Cherine's journal. He'd been tracking the rangers in the woods, so he knew where the crates of explosives were. We grabbed as many as we could find."

"So Cherine saved the northern weald?" Biski asked.

"That's a stretch," Merin countered. "His journal let others do it. It's not the same thing."

"You were about to skewer him because Reeve Brevin used his journal for evil," Biski countered. "Now you're going to say it doesn't matter what his information is used for?"

"It isn't just that the crates didn't explode," Triddle added. "Kia said that the oil spread the fire. So if we exploded the right locations, it could stop the spread from the fires we missed. I think *starve the fire* was how it was phrased."

Grax cooed something from the sidelines.

Triddle didn't understand the words, but something dislodged. "Oh! That's right, we used them to blow up the bridge, too. Otherwise, the southern weald fire would have spread over Glacial Run."

Kia tapped Biski's tail and whispered, "We used the crates to blow up the dam to flood the grasslands, too."

Biski looked behind her and realized that Zeph was missing. It wasn't good form to lose witnesses. She would have liked him to testify to that.

Instead, she asked Triddle, "Didn't you also use the crates gained from Cherine's journal to flood the grasslands to keep the eyrie fire from spreading to the weald?"

"Oh! Yes! It's exciting, using fire to make water fight fires," he stumbled over his tongue twister. "And we found this powder that stopped fires near the boxes. We used that to keep the eyrie fire from spreading, too!"

"Sounds like a lot of gryphons and opinici owe Cherine's research a debt of gratitude." Biski turned to Merin. "Heck, your own home would be ash if not for Cherine, right, Merry?"

"You should ask the fantails and feathermanes how grateful they are for his journal." Merin stood tall. "That attitude, only looking out for one's own well-being or the well-being of just their small part of the weald, burned the night of the fire. I'm not here because I'm thankful that my small strip of hunting grounds survived. I'm here for the prides who lost everything that night. I want to see them get justice."

He stopped in front of Biski and stared her down. "The crates of explosives didn't go off at my home, you say? Ask the feathermanes about the crates dropped on their nests. When Erlock returns, ask her about being lit on fire and only saved due to the intervention of Satra and the wingtorn. You can't excuse a scholar who caused the deaths of thousands because he saves thirty. You can't *calculate* life like that."

Biski puffed up her little mane and stood on her back paws to look him in the eye. "I'm not saying there weren't bad opinici who did terrible things. I'm not saying no one is responsible for the weald and eyrie fires. I'm saying Cherine isn't one of them."

"That's something the eyries and prides should decide on their own," Merin said. "Triddle, you look exhausted. Go back to our nesting grounds. Your pride will make sure you're taken care of."

Two of Merin's offspring landed to escort Triddle out of the ring. He cast a helpless look at Biski as he disappeared.

She had a bad feeling about this.

Merin looked back up at the stands. "Now, if we have time for one more witness today, perhaps Hatzel would be willing to answer a few questions?"

37

THE SABERBEAK WITNESS

Hatzel missed her cue. As Biski and Merin postured, she received an unexpected messenger.

"I found out what Foultner meant about Askel and Orlea being up to something," Zeph said. As the witnesses were being interviewed, he'd flown down to Orlea's nesting grounds and back. He filled Hatzel in on Askel starting the eyrie fire on Merin's orders. He'd just finished when Satra's prompt came.

"Pride Leader?" the head of the Ashen Weald prompted. "We can't compel you, of course, but you seemed chatty earlier. We'd love to hear what you have to say."

Hatzel adjusted her feathers. The gryphons she'd knocked down earlier when she spread her wings were already taking cover. She glided down into the center of the ring. Where the other witnesses had settled down on their back paws or all fours, she remained standing.

Merin stood to match her. The ring seemed much smaller with the two of them squaring off.

"Why did you help rescue Cherine?" Merin asked.

"I didn't know it was him," she said. "I met Kia earlier in the day, so I knew a scholar was missing. I didn't know who he was or that you'd kidnapped him. I only found out when we pulled him out of the river. At that point, he was nearly dead, so I left it up to the medicine gryphons to sort out."

"Can we ask the medicine gryphons about that?" Merin's voice showed he already knew the answer to his question.

"You may ask us absolutely anything," the old medicine gryphon said from her perch of soft leaves. "As long as it isn't about patients, of course."

"How kind," Merin monotoned before looking back to Hatzel. "What did you and Cherine talk about as you dragged him through the scree to the medicine caves?"

"He said he'd discovered explosives, and the weald was in danger. He urged me to warn everyone," Hatzel said. "That's why I called for the meeting. Orlea arrived soon after, wounded from her run-in with some rangers, and warned us that the eyries were capturing gryphons and cutting off their wings. When I returned home, Kia provided Cherine's journal and Satra's information, and I called the meeting of prides."

"Orlea, Satra, and Cherine were conspicuously absent in your original telling that night," Merin said.

"That's not true," the old medicine gryphon said. Her voice was rough and sticky, as always. "Satra was definitely mentioned. Parrotface here called her a little murderess."

The parrotface elder puffed up. "I suppose I did. I apologize. You've proven yourself a good leader, Satra. Even the taiga pride speaks well of you. If that doesn't put light to the dark rumors, I don't know what does."

Satra inclined her head.

"*Cherine* wasn't mentioned that night," Merin corrected. "Why not?"

"Well, I knew you were trying to kill him," Hatzel said. "I didn't really want you invading the medicine gryphon's cave to steal him. Before you get all huffy, remember that we can call Grax back to testify as to how you respect pride sovereignty."

The air was tense between the two pride leaders. A lost bee flew through the ring, passing right between Hatzel's saber beak and Merin's hooked beak on its way to find flowers.

"It's nice of you to care so much for him," Merin said. "Considering you'd met him only once?"

"I think kindly towards most gryphons or opinici who warn me about dangers," she countered.

"I see. Enough to offer him and Kia a place to hide in your pride?" he asked.

"It's as Biski says." Hatzel kept her eye on Merin. "He helped save the northern weald and gave us time to evacuate much of the southern weald. Kia was instrumental in taking down Reeve Brevin."

"So it was to say thank you?" Merin asked.

She thought. "No, that's not quite right. Many opinici and gryphons were starting over after the fire. They'd lost their homes, their careers, their possessions, their health, and sometimes the lives of their loved ones. I didn't turn away any who came to my pride seeking help."

"Including one of the rangers fleeing the battle of Sandpiper's Dune," Merin added.

"It feels like you're putting everyone on trial here except yourself," Hatzel said. She looked up to Satra. "You said free pride leaders may ask questions?"

Satra nodded.

"Excellent." Hatzel turned back to Merin. "Did you order Askel to burn down the Redwood Valley Eyrie?"

"You can ask questions of the witnesses, not of the advocates," Satra clarified. There was a murmur from the crowd. The question had seemed fanciful, but her comment and Merin's failure to immediately deny it was causing a stir.

Hatzel ignored Satra. She wanted answers. "Askel is in a cage outside the eyrie he burned down. He says he did it on your orders. He's awaiting sentencing."

Merin remained quiet.

"When Askel slipped away during the kjarr gryphlet rescue, I thought he was going to meet you," she continued. "But when I found you later, you were all by yourself. Did you order him to burn down the underbough then?"

The crowd quieted.

Hatzel remained in a hunter's crouch opposite Merin. "Ah, my mistake. I thought tonight was about justice for the victims of the fires, plural. In the Ashen Weald court, Cherine claims innocence. In the opinicus court, Askel admits guilt."

There was no quiet this time.

"Yes," Merin said. "I ordered Askel to burn down the eyrie."

38

THE NIGHT OF THE FIRE

Merin's memories were thick like oil. He was slow to move through them, and he left them covered in a film.

The night before the conflagration, he sat in a circle with the leaders of the weald prides. To his left, Hatzel advocated for saving Satra and then getting out of the eyrie. Though less than a year ago, she looked much younger. Her stomach and chest were unscarred. Her beak had not yet tasted her lover, Vosk's, blood. She kept looking north, the direction Kia and Zeph had disappeared to.

The parrotface elder bickered with Erlock Fantail, her forty-two feathers still intact, and Zrim Feathermane, not yet torn apart by starlings. Strix had a strange look in his eye. He knew more than he was saying. When Kia revealed the rangers sneaking into everyone's territory, he only seemed surprised that no one else knew.

The pride leaders had never gotten along. The old prides saw Hatzel and Merin as curiosities. If they'd had their way, the small prides would have been absorbed into the others. Even now, the fantails and feathermanes saw the crates of saltpeter as a northern problem. They didn't yet know that their own hunting grounds were rigged to explode.

A plume of fire lit up the night. Outside of Hatzel's nesting grounds, the first crate went off. Not rigged with oil, the fire was quickly contained. Only a scorched crater, a crater that still existed today, remained. All of the pride leaders agreed that Satra must be saved and the rest of the crates located.

But the night didn't end there. Askel had disappeared. While Triddle searched the nesting grounds for him, Merin ventured out to the scene of the explosion and found his wayward pridemate.

"Hard to look away, wasn't it?" he asked Askel.

The small, chestnut-colored gryphon was examining the few opinicus supplies that hadn't burned. "I don't think he set it right. The opinicus, I mean."

There was no knowing who the opinicus had been. Tiny bits of him had been flung across the weald. Of course, that mystery was short-lived by the arrival of the gryphon who was the real mastermind behind the eyrie fire.

Merin felt the soft sound of an owl nearby. It was a whisper barely perceptible. A single word spoken from a hundred yards above him at his left ear.

Move.

He stepped back, pulling Askel with him, as the body of a dead ranger fell out of the canopy.

The night sky flowed down after it, coalescing over the corpse as Strix.

"Crackling Sea," the owl pride leader said. "Hatzel's brightly colored scholar said there was only one. She lied.

The forests are full of them. Full of their saltpeter, their wildfire in a box."

"What's the Crackling Sea?" Askel asked.

Strix pulled himself up close. He was large for an owl. At night, there was no line between the darkness and his feathers. "It is by the kjarr. A lake larger than the weald. The water is salt. When the lightning cries out from above, the sea cries back, flashes of blue and green."

Kjarr was the word that stuck in Merin's mind. "You said Jun the Kjarr was your friend. Did you know they'd..." the words didn't come to Merin at first. He was having a hard time understanding he lived in a world where gryphons were hunted, where their wings were chopped off. "Wingtorn. Did you know he was wingtorn?"

"No." There was a touch of emotion to Strix's voice that hadn't been there before. "I was in the kjarr only briefly. I didn't know what happened to him until now."

Askel was shivering. Merin put a wing around the smaller gryphon.

Strix lifted the dead opinicus up with one paw, then ripped his harness off with the other. He pecked through the pockets, tossing a flint and dried tinder fungus on the ground and pointing at Askel.

"When you were young, you would sneak out at night," the owl said. "You spent hours with the flint, holding it in your beak, striking it against things to make sparks."

Askel froze.

"The plateau isn't my only home," Strix continued. "All of the night is my hunting territory. Wherever darkness shines, I am there. Weald, kjarr, Crackling Sea—even the eyries themselves. I have seen what our enemies do. But I have also seen what you do, Askel."

Even now, Merin didn't know the extent of Strix's knowledge. He would soon take that knowledge with him to the grave.

"These opinicus tools, the ones they used to try to burn down our home." The owl nudged one with his beak. "I can think of only one gryphon who knows how to use them."

Askel picked up the flint in his beak. He struck it against the rocks, igniting the dried tinder fungus.

Merin stomped it out before anyone saw.

"Opinici." Strix spoke without opening his slight beak. Where his sons knew only basic common, their father's words seemed to resonate within whomever he spoke to. "They will hunt you. They will burn most of you alive, but the rest, they will hold you down and tear off your wings. Then they will send you to kill other gryphons. They are doing it now with the fisherfolk. But there is an answer."

Merin looked at the dead ranger. Something had been feeding on it. Strix enveloped Askel and most of Merin with his wings, stopping anyone from overhearing his next words. When he spoke, Merin could smell carrion on the owl gryphon's breath.

The plan was simple. All it required was three gryphons and a few minutes in the center of the eyrie. It took Strix no time to explain, and then he disappeared into the night, leaving Askel and Merin alone with the kill.

"We don't have to do that," Askel said. "We could just save the Kjarr's daughter and the gryphlets and leave."

Merin was cold. He thought of his eldest son, of his father before he spoke. "The world seems large, Askel, but it's not. I sent my son west to find the starlings, but he never returned. No gryphon flies in the kjarr. The sea to the north is lightning. There's nowhere for us to go. The weald is our home. We live here or we die here."

With Strix gone, the night birds began to chirp again. Askel and Merin sat in silence. Merin was having doubts until the smaller gryphon said, "I don't want them to tear off Triddle's wings."

Merin looked down at the flint and tinder fungus. He used a large paw to pull them closer to Askel. "You can't tell Triddle."

MERIN'S EYES refocused in the present. He reiterated his statement. "I ordered Askel to burn down the eyrie."

"What?" Hatzel asked.

"Wait, what?" Biski echoed.

Merin's posture relaxed. "I ordered Askel to locate the butcheries where the flammable oil was stored, use the saltpeter taken from Cherine, and light it all on fire."

"Why?" This time, the question came from Satra. "You had to know the eyrie had thousands of inhabitants."

He looked her in the eye. "Everyone here wants to blame Reeve Brevin for the fires and Jonas for the wing-torn, but I think you know better. The northern quarter, the scholars, the military—it was the eyrie itself that was trying to kill us."

Satra didn't disagree with him, so he went on. "If we'd saved you and the gryphlets and left, the armies at the Crackling Sea and New Eyrie would have been recalled. The weald would have been purged by metal talon instead of flame. Jun, Urious, Thenca, and the wingtorn on this side of the taiga had nowhere to go. The eyrie was going to burn down the weald and raise livestock on its corpse. So I killed the eyrie."

Hatzel kept her eye on him.

He ignored her and paced, looking for a songbird opinicus to make eye contact with. "I'm sorry for the underbough opinici who died in the fire. I believe Reeve Brevin would have starved you eventually. I believe killing the eyrie freed you. To the reds who joined gryphon prides—we've kept you fed. We've kept you warm and safe.

"To the blues, I have a lot of respect for who you've become, but think of who you were before Jonas died. Reeve Brevin's aid came with a price. She provided food, you provided the wingtorn."

Not a single fantail in the audience showed signs of disagreeing with him. Of the feathermanes, only the medicine gryphons disapproved. There were only a pawful of Redwood Valley opinici in the audience.

"I don't mind standing in judgement for my actions," he continued. "I honestly believe both the opinici and gryphons of the Ashen Weald and free prides are better off because of it. But I'll let the underbough hear my words and judge me. Unlike Cherine, I don't deny the things I've done."

Up top, Foultner was whispering something to Satra. The Kjarr stood and addressed the audience. "I believe we've lost focus. We'll reconvene tomorrow. Cherine will be returned to his prison. Grax, tell Ninox to meet me at the Parrotface nesting grounds if she wishes to see her mate tonight."

With the help of Merin's pridemates and the Ashen Weald rangers who were providing security, the crowd dispersed, leaving Merin and Hatzel alone in the ring.

"More opinici died in the Redwood Valley than gryphons died in the weald," the saberbeak pride leader said. "I don't know how many the blackwings killed at the Crackling Sea. Did you kill more or fewer? How can you fly with that weight on your wings?"

Merin didn't back down, had never backed down from his closest neighbor. "Your entire pride is only alive because I had the courage to do what you were too afraid to."

"That night, the prides decided, together, to just save Satra and get out," Hatzel said. "You agreed, too. What changed?"

Strix wrapped his wings around the two gryphons. "With one spark, you need not ever be afraid again. With one spark, you go from prey to predator. With one spark, the eyrie will never threaten your pride again."

"The eyrie killed my father and didn't care," Merin said. "They were hungry, and their goliath birds stampeded right through our home. We didn't fight back then. We did nothing. We let them continue their experiments on the grasslands. Our lives as gryphons meant nothing to them."

To Hatzel's credit, she did seem to be trying to understand. She'd always had a good relationship with his father, something he'd been unable to replicate with her.

"The next time an eyrie got hungry, it created the wingtorn. And we did nothing. Didn't even notice." Merin was chastising himself as much as Hatzel. "And then the eyrie's hunger, the reeves' hunger, grew again, and we found it at our threshold once more. Saving Satra was never going to stop it, Hatzel. You can't feed an eyrie. Its hunger knows no end. You can only kill it."

Hatzel shook her head, but he knew it was true.

"It took one spark," he challenged. "Can you tell me we aren't better off now?"

"It was wrong." Her voice had conviction.

"So long as you appreciate that the only reason you're here to criticize me is because of the actions I took," he said. "As much as I'd like to stay here all night, I need to check on Askel and prepare tomorrow's witness."

He didn't turn back to see if Hatzel followed him. In the year since the fire, he'd never regretted his decision once. He hoped no harm came to Askel, but he knew they'd made the right choice.

39

THE FREE PRIDES, REDUX

Zeph feared for the worst until an opinicus messenger arrived with word that right after he'd left to catch Hatzel up, Orlea had found his missing fisher-folk and wanted to meet by the Summer Falls. Unlike the previous clandestine meetings, this message specifically said to bring gryphons who could fight with them.

Thanks to the flyway through the canopy, Zeph, Hatzel, Pink Paw, and ten of their best hunters arrived at the collapsed dam without attracting unwanted attention. It was dusk, the best time of day to remain unseen by both the diurnal and nocturnal inhabitants of the weald.

Pink Paw insisted on scouting the area first. She and Xavi often went hunting snakes in this territory. She returned with word that the area was clear but full of strange scents.

"Chalky and dry, like the taiga," she said. "But also sour. Maybe the taiga scouts are searching for new caves."

"Let the other leaders know as they approach," Hatzel ordered. "Just in case they want to find a new location."

Orlea, Quess, and Kia arrived on their own.

"I thought you said to bring hunters?" Zeph asked.

"They're all busy guarding Askel," Orlea replied. "Merin's there talking to him. I figured I'd let the gryphons take care of this one."

"We could have used them," Kia said. "We ran into scavengers when we skirted the Redwood Valley ruins."

"Padfeet?" Zeph asked.

Orlea shook her head. "A little of everything. Ashen Weald, free prides, even a few New Eyrie opinici come home to try their luck."

"What're they searching for?" Zeph asked.

"Beads, metal, red fern," Kia began.

"Surely that's gone by now," Zeph said. "Between the fire and the months since, there can't be anything of value left, can there?"

"Reeve's Nest," Orlea said. "The eyrie's coffers are still buried somewhere. Whoever locates them is going to find themselves the richest opinicus in the south."

Kia tapped her beak. "Strix and Wolden fought in the Reeve's Nest, didn't they? Ninox located Wolden's body. Shouldn't she know where it is?"

Orlea was about to say something when they were interrupted by the final arrival, the old medicine gryphon. She looked worse for wear after having to sit through the trial.

"I sent a fast flyer to Younce," she barked once she'd settled in. "He says he wants no part of what we're planning after Orlea stole Askel from the taiga."

Zeph frowned. While he didn't expect Younce to help with the rescue, it would be nice to have him here. "I suppose it's just us, then. We're the only free prides."

"Well, we do have one more guest," Kia said. "I caught

up to the brown-feathered owl before she returned north."

From the direction Kia had come, Zeph heard cooing. "Did she convince Ninox?"

"No." Grax, the brown owl gryphon, came through the underbrush. "She's meeting with Satra. I'm here to listen, not help."

"She isn't worried it's a trap?" Zeph asked.

Hatzel sniffed the air and looked back at the water. Her tail twitched.

Grax didn't reply to his question. Instead she looked to Quess. "You have a fisherfolk here, too?"

Quess looked ragged, but Zeph was glad she'd survived.

"What happened to you?" he asked her. "Was Cherine in the cave?"

"Well, he wasn't in *that* cave," she began. She filled them in on her adventure—and associated nap on the ride back north with the fisherfolk caravan. She'd met with Lei and Piprik coming back from the trial there, though they'd wisely remained behind with Carru and Gressle.

Zeph listened intently, but kept his eyes on Hatzel, who seemed aware of something that the copper hawk scouts weren't. Pink Paw was pawing at the water's edge curiously. "Well, we know where he's at. Now we just need to get him free. No chance the cave has a back entrance, is there?"

Quess shrugged. "I didn't go inside. There seemed to be a good number of Ashen Weald rangers guarding it."

"Well, now we know where the missing food was going." Kia looked crestfallen. "How are we going to get him out of there?"

"We could let Ninox handle it," Orlea suggested. "I don't see any other options. We're not warriors. We're hunters and poachers. You can't fight into a small cave and rescue someone without violence."

Grax remained silent.

"Unless Ninox already knew?" Kia prompted Grax. "Or is already headed there now?"

"How did she find out?" Zeph asked. Then he had a sudden sinking feeling. "She didn't find out from the blackwings, did she?"

Grax preened a stray feather. Orlea averted her gaze.

"Then why not tell us?" Kia asked. "We don't love the northern eyries, but we'd help get Cherine to safety."

Zeph took his eyes away from the river. "Unless it isn't Ninox who's going in there to get Cherine. Is it the black-wings' assassin?"

Grax remained silent.

Kia put it together first. "Are we here because Ninox wanted us away from the cave?"

Grax blinked. "You should be safe here."

Behind them, the water began to churn. It seemed Ninox's uneasy allies had a different idea about their safety.

40

JAILBREAK

C herine rubbed at his wing muscles. A flight so short wouldn't normally strain his wings, but Merin's children had roughed him up on the flight back, and he wished he had access to a hot springs.

"How was the trial?" the cockatiel asked with unusual cheer. He was surrounded by the dried leaf wrappers his daily dose of fern came in. "Think they're going to let you go?"

Cherine shook his head. "It would be nice, but something else is going on. The opinicus pride is holding a gryphon and saying he's responsible for the fire."

Once Cherine was back in his cell, Merin left to go spend time with Askel. The large room with the three fancy cells had two braziers across from the prisoners. Usually, these were left unlit. With the trial going on, some kind soul had left them ablaze, giving the cave a warmth it usually lacked.

The cockatiel's blackwing friend was back, though worse for wear.

"Is he going to be okay?" Cherine motioned to the scout. "He looks terrible."

"They're getting frustrated he won't talk." The cockatiel forger watched the door with an intensity he'd lacked for the past few months.

Cherine could hear the distant sound of a blue jay. "Did the blackwings do something to his syrinx, or is he just particularly quiet?"

The scout glared.

"Hey, I kept you fed, warm, and dry," Cherine protested. "At least the workshop had a breeze. This place is wet, and I'm getting tired of all the clicking. What is that sound?"

When the braziers were doused and the prisoners left alone, there was a clicking sound that came through the cracks in the walls.

"Bats," the cockatiel said exasperated sigh. "It's always bats. There are cave systems all over the weald. I heard about a gryphon who escaped by swimming upstream from one."

"Wait, you heard that from me," Cherine scolded. "Also, I have a theory about the bats; I don't think there really are any of them."

He'd just started his theory of wing-squirrel migration when two things happened. Well, three, if he counted the cockatiel forger making fake snoring noises.

Forger aside, the sound of a chirping blue jay from down the corridor intensified, and the blackwing scout began coughing loudly.

Cherine went to help him, but the cockatiel pulled him back.

"I'm sorry about your brother," the forger whispered out of the blackwing's hearing. "I don't know that there's anything I can do for you now, but I wanted you to know that. I worked with the plague victims. I saw you visit him. I made sure his burial was proper."

The sudden change in tone alarmed Cherine almost as much as the metallic clink with the scout's last cough. From the blackwing's crop to the floor of the jail cell flew a large key with a metallic clang. The sharp peacock design on top had been sanded down smooth.

"So, tired," the scout coughed, speaking for the first time since his capture, "of your talking."

Cherine's eyes grew wide. "Did you swallow that when *we* captured you? And it's been in your crop the whole time?"

The cockatiel slicked back his crest, picked up the key, and unlocked the first cell. "The night of the fire, I grabbed that key to unlock a different kind of vault. It was just fortuitous that the Redwood Valley only uses two types of keys."

Cherine stood back from the blackwing scout, who was giving him a dangerous look. He'd read every book he could get his talons on, so he knew the other vault the key opened. "You don't think they've found the treasury under Reeve's Nest in the months we've been held here?"

In the corner where the forger had been held were small slips of dried leaves that held his dose of red fern. They all had numbers on them written in merchant shorthand, counting down the days. Today's dose had a zero scrawled on it with the words *Be ready*.

"So much talk," the scout continued. "Don't you have a sense of self-preservation?"

"Well, sure," Cherine replied. "It's not as strong as my sense of curiosity. Otherwise, I wouldn't find myself in these situations."

The cockatiel and blackwing scout fetched their harnesses from pegs on the other side of the room. They'd been emptied and checked twice now, first by Ninox's owls, then by the Ashen Weald. The blackwing scout still managed to gnaw off the decorative end of a strap to reveal a small blade hidden inside.

"You won't get the door open," Cherine said. "It doesn't use the same key."

The blackwing scout started to move towards Cherine, but the cockatiel held him back.

"Not yet. Let's see what our orders are." The forger turned to Cherine. "Keep your beak closed. The head-master likes you. There's a good chance you'll survive tonight if you stick with us. If you make any noise, there's a one hundred percent chance they'll kill you."

Cherine endeavored to keep his beak shut. He felt like he was being watched from every crack in the cavern wall, though the clicking sounds had ceased.

Outside, the chirps came closer.

"Oh, dear me," a melodic blue opinicus said to the jailors outside their room. "Your friends outside subdued this blackwing trying to sneak in. Several guards were injured and are going to the medicine gryphons, but they said to lock him away before he wakes up!"

Cherine stood up to try to see through the small window atop the door. He could just make out all four guards reaching down to lift up an incapacitated figure. Beyond them, he thought he saw a familiar face from the old merchant square.

The guards lifted up the unconscious opinicus. They moved him to the door, and one reached for the key to the outer barrier. The cockatiel and blackwing scout tensed, but the guard suddenly dropped the key. All four guards, in fact, collapsed below where Cherine could see.

The opinicus who had played unconscious stood, picked up the key, and unlocked the door.

When the forger and the scout saw who it was, they both leapt back.

"They sent the bleeding Reeve's Bane," the cockatiel muttered.

"Lord Rybalt!" the scout squawked. "I'm glad to see you're free."

The opinicus, Rybalt, looked like he fit right in. Broken leather bindings adorned his person. There was a torn falconry hood, its bindings broken and hanging down, still on his head. It appeared he had clawed out holes to see through.

"It's *Reeve* Rybalt," he corrected. "I see you retained the peacock key. Good job. Give it to me."

The scout held out the key in a talon, keeping it as far from his body as possible. When Rybalt snatched it away, the scout leapt back.

"We have a little antidote," Didi the Merchant said from the back. "Do you want me to give it to the guards?"

Rybalt's eyes were on the blackwing opinicus when he said, "I have no love for jailors," but he turned to Cherine to ask, "How about yourself?"

"Is it your feathers or your fur that holds the toxin?" Cherine asked.

Rybalt raised an eyecrest. "Both. It's groomed from one to the other."

"I don't love jailors, but you should give them the cure," Cherine said. "They're not all bad opinici."

The Reeve's Bane shrugged. "You heard the scholar, Didi. Give it to them."

The merchant traitor, affectionately called Splotchy Blue by most who met her, fished through her harness for several vials of red liquid. Between the headmaster, the scholars, and her, Cherine was starting to wonder just how many of his friends at the eyrie had been spies.

"Is the headmaster okay?" the cockatiel asked. "Is he okay...with the northerners?"

Rybalt considered the small cockatiel for the first time. "Your master is fine. He's at Poisonmaw awaiting your return. I'll get you that far safely."

The Reeve's Bane stepped all the way into the room, allowing the three prisoners to slip past him and into the hallway. As Cherine slipped past, the assassin whispered, "I put no bonds on you, but your life will be in danger if you don't come with us and do as I say. Understand?"

Cherine nodded. Perhaps he was just trading one cell for another, but he'd stood no chance of escaping from Merin, who definitely wanted to kill him. He'd take his chances in the wider world.

They slipped past the bodies of more victims of the pitohui's venom, with Didi stopping to offer the cure to each as they went. Once they were outside, they joined up with a small force of pitohui and blackwings under the bridge.

Rybalt ordered them to wait. "Not until Iony gives us the signal."

The imprisoned scout moved to the safety of the other blackwings, never taking his eyes off the Reeve's Bane. Cherine stuck close to the cockatiel. If nothing else, they were both intent on having words with the headmaster.

"Why did you call him the Reeve's Bane?" Cherine whispered.

"The Crackling Sea reeve." The cockatiel wouldn't say more.

Rybalt looked back at the two scholars. "Your insatiable curiosity may enjoy this next bit. I understand the Redwood Valley has the occasional monitor mishap."

Cherine nodded. "Every few years, a massive number of them seem to just materialize. The gryphons get hit hardest, along with any gryphlets or chicks caught on the ground. Really, the whole underbough, too."

"And the plague they carry," the cockatiel added. "Nobody's sure where they come from."

Rybalt pointed a talon to the north. "Poisonmaw. We found a goliath trail that goes through caves, across ledges, and traverses the highlands."

Cherine shook his head. "Who would have the resources to create such a thing?"

"The creators of the Snowfeather Dam," the cockatiel said. "But if there was a goliath bird path headed north, we'd know about it. We'd see where it came out."

"Ah," said Rybalt, "that's just the thing. The last part is flooded now. It used to come out by the Summer Falls. Iony followed the path from Poisonmaw south. The monitors follow it and come out of the river itself."

Cherine's feathers rose. "Why are you telling us this? Are you sending the monitors through the pass?"

Rybalt grinned. It was a genuine emotion, only appearing off because his beak had scarring from a hundred battles. "We are. We've caught a surprisingly large number of monitors and corralled them at the entrance to the pass."

"Most of Orlea's pride are still living on the ground," Cherine protested. "You'd only be hurting the refugees."

"I trust they can fly," the assassin said. In the distance

came the soft sound of a saltpeter explosion muffled by rock. "Nothing as impressive as what Bario makes, all flash and noise, but still a nice incentive to keep the lizards moving."

A few curious onlookers flew up into the sky, but when no fires came, they settled back down. Avalanches weren't uncommon, and they sometimes sounded like saltpeter going off.

A sense of dread overtook Cherine. If the monitors came out at the Summer Falls, Hatzel and Orlea's prides would be right in the way.

"You need to warn them!" He stepped forwards but stopped when the pitohui reeve held up a dripping talon.

"Now, now. You said this is a natural occurrence that happens every few years," Rybalt chided. "I'm sure they've got a plan in place. And if not, this will be a nice test run for them."

The first cries of alarm came from the direction of the Summer Falls themselves, down below the rubble of the Snowfeather Dam. Cherine was reassured a little that two shapes shot off in different directions to warn the prides— a bright red opinicus who looked like Kia went towards Orlea's pride while a copper hawk moved towards Hatzel's.

"Terrible location to have a picnic," Rybalt muttered. The skies quickly filled with gryphons and opinici. Chaos settled in.

"Okay, now we fly. Head for the Redwood Valley ruins." Rybalt put the peacock key into his harness pocket. "Iony will meet us there. We have one more stop to make on our way north."

41

NINOX AND SATRA

S atra thought of herself as a fairly trusting gryphon, but she still brought a selection of her best body-guards when she went to the Parrotface hunting grounds to meet Ninox. She kept the guards out in the open so her guest wouldn't think it a trap. If there was one gryphon Satra didn't want to upset, it was Ninox. That was why the trial was so vexing.

Of course, it could be a trap *for* Satra. That thought had occurred to her. But if she were killed, Cherine's fate would be left up to chance. Ninox was an enigma, but she honestly seemed to want Cherine to be safe.

Satra hoped she wasn't misreading the situation. She'd sent Foultner and Blinky to prepare for tomorrow's trial and missed their counsel. In all honesty, Satra assumed this would be a waste of time. Ninox wouldn't show. No sane gryphon *would* show up to enemy territory alone to be escorted into a prison. It was unthinkable.

Still, Satra arrived at the meeting place just in case. She waited, and just when she was ready to head back to spend the rest of the evening planning Cherine's defense, a soft hoot greeted her ears.

The Kjarr looked up. Above them, Ninox made a show of floating to the ground. All of Satra's guards tensed, but Ninox paid them no mind. She walked up to Satra and licked her. Satra returned the grooming lick. It wasn't something modern prides did, but she'd seen Strix greet her father the same way.

"We can take you straight to Cherine, if that's easiest," Satra said. "He's not far from here."

Ninox made no moves towards following Satra.

"I'm sure the trial is stressful," Satra continued. "I hope he's found innocent, so he can be returned to you soon."

Ninox took to grooming her feathers, a very owl-like thing to do. "Why did you allow him to be captured?"

Ah, I suppose I'm the one on trial here, Satra mused. It was a fair question. She decided to err on the side of honesty. Her father said Strix could hear a lie in a gryphon's heartbeat. Had Jun lived long enough, Satra would have asked if that was true or not.

"I didn't," Satra said at last. "I knew Merin was chasing after scholars, Jonas loyalists, and blackwing spies, but I didn't think he'd end up at your doorstep. I didn't know you were even in there."

Ninox's ears were both on Satra as she spoke. "You could have released him."

"I'm not sure I could have," Satra countered. "Merin believes Cherine tried to blow up his nesting grounds. A trial was the best way to put things to rest."

"It has been months," Ninox said. "You should have released him to see his eggs hatch."

"I would have, if I'd known he had eggs," Satra said.

"You disappeared without a trace. All we knew about your relationship with Cherine were rumors. And you know how owls are—they hardly pay any mind to their mates. They're not opinici."

"But *Cherine* is an opinicus," Ninox said. "And he is my friend."

"Your friend, your mate, but not a member of your pride?" Satra prompted. "Grax's common is excellent. Good enough for her to lie if she thought it would save a life."

Ninox didn't answer the question. "Pride hunting grounds and nesting grounds used to mean something. My father helped yours. Jun the Kjarr would have released Cherine off that bond alone."

Satra took advantage of her first conversation with Ninox since the war to push back. "The world is growing, Ninox. There were ways for you to get Cherine back, but they didn't involve disappearing into the night and killing opinici to send a message. They involve diplomacy, conversations, understanding, and cultural exchanges.

"Neither of us are our fathers. Strix operated in secrecy, but you'd do better to forge bonds of friendship with your neighbors. My opportunities to fix this ended when you vanished."

"I have made friends," Ninox protested. "Cherine is my friend. So are Orlea, Hatzel, Kia, and Younce."

"Did you lean on them when things got bad?" Satra pushed. "I don't think you did. I think you disappeared. I'm not saying I couldn't have handled things better. But I think that, together, as friends, we could have fixed this months ago."

"This was because we did not let you see the black-wing?" Ninox asked.

"Partially, yes," Satra said. "The more we know about the northern eyries the better. The sooner we know it, the better we can plan together."

Ninox considered this.

"Half of being a leader is how you handle your enemies." Satra thought of Ranger Lord Grenkin as she said this. "The other half is how you handle your allies. You need to keep their feeling of safety in mind."

"I am keeping your safety in mind," Ninox said.

There was something to Ninox's tone that worried Satra. A feeling of dread was growing in her gut.

"What safety issue would I have to worry about?" she asked at last.

In the style that had become common for gryphons after the war, Ninox had a single leather bracer with the feathers of loved ones tied to it. A metal charm and vial of red liquid, possibly blood, were also attached to it.

Satra herself wore Mignet's feathers, though Mignet hadn't been a casualty of the war itself. Urious and Thenca had traded feathers—from their torn wings, retrieved from the bloody sands by Satra before the sail-fins got to them.

Ninox wore one of Cherine's feathers, golden eagle brown. There was another feather, black and burnt with the barest hint of red.

"Is that Strix's feather? Did you find his corpse?" Satra asked.

Ninox reached into her harness and pulled out a melted, metal talon and tossed it to Satra. "Commander Wolden."

While Satra's adventure the night of the fire had involved nearly cutting off Jonas's wings before her conscience—or, more specifically, Mignet's conscience—

caught up with her, she'd heard about Strix fighting the eyrie's commander over Reeve's Nest.

"Kia identified the talon." Ninox nuzzled the burnt black feather. "It was the only feather to survive."

A conversation came back to Satra. There were only three peacock keys. The headmaster had one. Reeve Brevin held one herself, removed from her grave by the Ashen Weald. And the last belonged to Commander Wolden.

"Did you find any other metal by the commander's body?" Satra asked.

Ninox tilted her head to the side. She dug through her bracer with her beak and pulled out a metal peacock tine like the sort the top of Brevin's key had been adorned with and threw it at the Kjarr's feet.

"I thought perhaps opinicus riches would buy his freedom," Ninox said. "But you think a trial is important to the Ashen Weald. That the Ashen Weald is more important than old friendships between prides. That is fine. That is the leader you are."

Satra's heart skipped a beat. "Did you find Reeve's Nest by your father's body? Did you open the treasury?"

"But I am not the sort of gryphon to leave the fate of my mate to chance." Ninox's voice increased in volume. "I do not trust your Ashen Weald allies to do the right thing. But I found someone who may accept metal beads in exchange for Cherine's safety."

Satra's first thought went to the guards at the prison. Would Ashen Weald rangers take a bribe? Considering the black market for food, it wasn't impossible. Not everyone was willing to trust on spring crops and fishing to feed them.

But there was another option that occurred to Satra,

an option that had Ninox seeking out the blackwings that roamed the night.

"Ninox, did you strike a deal with the blackwing's assassin?" she asked.

In the distance, the sound of a small avalanche echoed across the valley. Satra jumped in spite of herself. Ever since Bario detonated his workshop with Satra in it, she had no control over her body when a loud noise went off.

"You aren't here to visit Cherine, are you?" she asked.

Ninox bowed her head slightly. "I am here to keep you safe. I believe this new Reeve's Bane would kill you like a reeve if he had the chance. I am keeping you here with me until he has left the area."

"Like the depths you are," Satra shouted. "Ashen Weald, to Merin's territory, now!"

Satra's mistake was forgetting that Ninox was, like her father, a predator first and foremost.

The Kjarr was on her back with Ninox's beak at her throat before she could finish her sentence. Ten owls appeared from the trees and formed a barrier between Satra and her bodyguards. Belatedly, she regretted sending Blinky with Foultner. Neither of them ever put their guard down.

She pushed against Ninox, but it was like pushing against metal. Ninox tightened her beak, and Satra went limp.

This is a terrible way to die, she thought. But Mignet's death hadn't been any less terrible, and had Jun's death been any better?

Ninox didn't close her beak. Satra wondered what she was waiting for. In the distance, in the direction of the avalanche, came a cry for help. It didn't sound like the cry of a blackwing invasion. Instead, it sounded like...

Monitor lizards?

Ninox pushed a paw under Satra's neck, letting her claws dig in just a little, and moved her beak against Satra's ear.

"If Cherine survives, we will try your diplomacy." Ninox's whispers tickled Satra's ear tufts. "If he does not, I will kill Merin. Then I will kill the blackwing's assassin. Then I will kill you."

From the canopy, an eleventh owl sounded an all clear. Whether that meant Cherine was free or not, Satra didn't know.

"You are safe." Ninox removed her beak and claws from Satra's neck before adding, "For now."

Ninox and the Strix Pride rose into the sky as Satra's bodyguards rushed to her aid.

42

REEVE'S NEST

Whenever Cherine faltered, one of the pitohui would dive down at him with their poisonous plumage and force him to fly faster.

Several of their blackwing escorts were forced to hang back and deal with members of Merin's pride who challenged the procession heading north. When they passed over Orlea's nesting grounds, Didi the Merchant disappeared back into the crowds and helped couples get nests moved to higher ground before the monitors arrived.

Cherine had a bad feeling. If Didi wasn't worried about him knowing her status as a traitor, it didn't speak well to his ultimate fate.

When they arrived at the ruins of the Redwood Valley Eyrie, Cherine got to meet Rybalt's second-in-command, Iony, for the first time.

"You're a gryphon?" Cherine asked.

"Guess not all Redwood scholars are as bright as they say," the gryphon chided. His long grey ears and thick fur looked well-suited for the mountains.

With Iony came another twenty gryphons and twenty

opinici. Some of the opinici had burn wraps on them, leaving Cherine to speculate what had happened. There hadn't been any word of fires that had made its way down to his jail cell.

The distraction had worked. There were no scavengers or opinici in the ruins. Everyone who could fly had taken to the heights to avoid the monitors. It was just them.

When they reached Reeve's Nest, Rybalt pulled out the key only to find that the door had been opened.

"Watch yourselves," Rybalt said. "It's a trap."

Several blackwings put swirled metal talons on. The gryphons bristled. The pitohui rubbed their talons through their plumage until they glistened.

"Not a trap." Ninox's voice echoed through the ruins. Ash hung in the air.

"Ninox of the Strix," Iony mumbled. "She's come to make good on her threat. I always hated owl gryphons."

Cherine looked at Iony's grey owl visage and raised an eyecrest.

"I'll play along," Rybalt spoke to the darkness. "If not a trap, then what?"

"Open the vault." Ninox's voice came from behind them this time.

One of the blackwings pulled open the vault and called back. "There's maybe two thousand beads in here. It's nearly empty."

"I moved the rest near your camp," the Strix pride leader said. "If you turn over Cherine, I will tell you where."

"The headmaster was specific," a blackwing said. "We need to bring him Cherine. He has crucial information for putting down the insurrection."

Rybalt turned and looked at Cherine. "Does he? I see a

common opinicus who spent months trying to figure out our maps and intelligence. I don't believe he knows anything."

"That's not your call to make, trashbird," the until-recently-imprisoned scout pushed. "Orders are orders."

"That's *reeve* trashbird to you." Rybalt stepped in front of the scout. "And I don't think you know what our orders are. We weren't sent here to retrieve a scout. We were sent here to acquire an immense fortune and kill any remaining reeves."

He pushed against the scout, leaving a glistening stain behind. When the scout reached for a vial of the antidote, the Reeve's Bane snatched it out of his talons and tossed it to Cherine.

"I agree to your terms, weald gryphon." He stood very close to Cherine. "If you tell me where Reeve Brevin's fallen fortune is located, I will leave your mate here for you."

Ninox appeared a hundred yards away, between two rusted arches. "I will tell you once he makes it to me."

Rybalt lifted up Cherine's talons holding the antidote, then pushed the scholar towards Ninox. He'd made it three quarters of the way there when the toxin began to take effect.

"It is in the workshop where the cockatiel and scout were held," Ninox said. Several of her owls materialized and pulled Cherine towards the northern aneda forests before the Reeve's Bane could pursue them.

Cherine felt his mind fogging and his muscles beginning to twitch. He reached for the antidote and had the cork out of the plunger when Ninox sniffed it and knocked it out of his talons. She pulled out a different red vial from her bracer and gave that one to him. The spasms subsided.

"I've missed you," he said.

She blinked back. "You were a good mate, and you are a good friend. Come, we will show you your offspring, then we will get you to safety."

He was left to wonder why those two weren't the same thing as an escort of owls led him into the Owlfeather Highlands.

43

MONITOR ATTACK

K ia arrived as fast as she could fly, but the monitors were hot on her tail. Orlea's nesting grounds were abuzz. She looked around for someone in charge. Her eyes caught sight of Piprik and Lei near the fisherfolk, but she didn't want to draw attention to them. Instead, she headed towards the cage at the center of the town.

"What was the explosion?" Merin asked. "What do you mean monitor lizards?"

"I was by the Summer Falls with friends talking about the trial," Kia half-truthed, "and they erupted out of the water. Hundreds, maybe a thousand of them. They'll be here in minutes."

"Where's Orlea?" he asked.

"I don't know," and Kia really didn't. The last she'd seen the opinicus pride leader, Hatzel was saving her from a monitor.

"There's nobody in charge here," Merin grumbled. "They're not going to listen to me with Askel in the cage."

"They'll listen to me." Kia felt a confidence she wasn't sure she'd earned. "First things first, that cage won't survive a stampede of monitors. Break Askel out. Second, grab any large wreckage from the ruins. Toss it between the sheds and buildings. Let's force the monitors to go around as best we can."

For her first month at Luminaire, Kia had been soft-spoken. The fisherfolk, especially the Crane's Nest refugees, had taken her words as suggestions and didn't obey them.

Rorin had taken her aside and taught her to speak so her words were understood as orders. He told her that if she was going to organize food and supplies so everyone didn't starve, she needed to get gryphons and opinici to follow her.

Kia remembered Rorin's voice. It sounded like the deep, resonant sounding of an iron bell from across a long distance. She cleared her voice and aimed for 'iron bell.'

The fisherfolk were trained to listen to Rorin—when Gressle's caravan heard Kia's orders, they obeyed. Carru flew after his father to grab debris for barriers. Piprik, Lei, and Gressle began searching for eggs and nests that would need to be relocated.

Kia turned to the ex-Reeve's Guard watching Askel's cage and put her voice to the test. They looked confused and unsure what to do.

"Break apart the cage," she commanded. "Askel, you're a smart gryphon. Figure out where the barriers need to go to keep the monitors out of the city center."

"We need to keep an eye on him," one of the guards protested.

"They're not mutually exclusive," Kia said a little too sternly. "Stick close to him, *obey his orders,* help him protect the town."

At the edge of the grasslands, a capybara squealed. The monitors were entering the forest.

She shouted more orders. Opinici evacuated, taking eggs or chicks with them as they left. The first of the fastest monitors had hit the makeshift breakwater when a new problem arose.

"Askel, what're you doing!?" she shouted to the chestnut-colored gryphon. He was using the pieces of his jail to construct a makeshift cage around a large yet flimsy building on the far side of town.

"It's the wounded, those who can't fly," he said. "There's not enough time to evacuate all of them. This is sort of an opinicus medicine cave."

They'd only managed to fortify one side of the building, and already, the barricades on the other side of town were giving way.

Her eyes went from Merin and Carru to the hospital, then from the hospital to the forest filling up with giant lizards.

"Carru." She spoke in her usual voice.

He saw the hospital and understood. He chirped to Merin, and father and son went to stand guard at the unblocked entrance.

Kia looked around. Her mistake in evacuating the nesting grounds was that there weren't any opinici left to defend the hospital. Only the merchants remained atop their homes, afraid to leave them alone for fear of looting. They ignored Kia's pleas for help until she saw a familiar blue shape arrive.

"Didi!" Kia called out.

"Kia?" The blue merchant nearly jumped out of her skin.

"We didn't evacuate the hospital in time," Kia explained. "Get your merchant friends to help."

Didi tried her best, but the merchants wouldn't listen to her. "It's no use. They're more worried about themselves."

"Fine," Kia said. "You go help Carru; I'll try to get us help."

"C-carru is here?" Didi squeaked.

Kia didn't have time to ask how an opinicus merchant from the eyrie knew a gryphon fisherfolk from the shore. The outer huts, more makeshift rain barriers to keep out the wet and cold, collapsed as the monitors hit the edge of the city.

She flew up to shout for help. Below her, Piprik and Levin descended upon the hospital. Lei slipped on his mother's talons, giving both Kia and Piprik a small heart attack, and Piprik shoved him into the hospital building to protect the patients from any small monitors who wriggled in.

In the distance, Kia thought she could make out gryphons coming from the direction of Hatzel's nesting grounds.

MERIN STOOD GUARD WITH CARRU, father and son, together for the first time since Carru had left to become a fisherfolk.

The first monitors to slip through the barricades were small. They had the blue stripes of adolescence on their back.

"Don't forget their poison," Merin said.

"I know, Dad." Carru grinned. "I haven't been sleeping on the beach eating fish, you know."

"Lot of monitor lizards in the ocean?" Merin countered, but he was inwardly pleased. He'd missed his wayward sons. It was the way of some offspring to leave, to need to find their way in the world. Others wanted to stay closer to home and build bonds. He should have gone south to visit Carru, but it had never felt right. Becoming fisherfolk felt like a betrayal of the weald prides. Had Merin gone down to visit, he was worried he would say something he didn't mean. Still, he wanted his son to be happy.

"Did you and your opinicus mate ever have any gryphlets?" he asked after stomping on a small monitor.

Carru tossed a different lizard into the air. He kept his wings folded close, just like Merin had taught him. "She got cold paws at the last second. Couldn't leave behind her family's trade empire to eat fish."

"Then why did you stay away?" Merin's heart ached for his son.

"Because I think gryphons and opinici should live however they want," Carru said.

"The Ashen Weald agrees with you." Word of Carru's exploits at the Battle for Sandpiper's Dune had reached Merin's ears, and he was proud of his son.

There was a break in the wave of lizards as the larger ones continued trying to break through barriers and all of the small ones had been taken care of. A blue merchant flew down with resin and bandages.

"Didi?" Carru asked.

The opinicus's nares blushed red, a striking contrast with her blue feathers. "Hello, Carru. How have you been?"

Merin had a very specific memory of this opinicus. Of finding this opinicus and his son in the grasslands. "Wait, aren't you..."

Carru shushed his dad. "How's life treating you, Didi? Merchant business good?"

The building across from the hospital collapsed, putting an end to the small chat.

"I'll tell you all about it later," Didi chirped as she flew inside to help the wounded.

Out of the rubble rose up a nine foot long monitor lizard. Merin had forgotten they grew that large. Past migrations, while still dangerous, were mostly adolescents. This was something different.

"Carru," Merin said, "if there are more like that, you may need to leave."

Carru shook his head. Except for his blue plumage, he looked just like his father. "I'm not leaving you here. We never stand down. Like granddad, right?"

As the monstrous lizard caught Carru's scent, Merin was reminded of the words he'd spoken at trial about wanting the best for the opinicus refugees. Had he meant them? Had he meant the words he'd given Askel about standing and protecting the weald?

"Like my father." Merin clinked the bracelet on his tail against a nearby tree to get the monitor's attention away from his son and then leapt at its eyes.

While Merin and Carru battled the largest monitor the weald had seen in a generation, Askel shouted orders to his former jailors.

"No, not the berry juice, grab the rope!" he told one. "Wait, actually, is that starberry? Grab it, too!"

"Quick, fetch the extra-large harnesses from the flame-works," he told another. "Grab the ones that have buckles on them."

"Ooh, are those light-colored hides?" he said as they flew over a merchant's hut. "I need those, too."

"Where do we put these?" a third guard asked.

"On top of the trees!" Askel wasn't used to the questioning looks he was getting. Normally, his pridemates just assumed he knew what he was talking about. "Splash the hides with the juice, then put half the harnesses and rope next to them. Take the other half and start putting them on everyone in the hospital who's safe to move."

One guard scoffed. "Who're we leaving the harnesses for? Squirrels?"

"No, them." Askel pointed a paw to the south, where Merin's pride was coming to help, led by Triddle. Off in the west, he saw Hatzel and some copper hawks, but he didn't think they'd be big enough to lift out any of the wounded.

This would all be a lot easier if they'd let him use a little saltpeter. One or two explosions would encourage the monitor lizards to head elsewhere.

He followed his guards into the hospital. Unlike the sheds and hovels outside, this had been a real building before the wounded were moved in. This had been the Reeve's Guard outpost where poachers were held—and, in the case of Orlea's mate, executed. There were two hundred opinici who were in no shape to fly in here.

It was the kind of building that would have benefited from a moat of fire for just this sort of occasion.

"Kia," he called out.

"What's your plan with the harnesses?" Kia asked.

She arrived with a peacock fisherfolk and Didi in tow. The blue merchant was eyeing the peacock's ornamented talons with a sense of recognition that seemed to distract her from her helper duties.

"Break the roof off, fly everyone out of here," he said. "It'll take a few trips, but the monitors are getting bigger and bigger. Can you organize that?"

Kia looked around. She had a few helpers and some medicine gryphons in here. "We'll start having the healthy opinici strip. We'll find enough harnesses for everyone. How're things outside?"

"Not good," Askel said. "Carru and Merin won't hold out much longer. That's why we need to move everyone."

"Where, though?" Didi asked. "The monitors will be everywhere. There aren't any heights until the Strix Plateau."

"That's not true," Kia said. "Take them north to the Owlfeather Highlands."

Didi shivered. "That's not safe!"

"It's safer than here," the fisherfolk said. His voice was a little scratchy. "Ninox isn't going to attack refugees."

"We'll figure it out," Kia told Askel. "You get the roof off and bring your pride here."

Askel slipped outside and was above the nesting grounds when he realized he was free of supervision and guards. He cast a look west. If he was going to fly for it, now was his chance. He didn't have anywhere to go, and there was nowhere he wanted to be without Triddle.

He turned south and flew to greet the rest of his pride and tell them the plan, keeping an eye out for Triddle's blue crest.

A THICK TAIL struck Merin across the side of his head, sending him sprawling into the side of the hospital. Carru tried to grab the monitor by the back of the neck, but its hard, smooth scales wriggled out of his beak.

Carru rightfully flew out of range of the lizard's maw, leaving his father on the ground.

Merin stood. One eye was swollen shut. He'd lost count of the bite marks from the smaller lizards, but his whole body burned with their venom. Above the hospital, Askel and Triddle directed his pride to carry the wounded to safety. In the distance, he heard the cries of copper hawks and magpie pulling lizards off the side of the building.

On the ground, it was just Merin and his son.

"Dad, you need to get up," Carru said. The massive lizard snapped into the air, narrowly missing its quarry.

Merin saw a large gryphon with plumage too dark to be one of his own.

At least one of that pride is large enough to kill monitors.

He charged the lizard, distracting it while Carru dove and pushed its head against the ground, exposing its neck.

Hatzel the Saberbeak landed atop the exposed section of flesh and dug in. The monitor wriggled both Merin and Carru off, but the sabers on her beak gave Hatzel purchase. It took a minute or two, but the beast finally stopped moving.

"Don't you have your own nesting grounds to protect?" Merin grumbled.

"We built our nests up high to avoid just this sort of thing," Hatzel said. "You forget that I grew up at Poisonmaw with the monitors."

"I thought you grew up in the medicine gryphon caves because you were sick?" Carru asked.

Merin managed a laugh. "He has you there."

"My tailfeathers," Hatzel said. "Is that little Carru returned from the fisherfolk? How did you grow up so pretty with such an ugly father?"

"He looks just like me, don't you deny it," Merin said. He licked at his wounds, trying to get the venom out. Already, he could feel his body burning up.

"Now, now, don't crush his dreams of finding a mate while he's so young." Hatzel nuzzled Merin back up, making him realize that he'd been slumping down. "How're you doing? I think we need to get you out of here."

He coughed. "How many are left in the hospital?"

Hatzel didn't answer.

He took that to mean they needed more time. In the distance, more buildings collapsed. Two more of the megafauna began wriggling towards them.

Hatzel let out a cry and Zeph's familiar voice answered. "He says this is the last of the big ones."

Merin tried to stand, but his legs were shaking. As the new wave of monitors charged, the venom finally took its toll, and he collapsed.

44

EVACUATION

Piprik finished bringing the last of the evacuees to the roof. He was just tying the final few ropes when he heard a scream from downstairs.

The barriers blocking the entrances into the hospital gave way, and monitor lizards spilled in. Didi leapt towards the roof balcony when a lizard caught her out of the air. Only a timely intervention by Lei saved her from being a snack.

Despite the peafowl's small size—though much larger than when he'd first arrived at Luminaire—the sharpened talons slipped through lizard flesh like it was liquid.

Piprik reached a talon down and helped pull the merchant up. Once she had room to spread her wings, she flew north, leaving him alone with his apprentice and the last of the patients.

"That's the last of them." Lei's tail looked looked worse for wear. Lizards did better in close quarters than opinici. Where his train of covert feathers had been crushed, the emerald green faded to brown.

Not the prettiest color, but it'll help hide her identity. His identity, Piprik corrected himself. Levin had insisted they maintain the ruse in private, too, for fear of owl eavesdroppers.

"That merchant sure flew away fast, didn't she, Pip?" Lei said.

"I imagine the scare with the lizard downstairs took the last of her nerves." Piprik had known a few merchants in his time whose bravery was without question. The kind who braved the Jadebeak Mountains, the desert, and the Frozen Sea without a second thought and were willing to rescue a stranded opinicus trying to reach the fisherfolk shore. He hadn't met their like among the Redwood Valley merchants.

Several large, hook-beaked gryphons landed, and waited for the fisherfolk to tie ropes to their harnesses. They took all but the last three patients, who were unconscious.

Lei cleaned the blood off of his talons. "I didn't remember the weald being so exciting. I hadn't been born yet the last time there was a migration."

"Hmm." Piprik scratched at a feather under his chin. His talons came away with white. "Er, how do I look?"

"Old?" Lei ventured. Then he saw the paint. "Oh, it's still fine. The merchants at New Eyrie will have something sturdier."

Piprik wiped his talons off on an expensive hide that someone had splashed with berry juice to resemble the effigies gryphons use to mark their landing areas. These had been used to show Merin's pride where to find harnesses or pick up patients in need of evacuation.

"How about myself?" Lei adjusted his voice back to its scratchy tone. His disguise, the mixture of Tresh's necklace and Rorin's red paint, had stood up well, and Piprik told him so.

"The red is bleeding a bit." Lei wiped his own talons off on the hide.

"It's supposed to," Piprik said. "It's meant to look ferocious. They say Rorin the Hunter was pure white, and it was the blood of the crowncrest sea serpent who stained his chest red, a mixture of opinicus and serpent blood."

Lei's eyes got wide. "Is that true? What's a crowncrest sea serpent?"

"A water snake or eel, I imagine," Piprik said. "And probably not—Rorin's mother was a grosbeak, so he was always going to have those red feathers."

Lei had been his pupil for long enough that he knew what came next. "But it makes for a good story?"

Piprik nodded. "Precisely."

Merin's strongest flyers returned and Pip and Lei helped secure the harnesses and ropes for the last of the patients.

As they took off, a new set of gryphons and opinici arrived in the air.

"Speaking of crowncrest," Piprik muttered to Lei. "Put away your talons, now!"

Lei moved a wing to hide his talons from view, slipping off the weapon and putting it in his harness before standing straight.

Satra and her bodyguards flew over the hospital.

"Everyone has been evacuated!" Piprik shouted up, but Satra wasn't there for them. She was headed to where Carru and Merin had been guarding the entrance.

Piprik went to the edge of the roof. Below, Hatzel and Carru were protecting the unconscious body of Merin. Satra and her bodyguards helped retrieve his body.

Piprik turned his attention from the Kjarr to Reeve Brevin's youngest. "We need to go. Satra might recognize you even under the paint. She watched your mother's court for years."

Lei didn't take his eyes off Merin. "You're a medicine opinicus. You need to help him."

Khalim had been a scholar for years. He'd been an alchemist, an apprentice phoenix in the dark years before saltpeter, and even a farmer. He'd been all of those things for longer than he'd been Piprik.

How long could someone pretend to be a medicine opinicus before they truly became one? Had the elixir caused him to become—not Piprik, Eyes of the Seraph King—but Piprik, medicine opinicus to a small fisherfolk village?

"You remember your chemistry lessons?" He listed off a list of medicines, using the Redwood Valley terms for them, and ordered Lei to fetch them for him.

Down below, Hatzel and Carru were lifting Merin's body onto the hospital roof. There was little chance he could save the pride leader now, but Piprik could ease his suffering and give him a few more minutes of lucidity before he passed.

MERIN

HARPY EAGLE GRYPHON

45

MERIN

Satra stuck close to Merin, having to be shooed away by the fisherfolk's medicine opinicus when she got in the way. Things didn't look good.

A large number of his pride crowded the roof of the hospital. When the medicine fisherfolk demanded room to work, Satra was left to choose who would be able to see Merin's final moments. She chose Carru, Askel, and Triddle and prayed the rest of his offspring would forgive her.

"Go, track the monitors, make sure the other prides have evacuated any eggs or elderly," she ordered his other pridemates. "Merin didn't sacrifice himself just so your own nests would come under attack."

The last prompting worked, and the skies filled with harpy eagle gryphons seeking to do good in their pride leader's name. Satra's bodyguards refused to leave her side after the incident with Ninox but stood guard atop the trees nearby.

As the fisherfolk's medicine took effect, some clarity returned to Merin's eyes.

"Killed by monitors like a common saberbeak," he coughed.

Hatzel shook her head. "Save your words for your loved ones. You have more venom in your veins than a cobra."

Satra pushed Carru closer.

"I'm here, Dad," he said.

Merin didn't turn to look at him. "I don't blame you for your convictions and wanderlust, Carru. I want you to know that I love you just as much as your siblings."

Carru stared down at his paws.

"I need you to find Erlock," Merin continued. "And find out what happened to your brother. If he's…"

Coughing interrupted the rest of the message. Satra went to move Askel and Triddle closer, but Merin looked directly at her.

"You need to take care of the Ashen Weald," he said. "There are enemies, spies within. I didn't save you from the eyrie for you to give up."

"I'll take care of them. I promise," Satra said. She still remembered Merin finding her standing over the body of Jonas. He'd kept her secret. No one had asked her what had happened to Jonas. She didn't know if she'd be judged more harshly by her critics for trying to kill Jonas or for leaving him alive.

Satra looked at Merin's wings. They were both broken, and no one made any attempt to reset them. One of his paws had been crushed.

The medicine opinicus stepped back. "That's the highest dose I can give him. There shouldn't be any pain, but he won't last much longer."

She pushed down her feelings and made room for Askel and Triddle.

"You don't think about the consequences of your actions," Merin told Askel. "Some of that's on me. I could have done better to shield you from your worse nature, but I only encouraged it. Sometimes we saved lives. Many times, we took them."

Askel didn't respond. His ears and tail drooped.

"And you, Triddle," Merin coughed. "At the Crackling Sea, you stayed back when gryphons needed your help. You were too afraid to act, and it cost the lives of some of your pridemates. You get so caught up on what could go wrong that you miss your chance to do anything, which is just as bad."

Merin's eyes lost focus several times, then he found one last bit of lucidity. "But together, you're better than any other one gryphon I know. Askel and Triddle, I name you two pride leader. Let that damned Orlea lock you up, now!"

Merin's eyes remained unfocused after his final outburst. Distance, freezing water, cages, war, and armies had kept Satra from remaining by Mignet, Jun, or Vitra's sides. Here, on a cold spring day in the weald, she curled up next to her friend and stayed with him until he stopped breathing.

46

HOME AT LAST

Cherine followed Ninox past a flock of frost chickens, down a tunnel, and into the depths of the old Snowfeather nesting grounds. Supplies of all sorts lined the walls, including several scorched braziers taken from the eyrie ruins.

In a large chamber, two smaller braziers had been set against one wall to provide illumination. Against the other wall were nests, with a section hollowed out for the Strix Pride den mother and gryphlets.

Ninox cooed and three little ones squealed and rushed over to greet her. She licked their down-covered heads. There were two boys and a girl.

"This is Cherine," she said. "He is your father."

The gryphlets had wide eyes.

"Why is he so tall?" one of the boys asked.

"It is because he is a scholar," Ninox explained. "The cases of books are very tall, so scholars must be tall to reach the top shelf."

"Ooh," said all three gryphlets.

"He does not have long here," Ninox continued. "If

you wish to ask him questions or cuddle him, you must hurry."

Cuddles were definitely in the equation. He put his wing over the three gryphlets—*Two gryphlets and one chick*, he mentally corrected himself when the girl grabbed his talon in her own.

"What are your names?" he asked.

"They do not have names," Ninox said. "I did not know how opinici make such decisions."

"What do you call them?" he asked with a genuine curiosity.

Ninox attempted to groom the largest one's head. "I let them choose their own names for now."

The one whose face disappeared under her tongue said, "I am Squirrelbane."

"I'm sure the squirrels will quake in fear," Cherine said.

The sister of the bunch let out a squeaky roar and then said, "I am Sound of Snow."

Cherine used his beak to preen the last child. "What do they call you?"

"Marshmallow," the shy gryphlet responded.

"Marshmallow...bane?" Cherine asked.

"Just Marshmallow." The gryphlet slow blinked.

Cherine looked to Ninox, but she just shrugged and pointed to a stolen Crackling Sea crate of marshmallows. "There is one every nest year. The names are not permanent. We will decide on other ones if they survive to fledge. I need to ask you about Snow. She is small. Is that normal for an opinicus?"

Cherine lifted up his daughter. He examined her talons, her slight owl-like beak, and the nubs where her feathered tail would come in. "No, she seems normal.

Gryphlets mature faster, don't they? She'll probably be a year behind her brothers fledging, then lose another year to get out of the awkward fledgling stage."

The Sound of Snow looked disappointed, so he tossed her in the air and caught her.

"Your brothers are going to have to work a lot harder with their paws to keep up with your talons," he told her. "You're going to have a lot of time to hunt and be an adult. Enjoy an extra two years of childhood."

She seemed skeptical but flexed her tiny talons happily.

From a different passage than the one they'd taken, Grax cooed down a message for Ninox in owlish. The Strix Pride leader cooed back.

"There is not much time," she told Cherine. "It will not help your case that the blackwings freed you. I have a place for you to hide and write. While you are away, I will try to smooth things over."

His heart dropped. "Why can't I stay here with you and the kids?"

The little ones were already in the mass of downy owl gryphlets being watched by the den mother.

Ninox pushed him towards the passage where Grax waited. "I wish to open up my dens for trade again. I believe that is the way to get you pardoned. I hope Satra has realized she needs us."

"I've missed you," Cherine said. "I know you explained gryphon relationships before, but..."

"You may compete next mating season," Ninox said. "If incarceration has not dulled your intellect, maybe I will choose you."

Cherine grinned at her use of harder vocabulary. "Hey, maybe you'll have to compete for me next season."

"It is true, there could be competition." Ninox tilted her head to the side and pretended to size him up. "I have seen how Kia looks at you."

"Hey now," Cherine began.

"And Zeph," Ninox added.

Cherine blinked "What?"

"Oh, yes, he is always looking at your tailfeathers," Grax nodded.

"And Hatzel. And Orlea." Ninox started walking down the passage. "So many hearts were broken, as the opinici say. Perhaps even Grax."

"Oh, no," the brown-feathered owl said. "I am going to catch a taiga gryphon next year. The smart one."

Cherine laughed in spite of himself. He liked Ninox, would probably be jealous when she found someone else, but she'd been very clear when she came to him in the autumn as to what gryphon relationships were like.

Hopefully, his pardon would come in time and he'd be able to see his offspring and teach them. But he'd be mindful to treat Ninox as a friend, even if he missed their journey through the mountains exploring abandoned workshops together.

They reached the end of the passage. An old snow barrier covered in leaves hid the passage from the outside. Once it was open, he said his goodbyes.

"I'd have loved to become a member of your pride," he admitted. "It would have been an honor to be the first opinicus member of the Strix Pride."

"Second," Ninox corrected. "Do not forget The Sound of Snow."

He laughed. "Well, maybe later."

Grax and Ninox cooed back and forth for a moment. There seemed to be a disagreement of sorts.

"Grax will take you to the hiding place," Ninox said. "It is north, along a river. Stay in the aneda forest. There are scouts who watch the banks of the Crackling Sea. Do not go out there to fish. Do not leave the forest for any reason."

He nodded. That was a larger prison than he was used to. With any luck, it would be temporary, and he might get some visitors.

Ninox groomed one of his feathers back into place. "There is another thing. We have watched the blackwing scouts. They are at Poisonmaw. Do not go into the mountains. And be careful. Our scouts have come across something hunting them. I think it is the opinicus who owned the workshop."

Grax pulled out a white feather with a red barb. "It's not an opinicus. It's a monster."

"Mally was both." Cherine took the feather. What he'd taken to be blood seemed to be an iron disorder Redwood opinici were sometimes born with. His views on the Nighthaunt had changed when he saw the mass graves and the research notes. He had become more and more certain the scholar lived.

"I saw his shape in the taiga," Ninox said. "He does not look like any opinicus I have seen."

"The headmaster used to speak of him like an old friend," Cherine began, but both Grax and Ninox heard something in the distance and shoved him back in the tunnel.

A minute later, Didi the merchant flew overhead to return to her blackwing masters.

"Looks like she wasn't willing to risk the prison guards remembering her," Cherine mumbled.

The owls didn't respond, waiting for Didi to pass

them by.

"The first rule of hiding is not to speak while you are hiding," Ninox said. "You will need to remember that while you are north."

She slipped back in the passage, which Grax kicked dry leaves over to hide. "Come, scholar. Night will be here soon, and the darkness is not as safe as it once was. We would do best to cross the mountains now."

Cherine looked at the pile of leaves that led into Snowfeather Mountain where his children would be raised as gryphons. He wanted to stay and teach them, but he let Grax guide him northwest, skirting between the Crackling Sea and Poisonmaw Valley.

47

POISONMAW

Rybalt had always been good at sewing civil unrest. It worked best when his enemies didn't know he was there. With merchant caravans, he'd gone from eyrie to eyrie, letting slip the rumors he'd heard from other lands on his travels.

"Salt is so cheap here!" he'd have one of his merchant spies say in Redwood Valley trade quarter. "Have the shortages not reached this far south?"

When the merchant next returned, the cost of salt had doubled. It was a simple, easy thing to do. Thanks to his spies, he'd kept close eyes on most of the eyries east of the desert and a few to the west.

Every eyrie had its worries. The Argent Heights lacked the herbs needed to counteract diseases from the Emerald Jungle. The Crackling Sea Eyrie feared Crestfall shutting down trade.

Even the Blackwing Eyrie had its fears. Its opinici feared that their allies would rebel and join the Seraph King's armies. Rybalt had used that fear several times to

campaign for better living conditions for his eyrie's expa-
triates.

And the inclusion of gryphon prides, he thought as Iony
flew above him.

The pitohui opinici and glacier pride had long been
friends—odd, considering his eyrie was on a tropical
island and the glacier pride lived on a frozen mountain.
Even now, where a few blackwings flinched at gryphons
flying above them, the pitohui were grateful for the
support should Ninox or the Ashen Weald's forces catch
up with them.

While sowing unrest was a useful skill to have, it was
useless if an opinicus didn't know when it was time to
leave. A quick count of his forces showed that at least two
blackwings had been killed in their flight from the prison.
The Ashen Weald would put them together with the
monitors and the prison break tonight.

And if not them, Mally would have informed the
Seraph King's forces about the blackwing camp by now.
And there was no telling what Ninox would do now that
she had her mate back. It was time to move camp and
reassess.

They landed on the southern edge of Poisonmaw
Valley, and Rybalt and Iony made their way to meet with
the headmaster.

"We should have killed the Kjarr," Iony grumbled.
"Coming back with a treasury is great, but they didn't
release the Reeve's Bane from jail for him to come back
empty-beaked."

"It's a lot of beads. It would certainly refill my own
coffers." Rybalt sighed. "They want the reeve killed in a
land where there are no reeves. We could kill a random

opinicus off the street, put a tiara on his head, and they'd be none the wiser."

"No more reeves isn't such a bad idea," the long-eared gryphon said. "But you aren't taking this seriously enough, old friend. You cannot come back without a body."

"Perhaps we'll get lucky yet," Rybalt said with an open-beaked grin. "There's one more thing I'd like to finish up before we go."

They pushed through into the headmaster's quarters, and Rybalt made his demands of Neider.

The scholar had several maps of the bog unrolled around him. "I think you're making the wrong choice. But if you must know, here was the dig site. The landmarks will be hidden under the cypress and moss, but you can fly northeast from the bend in the Jadebeak River and find it."

Iony pawed at the corner of one of the maps. "The Nighthaunt isn't going to be sitting there waiting for you to show up, Rybalt. Neider's little spy ring has had assassins tracking him since before you were locked away."

Rybalt dismissed the blackwing guards to go prepare to retrieve the beads. He waited until they were out of hearing range to scold Neider. "It was a mistake to send them instead of me. Headmaster, you're a smart opinicus. You know I'm going there to burn the infested seraph. But I think you know the threat your old colleague poses, both to your own life and the lives of others. I'm going to ask you one more time—do you have a clear and accurate map of where the dig site is located?"

The headmaster stared the reeve in the eyes. "Did you bring back my assistant and Cherine?"

"Your forger is in one piece outside," Iony said. "Your protégé is... safer than he would be with the blackwings."

"We gave him to Ninox," Rybalt said. "I believe the blackwing reeve grows tired of Redwood scholars."

The headmaster seemed less than pleased. He put away the journal he'd been writing in when he was interrupted and pulled out a new map—one that had the most current landmarks.

"We retrieved this from the Clover Ranch," the headmaster said. "There's a bog witch and wingtorn who have been mapping the northern bog as they clear out starlings. They could be a little more diligent about putting away their things."

"Is the bog clear of starlings?" Iony asked.

"No." The headmaster left it at that.

Despite the speculation reported back from their spies in the Ashen Weald, Impir's use of the parasite had been a trial run. The starling incursions into the kjarr was something the best blackwing tacticians had guessed would happen. The way the starlings reacted to the parasite, their pack-minded response, was not.

Rybalt looked over the map. It was a long way to the bog. It would be a long way back when they were done. They'd want to bypass the Kjarr nesting grounds and Crackling Sea Eyrie at night.

A commotion from outside drew their attention away from maps and logistics. Two blackwing guards escorted in a small, blue merchant.

"She insisted, Reeve Rybalt," one of the guards said. "I told her pay would come through the usual trade channels."

"This couldn't wait," Didi said.

Iony bristled. "What could be so important at such a late hour?"

"You asked me to keep out an eye for any word on the reeves," Didi said. "Well, I found something."

The merchant pulled out a piece of parchment from her harness, rubbed a rounded talon into charcoal and began to sketch out a metal talon with gems.

"Quite the artist," the headmaster said.

"Looks like Redwood Valley design," Rybalt said. "Or maybe Reevesport. Definitely peafowl."

"It was Reeve Brevin's," the merchant corrected. "When she was buried, her necklace and metal talons were missing. Zeph and Kia took them from the body, but they disappeared at Hatzel's nesting grounds."

"And?" Iony asked.

"And I just saw a fisherfolk wearing them," she continued. "He might be hiding more relics or even one of the reeve's daughters."

"How many of Brevin's daughters were unaccounted for? The eldest and youngest?" Rybalt chewed a talon. He thought it unlikely either had survived. Bario and Impir were usually quite thorough. "This may be better left to the next team of scouts. We don't have time to return to the shore."

"I saw them at the Redwood Valley ruins," Didi said. "There's a fisherfolk caravan stationed there. I can find out where they're going. I know one of the fisherfolk."

Wealth, reeves, and a weapon too dangerous to allow even his own side to use it. Rybalt sighed. Things often went better when he had Iony by his side. Then again, there was something nice about having Iony in a position to come to his rescue if things went wrong.

"Fine." Rybalt pulled out a string of five hundred

metal beads. "Here's your payment up front and an advance. Find where they're going, then head to the meeting spot along the goliath pass."

Didi chirped a thank you and allowed the guards to escort her out.

"I thought it was bad form to pay an informant before they provided information?" Iony chided.

"Didi's a special case," Headmaster Neider said. "She's tried to leave several times now, but her family pulls her back in. She tried to run off with a fisherfolk once."

"Ah," Iony said.

"Five hundred pure metal beads from the treasury should help her decide where her loyalties lie," Rybalt said. "If she wants to run off, so be it. She has the money to do so. I trust her information better this way."

Iony spread the map out with his paws again. "Mally the Nighthaunt, at last."

"Not for you," Rybalt said. "You wait and find out if Didi's information is good first. You're my backup if things go awry."

Neider put away his other maps. "I'll be glad to leave this place behind. Will we be able to move a treasury's worth of wealth by ourselves?"

"Get as much of it as you can tonight," Rybalt said. "Iony's pride will help you."

Iony scratched idly at an ear. "I sent my fastest flyer the moment we got back. If we can get it north of Poison-maw, they'll take it up to my nesting grounds, where the blackwing reeve may pick it up at his leisure."

If the headmaster had doubts about where the beads would end up, he was smart enough not to show it in front of Rybalt. The Reeve's Bane collected the rest of his forces. Iony would look into the reeve's missing offspring. The headmaster and the rest of Iony's pride would start moving the wealth north, assuming Ninox hadn't betrayed them.

And Rybalt would hunt down the greatest war criminal of all time.

Well, the greatest war criminal who isn't on our side, he amended.

48

FOULTNER'S FLIGHT

Foultner couldn't stand to be in the weald. She'd been so caught up in the trial that she hadn't even considered the possibility that the blackwings would stage their jailbreak at the same time. What's more, they had their own keys, which suggested there were spies in the Ashen Weald she was unaware of.

She flew west. Merin was her friend, but she didn't have anything to say to Satra or his children. She felt like she'd failed him. At the waystation where she'd met the Ashen Weald, he'd been the first gryphon to say kind words to her. She'd often disagreed with him—they were rarely on the same side of an argument—but she'd always enjoyed his company.

Foultner looked back and was annoyed to see that Blinky was following her. As an opinicus, Foultner should be able to outfly a gryphon.

She worked her wings harder, gaining a little on her owl friend, and followed the pass through the taiga.

None of the taiga pride's patrols challenged her.

Having retrieved her black armor and claws from Orlea, Foultner had a distinct look.

Her wings should ache, but she felt numb. She flew over the kjarr nesting grounds. The prospect of spending the night alone there didn't appeal to her. With any luck, Henders would have stayed late at the ranch. She'd probably find him trying to teach Tilly the Goliath Bird to play fetch or something stupid like that.

The numbness faded, letting a few tears fall over the fields of sawgrass south of the Crackling Sea. She began to feel the ache in her wings just as the clover-shaped ranch came into view.

Blinky flew ahead of her, letting Foultner see her as she slowed down. "Stop flying. The night is not safe for you. We need to rest and go back."

"I'm not going back," Foultner said. "I'm finding Henders and going to bed."

True to life, Henders hadn't returned to New Eyrie. He was leading a few lost capybaras back into their pens.

Foultner began her descent. Blinky flew after her, but Urious and Soft Paws called up to get their attention. Foultner didn't hear what they said, didn't really care what they said, but their words pulled Blinky away.

Foultner was curled up with Henders in one of the loft nests when Blinky finally came up a half-hour later. Foultner had told Henders everything, and he was in the middle of explaining that Blinky was just worried about Foultner's safety when the owl gryphon interrupted them.

"You are needed downstairs," she said. "Soft Paws and Urious found something in the bog that needs our attention."

"There's nothing in the bog that can't wait until morning." Foultner stuffed her face under Henders's wing to hide from the owl.

"The white opinici have found what they are looking for," Blinky said. "The goliath birds you gave them are there, along with all of their forces."

Foultner didn't want to deal with this. "Soft Paws is a pride leader. Why can't she deal with it?"

"Fine," Blinky said. "I cannot force you to come. But what they found concerns Henders."

Blinky burrowed between the two opinici and pushed the ex-Reeve's Guard off the edge.

He squawked and spread his wings, gliding down to where Soft Paws and Urious waited.

Foultner tried to curl up with Blinky, but the owl gryphon put a paw in Foultner's face and removed herself from the nest. "Why do you need Henders?"

Blinky groomed a few feathers back in place before leaping down. "The white opinici are after the mummy he found in the swamp."

Foultner's body groaned in protest, but she wiped off her tears and followed Blinky down to the common area.

FOULTNER WARMED her talons at the brazier. The breeze coming off the sea kept the ranch cold even in spring. She settled in to listen to Urious and Soft Paws.

Henders, ever concerned with hospitality even when he wasn't the host, retrieved some spiked eels to warm over the fire.

"It's a reunion of sorts," Urious said. "All of us have been to the dig site except for Foultner, though not at the same time. Henders and I were there together with the expedition."

"I was there watching Soft Paws," Blinky confirmed.

Soft Paws eyes widened. "I didn't go to the dig site itself, but I've picked flowers near it. The elder witches didn't like the younger ones to get close."

Blinky considered this. "It is true. I had forgotten. You followed Vitra away. I watched the elder witches."

"That's who we've been tracking," Urious said. "Officially, we're in there clearing out starlings. And that is most of our work. But unofficially, we've been trying to track down Black Mask and the last of Vitra's bog witches."

While Henders divvied out roasted eel, Foultner made her own talons useful and fetched the bog map off the wall. It was made of leather with painted glyphs marked over areas or scratched off based on starling sightings. For the most part, the kjarr half was safe. The boardwalk, Flower, and raftworks all had fairly large wingtorn and ranger contingents at them, with Bogwash catching any starlings who managed to sneak east.

The western bog was still full of starlings. The bog pride sent expeditions to the Heart of the Bog, though the only permanent inhabitants of the sunken eyrie were giant matamata turtles now. The bog north of the Heart was impossible to keep clear of starlings for reasons Foultner was about to learn.

Blinky pointed to the dig site. "This is where the starlings are infected. When I was following the elder crones, I saw a starling expedition turn on itself."

"While we stayed there," Urious added, "we saw an infected starling cry out and little mites came out of the opinithing."

"What's an opinithing?" Foultner asked. She finished her sixth eel and sent Henders to get more. Her body cried out for more salt.

He returned with more spits for the fire and a sketch. "I drew this while we were there."

"Is that a gryphon burial shroud?" she asked. "Why does it have flight feathers on its legs?"

"I don't know," Urious said. "Its back legs were funny, too. They weren't talons or claws. They were kind of both."

"I saw little six wing drawings all over the ruins," Henders added.

"Yes, perhaps they built the eyrie that collapsed. The bog sometimes preserves things." Soft Paws recoiled a little at how much salt Foultner was eating and pushed a bowl of mint water over to her. "Drink this before you, too, end up a preserved mummy."

"Okay, I'm caught up—and full, thank you, Henders," Foultner said. "So there's a mummy full of parasites, and the Seraph King's opinici are here to take it away. Do they know it's infected?"

Urious looked at Soft Paws, who returned his shrug. "We didn't think of that. We assumed they knew."

"When it was submerged, the bugs didn't come out," Henders said. "Erlock spent hours staring at it. It was only when it dried out several days later that we found out. How wet is that part of the bog right now? Was the pond full?"

"I didn't think to look," Urious said. "The lowlands had standing water."

"I believe it was underwater." Soft Paws had out more blue paint and was refreshing her flowery camouflage.

Foultner swore internally, but not anything too

profane lest Henders could read her thoughts. If the bog witch needed new paint, that meant they were going out there tonight.

"Fine. We've had a blackwing attack already," Foultner said without realizing that Soft Paws and Urious would have no idea. "Let's take the full might of the Ashen Weald and squash their expedition. We can send their bodies with a blackwing or two and explain that they were ambushed and the Seraph Emperor or whoever won't be any wiser."

"There is no one to send," Blinky said. "Everyone who could fly went east to pay their respects to Merin. Everyone who can walk won't make it here in time."

"Why does Merin need anyone to pay him respects?" Urious asked.

"What attack?" Soft Paws added.

Blinky saved Foultner the pain of explaining it by giving a short version. Soft Paws hadn't known Merin except for council meetings, but Urious had fought with him at two eyries.

"He's with Zrim and Jun now." The wingtorn kept his voice even.

Foultner looked up and realized how few ranch hands were still here, none of whom had any experience fighting. The trade caravan must have left to take supplies from the Crackling Sea to the Redwood Valley. "Wait, are you suggesting us five go in and stop them?"

"There's no one else," Urious said. "We should at least see what they're up to."

Blinky looked east. "There are more we can ask. I saw them flying after us. They, too, fled the weald when Foultner did."

"I wasn't fleeing," Foultner corrected her owl friend. "But how can we trust anyone who was? Who are they?"

"Fisherfolk and free pride." Blinky moved to the eastern threshold of the common area and looked out into the night. "They are nearly here."

Foultner got up to look out at the night sky. She couldn't see anything at first. It wasn't until their visitors landed and she saw who they were that she groaned.

"Bleeding depths, not the Reeve's Bane again." Foultner watched Henders's nares turn red.

"Hello!" Zeph called out as he landed. His ears and tail were far too perky for the late hour.

"It's nice to meet you again," Kia added. "Foultner, isn't it?"

Behind them were three fisherfolk. The white one and the peacock stayed out of the light, but the third one charged right in.

"Oh, hey, is it a reunion party?" Quess ran up and gave Soft Paws a big hug. "How've you two been? And Henders! I tried your knife fish recipe with some ocean eels. It took a few tries and a lot less salt, but I got it working."

Foultner was torn between wanting to hide, cry, sleep, or fly to New Eyrie and ignore the world. Instead, she just said, "Well, come on in. There's eels over the fire. We may as well catch everyone up."

49

THE NEW EXPEDITION

Т he common area on the ground floor of the Clover
Ranch looked to Piprik more or less as he'd had it
described to him by Tresh after her adventures in the bog.
The ranch had one main purpose: to move supplies from
the eyries down into the bog. To that end, it had the
largest concentration of goliath birds, and the bottom
floor of the inside of the ranch was piled high with crates.

Urious and Soft Paws had a small planning space set
up away from the loading area for their search, and maps
lined the wall here. Quess found a couple small braziers,
lit them, and brought them over for the group, along with
several cushions for the opinici.

Zeph, Kia, and Piprik formed a barrier in front of
Levin. Piprik settled in around just the sort of observant,
powerful gryphons and opinici he had hoped to avoid by
coming out to the Clover Ranch.

Quess had arranged several nests for them here to
allow them to trade salt with New Eyrie and the Crackling
Sea Eyrie. After getting so close to Satra, they decided

they should leave before anyone put them under closer scrutiny. Kia and Zeph, fearing the skies were still full of blackwing spies, came with them. Hatzel would have come along, too, had she not needed to stay for Merin's funeral.

Then again, those gathered here weren't quite strangers, either, as Quess's reaction had attested to.

"We never made it to the dig site ourselves," Quess said. "The lone survivor from the Flower talked about it. He said Headmaster Neider had led the expedition there. He seemed to think it was cursed."

"What happened to him?" Foultner asked. "We should get his account later."

"I killed him," Quess said.

"Oh." Foultner blinked. "Infected?"

"Sadly, no." Quess's voice hardened when she spoke about the bog. "A failed escape attempt that cost the life of my partner. He was guarding us and failed to check for my spare gutting knife."

"Ah," Foultner said.

"We've all heard about the expedition," Piprik lied. "Bruen, Quess, Tresh, and the rangers who sought sanctuary filled us in. What's going on in the bog? What do you need us for?"

"Northern eyries seeking to cause trouble," Foultner said.

"We had a little of that on the shore," Quess said. "Piprik here blew them up."

Piprik would have preferred to keep that part quiet. Along with his full name, false though it was.

"So the blackwings hit the jails, the eyrie, and the dig site all on the same night?" Kia asked.

"Not blackwings, no, this is the Seraph King." Urious scratched at an ear like he was thinking. "Piprik, weren't you the one who gave Soft Paws the information on them?"

"I'd rather it not be well known I'm here." Most of the gryphons and opinici Piprik was familiar with, but Foultner, Henders, and Urious were unknown to him except by reputation.

"That's fine," Foultner said, "but we could use some help. I'd like to know what they're up to."

He filled them in with the basics, leaving out some information on himself. He begged off details of the Alabaster Eyrie and Argent Heights, claiming he'd been a farmer to the east. Which wasn't a lie—his family did own a goliath bird ranch to the east, just much farther east than he was letting on.

Blinky poked her head down from the roof. "Are we done talking? We should go now."

While Henders and Foultner tracked down a few extra pumpkin vials and a harness for Zeph to wear, Piprik tried to convince Lei to stay.

"It's dangerous out there," he said, but Lei wasn't listening.

"It's dangerous everywhere," the peacock countered. He'd become emboldened by helping evacuate the underbough from the monitors. "And they could be taking the opinici from New Eyrie into the bog. I want to see for myself."

Piprik spared a glance for Foultner and Urious. "Fine, but keep your talons tucked away this time."

Lei nodded.

Piprik led his young charge towards the strangers. "I'll

be your medicine opinicus for this expedition. I under-stand you had Biski last time. This is Lei, my assistant. He'll be carrying my supplies. He's an islander, so if he says anything strange, that's just how they are."

Kia shot Piprik a disapproving glance, but he shrugged it off. Lei had handled himself well with the monitor lizards, and his fledgling feathers were mostly gone. While Piprik would prefer the peacock stay hidden on an island, he'd had younger assistants in his time.

"We have a medicine gryphon already," Soft Paws said.

He looked at her strange harness pouch with flowers and vines sticking out of it. "It never hurts to have a backup in case one of us is injured."

"Okay," Urious said. "I'll be going in by foot, but we've cleared out enough starlings that you can fly most of the way there. Just stay low so the white opinici don't see you."

"Wait, you're not coming with us?" Foultner said.

Urious took a bow, showing off the long scars where his wings once were. "You don't have time for me to walk all the way into the bog. I'm going to head directly west and find a good vantage point. With their goliath birds, they're going to have to walk out. I want to be there to see what they're carrying. Besides, you're in good paws. Soft paws, one might even say."

Soft Paws rolled her eyes. "Once we're on the ground, stick close. Stay away from water. This isn't the expedition where you want to find out what a knife fish is for the first time."

Everyone from the previous expedition looked at Henders.

FLYING over the bog gave Piprik flashbacks to his own flight from the Emerald Jungle. He'd followed the Jadebeak Mountains—almost hills by comparison with the taiga in the east—dodging bog gryphons and starlings as best he could. He'd ultimately ended up stranded on an island south of the Emerald Jungle after several mishaps. Only luck and a parakeet smuggler had brought him the rest of the way to Swan's Rest.

Even knowing they would stop long before the starling's home, a feeling of panic sent his heart into a tizzy at the thought of flying *towards* the Jadebeak Mountains. He held a lot of regrets in this direction. He felt a small pang of regret for giving Erlock his eyrie badge. Each day that passed without her return made him fear for the worst.

As they approached the dig site, they could see the light of a giant bonfire. They landed out of view and let Soft Paws lead them the rest of the way on foot.

"They're brave to use so much light," Kia said. "Aren't they worried the bog pride will see them? Or the Ashen Weald?"

"By tomorrow, they'll be gone," Foultner replied. "This is what they were after, not diplomacy, it seems."

"Wait, how will they return the goliath birds if they leave tomorrow?" Henders asked.

Blinky shushed them.

Soft Paws held up a back paw to tell them to wait, then slipped ahead.

"There's a ledge up ahead," Henders explained. "It'll give her a good look at the dig site."

While their bog witch went off to scout, the others settled in to wait. Only Lei went to explore a little on either side. He'd heard about the types of bog medicines from Soft Paws during her stay at Sandpiper's Dune and retrieved some thorn vine.

Henders went to relieve himself away from the group, an act that was followed by a small yelp.

Everyone leapt to their feet. Blinky and Zeph both slunk down low with their stomachs nearly touching the ground and prowled towards the sound.

They found Henders—and five dead bodies.

"Starlings?" Foultner comforted poor Henders.

"Sorry," Henders said. "I didn't mean to yelp. I think they're dead."

Lei had gone close to inspect them. He put his talons on a starling's chest. "This one is still breathing."

Blinky went from starling to starling and made sure they were dead. Foultner pulled out a vial of pumpkin to dose her with.

"It is strange," Blinky said. "I am starting to like the taste of pumpkin."

"The newer vials use roasted pumpkin instead of raw tincture in alcohol," Piprik said. "I helped design the new mixture last time I was up north."

"Medicine is no good if you throw it back up," Zeph said. "Younce taught us that."

"Mmm," Piprik said. He turned to say something to Lei, which was when he saw his apprentice on the ground twitching.

"Depths," he whispered.

Foultner went to grab another pumpkin vial, but he shoved her away.

"This is something different." He pulled out a vial of red liquid and got some of it down Lei's throat. The twitching subsided, then his beak stopped chattering.

"Pitohui?" the peacock asked.

"We're not alone," Piprik said. "The blackwings' forces are here, too, chasing after the Seraph King's expedition. Nobody touch the dead starlings. Keep watch on Blinky in case she got their poison on her."

They slipped back to their waiting spot, but every shadow felt sinister.

"Is the headmaster here?" Kia asked. "Did he bring Cherine with him?"

"It's the Reeve's Bane," Zeph said. "He kills reeves, right? The opinicus called Silver is the reeve of a small eyrie north of here."

"He doesn't just kill reeves," Quess said. "He went after Piprik, too. He seems to have something against scholars."

All eyes were on Piprik again. He supposed it was better than having them on Lei. "The Blackwing Eyrie's spy network misunderstands my desire to find Mally the Nighthaunt. They believe me one of his allies when all I want is to see him held accountable."

"It's hard to believe someone like that is real," Foultner said.

"I saw his portrait hanging in the headmaster's office," Kia said. "He was a peregrine falcon with white feathers and a hint of red. Cherine's letters said he found one of Mally's workshops and several mass graves in the mountains. I suppose the stories were real."

Piprik thought back to the crates of purple salts with the seal of Crestfall stamped on them. He had doubts that his old mentor still resembled a peregrine falcon but kept his beak shut. If Mally was here, they'd find out soon enough.

Soft Paws returned. "They have nearly retrieved the

opinithing. The goliath birds are already on their way north carrying the rest of their findings."

"Supplies?" Foultner thought of the Reeve's Nest treasury fortune hunters were looking for. "Like bog flowers or what? Is there treasure out here?"

"Stormcloth," Henders said. "All the stormcloth stolen from the Crackling Sea over the years was by the bog pride's nesting grounds."

Soft Paws nodded. "We had yet to retrieve it. There didn't seem to be a polite way to carry a fortune worth of stolen stormcloth past our opinicus allies at the Flower and raftworks, so we left it."

"We're not alone out here. The Reeve's Bane is making his move." Piprik divvied up the last of his vials of pitohui antivenom to members of the expedition with versatile talons.

Zeph looked at the bottle given to Kia. "You should give the Ashen Weald the recipe for it. And make more. A lot more."

"The recipe needs scarabs," Piprik said. "There's no easy way to get them this far south."

"I thought you drank the last vial when they attacked?" Lei asked. "You got all that out of the one scarab we found?"

Quess winced, having just figured out the answer. She'd set aside the dead bodies of the opinici killed in the explosion for Piprik to *give proper burial rites* to.

He confirmed her suspicions. "Dead pitohui also work, if you scrape the venom off their feathers."

Lei made a face.

"Making the elixir this way isn't nearly as effective, so try not to hug any for too long." Piprik had learned several recipes from Mally the Nighthaunt that he didn't share in polite company—alchemical constructs that required ingredients from gryphons and opinici. Often blood.

They began their crawl towards the dig site when a shout for help broke the quiet night air.

50

THE DIG SITE, REVISITED

Zeph crested the top of the rise overlooking the chaos. The opinithing was out of the pond and atop a wagon secured to four goliath birds. When Henders had explained it, Zeph hadn't understood. He'd thought the feathers on the legs had been added later as decorations. That wasn't the case. These were some sort of flight feathers connected right to the legs.

The opinicus who had called himself Goldfeather was wounded and at Rybalt's feet. The rest of his guards had been killed, along with the laborers.

"Stay back," Zeph hissed to the gryphons behind him. Whatever side they wanted to help, it appeared to be too late.

"Do you see Silver?" Foultner asked. There was a touch of genuine concern in her voice.

"She must have gone north with the stormcloth," Zeph guessed.

Goldfeather was rambling. There was a touch of red on his beak, either blood or antivenom, and he went on about reeves and kings while Rybalt searched the area.

"Where are you hiding, Mally?" the Bane of the Crackling Sea Reeve shouted. "The Blackwing Eyrie doesn't take kindly to traitors."

No reply came. The pitohui and blackwings, about fifteen remaining, gathered around the bonfire. Rybalt lit a torch with the fire and carried it to the wagon in his beak. The mummy was still dripping wet from being pulled out of the pond.

"Still hiding?" He transferred the torch to his talons. "Bario has been busy carrying on in his father's name. Did the headmaster tell you about his work?"

The blackwing opinici began to douse the mummy in a new type of oil.

"Last chance," Rybalt challenged. "I know you're out there. How will the king feel about your experiments if you let this seraph burn?"

The screech that came from overhead was unlike anything Zeph had heard before. Everyone flattened themselves to the ground.

Several pouches of white powder hit the bonfire, extinguishing all light except for Rybalt's torch.

Rybalt held the torch out to look for Mally. He held it high for several minutes, then turned it towards the bonfire.

The moment he turned his back to the mummy, two pale and red wings spread from behind it and a long form slithered out from its hiding place.

Rybalt's instincts were good, and he turned around and ducked just in time to keep his head. The last torch went flying, landing by the pond, as the Reeve's Bane and the Nighthaunt rose into the sky together, blood raining down on those below.

Zeph had hunted a lot of things in the last few years,

from the parrots and monitors of the weald to starlings and goliath birds. He'd even gone with Rorin on a deep sea hunt and caught glimpses of crowncrest sea serpents, serpentine whales, and sharks. He'd never seen anything quite like the afterimage of the Nighthaunt that flashed across his vision.

The mummified seraph was a thing of beauty in a state of decay, a creature of six 'wings' that was neither gryphon nor opinicus. Mally the Nighthaunt was not a thing of beauty. He was an opinicus who had become a monster. His eyes were pure black, his neck and body too long. The feathers growing from his arms and legs were flight feathers in shape only; they didn't look like anything other than a strange mutation.

The mummy and Nighthaunt were a study in how the same design could be both beautiful and monstrous, decayed and twisted, based on who the painter was.

The blackwings and pitohui rose up after Mally and Rybalt, lost in the dark night.

The Nighthaunt was a formless shape, a long beam of moonlight that twisted and flowed like a fantail's feathery train. Still, he was outnumbered fifteen to one.

He let out another preternatural screech and the sky changed. If Mally was the moonlight, Silver and her opinici were shooting stars.

Where the silvery opinici collided with blackwings and pitohui on their way down, their enemies fell limp and dropped to the ground.

Zeph watched the torch get knocked closer to the standing water. "We can't let them take the opinithing and spread the parasite. It's better if it burns."

"It seems safer to wait and see who wins," Foultner said.

"It's going to be a lot harder to burn it if the Nighthaunt wins," Zeph said. "Who has flint and tinder fungus?"

Lei and Kia raised their talons.

"You two get to the wagon and start the fire burning," Zeph said. "The rest of us will grab the torch and see if we can draw their attention."

Zeph and Blinky leapt off the ledge and went for the torch. Kia, Lei, and the other opinici went for the wagon.

Only one fisherfolk remained. Before Zeph could give him a warning, Piprik flew straight towards where Rybalt and Mally were facing off.

BELATEDLY, it occurred to Piprik that he could be mistaken for one of the Seraph King's forces in the dark. Still, he'd waited years for this moment.

Mally had knocked Rybalt out of the sky and was diving into him when Piprik collided with his old master.

Rybalt watched up with surprise as the two grappled above him. When some of the paint smeared away, he said, "Piprik?"

Mally's eyes were black orbs, nothing like the kind blue eyes they'd been when Piprik first met him. His words seemed to come from everywhere when he spoke.

—*I never took you for a traitor, Piprik.*

—*You are strong for your age, Piprik.*

—*Do you remember when we first met in the cathedral of painted glass, Piprik?*

—*I thought you were rotting in the belly of a starling, Piprik.*

—It will break your brother's heart to hear of your betrayal, Piprik.

Piprik ignored the whispers. The Reeve's Bane had tired Mally out. His old master had failed to dose himself properly with antivenom and was slowing.

Four sets of clawed-talons slashed out at Piprik and missed. Piprik pushed close, the way he'd taught Levin to imitate a pitohui, and his momentum brought Mally to the ground.

"My name is Khalim," he whispered. As soon as the words left his beak, he knew it had been a mistake. If Mally survived, Khalim would no longer be able to hide.

—My missing apprentice!

—I mourned you.

—I told your family of your death myself.

—Your widow cried.

—Was it just you who drank of my elixirs, little Khalim?

—I will find the other scholars. They will not hide. I will take them apart for my experiments.

—The night is long and covers all lands.

—I will find them.

Piprik had trained for years to fight. He had studied the styles of gryphon prides and eyries. He had looked forward to this moment for years.

Had he hesitated for only one moment, Mally would be dead. But he hesitated for two, and Silver's pounce caught him off balance and sent him sprawling.

Silver lifted Piprik up with a strength he wouldn't have guessed by her size. She lifted him to dive down and crush him. Just as she reached the heights, Rybalt caught up with them.

A single slash sent Piprik falling as his bright adversary dropped him. He managed to get his wings open and slow his fall.

Rybalt and Silver flashed through the air, but she was the bloodier of the two when she fell to the north.

Piprik landed on all fours. His whole body, Piprik's old body, shook.

Rybalt landed next to him. "I didn't believe you. You should join us up north. With your knowledge of the Seraph King, you could find yourself a cozy nest somewhere."

Piprik didn't correct Rybalt's misconception as to his real identity. He didn't have the breath to talk.

Lei, who should have been running to the wagon, must have seen him fall. He appeared with talons drawn and threatened the Reeve's Bane.

"Step away from him!" Lei shouted.

Rybalt seemed amused—until he saw the talons. "Oh, I thought I'd have to go searching for you. Who are you, little one? Where did you get those trinkets?"

Lei hissed at him. "Lei of Ashfoot Isle."

"A place I've never heard of. How quaint." Rybalt seemed to be looking at the paint, the crushed tailfeathers, and the metal talons. "But are you, really?"

He kicked dirt towards Lei's face, then used his size to knock Lei down. Rybalt lifted Lei up with one set of talons, then used the others to snap off his harness and look through the pockets with his beak.

The Reeve's Bane pulled out the twined snake necklace and tossed it on the ground. "Now why would the Bane of the Redwood Valley Reeve give you those? I imagine they'd fetch a lot of beads. What did you say your name was? Because I believe I know who you really are, little peahen."

Rybalt turned to look back at a twitching, incapacitated Lei. After Lei's run-in with the starling on their way here, he'd already been dosed with the antivenom and was fully conscious. Piprik had taught his apprentice well, and Rybalt, like all short-necked opinici, made an error of distance.

Lei struck like a snake, his beak nearly catching the pitohui's eye.

Rybalt let go, and Lei's talons cut through his chest feathers like water.

The Reeve's Bane fell back, seeing Kia striking her flint and tinder for the first time. "No, if you light it, he'll disappear again!"

Kia didn't heed his warnings. The seraph, the mummified opinithing as the first expedition called it, burst into flames.

In the dancing firelight, Piprik looked back at where his old master had been. The flames lit up a form unlike the peregrine opinicus he'd known in the Emerald Jungle. Black eyes, thin wings, a body far too long, a feathered tail that split at the end. He had more in common with the fiery seraph than the Redwood Valley opinicus he'd once been.

As though burned in effigy, the Nighthaunt disappeared into the darkness. Moments later, icy grey gryphons descended from the sky and finished off the Seraph King's remaining forces.

Lei helped Piprik up. The rest of their expedition, except Henders, Soft Paws, and Foultner, stood side-by-side in the firelight and looked at the blackwing forces.

The grey, long-eared gryphons had them surrounded.

When one of them got near Lei, Piprik kicked dirt at him and said, "Stay away from my assistant."

Rybalt looked at the medicine bag around Piprik's neck. "Did you become a medicine opinicus after you retired, Piprik? Come here and stitch me up. Your apprentice is deadly."

Piprik did as he was told. When he was close, he whispered to Rybalt, "There are no more reeves here for you to kill."

Rybalt didn't flinch as needle and thread brought his flesh back together. "Your hatred for Mally is all that keeps me from killing you. I abhor surprises."

Piprik nodded.

"The price for your friends here is the Seraph King." Rybalt motioned to Iony to check on the wagon.

Piprik frowned. "I don't understand."

"I was told Mally had become a monster," Rybalt continued. "I was also told he keeps the Seraph King immortal. Both lies, I assumed until I saw the Nighthaunt with my own eyes."

Piprik finished the stitches.

"What's the secret to his alchemy?" Rybalt asked. "If you tell me that, I'll let everyone go."

Piprik didn't know, but he had a guess. He thought back to the crates of elixir that showed up mysteriously in the jungle. The crates full of elixir he'd used on himself.

Piprik put away his supplies. "Crestfall."

"There's nothing left there," Rybalt said. "The glassworks and eyrie are gone. The pink reeve held onto his neutrality for too long, and the Seraph King's forces got there before we did."

"A desert always appears barren until you look closer," Piprik said.

Rybalt seemed to weigh this advice against the lives of so many Ashen Weald members.

"Let them go," he ordered the glacier pride. "When we next return, it'll be with armies and without patience. Before then, you should either surrender or stop your infighting."

Zeph stepped forwards. "Would you have burned the opinithing on your own, or would you have let all of those opinici die to the parasite?"

"Ah, the Bane of the Red Reeve," Rybalt said. "I'm sad I promised to let you all go. I might have changed my mind if I'd seen you here."

Zeph didn't stand down.

"I would have burned it," Rybalt said. "I never stood for disease and parasites as warfare. I believe with a few kills you can free an eyrie of tyranny. That view has never changed."

"Do your allies know that?" Lei asked. The blackwing opinici were shifting uncomfortably. They seemed to believe threatening to burn the seraph was a ruse to catch the Nighthaunt.

Rybalt nodded to Iony, who picked up Reeve Brevin's snake necklace off the ground.

"I hear there are no more reeves in the south," Rybalt said. "We'll be taking these to keep the Ashen Weald from dressing up another peacock as leader."

"Did you let the seraph burn?" a blackwing scout said. "You know our orders."

As though by choreographed accident, all of the pitohui stepped forwards, bumping their blackwing allies. The blackwings grumbled and quickly downed their antivenom vials.

Rybalt didn't look back at his questioner, instead addressing the Ashen Weald and free pride prisoners. "I don't always agree with my masters, as I'm sure the blackwings here would be quick to tell them when they return home... had I not replaced their antivenom with poison."

True to form, the blackwings began to twitch and collapse. The last one muttered "trashbird" as he died.

Rybalt stretched his wings, testing the stitches. "Unfortunate that none of them survived Mally the Nighthaunt's ambush, but all of them once served as jailors in the black reeve's prison system. I don't believe they'll be missed."

"And that the treasury was never found," Iony mumbled. At least, that's what Piprik thought he heard.

Rybalt nudged Goldfeather's unconscious body with a talon. "We'll take him. I'm sure our allies at Blacktalon will have questions for him. Iony, you find the argent reeve. She crashed north of here. She'll make a nice prize for the blackwings. Maybe with my old cell full, they'll reconsider where they want to send me."

The pitohui and glacier gryphons departed the dig site, leaving behind the Ashen Weald and a large number of dead bodies from both sides.

Piprik held his breath until all of the pitohui and glacier gryphons had left. "I didn't think they'd really let us live."

Quess looked around. "Where did Foultner, Henders, and Soft Paws go?"

51

THE ARGENT REEVE

F oultner had been feeling more like part of the crowd and less like a valuable member of the Ashen Weald until she saw Silver fall out of the sky. In that moment, she remembered her value to Satra.

Foultner grabbed Henders and pulled him away from the fighting. She called out to Soft Paws, who followed, confused.

"Did you see that opinicus crash?" Foultner asked.

Soft Paws nodded.

"Take us there. Stay out of sight, but let Henders and I come upon her. Got it?"

Soft Paws looked around. Her eyes settled on the roots of an exposed tree, and true to bog witch form, there was a path hidden behind a spike palm there.

Foultner didn't have much time to prepare Henders. He'd never been a spy, but he had a good heart, and kindness was a type of espionage.

Foultner took a few supplies out of Soft Paws's bag when they came close. With luck, Silver would still be alive.

Luck was on their side.

Soft Paws put a wing over her face, turning into a flower bush from a distance. Henders started walking towards Silver, but Foultner directed him in a slightly different direction.

"I give up!" Foultner shouted. "That stupid capybara can spend the night in the bog for all care. Let a starling eat him."

"That's not nice," Henders said. "Billy is a good capy. He just has an inflated sense of adventure."

"Yeah, well, I'm not getting devoured by sailfins searching for him," Foultner said. "We're headed back. I don't get paid enough for this."

They continued on in silence, coming close to where Soft Paws thought Silver was located. Foultner and Henders were careful to make noise. With any luck, Silver would fall for the ruse.

They were nearly past her hiding spot before she called out. "Help! Is anyone there?"

"Billy?" Henders asked.

Foultner hit him. "Hello? Is someone out here?"

"Foultner?" came the reply. "It's Silver."

Henders made it to her first. "Oh, my goodness, what happened!?"

Foultner didn't need to let loose a fake gasp. There was enough damage here to justify a real one. Silver's feathers were shredded, though her wings weren't broken. It looked like she'd tried to soften her fall with her front legs, both of which definitely were broken.

"You poor dear!" Foultner went through Soft Paw's pouch, pretending she knew what the various vines and flowers were for. Thankfully, there were splints at the bottom.

Henders pulled out two roots and began to mash them. "This is kashow root. It'll make you sneeze, but it kills the pain."

"Uh, yeah." Foultner was taken aback at Henders being good in an emergency. "Here are some splints. Do you think you have enough feathers to get airborne?"

Silver spread her wings, confirming they were unbroken, but the primaries were in terrible condition. "I don't think so. It would be tricky to get into the air with just my back legs even if the feathers were good."

Foultner hadn't heard of an opinicus using the four-legged leap to get into the air. That had always been more of a gryphon thing.

"What happened to you?" she asked. It was a dangerous question, since if she let on too much, her mark would figure out the ruse. Still, normal, nice people asked questions like that, so it was necessary she do so, too.

Silver stiffened. "I was out too late looking for roots. A starling caught me off guard in the air. It died on impact but left me in this condition."

It was a good lie. It explained the bite and claw marks on her.

"You're lucky more didn't come," Foultner said. "Though it's bad luck to have starlings so far north."

"Bog turtle luck." Henders finished with the splints. "We can probably get you to the Clover Ranch. There's a goliath bird vet who can do a better job than me."

"If you can get me north, there's a doctor at New Eyrie," Silver ventured.

Foultner doubted that was true, but she was willing to take Silver wherever she felt safest.

"How do we do this?" Foultner asked. "How do we actually move her?"

"Oh, I saw this once when I was, um, adventuring with friends," Henders said. Thankfully, Henders was always a little weird, so Silver didn't even begin to suspect he meant an Ashen Weald expedition to the very dig site she'd just come from. "Put her on top of me."

"What?" Foultner was sure she'd misheard him.

"Oh, I see," Silver said. "So I just ride you back to town?"

Foultner didn't really want anyone riding Henders, but her brain was still out of sorts from the day.

"Right!" Henders said. "We should hurry in case the starlings come back."

A little uncomfortable with opinici riding other opinici, Foultner got underneath Silver and helped lift her atop Henders with her feet hanging down. It looked painful, but the kashow root's numbing properties were strong.

"Okay, you stay behind me, Foult, and make sure Silver doesn't fall off," Henders said.

"Sure thing," Foultner replied. She looked back at where Soft Paws had hidden, but the gryphon was gone. "This isn't weird at all."

"You must do a lot of flying," Henders said to his passenger. "Your stomach muscles are like iron."

"Thanks!" Silver said. "I do fly a lot. We run drills every day."

"I'd rather have a full stomach than an iron stomach," Foultner groused.

"I miss running drills," Henders said. "We used to do that in the Reeve's Guard, back before I was a rancher. Oh! But I've been building shoulder muscles. Can you feel?"

"Nope, both legs are splinted," Silver said. "I'm sure Foultner can feel, though, for me?"

Henders paused so Foultner could feel. She suppressed a sigh, but said, "Yep, definitely getting some muscle there."

Henders looked happy. He continued chatting as they worked their way across the sawgrass fields towards New Eyrie. Foultner had to give it to him, no one would ever expect either of them to be spies. Even she was starting to think they were just taking a friend to get help. And, in a way, that's what they were doing. There was no way to know when either of them may need a favor later.

"Okay, I can't go on anymore," Henders said. "Move in front of me and I'll lower her on top of you, Foult."

Foultner allowed Silver to be lowered on top of her. Her whole body ached after the flight, but they were nearly to the city limits. How much of the night was gone?

"Am I too heavy for you?" Silver asked.

"Nope," Foultner lied. "My muscles are like iron vines. I just keep a layer of fat around them for warmth. It's a southern thing."

That was the last of the energy she had for chat. She let Henders continue to question their guest about drills and exercise the rest of the way. Despite Henders's excitement and promises they'd wake up at dawn each day and practice aerial acrobatics, Foultner felt certain she'd be sleeping in every day until summer after tonight.

The sun was just starting to come up when they dropped off Silver with the last of the Seraph King's envoys in New Eyrie who were packing up to go. While Silver offered gracious thanks, Foultner and Henders limped to the small, misnumbered tent outside the walls.

They collapsed together in his nest, most of their limbs spilling out from its confines.

"Hey, the sun is up," Henders mumbled. "Does today count for our exercise routine?"

"Sure," Foultner mumbled. She pushed her soft stomach against his back, mindful of his wings, and wrapped her talons around his cozy middle. It had been a hard day, but she'd come to realize something. She wasn't perfect, her inability to predict the jailbreak and monitors proved that, but she was useful.

Useful, she thought. *I can live with that.*

She listened to Henders's light snoring, thought about Merin, and cried a little before falling asleep herself.

52

THE HEADMASTER AND THE
NIGHTHAUNT

Back at Poisonmaw Valley, Headmaster Neider watched from a safe distance as Didi pretended to pick the lock on the cages holding the prisoners and escorted them out through the same path the monitors had taken. The Reeve's Bane may want them killed, but the headmaster didn't see any harm in letting them go. It also provided Didi with a cover story should someone recognize her part in the events of the last few days.

Most of Neider's value to his blackwing allies came from his informants in the south, of whom Didi was one of the last. Most had been killed by fire, wingtorn, starlings, or inquisitors, but he suspected many of them were simply laying low to see what happened next.

The merchant spy made a great show of unlocking a cage that was already unlocked and freeing several captured gryphons, including the taiga gryphon whose identity Iony had borrowed to sneak around the weald and eyries. The glacier pride leader had been surprised to see a gryphon like himself wearing a medicine gryphon harness.

As the prisoners crept away, Neider settled in and finished writing down his notes for Cherine. He was getting too old to lead a spy ring. He no longer had the faith he'd once had as a young opinicus. The game no longer felt like a puzzle he had to solve.

By his own accounting, he'd only done a few truly terrible things in his years. For the most part, he'd helped people who needed help. He'd given guidance to the disenfranchised, allowed them to shape the world in less conventional ways.

The worst things to happen hadn't been his idea. Reeve Brevin came up with burning down the weald on her own. That nasty business with the Crackling Sea reeve had been all Rybalt. Even though Neider's expedition had found the parasite, others had weaponized it.

But he had let those things happen. At some point, he'd stopped influencing others and allowed himself to be influenced. Which was a shame. He'd joined Felicio's spy ring, took it over after his friend's death, because he honestly believed it was the best way to protect the Redwood Valley Eyrie in the long term.

He looked down at the journal. It was the same type Cherine used to write in. When the headmaster looked at Cherine and Kia, he saw the offspring he'd never had. He saw young scholars who wanted to make the world a better place. Bright and passionate, with a love of learning.

This journal was his last message to his former pupils. In whatever capacity the university still existed, he awarded Kia full scholar status. To Cherine, he left behind one of his brother's feathers, treated to be free of plague, and a story about how important Cherine's family had been in Neider discovering the cure.

Neider left out the bit about dissecting Cherine's brother. He hadn't become headmaster without understanding tact. And to both, he left behind detailed research on crops, livestock, and a list of plants that northerners had known were edible but which Redwood Valley opinici had yet to try. He thought Kia in particular would appreciate the trick to making rhubarb safe to eat. Between the two of them, they should also be able to read between the lines and figure out the secret of his egg treatments in case they could be improved upon.

He secured the journal in its hiding place and rubbed mint around it. Ninox's scouts would certainly show up to make sure the blackwing forces had left. When they smelled the mint, they'd bring the journal to Cherine. At least, that's how it went in his mind.

The headmaster doused the fire where he'd burned some of his other maps of the region. The cockatiel and Iony's pride were waiting for him just north. He should catch up before he was left behind. The flight up through the mountains was terrible without someone to talk to.

He stepped out of his cave and into the light, where a bloody mess awaited him.

"Mally," he said.

The shape of his old friend coughed.

—*You told them where I was located.*

"Yes," the headmaster said.

—*You sent assassins to kill me.*

"Would you not have killed me last time we met if I hadn't lit the light in time?"

—*It wasn't personal. We are friends.*

The headmaster looked down upon his old comrade. He didn't trust the wounds he saw. Mally's elixirs had healed him from worse.

"Is the Reeve's Bane dead?" Neider asked.

—*He lives. He burned the seraph.*

The Nighthaunt breathed heavily. Blood pooled at his feet. In the daylight, he looked less like a monster and more like a curiosity from the taxidermy section of the zoo.

The headmaster clenched both sets of talons. The talons on his left were sharp. The ones on his right had been sanded down to allow him use of a quill pen.

Rybalt had made a mistake in burning the seraph. The parasite could have ended the war. Now, the only remaining seraph was frozen in ice atop the glacier pride's icy mountain. There was no keeping a zealot from his prize. The Seraph King would find a way there. Rybalt's actions had only put Iony's pride in grave danger.

—*You sent him to kill me.*

"Yes," Neider confirmed. "All of them. From the moment I had you banished, I realized my mistake. You are too dangerous to live. Every assassin who has plagued your steps came from me. The world is better without you."

The thing that was once Mally the Nighthaunt let out a screech that deafened the headmaster's sensitive hearing and pounced. The headmaster slashed, felt the dulled tips of his digits against the white feathers of his opponent's throat, and belatedly realized he'd slashed with the wrong talons.

The Nighthaunt's beak opened large, far too large, and the last thing the headmaster saw was the iron-red maw at the center of the white feathers.

EPILOGUE
HEIR TO THE BLUE THRONE

S atra allowed herself to be pulled from the weald to
the Crackling Sea Eyrie only after she'd spent time
with all of Merin's loved ones.

Gryphons were resilient. She hoped they'd all be okay,
but she wanted them to know they weren't alone or
forgotten in their grief.

Orlea was recovering from a monitor bite at Hatzel's
nesting grounds. She wasn't safe to fly, and the weald was
now unsafe for walking until the last of the rogue lizards
were cleared out, but she sent word that, with Merin's
death, they wouldn't be prosecuting his successor, Askel.

Cherine's disappearance raised too many questions
for Satra to pardon him, despite Zeph and Kia's pleas. The
Kjarr hoped that with Triddle serving as co-leader of the
pride, he'd eventually bring his pridemates around.
Besides, since no one knew where Cherine was, there was
no one to forgive or prosecute for the time being.

The only reason Satra felt certain Cherine was even
alive was the arrival of the strangest guest to the funeral—
Ninox, complete with three fuzzy gryphlets in tow. Had

there been any doubt about Ninox and Cherine's relationship, Sound of Snow's feathered down had turned a slight golden color, and she kept pulling her brothers' tails with her opinicus talons.

After the blackwing sightings in the bog, kjarr, sea, and weald, everyone was willing to chalk up the deaths to the northern Reeve's Bane and breathe a sigh of relief that Ninox was watching their northern border again.

Which brought Satra back across the taiga to the eyrie that had served as the background to her greatest accomplishments and darkest moments: the Crackling Sea.

She sat with Grenkin in the throne room and filled him in on the funeral. He was still recovering from his assassination attempt and hadn't been able to make the flight.

He slid over a bowl with more than just mint water in it. "To Merin."

"To the co-consorts, Askel and Triddle." She took a lap. The alcohol burned a little on its way down.

Grenkin's eye patch and prosthetics were on the ground next to him in case he had to look presentable in a hurry. Behind them was a plain tapestry draped over the only furniture in the room.

"You threw a sheet over the throne?" she asked.

"I'm trying to find a way to remove it entirely," he said, "but it seems to actually be carved into the mountain itself."

She laughed. "That's such an opinicus way to make a chair."

"Instead, I'm having more perches added around it," he said. "Half of the refugees at New Eyrie went with the Seraph King's forces. The other half are keen to rejoin eyrie life."

"About time," Satra said. "How do your blues feel about having so many reds living with them?"

"Like siblings sharing a nest," the ranger lord said. "They'll get used to it, though. I've decided it's time for the Crackling Sea to stop being afraid of having leaders. Obviously, it didn't deter the assassins. With your blessing, I'll be taking over in an official capacity."

Satra nodded her approval. "You already do the job. Ranger lord may as well be a synonym for reeve out here. I know the Redwood Valley Eyrie had an ornate, intertwined snake necklace and matching talons that disappeared with Brevin. What does the Crackling Sea reeve wear?"

"The Crackling Sea crown has metal tentacles designed to flow down a long neck," he explained. "Same for the talons; the metal wraps up around the bindings on the leg. We left them in the old reeve's quarters."

"How properly ostentatious for a reeve. I can't imagine how you fly around without it falling off," Satra laughed. Then she inclined her head. "Reeve Grenkin."

"Ah, about that," he said. "I've decided to take the title of pride leader. It's hard to run the rangers and the eyrie, and it's a conflict of interest. I'm assigning one of the reds as new ranger lord. One of the blues will serve in a new role, one that manages eyrie logistics."

The echoes of pigeons came from down the hall behind the throne. She remembered gulls and herons sneaking in to steal fish from her time here, but pigeons usually stayed above the eyrie in the gardens.

Grenkin took another drink. "I've decided that, to stop another Brevin or Jonas, we need more than one person in charge of our eyrie."

"It's been nice to share Ashen Weald leadership with

the other prides," Satra said. "I've been looking at ways to bring in the so-called free prides. Some sort of agreement that keeps us all working together even if they don't want to be called Ashen Weald."

"It's a smart idea," Grenkin said.

"Thanks, Orlea and Foultner thought of it." Satra grinned. "I hope your own co-rulers are so smart."

"Well, I've picked out Mia as the new Ranger Lord," he said. "She's been skulking around here lately with her sister and Biski. They finally fessed up to finding some of the old reeve's tunnels."

"You should clear those out with fire." Satra regretted her choice of words. The last time she'd been in a hidden passage here, it had blown up, nearly killing her and Merin. "Sounds like some pigeons got into the passages."

Grenkin stretched his neck up. "You're right. Want to come with me to help close them up?"

"Afraid to go alone?" Satra's tone was jovial and inebriated, but a sense of dread came to her. The old reeve's quarters felt haunted. She'd spent many hours outside the sealed-up door hiding from Jonas, who wouldn't come anywhere near that section of the eyrie.

Grenkin didn't laugh. He grabbed a small, portable brazier and brought it along with him, using it to light the larger ones along the way. Half still worked, though they smelled strongly of fish.

To their surprise, there were no pigeons. They hit the door, seals removed but rusted shut, and heard the birds from the other side.

"Did someone open it?" Satra asked.

"It's possible." Grenkin pushed against the entryway, but it was wedged shut. It took both of them shoving to finally break the last of the seal.

They stumbled inside, startling the pigeons. Satra looked at the large bed with its four decorated columns. Where Brevin's Reeve's Nest building was intricate and showed off her wealth and metalworking, this was a bedroom of carved stone and power.

One entire wall had been carved with depictions of a storm over the sea. Lightning and jellyfish were everywhere. Mother of pearl had been used liberally. Sitting at the center was a carved heron opinicus.

Grenkin rushed over to it. "They're gone."

Satra blinked. "What's gone?"

He ran his good talons over the statue's head and legs. "When we locked up the room, we left the reeve's crown and talons here. They've been taken."

"Was it Mia and Biski?" Satra asked. "Surely they wouldn't steal them and then tell you?"

One of the alarmed pigeons flew towards the far wall, where another hidden door marked with a seahorse was open.

They shared a look and ventured deeper inside. The passage led to an adjoining room. It looked similarly ransacked.

Grenkin explored the mosaics, but Satra stared at the pile of bandages and ointments. She reached down to touch one. When she pulled back her paw, it had wet blood on it.

"I'd forgotten about that old passage," Grenkin admitted. "I suppose it makes sense. No one wants to wake their guards and traipse through the hallways just to visit their mate in the night."

Satra's body tensed. The smell was a familiar one. Her fur stood on end.

Grenkin lit the large braziers, filling the consort's

chamber with light. From the corner of the pile of bandages came a glint.

Satra reached out a shaking paw and pushed aside the bandages. Beneath them was a saw with scorch marks on it. The one she'd paid a metalworker to modify. The one she'd planned to use on an unconscious opinicus hidden in her chambers the night the Redwood Valley Eyrie burned down.

"Jonas."

K. VALE NAGLE

THE RUINS OF CRESTFALL

GRYPHON INSURRECTION: BOOK FIVE

A QUICK NOTE ON REVIEWS
THEN MORE GRYPHONS

Thank you for reading Reevesbane! If you're enjoying the Gryphon Insurrection series, please considering leaving a review at your favorite online retailer or Good Reads. Reviews help other readers find books they like and let them know that, yes, this really is a series about gryphons.

AUTHOR'S NOTE
THE PROBLEM WITH GRYPHONS

All gryphon authors are faced with a problem when they start writing their series—a gryphon problem, if you will. (Chimaera conundrum also works, as you'll soon see.) Here's the problem in brief.

You're writing an animal that is composed of two different organisms, a cat and a bird. How did such a creature come to exist? Is it actually half cat, half bird? Or does it just resemble them? What does it mean for the world you're writing to have such a magnificent beast in existence?

Gryphon authors approach this in several ways. If it's a science fiction setting, maybe your gryphons came from genetic engineering. If it's a fantasy setting, perhaps your gryphons were created through magic when a bird and a cat entered an arcane portal and things got mixed up. For gryphons that are truly half cat and half bird, that's a common solution.

Sometimes, however, the gryphons don't really resemble a specific feline and avian. They're just a creature with a beak, wings, mammal-like musculature, and a tail. Heck, if you remove the wings, we're talking about a duck-billed platypus or hard-beaked echidna here, aren't we?

These gryphons are their own distinct creatures. Sometimes, they're created via magic, like Mercedes Lackey's Skandranon, whose fur is actually microfeathers. Sometimes, they evolve naturally. Most four-limbed life evolved from the four limbs of the lobe-finned fish, so it's not uncommon for fantasy settings to have dragons and other hexapodal creatures with a six-limbed fish ancestor. It's a nice solution. Who doesn't love their dragons and gryphons to have wings and four legs?

Let's back up a moment here, however, to discuss a different gryphon problem: descriptions. I promise it's related. Having read eighty excellent gryphon books over the last two years, I noticed something many of us do. Allow me to illustrate with a few sentences. *The green and brown gryphon sat down next to a black and red gryphon who was chirping at a white and red gryphon.*

If you're like me, you've probably already forgotten the colors of those gryphons unless you have reason to believe it's very important to the plot, such as authors' tendencies to make red gryphons be special. If pressed, you probably imagined the gryphons to be vaguely eagle- and lion-shaped. Colorful descriptions paint a fairly boring portrait of gryphon diversity if no readers can remember them.

Let's try that same sentence again and see if it brings a different set of images to mind. *The peacock opinicus sat down next to a black owl gryphon with a red undercoat who was chirping at a Japanese crane opinicus with a splash of red on his chest.* Hopefully, you didn't imagine Levin, Ninox, and Rorin as all looking the same in the second sentence.

I knew from the start of *Eyrie* that I wanted the gryphons and opinici to be as diverse and wonderful as all the birds and cats in the world. Part of my writing style is animal facts, whether they're about diving petrels (Tresh), poisonous hooded pitohui birds (Rybalt), leaping caracals (Jun and Satra), or cobra-slaying green peafowl (Brevin and Levin).

Of course, having read the start of this Author's Note, you've already figured out my problem: I'm writing a low epic fantasy without any magic or humans. There's no genetic engineering facility splicing kitties and birds together. The closest thing to magic in my world is Rorin's dreamy voice, or so the fanfic writers tell me. I see what you've been up to, "Trorish" shippers.

So what's an author to do?

Well, I already knew the answer: horizontal gene transfer. Wait, come back, this isn't a biology textbook! And horizontal gene transfer is kind of cool.

You probably know vertical gene transfer: those are all of the genes your parents passed on to you. By contrast, horizontal transfer means you're not passing them down to offspring, you're getting them straight from other organisms. Griffith's Experiment back in the `50s showed that you could have genes transferred between one virus or bacteria to another type. Basically, some organisms could steal DNA from others.

Once we saw it happening on a small scale, we began to see it in some larger organisms, such as plants (especially the parasitic types) and rarely in animals. To me, taking horizontal gene transfer to the extreme just makes the most sense for gryphons who resemble animals.

Thin-coated gryphons arrive in the frozen taiga and have a hard time adapting, but under stress, they end up consuming the gyrfalcons and snowy owls who make their home there. As part of their evolutionary survival adaptations, they pass those genes onto their chicks. Eventually, the gryphons have adapted to a new ecosystem. It made sense that wherever gryphons struggled to survive, they'd need to adapt. It explained how you could have a wide variety of gryphon appearances or morphs for a single species.

Hopefully, in a nature fantasy setting grounded mostly in real animals and plants, this isn't a step too far. I was nervous when I handed in *Reevesbane* to my beta readers and then editors, but everyone was on board with the idea or had already guessed it. I seeded the gene transfer in back at the end of *Eyrie* when Impir tells Askel he used his alchemical skills to make sure all of Reeve Brevin's children hatched as emerald peafowl. I expanded upon it a bit further in *Ashen Weald* and *Starling*.

So that's the problem every gryphon author faces. How do you have a creature that's half of one thing and half of something else? There's another solution I didn't mention above: just ignore it! A lot of great gryphon fiction never explains why gryphons look the way they do. If solving the gryphon problem inspires you to write your own gryphon novel, excellent. If it doesn't, keep writing anyways, because the world needs more gryphon books.

We're now about over halfway through the main story arc of the Gryphon Insurrection. Up next, it's time to visit *Crestfall* and see what's going on with the flamingo reeve. With the Blackwing Eyrie finally making its moves and the white reeve on the hunt for the final seraph, the stage is set for the final novels. I hope you're having as much fun as I am. I'll see you in the Author's Note for *Crestfall*!

-Vale

ALSO BY K. VALE NAGLE

THE GRYPHON INSURRECTION

Eyrie

Ashen Weald

Starling

Reevesbane

The Ruins of Crestfall

The Crackling Sea

Opinicus

Pridelord

SHORT STORY COLLECTIONS & ANTHOLOGIES

Blue Eyes and Other Tales

Tales of Feathers and Flames

Need more gryphons while you wait for *The Ruins of Crest-fall* to come out? Sign up for my newsletter at kvalenagle.-com/mailinglist and receive a free ebook copy of *Blue Eyes and Other Tales*, a short story collection set right after *Starling*. This book is currently only available to newsletter and Patreon.com/kvalenagle subscribers.

Enjoy this complete short story from the Blue Eyes collection, "Silver Eyes," starting on the next page!

SILVER EYES
A BLUE EYES SHORT STORY

"There's been another outbreak." Deracho spread his wings to help shield his team from the wind. Several members were shivering, and while there were a few fellow taiga gryphons coming along for this mission, the bulk of his forces were Ashen Weald. Several rangers had been stationed nearby to guard the builders working on the path, and they'd offered their aid. The Ashen Weald was better equipped to deal with the infection, if not the snowstorm. He was grateful for their help.

He nodded to Thenca. She wore fur-lined armor designed by opinicus tailors and was flanked by two bog witches. While she'd gone back and forth from the taiga to the kjarr once a small path was made, Deracho's arrival in Snowfall had brought her back to the icy mountains to see him.

As long as he was in charge of Hoarfrost, they weren't able to spend any time together. She couldn't cross south of Glacial Run because of the wingtorns' pact with the fisherfolk. For the first time in years, they'd had an opportunity to have gryphlets together—right in time for him to be sent south. Now they struggled to find more than a few minutes in each other's company. Not that their current mission would afford them that opportunity.

The bog witches Thenca was mentoring were too inexperienced to risk in combat. They were younger than they first appeared. Once the infected were killed, however, they'd be in charge of burning the bodies. Their natural immunity to the parasite made them a necessity— they wouldn't become sick by handling the dead. The weald medicine gryphons had told them what precautions they needed to take so they didn't accidentally spread the infection to the rest of the team.

Several opinicus rangers shivered in the back. They tucked their long, blue heron necks against their bodies. They'd started complaining back at Snowfall Mountain and hadn't let up since.

Deracho hooted to his taiga gryphon pridemates, and they surrounded the blue opinici to keep them warm. "This is the resistant strain, but I don't want any of you to worry. We brought more than enough pumpkin to take care of all of us, should it come to that."

"I thought the resistant strain was only in the south, around Sandpiper's Dune and Hoarfrost," the male bog witch said. "Do we know how it got up here?"

The bog witches were all stolen eggs. They'd been raised as gryphlets without parents or a den mother, and their social niceties around other prides were still a little lacking. They could be a bit blunt at times.

"It's not clear." Deracho had his suspicions. One of the scouts who survived the initial starling attack on Hoarfrost, a snowy owl gryphon named Lenti, had gone missing. Over the last few months, the medicine gryphons had been treating him for the resistant strain. He'd fluctuated between recovering and getting worse up until a week ago, when he'd disappeared. Yesterday, one of the gryphons Biski assigned to check the taiga wildlife caught signs of an outbreak where he'd last been seen.

"There's at least one scout missing," Thenca said. As the only wingtorn, getting her out here had been a logistical nightmare, but her familiarity with the taiga made her the natural choice to lead the Ashen Weald side of the joint operation. "That's why we're grateful for the rangers' help. We'd like to capture him alive if he's infected. We'll burn the wildlife. There isn't enough pumpkin to make curing them reasonable at this point."

She went through several safety precautions. After New Eyrie and the stories from the bog expedition, they all had a good idea of what to expect from the infected. Nobody liked to be near them, but everyone here was a volunteer, even the grouchy rangers.

The storm howled, and Thenca shivered. "I know the snow and winds aren't ideal, and they're only going to get worse over the next few days. That's just what winter is like in the taiga. This is probably our best opportunity to stop the spread."

"Thenca and our bog friends will set up camp in the cave over there." Deracho belatedly realized that they could be having this conversation inside the cave, but it was a good opportunity to help their Ashen Weald friends build character. "Once the rangers get a fire going and a snow barrier up, they'll wait at the entrance while the taiga pride locate wildlife and, hopefully, our missing scout. Then it's their turn."

One of the rangers, a captain, stretched out his long, blue heron neck. "The taiga gryphons will take care of any frost chickens or small birds they find. If they see a goliath, they'll send one gryphon to fetch us while another flies above the bird to mark its location. And if anyone locates the scout, it'll be up to all of us working together to subdue him safely."

The other rangers didn't complain, either because the captain outranked them or because their beaks had frozen shut. Deracho made a cooing sound, and the blue-eyed taiga gryphons headed into the snow-covered aneda forest to begin searching. With any luck, they'd finish before the snowstorm forced them to stay the night.

ONCE THE RANGER'S fire was in full swing, Thenca knew how to keep it burning. The opinici set up a barrier of pelts to keep the worst of the wind and snow out of the cave, then settled in to wait for word.

Thenca conversed with the bog witches. Bringing them along on this excursion provided her with an opportunity to help teach them what it meant to be a part of the Ashen Weald. The male asked a lot of questions about what the bog pride was like before he was born. She did her best to answer them, but she'd been a gryphlet back then.

She'd assumed the other bog gryphon was just quiet, but when the male ran off to ask the rangers some questions, his associate finally opened up to Thenca.

"Are you my mother?" the bog witch asked.

"No." This was not a question Thenca was prepared for, but she definitely knew the answer. "What's your name?"

"My friends call me Petal." Her nares blushed with

embarrassment. "I didn't mean to insult you. It's just that we look a lot alike."

Thenca would have to take her word for it since it was impossible to tell what Petal looked like under all of that blue paint. While her face and undersides were covered with skeletal patterns, the tops of her wings had been painted to look like aneda needles.

"Gryphons don't always look like their parents," Thenca explained, "and I didn't have an egg before we were captured, so I think it's safe to say I'm not your mother."

Petal sat in silence.

"Are a lot of the bog witches looking for their parents?" Thenca asked.

Petal nodded.

"I don't think there's any way for them to find out, not for certain," Thenca said. It'd been two and a half years since the bog witches had all been stolen and raised in a sunken eyrie. Since their recent reunion with the remains of the wingtorn, there'd been relief but also confusion. Many of them had been kjarr eggs, and none of them knew who their parents were. Before they'd even hatched, they'd been taken first by the rangers, and then by a rogue faction of bog gryphons, most of whom were now dead.

Petal fidgeted, and Thenca was still searching for some words of kindness when the first of the taiga scouts came through the pelts and into the cave.

"We found some gryphon tracks nearby, on the other side of the mountain." The taiga gryphon's eyes were so blue they glowed in the firelight. "Deracho's following them, but he wants all the rangers to come out and be ready with their nets."

The taiga gryphons and rangers left, leaving Thenca

alone with Petal and the other bog witch to tend the fire. Thenca didn't know any more tales from the bog, so she started telling them about her and her brother's adventures with the Ashen Weald.

"The walls of New Eyrie were lined with spikes, and the sky was full of opinici. There was a horde of infected starlings to the south, but Urious didn't know that yet..."

DERACHO USED his wings to shield his face against the winds. When he'd put together this mission, he'd been worried he wouldn't find any trace of Lenti. Instead, he was actually finding too much evidence.

Tracks went off in all directions. Over the last week, the infected scout had walked all over the mountain. Snow slides had covered some tracks, winds had obscured others, and Deracho was having a hard time finding anything fresh. He worried that meant the gryphon had either frozen to death or left the area. Neither were outcomes he wanted to consider. Not when Lenti had eggs back home that would hatch come spring.

Deracho followed a set of tracks south, taking care of a few frost chicken dens on his way, until they disappeared into a snowbank. There was a lump buried under a foot of snow.

Is this him? He began to dig.

"Please be okay in there, friend," Deracho whispered. He made it through the snow and his paws touched wet feathers. He left his foreleg there for a moment and thought he could detect a slight heartbeat.

His hopes rose until he burrowed a little further and

got a glimpse of grey. The mound of snow began to shake, and a feral goliath bird freed itself with an angry *Mronk!*

Instinct took over, and Deracho jumped straight up to escape.

His heart leapt into his stomach as the goliath got the better of him. It pulled him out of the air and slammed him into the ground.

The snow crunched beneath his fall. The air was knocked out of him. His head spun. He shouted for help with a touch of panic in his voice. He'd been so worried about finding Lenti, he let his guard down.

The goliath's eyes didn't have a silver sheen, but that didn't mean it wasn't in the early days of infection. The silver took a while to set in, and a healthy goliath was just as deadly as an infected one.

Deracho stood up on his back paws and spread his wings as wide as they would go. It was common knowledge that if you ran from one of these birds, they knew you were prey. Instead, he backed up slowly towards the woods. If he could get an aneda tree between him and his opponent, he could buy himself enough time to get airborne.

"Mronk!" the bird repeated. It crouched down, bringing it to eye level with Deracho. Closer to Hoarfrost, the feral goliaths could reach fifteen feet tall. This one was still growing and stood only three feet higher than a gryphon.

He had to lower himself to all fours to back up farther, but he kept his wings out wide and his tail straight up. He waved it a bit. With any luck, the goliath would attack the black spot on the tip before it attacked him. At least, he hoped that wasn't an old medicine gryphon tale. This would be his first time putting it to the test. Normally, he was smart enough not to fight goliaths on the ground.

Luck was on his side. Several taiga gryphons and rangers appeared in the sky above him, but the goliath bird looked about ready to take a bite out of him just to sate its curiosity.

Deracho rose up again on two legs to look more intimidating. It was working until he took a step. His foot caught in a hole in the snow, and he fell onto his back, twisting his paw.

The goliath bird charged him, biting down to try to catch his throat. Deracho rolled out of the way, but the bird caught his hip in its beak.

He stuck all four sets of claws into its face and pushed off. The bird screeched and fell backwards.

Deracho leapt onto his paws and groomed his side and hip to see how the damage was. To his surprise and relief, the goliath had come away with a beakful of fur and no flesh.

Thenca would have killed me if that bird had bitten anything important. He considered what she'd say when she found out that he'd dug a goliath out of its burrow instead of letting the rangers handle it. *She may still kill me yet.*

The goliath regained its footing. It shook its head, splattering the snowy hillside with drops of blood. He'd missed its eyes and made it mad.

The bird reared up and tried to stomp on Deracho, but by then, his mind had found its hunting calm. He slipped to the side. When the bird's massive foot landed, becoming lodged in the same snow he'd tripped over, he leapt up and caught its neck with his beak.

Its heavy, fur-like feathers and thick hide kept it safe. It shook him off the same way it had the blood. Just when it turned to stomp again, one of the ranger's nets enveloped it and brought it down. Another ranger with jelly toxin arrived to render it unconscious while they killed it and prepared to burn the body.

"Are you okay?" The ranger captain was looking at his waist, where there was a huge clump of missing fur. "Let's get a dose of pumpkin into you."

Deracho accepted the orange vial, letting the ranger pull out the stopper. No one knew how cooking the pumpkin or adding spices would affect its medicinal properties, so for the moment, everyone was drinking it raw in an alcohol-based tincture.

Deracho coughed once but didn't spit it back up. "I was looking for the missing scout, but I found a goliath bird instead."

"This area seems to be full of them," the captain said. "Your pridemates flagged around a dozen. We have our work cut out for us. I hear this is called Goliath Mountain? It's well-named."

"If the scout is infected and we don't find him, this'll just start anew." Deracho didn't confirm the mountain's name. One of the games they played with the weald and kjarr gryphons was making up names for different mountains. In truth, the only mountains that had names were the ones where prides had lived: Hoarfrost, Williwaw, Snowfall, and Snowfeather.

He looked down at his twisted back paw. It hurt but not enough for him to head back and give up looking for his friend. He searched for what he'd tripped over. Frost chickens built dens under the snow. It would be safer to kill and burn them now if that's what he'd stumbled over.

He followed the burrow back another ten feet. Before he located the chickens, however, he stumbled across fresh gryphon tracks headed back towards the mountain. Lenti still lived.

"There are some chickens here that need to be taken care of," he told a nearby ranger. "I'm going to stop in at the base camp and get some ointment for the scratches. Tell your captain we should finish checking this area in another couple of hours, then we can head back to Snowfall and get something to eat, assuming the weather holds."

The ranger saluted and flew off. By the way the snow was starting to come down, the weather wouldn't hold.

THENCA WAS JUST TELLING the bog witches about her various mountain-climbing efforts when the makeshift snow barrier was pulled up and a ranger came in, leaving it open behind her.

"What news of the storm?" Thenca asked. "Need our help yet?"

The ranger nodded. "We've killed a dozen goliaths now. At least a couple were showing signs. Deracho himself decided to go paw-to-claw with one on the ground. I think he's coming to get patched up, but after that, it's about time to move the bodies into the other cave and get a pyre going. I'll leave that to you and the other immune."

The bog witches looked relieved that they wouldn't have to kill the goliath birds themselves. They went through their supplies. Most of their treatments involved pastes made from flowers or fish of different sorts, but the local medicine gryphons had given them pumpkin and aneda poultices, too.

Thenca was about to tell the ranger to close the snow barrier when her eyes rested on a familiar sight: the outline of a snowy owl gryphon. Deracho was making his way towards the cave from around twenty feet out.

She watched him run closer, wondering why he hadn't landed by the entrance. Her hackle feathers rose. He never had that effect on her. She looked into his eyes to see what was wrong, but the eyes that looked back at her weren't blue.

They were silver.

This wasn't Deracho. It was the missing taiga gryphon.

"Close the barrier!" she shouted to the ranger, but it was too late. The infected scout crashed through it, smashing the opinicus against the cave wall. It chomped down on her with its beak.

"Behind the fire!" Thenca pushed the bog witches. Then she charged into the infected taiga gryphon, sending them both sprawling out into the snow.

They went tail-over-beak down the mountain in a tangle. Just when she thought she'd found purchase under the layer of snow, she came away with a pawful of scree and roots. They finally crashed twenty feet down into a small crevasse.

Luckily for her, the infected gryphon took the brunt of the fall. Its wings must have broken, but it didn't show any indication it was in pain. It bit at Thenca but was rebuffed by her leather armor.

She shouted, letting the stone on either side of her amplify her voice. No response came, but there was a slight tremor on the ledge above them. She cried out a second time, but the tremor grew, and she feared an avalanche.

The infected bit and clawed at her. She resisted the

urge to kill it and instead worked to create some distance between them. Lenti had a family back at Snowfall. While Deracho hadn't mentioned it to prevent putting the team in unnecessary danger, she knew he was hoping to save this gryphon.

The snowstorm's intensity grew. She cried out a third time, and instead of a ranger or taiga scout, the two bog witches looked down over the ledge at her.

Great, she thought. *I end up with the only two bog witches who don't have experience hunting the infected.*

The scout attacked again, and this time it managed to get its claws through her armor.

She yelped in pain, then shouted up at the young gryphons. "Fetch Deracho or the captain!"

The male bog witch disappeared, but Petal tried to fly down. She made it partway when a gust of wind slammed her against the rock face. She tumbled into the crevasse behind the infected.

At the young witch's cry, the infected turned towards the sound. He stalked towards her, his large paws finding purchase atop the snow.

While Petal screamed in terror, and Thenca found something rocky to push off from. She leapt onto the scout's back. If it came down to the taiga gryphon or Petal, Thenca would choose the uninfected every time. There was no guarantee that they'd be able to bring him back.

The scout shook Thenca off, sending her flying with pawfuls of shed fur. In a last ditch attempt to draw him away from Petal, Thenca used her mockingbird talents to roar at it in Jun the Kjarr's loudest voice.

This time, the snow on the ledge above didn't just rumble, it collapsed into the crevasse, burying all three gryphons.

DERACHO ARRIVED at the cave and found a wounded ranger and a trail of displaced snow leading down the mountain. The opinicus had a nasty bite taken out of her, but an aneda poultice was holding the important bits in, at least for now. Before she could tell him what was going on, one of the bog witches showed up.

"Deracho!" the male witch said. "Thenca's with an infected gryphon in a canyon. Petal fell in after them. They need your help."

Deracho didn't waste any time. "Go fetch the ranger captain. I'll help Thenca and Petal."

He ignored the heavy winds and followed the trail. If Thenca had gone over the edge, he didn't know what he'd do. Younce, the new taiga pride leader, had warned Deracho this would be a difficult section of the taiga for her to reach by paw, but he hadn't listened. Instead, he'd let his desire to spend time with her override any safety concerns.

The trail went over the edge and into a crevasse full of snow. His first thought was that they must have rolled past it. He began to fly by when he noticed that the trail didn't continue on the other side. There was also a sound coming from beneath the ground.

His owl-like hearing caught the sound of scratching and shuffling under him. He burrowed into the ground, trying to track the sound through the snow. He extended his claws to try to displace the snow faster. His claws went into her beak, but he didn't have time to apologize.

"Petal's also buried," Thenca's scratched beak said. "I have my armor. She's not wearing anything. She'll freeze if you don't get her out."

He assumed Petal was the other bog witch. He hadn't learned their names yet. All sorts of Ashen Weald came and went in the taiga as construction on the path progressed. Gryphons with skull face paint weren't any stranger than the fantails with their long, feathered tails or the parrotfaces who insisted on walking everywhere.

He thought he heard sounds coming from a few feet away, so he began to dig again. This time, the beak he unearthed tried to bite him. It was Lenti.

He grabbed a branch off an aneda tree growing out of the rock face and stuffed it in his friend's mouth. While Lenti chewed on the bitter bark, he dug where the snow was lumpy.

The infected thrashed around, but with its wings buried under the avalanche, it was having trouble making any headway. Thenca, meanwhile, used her beak to free one of her paws and was nearly above the snow. She shivered.

Deracho located a third gryphon under the snow. This time, he remembered to retract his claws. "Can you hear me? Are you okay?"

"It was so c-c-c-old," Petal stuttered, "but now I feel like my paws are on fire."

Deracho frowned. There was a point where the feeling of cold was replaced by heat. What came next was frost-bite—and worse.

He redoubled his efforts until a loud hiss come from behind him.

"Stay with it," Thenca shouted. "I'm just about free. I'll keep Lenti off you."

The hissing grew louder.

THENCA LIBERATED her second forepaw and started to wriggle free. Her brother had teased her mercilessly about the warm armor, but he wasn't spending half of his time in the mountains. The warmth had kept her from going into shock, and she was grateful, but she had some ideas about improvements that could be made in the future, especially around the paws.

The infected scout shook his entire body, dislodging the last of the snow entombing him. Whether this was a primal instinct or something taiga gryphons were taught, she didn't know. He pulled himself up with a loud hiss.

"Stay with it," she shouted to Deracho. "I'm just about free. I'll keep Lenti off you."

"She says her paws feel hot," he shouted back.

Thenca knew what that meant. They didn't have much time.

She pulled her back legs out of the snow and shook as hard as she could. She didn't give Lenti an opportunity to go for her mate. While his attention was on Deracho, she leapt on top of the infected scout. He rolled onto his back to bite and scratch at her, but her armor took the worst of it. She pinned him against the rock face.

"Got her!" Deracho freed Petal from the snow. She was limp. He tried to get airborne, but her fur and feathers were soaked through, and she weighed too much. He started dragging her towards the side of the crevasse and up to the surface.

Thenca cried out when one of the scout's claws pierced her armor.

Deracho started to come back for her.

"Don't stop!" she shouted. "Get Petal to warmth. I can hold him here."

More claws found purchase, and she stifled a scream.

"Where are the rangers?" Deracho's words were barely audible over the snowstorm. He hesitated, unable to leave her, but unable to do anything about it. Finally he extended his claws and came towards the scout. There was a determination in his blue eyes that she didn't like the look of.

"Don't do it!" she shouted. "I'll be okay. We'll cure him. Just get Petal to safety."

He pulled back his paw but couldn't bring himself to finish Lenti. Deracho raised and lowered his claws several times, and just when he looked determined enough to do it, a haunting heron cry came from overhead. The ranger captain landed.

A dose of jelly toxin finally rendered the scout limp. With the arrival of the rest of the rangers and the taiga gryphons, they were able to use their largest net to transport Petal to the cave before they returned for the infected taiga gryphon.

With some assistance, Thenca got her paws back on solid ground. She hurt all over, and her armor was shredded. By the time she reached the cave, they had another problem.

"The storm is getting worse," the captain said. "If you want us to airlift one of you out of here, now's the time."

He looked at Petal, Thenca, the chomped ranger, and the infected scout in turn. The ranger's wounds had been tended to enough to let her fly.

"Take Lenti to the medicine gryphons first," Thenca said. "We'll keep Petal warm here and help raise her temperature. If the storm obliges, come back for her."

"What about you?" The male bog witch looked at her lack of wings. "You don't want to get trapped here, do you?"

Thenca shook her head. "I'm happy enough staying here by the fire with Deracho until we get a break in the weather."

The rangers were unsure, but a taiga gryphon came in to say that the storm was getting worse by the minute. They wrapped the lost scout in a net, secured the snow barrier as best they could, and vanished into the snowy sky, weighed down by their cargo. The taiga gryphons also departed, leaving Thenca and Deracho alone with the two bog witches. They'd refused to be separated.

There were several pelts left over from the barrier, which Thenca turned into a burrow for Petal and the others. Deracho lent his warmth to the endeavor, and every so often, the male bog witch checked Petal and Thenca's wounds and gave Deracho another vial of pumpkin to drink.

Once Petal was warm enough to be out of danger, he relaxed a little but also sighed. "She really thought you were her mother. She seemed sure of it."

Thenca opened a sleepy eye. "I already told her it couldn't be true. I never had any children."

It was always possible Petal was one of Urious's offspring. Thenca had never come out and asked her brother directly. Instead, she'd just assumed he'd spent every mating season pining over Ari, who'd only had eyes for Jun back then.

"You seem old," the young bog witch said. "Did you just not want gryphlets?"

Deracho puffed up, but Thenca put a paw on his beak to settle him down.

"I suppose I feel old after all that's happened," she said. "In the time since I met Deracho, generations have gone by. First, Mignet and Satra grew up. Then half of the next hatch year was kept in cages. You were the other half, still eggs, who hatched soon after. We were dosed with red fern in captivity, so you were the last batch. Until spring comes, you're the youngest gryphons in our pride."

"Isn't the kjarr den mother taking care of you?" Deracho asked. "You're only just adults."

The male bog witch considered his next words. "The kjarr pride is more concerned about the children they know are theirs. They're not really sure what to do with us."

Thenca and Deracho shared a look. There was enough of a history between them that she already knew what he was thinking.

"You're needed at Hoarfrost," she told him. "Another few years and you could be made pride leader of the first new taiga pride since the Connixation."

"Why would I want to be leader of a pride situated where you can't go?" There was a sparkle in his eye. "We've talked about having an egg together, opinicus-style. Why don't we go help the lost-and-found bog gryphons?"

Curled up by the fire, Petal opened an eye.

"They're not gryphlets." Thenca turned to the male bog witch. "No offense intended. But you're adults, even if just. You don't really need a den mother."

There was a time in her life when being a den mother was inconceivable to her, but after all that had happened, she was starting to reconsider. She'd basically raised Satra already, and she spent a good deal of her time at Snowfall playing with the gryphlets.

More than that, there was something honest and refreshing about being away from the politics and horrors of the last three years. She wanted this to be a time of

rebuilding, and part of that was raising the next generation to make sure they didn't repeat their parents'
mistakes. This was something she could do that would
make a real difference.

But this wouldn't be a conventional den mother role.
Unlike the hostage gryphlets who had taken an extra year
to fledge because of malnutrition, the gryphons hatched
from the stolen eggs had matured at their normal rate.
The things they had seen and done in the bog had the
unintentional effect of making them seem older than the
other half of their hatch-year who'd been kidnapped to
the Redwood Valley.

"We need something," the male bog witch said. "Just
someone to ask questions of. Maybe not a den mother, but
the world is different from how we were taught. When we
realized we weren't going to find our parents, many of us
retreated back to the new settlement, Bogwash. I worry
that if we don't do something, many of us are going to turn
feral again."

Thenca was thinking it through. Deracho, showing
uncharacteristic wisdom, kept his beak shut. She looked
from Petal to the other bog witch. She and Deracho were
only just now considering if they wanted gryphlets. And,
if they did, whether they'd be handing them off to the
taiga den mother or trying to raise them like opinici
might.

The Ashen Weald's new Crackling Sea opinicus
members had started to normalize mating for life even
among its gryphon members. While the fisherfolk had
always been like that, she'd been barred from coming
anywhere near the shore, which limited their options. In
the last few months, many Ashen Weald gryphon couples
decided they wanted recognition of their bond, opening

an opportunity for Deracho when they ultimately made that decision.

But there was a lot she still didn't know about raising offspring. Den mothers normally trained for years. This might be an opportunity to speed up her own learning by finding out what the recovered bog pride felt they still needed to learn.

"Okay," she said at last. "We'll go down to Bogwash. We'll answer everyone's questions about the world. We'll spend the spring there doing what we can. But *just* the spring. I'm not spending summer among the mangroves. I'm not grooming swamp gunk and sea salt out of your fur in the blistering heat. The moment the weather turns, we head home."

Next to her, still mostly buried in blankets, Petal smiled.

Thenca rolled her eyes and looked at Deracho's missing clump of fur. "You know, last time we were caught in a cave during a snowstorm, things were a lot more romantic."

This time, it was Deracho who put a paw over her beak. "Not in front of the gryphlets."

His blue eyes twinkled right before she hit him in the face.

www.ingramcontent.com/pod-product-compliance
Lightning Source LLC
Chambersburg PA
CBHW051552100726
47898CB00001B/68